Praise for E. E. 'Doc' Smith

'Smith [has the] ability to create planets with truly original climates and inhabitants' *New York Times*

'What John Ford is to horse-opera – Grade A, homogenized – Doc Smith is to space-opera' *Astounding Science Fiction*

'With the exception of the works of H. G. Wells, possibly those of Jules Verne – and almost no other writer – it has inspired more imitators and done more to change the nature of all the science fiction written after it than almost any other single work' Frederik Pohl

'Adventure of an unprecedented kind ... the first great "classic" of American science fiction' Isaac Asimov

Also By E. E. 'Doc' Smith

SKYLARK

1. The Skylark of Space (1928)
2. Skylark Three (1948)
3. Skylark of Valeron (1949)
4. Skylark DuQuesne (1966)

LENSMAN

1. Triplanetary (1934)
2. First Lensman (1950)
3. Galactic Patrol (1950)
4. Grey Lensman (1951)
5. Second Stage Lensmen (1953)
6. Children of the Lens (1954)
7. The Vortex Blaster (aka *Masters of the Vortex*) (1960)

SUBSPACE

1. Subspace Explorers (1965)
2. Subspace Encounter (1983)

FAMILY D'ALEMBERT (WITH STEPHEN GOLDIN)

1. Imperial Stars (1976)
2. Stranglers' Moon (1976)
3. The Clockwork Traitor (1976)
4. Getaway World (1977)
5. Appointment at Bloodstar (aka *The Bloodstar Conspiracy*) (1978)
6. The Purity Plot (1978)
7. Planet of Treachery (1981)
8. Eclipsing Binaries (1983)
9. The Omicron Invasion (1984)
10. Revolt of the Galaxy (1985)

LORD TEDRIC (WITH GORDON EKLUND)

1. Lord Tedric (1978)
2. The Space Pirates (1979)
3. Black Knight of the Iron Sphere (1979)
4. Alien Realms (1980)

NON-SERIES NOVELS AND COLLECTIONS

Spacehounds of IPC (1947)
The Galaxy Primes (1965)
Masters of Space (1976) (with E. Everett Evans)

GOLDEN AGE
MASTERWORKS

Children of the Lens

E. E. 'DOC' SMITH

This edition first published in Great Britain in 2019 by Gollancz
an imprint of the Orion Publishing Group Ltd
Carmelite House, 50 Victoria Embankment
London EC4Y ODZ

An Hachette UK Company

1 3 5 7 9 10 8 6 4 2

A CIP catalogue record for this book is
available from the British Library.

ISBN 978 1 473 22473 5
eBook ISBN 978 1 473 22036 2

Typeset at The Spartan Press Ltd,
Lymington, Hants

Printed and bound by CPI Group (UK) Ltd,
Croydon, CRO 4YY

www.gollancz.co.uk

INTRODUCTION

I discovered the Lensman series back in the 1970s, when I was in my mid-teens. My sci-fi habit was hitting its first big peak, and I was perpetually hungry for something new to read. I prowled the bookshops of Liverpool on a daily basis. Actually, I mostly scoured the newsagents, which were nearer to hand and generally had a spinner-rack stuffed full of paperbacks. The selection changed unpredictably, though, so whenever you found anything that was even halfway interesting, the best tactic was to grab it and sweat the details afterwards.

One day in the middle of February, I grabbed *Triplanetary*. I was bemused at first by its stop-start structure, as it compressed thousands of years of history (and millions of years of pre-history) into a series of staccato set pieces. But then I got my eye in and I was hooked. I worked my way through the entire series, quickly catching up to their publishing schedule so I was searching out each title as it appeared. These were the Panther paperback reprints, with all-but-irresistible Chris Foss covers.

I was pretty much omnivorous back then. If a story had a cool premise or some exciting action, that was enough for me. I didn't worry about fripperies like style or characterisation. I knew what it was that gave me the hit I craved. It was both very simple and fairly abstract. I wanted big, insane ideas, unfeasible vistas, vast distances from the everyday. E. E. Smith delivered. How could he fail? The Lensman series starts with two galaxies colliding and it just goes on getting bigger from there.

I enjoyed the books enough to re-read them, more than once. In fact, there aren't many novel cycles that I've re-read so many times. At a rough estimate, I'd say there are three.

The other authors in that short, prestigious list are Ursula Le Guin (Earthsea), Gene Wolfe (the Torturer quartet) and China Miéville (Bas-Lag).

Smith is the odd one out, in a number of ways. With those other three series, I've re-read the works at regular intervals throughout my life. Most of my re-readings of Smith came when I was still in my teens and twenties. And whereas my love for Le Guin, Wolfe and Miéville has never wavered, I had a period of deep ambivalence about Smith's writing.

Reading the Lensman books as a grown-up was different from reading them as a teen. On later visits, I raised my eyebrows at things that had slipped under my radar as a kid. The dodgy politics, the addiction to superlatives and to a set of adjectives describing the brightness of energy weapons (*lambent* and *coruscating*, I'm looking at you), the two-fisted heroes who were more or less interchangeable, and most of all the general absence of female characters (there are six of any substance, across the entire series). For a while – a long while – Smith was a guilty pleasure, and whenever I discussed him I'd always throw out a defensive array of criticism of his gender politics, his innate conservatism and his unvaryingly perfect male protagonists.

It wasn't the first time I'd had this experience. I'd already gone through it with another favourite series, Mary Norton's *Borrowers* books. There too, I found that my enjoyment of the books came to be modulated by a wariness about the world view they expressed. Norton, like Smith, struggled with her female characters. She made Arrietty her main protagonist, but never seemed at ease with giving her full agency. The girl who trains under her father to be the chief provider for her hunter-gatherer family has her story truncated, finally, to a romantic liaison with an acceptably middle-class suitor (in the fifth book, after Spiller has been ushered off-stage).

For much of the Lensman series, Smith is more unequivocal in focusing entirely on his male protagonists – but there's a reverie going on under the surface, and it resolves in a fascinating way. To begin with, Smith just sidesteps the whole issue.

He doesn't want to write about women, and he rules them out with an immaculate piece of straight-faced nonsense. You just can't wear a lens if you're a woman. There's a fundamental incompatibility, full stop.

Then he gives us Clarissa MacDougall, the red lensman. But he's at pains to make it clear that she's a unique exception, the result of literally millions of years of Arisian breeding programs. And having brought her into the story, he never finds very much to do with her. She's a hostage victim a few times, a shoulder to cry on for Helen of Lyrane, and a sort of pin-up girl for the men (and other male entities) of the Galactic Patrol. Then she hangs up her lens, marries and becomes a stay-at-home mother.

Clarissa's four daughters are much more satisfying, in terms of the role they play in the series. It's significant that only one of the children of the lens is male, and that he's the only one who graduates from the Academy and goes into the Patrol. His four sisters have to work in secret, their abilities unknown and unrecognised. They strive to save the universe without ever blowing their cover as demure, proper young women.

By this point, Smith has put gender at the heart of the story in an unexpected way, which I won't discuss here for fear of spoilers. There's a sense in which you can see him pushing back against his own prejudices in the later books, and it's very gratifying when it comes.

When I last returned to the series, for the purposes of writing this introduction, I'd stopped believing that guilty pleasures were really a valid concept. You either enjoy something or you don't, and since everyone's fave is problematic there's no point in apologising for the texts (books, TV series, movies, whatever) that happen to float your boat. There *is* very much a point in interrogating those texts, and unpicking the attitudes that underpin them. But pleasure isn't a moral response, even in moral people. You like the things you like, and the argument comes afterwards.

However that may be, on this most recent outing with the Lensman Corps, I had a different reaction both to the style of the stories and to their substance – and in some ways I appreciated them more than ever.

Smith's spaceships may run on valves and transistors, but his space battles are immersive and enthralling. Whether he's describing a ship-on-ship dogfight, a cat-and-mouse pursuit, a siege or a mass engagement, he puts you in the action and he follows through relentlessly on his ideas. He's also realistic about how arms races work – how a small advantage has to be exploited quickly, before the other side figures out what you're doing and retro-engineers it.

As for Smith's style, it may be highly coloured but it's wonderfully fit for purpose. His repetitions are a bit like the repetitions of Homer, who had a store of stock phrases that he used again and again so he could keep his powder dry for the bits where he really wanted to cut loose. That may seem like a pretty outrageous comparison, but Smith's main business wasn't that different from Homer's. They were both aiming to narrate epic events as evocatively as possible. And in that respect the Lensman novels deliver again and again. They tell a huge story against a huge backdrop, in a way that induces the same sense of awe and wonder in me now as they did when I first encountered them more than forty years ago.

Mike Carey
2018

Message of Transmittal

Subject: The Conclusion of the Boskonian War; A Report:
By: Christopher K. Kinnison, L3, of Klovia:
To: The Entity Able to Obtain and to Read It.

To you, the third-level intellect who has been guided to this imperishable container and who is able to break the Seal and to read this tape, and to your fellows, greetings.

For reasons which will become obvious, this report will not be made available for an indefinite but very long time; my present visualization of the Cosmic All does not extend to the time at which such action will become necessary. Therefore it is desirable to review briefly the most pertinent facts of the earlier phases of Civilization's climactic conflict: information which, while widely known at present, will probably in that future time exist otherwise only in the memories of my descendants.

In early Civilization law enforcement lagged behind crime because the police were limited in their spheres of action, while criminals were not. Each technological advance made that condition worse until finally, when Bergenholm so perfected the crude inertialess space-drive of Rodebush and Cleveland that commerce throughout the galaxy became an actuality, crime began to threaten Civilization's very existence.

Of course it was not then suspected that there was anything organized, coherent, or of large purpose about this crime. Centuries were to pass before my father, Kimball Kinnison of Tellus, now galactic coordinator, was to prove that Boskonia – an autocratic, dictatorial culture diametrically opposed to every ideal of Civilization – was in fact back of practically all the pernicious activities of the First Galaxy. Even he, however, has never had any inkling either of the eons-long conflict between the Arisians and the Eddorians or of the fundamental *raison d'être* of the Galactic Patrol – material which can never be revealed to any mind not inherently stable at the third level of stress.

Virgil Samms, then chief of the Triplanetary Service, perceived the general situation and foresaw the shape of the inevitable. He realized that unless and until his organization could secure an identifying symbol which could not be counterfeited, police work would remain relatively ineffectual. Tellurian science had done its best in the golden meteors of the Service, and its best was not good enough.

Through one Dr. Nels Bergenholm, an Arisian-activated form of human flesh, Virgil Samms became the first wearer of Arisia's Lens, and during his life he began the rigid selection of those worthy of wearing it. For centuries the Patrol grew and spread. It became widely known that the Lens was a perfect telepath, that it glowed with colored light only when worn by the individual to whose ego it was attuned, that it killed any other living being who attempted to wear it. Whatever his race or shape, any wearer of the Lens was accepted as the embodiment of Civilization.

Kimball Kinnison was the first Lensman to realize that the Lens was more than an identification and a telepath. He was thus the first Lensman to return to Arisia to take the second stage of Lensmanship – the treatment which only an exceptional brain can withstand, but which gives the Second-Stage Lensman any mental power which he needs and which he can both visualize and control.

Aided by Lensmen Worsel of Velantia and Tregonsee of Rigel IV – the former a winged reptile, the latter a four-legged, barrel-shaped creature with the sense of perception instead of sight – Kimball Kinnison traced and surveyed Boskone's military organization in the First Galaxy. He helped plan the attack on Grand Base, the headquarters of Helmuth, who 'spoke for Boskone'. By flooding the control dome of Grand Base with thionite, that deadly drug native to the peculiar planet Trenco, he made it possible for Civilization's Grand Fleet, under the command of Port Admiral Haynes, to reduce that base. He, personally, killed Helmuth in hand-to-hand combat.

He was instrumental in the almost-complete destruction of the Overlords of Delgon; those sadistic, life-eating reptiles who were the first to employ the hyperspatial tube against humanity.

He was wounded more than once; in one of his hospitalizations becoming acquainted with Surgeon-Marshal Lacy and with Sector Chief Nurse Clarrissa MacDougall, who was later to become the widely-known 'Red' Lensman and, still later, my mother.

In spite of the military defeat, however, Boskonia's real organization remained intact, and Kinnison's further search led into Lundmark's Nebula, thenceforth called the Second Galaxy. The planet Medon, being attacked by Boskonians, was rescued from the enemy and was moved across intergalactic space to the First Galaxy. Medon made two notable contributions to Civilization: first, electrical insulation, conductors, and switches by whose means voltages and amperages theretofore undreamed-of could be handled; and later Phillips, a Posenian surgeon, was able there to complete the researches which made it possible for human bodies to grow anew lost members or organs.

Kinnison, deciding that the drug syndicate was the quickest and surest line to Boskone, became Wild Bill Williams the meteor-miner; a hard-drinking, bentlam-eating, fast-shooting space-hellion. As Williams he traced the zwilnik line upward, step by step, to the planet Jarnevon in the Second Galaxy. Upon Jarnevon lived the Eich; frigid-blooded monsters more intelligent, more merciless, more truly Boskonian even than the Overlords.

He and Worsel, Second-Stage Lensmen both, set out to investigate Jarnevon. He was captured, tortured, dismembered; but Worsel brought him back to Tellus with his mind and knowledge intact – the enormously important knowledge that Jarnevon was ruled by a council of nine of the Eich, a council named Boskone.

3

Kinnison was given a Phillips treatment, and again Clarrissa MacDougall nursed him back to health. They loved each other, but they could not marry until the Grey Lensman's job was done; until Civilization had triumphed over Boskonia.

The Galactic Patrol assembled its Grand Fleet, composed of millions of units, under the flagship $Z9M9Z$. It attacked. The planet of Jalte, Boskonia's director of the First Galaxy, was consumed by a bomb of negative matter. Jarnevon was crushed between two colliding planets; positioned inertialess, then inserted especially for that crushing. Grand Fleet returned, triumphant.

But Boskonia struck back, sending an immense fleet against Tellus through a hyperspatial tube instead of through normal space. This method of approach was not, however, unexpected. Survey-ships and detectors were out; the scientists of the Patrol had been for months hard at work on the 'sunbeam' – a device to concentrate the energy of the sun into one frightful beam. With this weapon re-enforcing the already vast powers of Grand Fleet, the invaders were wiped out.

Again Kinnison had to search for a high Boskonian; some authority higher than the Council of Boskone. Taking his personal superdreadnought, the *Dauntless*, which carried his indetectable, non-ferrous speedster, he found a zwilnik trail and followed it to Dunstan's Region, an unexplored, virtually unknown, outlying spiral arm of the First Galaxy. It led to the planet Lyrane II, with its humanoid matriarchy, ruled by Helen, its queen.

There he found Illona Potter, the ex-Aldebaranian dancer; who, turning against her Boskonian masters, told him all she knew of the Boskonian planet Lonabar, where she had spent most of her life. Lonabar was unknown to the Patrol and Illona knew nothing of its location in space. She did, however, know its unique jewelry – gems also completely unknown to Civilization.

Nadreck of Palain VII, a frigid-blooded Second-Stage Lensman, with one jewel as a clue, set out to find Lonabar;

while Kinnison began to investigate Boskonian activities among the matriarchs.

The Lyranians, however, were fanatically non-cooperative. They hated all males; they despised and detested all foreigners. Kinnison, with the consent and assistance of Mentor of Arisia, made Clarrissa MacDougall an Unattached Lensman and assigned to her the task of working Lyrane II.

Nadreck found and mapped Lonabar; and to build up an unimpeachable Boskonian identity Kinnison became Cartiff the jeweler – Cartiff the jewel-thief and swindler – Cartiff the fence – Cartiff the murderer-outlaw – Cartiff the Boskonian big shot. He challenged and overthrew Menjo Bleeko, the dictator of Lonabar, and before killing him took from his mind everything he knew.

The Red Lensman secured information from which it was deduced that a cavern of Overlords existed on Lyrane II. This cavern was raided and destroyed, the Patrolmen learning that the Eich themselves had a heavily fortified base on Lyrane VIII.

Nadreck, master psychologist, invaded that base tracelessly; learning that the Eich received orders from the Thralian solar system in the Second Galaxy and that frigid-blooded Kandron of Onlo (Thrallis IX) was second in power only to human Alcon, the Tyrant of Thrale (Thrallis II).

Kinnison went to Thrale, Nadreck to Onlo; the operations of both being covered by the Patrol's invasion of the Second Galaxy. In that invasion Boskonia's Grand Fleet was defeated and the planet Klovia was occupied and fortified.

Assuming the personality of Traska Gannel, a Thralian, Kinnison worked his way upward in Alcon's military organization. Trapped in a hyperspatial tube, ejected into an unknown one of the infinity of parallel, co-existent, three-dimensional spaces comprising the Cosmic All, he was rescued by Mentor, working through the brain of Sir Austin Cardynge, the Tellurian mathematician.

Returning to Thrale, he fomented a revolution, in which he killed Alcon and took his place as the Tyrant of Thrale. He then discovered that his prime minister, Fossten, who concealed his true appearance by means of a zone of hypnosis, had been Alcon's superior instead of his adviser. Neither quite ready for an open break, but both supremely confident of victory when that break should come, subtle hostilities began.

Gannel and Fossten planned and launched an attack on Klovia, but just before engagement the hostilities between the two Boskonian leaders flared into an open fight for supremacy. After a terrific mental struggle, during which the entire crew of the flagship died, leaving the Boskonian fleet at the mercy of the Patrol, Kinnison won.

He did not know, of course, then or ever, either that Fossten was in fact Gharlane of Eddore or that it was Mentor of Arisia who in fact overcame Fossten. Kinnison thought, and Mentor encouraged him to believe, that Fossten was an Arisian who had been insane since youth, and that Kinnison had killed him without assistance. It is a mere formality to emphasize at this point that none of this information must ever become available to any mind below the third level; since to any entity able either to obtain or to read this report it will be obvious that such revealment would set up an inferiority complex which must inevitably destroy both the Patrol and Civilization.

With Fossten dead and with Kinnison already the despot of Thrale, it was comparatively easy for the Patrol to take over. Nadreck drove the Onlonian garrisons insane, so that all fought to the death among themselves; thus rendering Onlo's mighty armament completely useless.

Then, thinking that the Boskonian War was over – encouraged, in fact, by Mentor so to think – Kinnison married Clarrissa, established his headquarters upon Klovia, and assumed his duties as galactic coordinator.

Kimball Kinnison, while in no sense a mutant, was the penultimate product of a prodigiously long line of selective, controlled breeding. So was Clarrissa MacDougall. Just what course the science of Arisia took in making those two what they are I can deduce, but I do not as yet actually know. Nor, for the purpose of this record, does it matter. Port Admiral

Haynes and Surgeon-Marshal Lacy thought that they brought them together and promoted their romance. Let them think so – as agents, they did. Whatever the method employed, the result was that the genes of those two uniquely complementary penultimates were precisely those necessary to produce the first, and at present the only, Third-Stage Lensmen.

I was born on Klovia, as were, three and four galactic-standard years later, my four sisters – two pairs of non-identical twins. I had little babyhood, no childhood. Fathered and mothered by Second-Stage Lensmen, accustomed from infancy to wide-open two-ways with such beings as Worsel of Velantia, Tregonsee of Rigel IV, and Nadreck of Palain VII, it would seem obvious that we did not go to school. We were not like other children of our ages; but before I realized that it was anything unusual for a baby who could scarcely walk to be computing highly perturbed asteroidal orbits as 'mental arithmetic', I knew that we would have to keep our abnormalities to ourselves, insofar as the bulk of mankind and of Civilization was concerned.

I traveled much; sometimes with my father or mother or both, sometimes alone. At least once each year I went to Arisia for treatment. I took the last two years of Lensmanship, for physical reasons only, at Wentworth Hall instead of the Academy of Klovia because upon Tellus the name Kinnison is not at all uncommon, while upon Klovia the fact that 'Kit' Kinnison was the son of the coordinator could not have been concealed.

I graduated, and with my formal enlensment this record properly begins.

I have recorded this material as impersonally as possible, realizing fully that my sisters and I did only the work for which we were specifically developed and trained; even as you who read this will do that for which you shall have been developed and are to be trained.

Respectfully submitted,
Christopher K. Kinnison, L3, Klovia.

1
Kim and Kit; Grey Lensmen

Galactic Coordinator Kimball Kinnison finished his second cup of Tellurian coffee, got up from the breakfast table, and prowled about in black abstraction. Twenty-odd years had changed him but little. He weighed the same, or a few pounds less; although a little of his mass had shifted downward from his mighty chest and shoulders. His hair was still brown; his stern face was only faintly lined. He was mature, with a conscious maturity no young man can know.

'Since when, Kim, did you think you could get away with blocking *me* out of your mind?' Clarrissa Kinnison directed a quiet thought. The years had dealt as lightly with the Red Lensman as with the Grey. She had been gorgeous; she was now magnificent. 'This room is shielded, you know, against even the girls.'

'Sorry, Cris – I didn't mean it that way.'

'I know,' she laughed. 'Automatic. But you've had that block up for two solid weeks, except when you force yourself to keep it down. That means you're way off the green.'

'I've been thinking, incredible as it may seem.'

'I know it. Let's have it, Kim.'

'QX – you asked for it. Queer things have been going on; all over. Inexplicable things ... no apparent reason.'

'Such as?'

'Almost any kind of insidious deviltry you care to name. Disaffections, psychoses, mass hysterias, hallucinations; pointing toward a Civilization-wide epidemic of revolutions and

8

uprisings for which there seems to be no basis or justification whatever.'

'Why, Kim! How could there be? I haven't heard of anything like that!'

'It hasn't got around. Each solar system thinks it's a purely local condition, but it isn't. As galactic coordinator, with a broad view of the entire picture, my office would of course see such a thing before anyone else could. We saw it, and set out to nip it in the bud... but...' He shrugged his shoulders and grinned wryly.

'But what?' Clarrissa persisted.

'It didn't nip. We sent Lensmen to investigate, but none of them got to the first check-station. Then I asked our Second-Stage Lensmen – Worsel, Nadreck, and Tregonsee – to drop whatever they were doing and solve it for me. They hit it and bounced. They followed, and are still following, leads and clues galore, but they haven't got a millo's worth of results so far.'

'What? You mean it's a problem *they* can't solve?'

'That they haven't, to date,' he corrected, absently. 'And that "gives me furiously to think".'

'It would,' she conceded, 'and it also would make you itch to join them. Think at me, it'll help you correlate. You should have gone over the data with me right at first.'

'I had reasons not to, as you'll see. But I'm stumped now, so here goes. We'll have to go a way back, to before we were married. First; Mentor told me, quote, only your descendants will be ready for that for which you now so dimly grope, unquote. Second; you were the only being ever able to read my thoughts without a Lens. Third; Mentor told us, when we asked him if it was QX for us to go ahead, that our marriage was *necessary*, a choice of phraseology which bothered you somewhat at the time, but which I then explained as being in accord with his visualization of the Cosmic All. Fourth; the Patrol formula is to send the man best fitted for any job to do that job, and if he can't swing it, to send the Number One graduate of the current class of Lensmen. Fifth; a Lensman has got to use everything and everybody available, no matter what or who it is. I used even you, you remember, in that Lyrane affair and others. Sixth; Sir Austin Cardynge believed to the day of his death that we were thrown out of that hyperspatial tube, and out of space, deliberately.'

'Well, go on. I don't see much, if any, connection.'

'You will, if you think of those six points in connection with our present predicament. Kit graduates next month, and he'll rank number one of all Civilization, for all the tea in China.'

'Of course. But after all, he's a Lensman. He'll have to be assigned some problem; why not that one?'

'You don't see yet what that problem is. I've been adding two and two together for weeks, and can't get any other answer than four. And if two and two are four, Kit has got to tackle Boskone – the *real* Boskone; the one I never did and probably never can reach.'

'No, Kim – no!' she almost shrieked. 'Not Kit, Kim – he's just a boy!'

Kinnison waited, wordless.

She got up, crossed the room to him. He put his arm around her in the old but ever new gesture.

'Lensman's load, Cris,' he said, quietly.

'Of course,' she replied then, as quietly. 'It was a shock at first, coming after all these years, but... if it has to be, it must. But he – surely we can help him, Kim?'

'Surely.' The man's arm tightened. 'When he hits space I go back to work. So do Nadreck and Worsel and Tregonsee. So do you, if your kind of a job turns up. And with us to do the blocking, and with Kit to carry the ball...' His thought died away.

'I'll say so,' she breathed. Then: 'But you won't call me, I know, unless you absolutely *have* to... and to give up you and Kit both... why did we have to be Lensmen, Kim?' she protested, rebelliously. 'Why couldn't we have been ground-grippers? You used to growl that thought at me before I knew what a Lens really meant...'

'Vell, some of us has got to be der first violiners in der

orchestra,' Kinnison misquoted, in an attempt at lightness. 'Ve can't all push vind t'rough der trombone.'

'I suppose that's true.' The Red Lensman's somber air deepened. 'Well, we were going to start for Tellus today, anyway, to see Kit graduate. This doesn't change that.'

And in a distant room four tall, shapely, auburn-haired girls stared at each other briefly, then went en rapport; for their mother had erred greatly in saying that the breakfast room was screened against their minds. Nothing was or could be screened against them; they could think above, below, or, by sufficient effort, straight through any thought-screen known to Tellurian science. Nothing in which they were interested was safe from them, and they were interested in practically everything.

'Kay, we've got ourselves a job!' Kathryn, older by minutes than Karen, excluded pointedly the younger twins, Camilla and Constance – 'Cam' and 'Con'.

'At last!' Karen exclaimed. 'I've been wondering what we were born for, with nine-tenths of our minds so deep down that nobody except Kit even knows they're there and so heavily blocked that we can't let even each other in without a conscious effort. This is it. We'll go places now, Kat, and really do things.'

'What do you mean *you'll* go places and do things?' Con demanded, indignantly. 'Do you think for a second you carry screen enough to block *us* out of all the fun?'

'Certainly,' Kat said, equably. 'You're too young.'

'We'll let you know what we're doing, though,' Kay conceded, magnanimously. 'You might, just conceivably, contribute an idea we could use.'

'Ideas – phooey!' Con jeered. 'A real idea would shatter both your skulls. You haven't any more plan than a . . .'

'Hush – shut up, everybody!' Kat commanded. 'This is too new for any of us to have any worthwhile ideas on, yet. Tell you what let's do – we'll all think this over until we're aboard the *Dauntless*, half-way to Tellus; then we'll compare notes and decide what to do.'

They left Klovia that afternoon. Kinnison's personal super-dreadnought, the mighty *Dauntless* – the fourth to bear that name – bored through inter-galactic space. Time passed. The four young redheads convened.

'I've got it all worked out!' Kat burst out, enthusiastically, forestalling the other three. 'There'll be four Second-Stage Lensmen at work and there are four of us. We'll circulate – percolate – you might say – around and through the universe. We'll pick up ideas and facts and feed 'em to our Grey Lensmen. Surreptitiously, sort of, so they'll think they got 'em themselves. I'll take dad for my partner, Kay can have...'

'You'll do no such thing!' A general clamor arose, Con's thought being the most insistent. 'If we aren't going to work with them all, indiscriminately, we'll draw lots or throw dice to see who gets him, so there!'

'Seal it, snake-hips, please,' Kat requested, sweetly. 'It is trite but true to say that infants should be seen, but not heard. This is serious business...'

'Snake-hips! Infant!' Con interrupted, venomously. 'Listen, my steatopygous and senile friend!' Constance measured perhaps a quarter of an inch less in gluteal circumference than did her oldest sister; she tipped the beam at one scant pound below her weight. 'You and Kay are a year older than Cam and I, of course; a year ago your minds were stronger than ours. That condition, however, no longer exists. We too are grown up. And to put that statement to test, what can you do that I can't?'

'This.' Kathryn extended a bare arm, narrowed her eyes in concentration. A Lens materialized about her wrist; not attached to it by a metallic bracelet, but a bracelet in itself, clinging sentiently to the smooth, bronzed skin. 'I felt that in this work there would be a need. I learned to satisfy it. Can you match that?'

They could. In a matter of seconds the three others were similarly enlensed. They had not previously perceived the need, but at Kathryn's demonstration their acquisition of full knowledge had been virtually instantaneous.

Kat's Lens disappeared.

So did the other three. Each knew that no hint of this knowledge or of this power should ever be revealed; each knew that in any moment of stress the Lens of Civilization could be and would be hers.

'Logic, then, and by reason, not by chance.' Kat changed her tactics. 'I still get him. Everybody knows who works best with whom. You, Con, have tagged around after Worsel all your life. You used to ride him like a horse . . .'

'She still does,' Kay snickered. 'He pretty nearly split her in two a while ago in a seven-gravity pull-out, and she almost broke a toe when she kicked him for it.'

'Worsel is nice,' Con defended herself vigorously. 'He's more human than most people, and more fun, as well as having infinitely more brains. And *you* can't talk, Kay – what anyone can see in that Nadreck, so cold-blooded that he freezes you even through armor at twenty feet – you'll get as cold and hard as he is if you don't . . .'

'And every time Cam gets within five hundred parsecs of Tregonsee she goes into the silences with him, contemplating raptly the whichnesses of the why,' Kathryn interrupted, forestalling recriminations. 'So you see, by the process of elimination, dad's mine.'

Since they could not all have him it was finally agreed that Kathryn's claim would be allowed and, after a great deal of discussion and argument, a tentative plan of action was developed. In due course the *Dauntless* landed at Prime Base. The Kinnisons went to Wentworth Hall, the towering, chromium-and-glass home of the Tellurian cadets of the Galactic Patrol. They watched the impressive ceremonies of graduation. Then, as the new Lensmen marched out to the magnificent cadences of 'Our Patrol', the Grey Lensman, leaving his wife and daughters to their own devices, made his way to his Tellurian office.

'Lensman Christopher K. Kinnison, sir, by appointment,' his secretary announced, and as Kit strode in Kinnison stood up and came to attention.

'Christopher K. Kinnison of Klovia, sir, reporting for duty.' Kit saluted crisply.

The coordinator returned the salute punctiliously. Then: 'At rest, Kit. I'm proud of you, mighty proud. We all are. The women want to heroize you, but I had to see you first, to clear up a few things. An explanation, an apology, and, in a sense, commiseration.'

'An apology, sir?' Kit was dumbfounded. 'Why, that's unthinkable...'

'For not graduating you in Grey. It has never been done, but that wasn't the reason. Your commandant, the board of examiners, and Port Admiral LaForge, all recommended it, agreeing that none of us is qualified to give you either orders or directions. I blocked it.'

'Of course. For the son of the coordinator to be the first Lensman to graduate Unattached would smell – especially since the fewer who know of my peculiar characteristics the better. That can wait, sir.'

'Not too long, son.' Kinnison's smile was a trifle forced. 'Here's your Release and your kit, and a request that you go to work on whatever it is that's going on. We rather think it heads up somewhere in the Second Galaxy, but that's just a guess.'

'I start out from Klovia, then? Good – I can go home with you.'

'That's the idea, and on the way there you can study the situation. We've made tapes of the data, with our best attempts at analysis and interpretation. The stuff's up to date, except for a thing I got this morning... I can't figure out whether it means anything or not, but it should be inserted...' Kinnison paced the room, scowling.

'Might as well tell me. I'll insert it when I scan the tape.'

'QX. I don't suppose you've heard much about the unusual shipping trouble we've been having, particularly in the Second Galaxy?'

'Rumor – gossip only. I'd rather have it straight.'

'It's all on the tapes, so I'll just hit the high spots. Losses are twenty-five percent above normal. A few very peculiar derelicts have been found – they seem to have been wrecked by madmen. Not only wrecked, but gutted, and every mark of identification wiped out. We can't determine even origin or destination, since the normal disappearances outnumber the abnormal ones by four to one. On the tapes this is lumped in with the other psychoses you'll learn about. But this morning they found another derelict, in which the chief pilot had scrawled "WARE HELLHOLE IN SP" across a plate. Connection with the other derelicts, if any, obscure. If the pilot was sane when he wrote that message it means something – but nobody knows what. If he wasn't, it doesn't, any more than the dozens of obviously senseless – excuse me, I should say apparently senseless – messages on the tapes.'

'Hm ... m. Interesting. I'll bear it in mind and tape it in its place. But speaking of peculiar things, I've got one I wanted to tell you about – getting my Release was such a shock I almost forgot it. Reported it, but nobody thought it was anything important. Maybe – probably – it isn't. Tune your mind up to the top of the range – there – did you ever hear of a race that thinks on that band?'

'I never did – it's practically unreachable. Why – have you?'

'Yes and no. Only once, and that only a touch. Or, rather, a burst; as though a hard-held mind-block had exploded, or the creature had just died a violent, instantaneous death. Not enough of it to trace, and I never found any more of it.'

'Any characteristics? Bursts can be quite revealing.'

'A few. It was on my last break-in trip in the Second Galaxy, out beyond Thrale – about here.' Kit marked the spot upon a mental chart. 'Mentality very high – precisionist grade – possibly beyond social needs, as the planet was a bare desert and terrifically hot. No thought of cities. Nor of water, although both may have existed without appearing in that burst of thought. The thing's bodily structure was RTSL, to four places. No gross digestive tract – atmosphere-nourished or an energy-converter, perhaps. The sun was a blue giant. No spectral data, of course, but at a rough guess I'd say somewhere around class B_5 or AO. That's all I could get.'

'That's a lot to get from one burst. It doesn't mean a thing to me right now ... but I'll watch for a chance to fit it in somewhere.'

How casually they dismissed as unimportant that cryptic

burst of thought! But if they both, right then, together, had been authoritatively informed that that description fitted exactly the physical form forced upon its denizens in its summer by the accurately-described simply hellish climatic conditions obtaining during that season on the noxious planet Ploor, the information would still not have seemed important to either of them – then.

'Anything else we ought to discuss before night?' The older Lensman went on without a break.

'Not that I know of.'

'You said your Release was a shock. You've got another one coming.'

'I'm braced – blast!'

'Worsel, Tregonsee, Nadreck, and I are quitting our jobs and going Grey again. Our main purpose in life is going to be rallying round at max whenever you whistle.'

'That *is* a shock, sir ... Thanks ... I hadn't expected – it's really overwhelming. And you said something about *commiserating* me?' Kit lifted his red-thatched head – all of Clarrissa's children had inherited her startling hair – and grey eyes stared level into eyes of grey.

'In a sense, yes. You'll understand later ... Well, you'd better go hunt up your mother and the girls. After the clambake is over ...'

'I'd better cut it, hadn't I?' Kit asked, eagerly. 'Don't you think it'd be better for me to get started right away?'

'Not on your life!' Kinnison demurred, positively. 'Do you think I want that mob of redheads snatching me bald? You're in for a large day and evening of lionization, so take it like a man. As I was about to say, as soon as the brawl is over tonight we'll all board the *Dauntless* and do a flit for Klovia, where we'll fix you up an outfit. Until then, son ...' Two big hands gripped.

'But I'll be seeing you around the Hall!' Kit exclaimed. 'You can't ...'

'No, I can't run out on it, either,' Kinnison grinned, 'but we won't be in a sealed and shielded room. So, son ... I'm proud of you.'

'Right back at you, big fellow – and thanks a million.' Kit strode out and, a few minutes later, the coordinator did likewise.

The 'brawl', which was the gala event of the Tellurian social year, was duly enjoyed by all the Kinnisons. The *Dauntless* made an uneventful flight to Klovia. Arrangements were made. Plans, necessarily sketchy and elastic, were laid.

Two big, grey-clad Lensmen stood upon the deserted space-field between two blackly indetectable speedsters. Kinnison was massive, sure, calm with the poised calmness of maturity, experience, and power. Kit, with the broad shoulders and narrow waist of his years and training, was taut and tense, fiery, eager to come to grips with Civilization's foes.

'Remember, son,' Kinnison said as the two gripped hands. 'There are four of us – old-timers who've been through the mill – on call every second. If you can use any one of us or all of us don't wait – snap out a call.'

'I know, dad... thanks. The four best. One of you may make a strike before I do. With the thousands of leads we have, and your experience and know-how, you probably will. So remember it cuts both ways. If any of you can use me any time, *you* whistle.'

'QX. We'll keep in touch. Clear ether, Kit!'

'Clear ether, dad!' What a wealth of meaning there was in that low-voiced, simple exchange of the standard *bon voyage!*

For minutes, as his speedster flashed through space, Kinnison thought only of the boy. He knew exactly how he felt; he relived in memory the supremely ecstatic moments of his own first launching into space as a Grey Lensman. But Kit had the stuff – stuff which he, Kinnison, could never know anything about – and he had his own job to do. Therefore, methodically, like the old campaigner he was, he set about it.

2
Worsel and the Overlords

Worsel, the Velantian, hard and durable and long-lived as Velantians are, had in twenty Tellurian years changed scarcely at all. As the first Lensman and the only Second-Stage Lensman of his race, the twenty years had been very fully occupied indeed.

He had solved the varied technological and administrative problems incident to the welding of Velantia into the structure of Civilization. He had worked at the many tasks which, in the opinion of the Galactic Council, fitted his peculiarly individual talents. In his 'spare' time he had sought out in various parts of two galaxies, and had ruthlessly slain, widely-scattered groups of the Overlords of Delgon.

Continuously, however, he had taken an intense sort of god-fatherly interest in the Kinnison children, particularly in Kit and in the youngest daughter, Constance; finding in the girl a mentality surprisingly akin to his own.

When Kinnison's call came he answered it. He was now out in space; not in the *Dauntless*, but in a ship of his own, under his own command. And what a ship! The *Velan* was manned entirely by beings of his own race. It carried Velantian air, at Velantian temperature and pressure. Above all, it was built and powered for inert maneuvering at the atrocious accelerations employed by the Velantians in their daily lives; and Worsel loved it with enthusiasm and elan.

He had worked conscientiously and well with Kinnison and with other entities of Civilization. He and they had all known, however, that he could work more efficiently alone or with others of his own kind. Hence, except in emergencies, he had done so; and hence, except in similar emergencies, he would so continue to do.

Out in deep space, Worsel entwined himself, in a Velantian's idea of comfort, in an intricate series of figures-of-eight around a pair of parallel bars and relaxed in thought. There were insidious deviltries afoot, Kinnison had said. There were disaffections, psychoses, mass hysterias, and – Oh happy thought! – hallucinations. There were also certain revolutions and sundry uprisings, which might or might not be connected or associated with the disappearances of a considerable number of persons of note. In these latter, however, Worsel of Velantia was not interested. He knew without being told that Kinnison would pounce upon such blatant manifestations as those. He himself would work upon something much more to his taste.

Hallucination was Worsel's dish. He had been born among hallucinations; had been reared in an atmosphere of them. What he did not know about hallucinations could have been printed in pica on the smallest one of his scales.

Therefore, isolating one section of his multi-compartmented mind from all others and from any control over his physical self, he sensitized it to receive whatever hallucinatory influences might be abroad. Simultaneously he set two other parts of his mind to watch over the one to be victimized; to study and to analyze whatever figments of obtrusive mentality might be received and entertained.

Then, using all his naturally tremendous sensitivity and reach, all his Arisian super-training, and the full power of his Lens, he sent his mental receptors out into space. And then, although the thought is staggeringly incomprehensible to any Tellurian or near-human mind, he *relaxed*. For day after day, as the *Velan* hurtled randomly through the void, he hung blissfully slack upon his bars, most of his mind a welter of the indescribable thoughts in which it is a Velantian's joy to revel.

Suddenly, after an unknown interval of time, a thought impinged: a thought under the impact of which Worsel's long body tightened so convulsively as to pull the bars a foot out of true. Overlords! The unmistakable, the body-and-mind-paralyzing hunting call of the Overlords of Delgon!

His crew had not felt it yet, of course; nor would they feel it. If they should, they would be worse than useless in the conflict to come; for they could not withstand that baneful influence. Worsel could. Worsel was the only Velantian who could.

'Thought-screens all!' his commanding thought snapped out. Then, even before the order could be obeyed: 'As you were!'

For the impenetrably shielded chamber of his mind told him instantly that this was no ordinary Delgonian hunting call; or rather, that it was more than that. Much more.

Mixed with, superimposed upon the overwhelming compulsion which generations of Velantians had come to know so bitterly and so well, were the very things for which he had been searching – hallucinations! To shield his crew or, except in the subtlest possible fashion himself, simply would not do. Overlords everywhere knew that there was at least one Velantian Lensman who was mentally their master; and, while they hated this Lensman tremendously, they feared him even more. Therefore, even though a Velantian was any Overlord's choicest prey, at the first indication of an ability to disobey their commands the monsters would cease entirely to radiate; would withdraw at once every strand of their far-flung mental nets into the fastnesses of their superbly hidden and indetectably shielded cavern.

Therefore Worsel allowed the inimical influence to take over, not only the total minds of his crew, but also the unshielded portions of his own. And stealthily, so insidiously that no mind affected could discern the change, values gradually grew vague and reality began to alter.

Loyalty dimmed, and *esprit de corps*. Family ties and pride of race waned into meaninglessness. All concepts of Civilization, of the Galactic Patrol, degenerated into strengthless gossamer, into oblivion. And to replace those hitherto mighty motivations there crept in an overmastering need for, and the exact method of obtainment of, whatever it was that was each Velantian's deepest, most primal desire. Each crewman stared into an individual visiplate whose substance was to him as real and as solid as the metal of his ship had ever been; each saw upon that plate whatever it was that, consciously or unconsciously, he wanted most to see. Noble or base, lofty or low, intellectual or physical, spiritual or carnal, it made no difference to the Overlords. Whatever each victim wanted most was there.

No figment was, however, even to the Velantians, actual or tangible. It was a picture on a plate, transmitted from a well-defined point in space. There, upon that planet, was the actuality, eagerly await; toward and to that planet must the *Velan* go at maximum blast. Into that line and at that blast, then, the pilots set their vessel without orders, and each of the crew saw upon his non-existent plate that she had so been set. If she had not been, if the pilots had been able to offer any resistance, the crew would have slaughtered them out of hand. As it was, all was well.

And Worsel, watching the affected portion of his mind accept those hallucinations as truths and admiring unreservedly the consummate artistry with which the work was being done, was well content. He knew that only a hard, solidly-driven, individually probing beam could force him to reveal the fact that a portion of his mind and all of his bodily controls were being withheld; he knew that unless he made a slip no such investigation was to be expected. He would not slip.

No human or near-human mind can really understand how the mind of a Velantian works. A Tellurian can, by dint of training, learn to do two or more unrelated things simultaneously. But neither is done very well and both must be more or less routine in nature. To perform any original or difficult operation successfully he must concentrate on it, and he can concentrate upon only one thing at a time. A Velantian can and does, however, concentrate upon half-a-dozen totally unrelated things at once; and, with his multiplicity of arms, hands, and eyes, he can perform simultaneously an astonishing number of completely independent operations.

The Velantian's is, however, in no sense such a multiple personality as would exist if six or eight human heads were mounted upon one body. There is no joint tenancy about it. There is only one ego permeating all those pseudo-independent compartments; no contradictory orders are, or ordinarily can be, sent along the bundled nerves of the spinal cord. While individual in thought and in the control of certain actions, the mind-compartments are basically, fundamentally, one mind.

Worsel had progressed beyond his fellows. He was different; unique. The perception of the need of the ability to isolate certain compartments of his mind, to separate them completely from his real ego, was one of the things which had enabled him to become the only Second-Stage Lensman of his race.

L2 Worsel, then, held himself aloof and observed appreciatively everything that went on. More, he did a little hallucinating of his own. Under the Overlords' compulsion he was supposed to remain motionless, staring raptly into an imaginary visiplate at an orgiastic saturnalia of which no description will be attempted. Therefore, as far as the occupied portion of his mind and through it the Overlords were concerned, he did so. Actually, however, his body moved purposefully about, directed solely by his own grim will; moved to make ready against the time of landing.

For Worsel knew that his opponents were not fools. He knew that they reduced their risks to the irreducible minimum. He knew that the mighty *Velan*, with her prodigious weaponry, would not be permitted to be within extreme range of the cavern, if the Overlords could possibly prevent it, when that cavern's location was revealed. His was the task to see to it that she was not only within range, but was at the very portal.

The speeding space-ship approached the planet... went inert... matched the planetary intrinsic... landed. Her airlocks opened. Her crew rushed out headlong, sprang into the air, and arrowed away en masse. Then Worsel, Grand Master of Hallucinations, went blithely but intensely to work.

Thus, although he stayed at the *Velan's* control board instead of joining the glamored Velantians in their rush over the unfamiliar terrain, and although the huge vessel lifted lightly into the air and followed them, neither the fiend-possessed part of

Worsel's mind, nor any of his fellows, nor through them any one of the many Overlords, knew that either of those two things was happening. To that part of his mind Worsel's body was, under full control, flying along upon tireless wings in the midst of the crowd; to it and to all other Velantians and hence to the Overlords the *Velan* lay motionless and deserted upon the rocks far below and behind them. They watched her diminish in the distance; they saw her vanish beyond the horizon!

This was eminently tricky work, necessitating as it did such nicety of synchronization with the Delgonians' own compulsions as to be indetectable even to the monsters themselves. Worsel was, however, an expert; he went at the job not with any doubt as to his ability to carry it through, but only with an uncontrollably shivering physical urge to come to grips with the hereditary enemies of his race.

The flyers shot downward, and as a boulder-camouflaged entrance yawned open in the mountain's side Worsel closed up and shot out a widely enveloping zone of thought-screen. The Overlords' control vanished. The Velantians, realizing instantly what had happened, flew madly back to their ship. They jammed through the airlocks, flashed to their posts. The cavern's gates had closed by then, but the monsters had no screen fit to cope with the *Velan*'s tremendous batteries. Down they went. Barriers, bastions, and a considerable portion of the mountain's face flamed away in fiery vapor or flowed away in molten streams. Through reeking atmosphere, over red-hot debris, the armored Velantians flew to the attack.

The Overlords had, however, learned. This cavern, as well as being hidden, was defended by physical, as well as mental, means. There were inner barriers of metal and of force, there were armed and armored defenders who, dominated completely by the monsters, fought with the callous fury of the robots which in effect they were. Nevertheless, against all opposition, the attackers bored relentlessly in. Heavy semi-portables blazed, hand-to-hand combat raged in the narrow confines of that noisome tunnel. In the wavering, glaring light of the contending beams and screens, through the hot and rankly stinking steam billowing away from the reeking walls, the invaders fought their way. One by one and group by group the defenders died where they stood and the Velantians drove onward over their burned and dismembered bodies.

Into the cavern at last. To the Overlords. Overlords! They who for ages had preyed upon generation after generation of helpless Velantians, torturing their bodies to the point of death and then devouring ghoulishly the life-forces which their mangled bodies could no longer retain!

Worsel and his crew threw away their DeLameters. Only when it is absolutely necessary does any Velantian use any artificial weapon against any Overlord of Delgon. He is too furious, too berserk, to do so. He is scared to the core of his being; the cold gruel of a thousand fiendishly eaten ancestors has bred that fear into the innermost atoms of his chemistry. But against that fear, negating and surmounting it, is a hatred of such depth and violence as no human being has ever known; a starkly savage hatred which can be even partially assuaged only by the ultimate of violences – by rending his foe apart member by member; by actually feeling the Delgonian's life depart under gripping hands and tearing talons and constricting body and shearing tail.

It is best, then, not to go into too fine detail as to this conflict. Since there were almost a hundred of the Delgonians, since they were insensately vicious fighters when cornered, and since their physical make-up was very similar to the Velantians' own, many of Worsel's troopers died. But since the *Velan* carried over fifteen hundred and since less than half of her personnel could even get into the cavern, there were plenty of them left to operate and to fight the space-ship.

Worsel took great care that the opposing commander was not killed with his minions. The fighting over, the Velantians chained this sole survivor into one of his own racks and stretched him out into immobility. Then, restraining by main strength the terrific urge to put the machine then and there to its fullest ghastly use, Worsel cut his screen, threw a couple of turns of tail around a convenient anchorage, and faced the Boskonian almost nose to nose. Eight weirdly stalked eyes curled out as he drove a probing thought-beam against the monster's shield.

'I could use this – or this – or this,' Worsel gloated. As he touched various wheels and levers the chains hummed slightly sparks flashed, the rigid body twitched. 'I am not going to, however – yet. While you are still sane I shall take your total knowledge.'

Face to face, eye to eye, brain to brain, that silently and motionlessly cataclysmic battle was joined.

As has been said, Worsel had hunted down and had destroyed many Overlords. He had hunted them, however, like vermin. He had killed them with bombs and beams, with talons, teeth, and tail. He had not engaged an Overlord mind to mind for over twenty Tellurian years; not since he and Nadreck of Palain Seven had captured alive the leaders of those who had been preying upon Helen's matriarchs and warring upon Civilization from their cavern on Lyrane II. Nor had he ever dueled one mentally to the death without powerful support; Kinnison or some other Lensman had always been near by.

But Worsel would need no help. He was not shivering in eagerness now. His body was as still as the solid rock upon which most of it lay; every chamber and every faculty of his mind was concentrated upon battering down or blasting through the Overlord's stubbornly-held shields.

Brighter and brighter flamed Worsel's Lens, flooding the gloomy cave with pulsating polychromatic light. Alert for any possible trickery, guarding intently against any possibility of counterthrust, Worsel slammed in bolt after bolt of mental force. He surrounded the monster's mind with a searing, constricting field. He squeezed; relentlessly and with appalling power.

The Overlord was beaten. He, who had never before encountered a foreign mind or a vital force stronger than his own, knew that he was beaten. He knew that at long last he had met that half-fabulous Velantian Lensman with whom not one of his monstrous race could cope. He knew starkly, with the chilling, numbing terror possible only to such a being in such a position, that he was doomed to die the same hideous and long-drawn-out death he had dealt out to so many others. He did not read into the mind of the bitterly vengeful, the implacably ferocious Velantian any more mercy, any more compunction, than were actually there. He knew perfectly that there was no slightest trace of either. Knowing these things with the black certainty that was his, he quailed.

There is an old saying that the brave man dies only once, the coward a thousand times. The Overlord, during that lethal combat, died more times than it is pleasant to contemplate. Nevertheless, he fought. His mind was keen and powerful; he brought to the defense of his beleaguered ego every resource of skill and of trickery and of sheer power at his command. In vain. Deeper and deeper, in spite of everything he could do, the relentless Lensman squeezed and smashed and cut and pried and bored; little by little the Overlord gave mental ground.

'This station is here ... this staff is here ... I am here, then ... to wreak damage ... all possible damage ... to the commerce ... and to the personnel of ... the Galactic Patrol ... and Civilization in every aspect ...' the Overlord admitted haltingly as Worsel's pressure became intolerable; but such admissions, however unwillingly made or however revealing in substance, were not enough.

Worsel wanted, and would be satisfied with nothing less than, his enemy's total knowledge. Hence he maintained his assault until, unable longer to withstand the frightful battering, the Overlord's barriers went completely down; until every convolution of his brain and every track of his mind lay open, helplessly exposed to Worsel's poignant scrutiny. Then, scarcely taking time to gloat over his victim, Worsel did scrutinize.

Hurtling through space, toward a definite objective now, Worsel studied and analyzed some of the things he had just learned. He was not surprised that this Overlord had not known any of his superior officers in things or enterprises Boskonian;

that he did not consciously know that he had been obeying orders or that he had superiors. That technique, by this time, was familiar enough. The Boskonian psychologists were able operators; to attempt to unravel the unknowable complexities of their subconscious compulsions would be a sheer waste of time.

What the Overlords had been doing, however, was clear enough. That outpost had indeed been wreaking havoc with Civilization's commerce. Ship after ship had been lured from its course; had been compelled to land upon this barren planet. Some of those vessels had been destroyed; some of them had been stripped and rifled as though by pirates of old; some of them had been set upon new courses with hulls, mechanical equipment, and cargoes almost untouched. No crewman or passenger, however, escaped unscathed; even though only ten percent of them died in the Overlordish fashion Worsel knew so well.

The Overlord himself had wondered why they had not been able to kill them all. They wanted intensely enough to do so; their lust for life-force simply could not be sated. He knew only that *something* had limited their killing to ten percent of the bag.

Worsel grinned wolfishly at that thought, even while he was admiring the quality of the psychology able to impress such a compulsion upon such intractable minds as those. That was the work of the Boskonian higher-ups; to spread confusion wider and wider.

The other ninety percent had merely been 'played with' – a procedure which, although less satisfying to the Overlords than the ultimate treatment, was not very different as far as the victims' egos were concerned. For none of them emerged from the ordeal with any memory of what had happened, or of who or what he had ever been. They were not all completely mad; some were only partially so. All had, however, been . . . altered. Changed; shockingly transformed. No two were alike. Each Overlord, it appeared, had tried with all his ultra-hellish might to excel his fellows in the manufacture of an outrageous something whose like had never before been seen on land or sea or in the depths of space.

These and many other things Worsel studied carefully. He'd head for the 'Hell-Hole in Space', he decided. This planet, the Overlords he had just slain, were not the Hell-Hole; could have had nothing to do with it – wrong location.

He knew now, though, what the Hell-Hole really was. It was a cavern of Overlords – couldn't be anything else – and in himself and his crew and his mighty vessel he, the Overlord-slayer supreme of two galaxies, had everything it took to extirpate any number of Overlords. That Hell-Hole was just as good as out, as of that minute.

And just then a solid, diamond-clear thought came in.

'Worsel! Con calling. What goes on there, fellow old snake?'

3
Kinnison Writes a Space-Opera

Each of the Second-Stage Lensmen had exactly the same facts, the same data, upon which to theorize and from which to draw conclusions. Each had shared his experiences, his findings, and his deductions and inductions with all of the others. They had discussed minutely, in wide-open four-ways, every phase of the Boskonian problem. Nevertheless the approach of each to that problem and the point of attack chosen by each was individual and characteristic.

Kimball Kinnison was by nature forthright; direct. As has been seen, he could use the approach circuitous if necessary, but he much preferred and upon every possible occasion employed the approach direct. He liked plain, unambiguous clues much better than obscure ones; the more obvious and factual the clue was, the better he liked it.

He was now, therefore, heading for Antigan IV, the scene of the latest and apparently the most outrageous of a long series of crimes of violence. He didn't know much about it; the request had come through regular channels, not via Lens, that he visit Antigan and direct the investigation of the supposed murder of the Planetary President.

As his speedster flashed through space the Grey Lensman mulled over in his mind the broad aspects of this crime-wave. It was spreading far and wide, and the wider it spread and the intenser it became the more vividly one salient fact stuck out. Selectivity – distribution. The solar systems of Thrale, Velantia, Tellus, Klovia, and Palain had not been affected. Thrale, Tellus, and Klovia were full of Lensmen. Velantia, Rigel, Palain, and a

29

good part of the time Klovia, were the working headquarters of Second-Stage Lensmen. It seemed, then, that the trouble was roughly in inverse ratio to the numbers or the abilities of the Lensmen in the neighborhood. Something, therefore, that Lensmen – particularly Second-Stage Lensmen – were bad for. That was true, of course, for all crime. Nevertheless, this seemed to be a special case.

And when he reached his destination he found out that it was. The planet was seething. Its business and its everyday activities seemed to be almost paralyzed. Martial law had been declared; the streets were practically deserted except for thick-clustered groups of heavily-armed guards. What few people were abroad were furtive and sly; slinking hastily along with their fear-filled eyes trying to look in all directions at once.

'QX, Wainwright, go ahead,' Kinnison directed brusquely when, alone with the escorting Patrol officers in a shielded car, he was being taken to the Capitol grounds. 'There's been too much pussyfooting about the whole affair.'

'Very well, sir,' and Wainwright told his tale. Things had been happening for months. Little things, but disturbing. Then murders and kidnappings and unexplained disappearances had begun to increase. The police forces had been falling farther and farther behind. The usual cries of incompetence and corruption had been raised, only further to confuse the issue. Circulars – dodgers – handbills appeared all over the planet; from where nobody knew. The keenest detectives could find no clue to paper-makers, printers, or distributors. The usual inflammatory, subversive, propaganda – 'Down with the Patrol!' 'Give us back our freedom!' and so on – but, because of the high tension already prevailing, the stuff had been unusually effective in breaking down the morale of the citizenry as a whole.

'Then this last thing. For two solid weeks the whole world was literally plastered with the announcement that at midnight on the thirty-fourth of Dreel – you're familiar with our calendar, I think? – President Renwood would disappear. Two weeks warning – daring us to do our damndest.' Wainwright got that far and stopped.

'Well, go on. He disappeared, I know. How? What did you fellows do to prevent it? Why all the secrecy?'

'If you insist I'll have to tell you, of course, but I'd rather not.' Wainwright flushed uncomfortably. 'You wouldn't believe it. Nobody could. I wouldn't believe it myself if I hadn't been there. I'd rather you'd wait, sir, and let the vice-president tell you, in the presence of the treasurer and the others who were on duty that night.'

'Um...m...I see...maybe.' Kinnison's mind raced. 'That's why nobody would give me details? Afraid I wouldn't believe it – that I'd think they'd been...' He stopped. 'Hypnotized' would have been the next word, but that would have been jumping at conclusions. Even if true, there was no sense in airing that hypothesis – yet.

'Not afraid, sir. They *knew* you wouldn't believe it.'

After entering Government Reservation they went, not to the president's private quarters, but into the Treasury and down into the sub-basement housing the most massive, the most utterly impregnable vault of the planet. There the nation's most responsible officers told Kinnison, with their entire minds as well as their tongues, what had happened.

Upon that black day business had been suspended. No visitors of any sort had been permitted to enter the Reservation. No one had been allowed to approach Renwood except old and trusted officers about whose loyalty there could be no question. Airships and space-ships had filled the sky. Troops, armed with semi-portables or manning fixed-mount heavy stuff, had covered the grounds. At five minutes before midnight Renwood, accompanied by four secret-service men, had entered the vault, which was thereupon locked by the treasurer. All the cabinet members saw them go in, as did the attendant corps of specially-selected guards. Nevertheless, when the treasurer opened the vault at five minutes after midnight, the five men were gone. No trace of any one of them had been found from that time on.

'And that – every word of it – is TRUE!' the assembled minds yelled as one, all unconsciously, into the mind of the Lensman.

During all this telling Kinnison had been searching mind after mind; inspecting each minutely for the tell-tale marks of mental surgery. He found none. No hypnosis. This thing had actually happened, exactly as they told it. Convinced of that fact, his eyes clouded with foreboding, he sent out his sense of perception and studied the vault itself. Millimeter by cubic millimeter he scanned the innermost details of its massive structure – the concrete, the neocarballoy, the steel, the heat-conductors and the closely-spaced gas cells. He traced the intricate wiring of the networks of alarms. Everything was sound. Everything functioned. Nothing had been disturbed.

The sun of this system, although rather on the small side, was intensely hot; this planet, Four, was pretty far out. Well beyond Cardynge's Limit. A tube, of course ... for all the tea in China it had to be a tube. Kinnison sagged; the indomitable Grey Lensman showed his years and more.

'I know it happened.' His voice was grim, quiet, as he spoke to the still protesting men. 'I also know how it was done, but that's all.'

'HOW?' they demanded, practically in one voice.

'A hyperspatial tube,' and Kinnison went on to explain, as well as he could, the functioning of a thing which was intrinsically beyond the grasp of any non-mathematical three-dimensional mind.

'But what can we or anybody else *do* about it?' the treasurer asked, numbly.

'Nothing whatever.' Kinnison's voice was flat. 'When it's gone, it's gone. Where does the light go when a lamp goes out? No more trace. Hundreds of millions of planets in this galaxy, as many in the Second. Millions and millions of galaxies. All that in one universe – our own universe. And there are an infinite number – too many to be expressed, let alone to be grasped – of universes, side by side, like pages in a book except thinner, in the hyper-dimension. So you can figure out for yourselves the chances of ever finding either President Renwood or the Boskonians who took him – so close to zero as to be indistinguishable from zero absolute.'

The treasurer was crushed. 'Do you mean to say that there's no protection at all from this thing? That they can keep on doing away with us just as they please? The nation is going mad, sir, day by day – one more such occurrence and we will be a planet of maniacs.'

'Oh no – I didn't say that.' The tension lightened. 'Just that we can't do anything about the president and his aides. The tube can be detected while it's in place, and anyone coming through it can be shot as soon as he can be seen. What you need is a couple of Rigellian Lensmen, or Ordoviks. I'll see to it that you get them. I don't think, with them here, they'll even try to repeat.' He did not add what he knew somberly to be a fact, that the enemy would go elsewhere, to some other planet not protected by a Lensman able to perceive the intangible structure of a sphere of force.

Frustrated, the Lensman again took to space. It was terrible, this thing of having everything happening where he wasn't and when he got there having nothing left to work on. Hit-and-run – stab-in-the-back – how could a man fight something he couldn't see or sense or feel or find? But this chewing his fingernails to the elbow wasn't getting him anywhere, either; he'd have to find something that he *could* stick a tooth into. What?

All former avenues of approach were blocked; he was sure of that. The Boskonians who were now in charge of things could really think. No underling would know anything about any one of them except at such times and places as the directors chose, and those conferences would be as nearly detection-proof as they could be made. What to do?

Easy. Catch a big operator in the act. He grinned wryly to himself. Easy to say, but not . . . however, it wasn't impossible. The Boskonians were not super-men – they didn't have any more jets than he did. Put himself in the other fellow's place – what would he do if he were a Boskonian big shot? He had had quite a lot of experience in the role. Were there any specific groups of crimes which revealed techniques similar to those which he himself would use in like case?

He, personally, preferred to work direct and to attack in force. At need, however, he had done a smooth job of boring from within. In the face of the Patrol's overwhelming superiority of armament, especially in the First Galaxy, they would have to bore from within. How? By what means? He was a Lensman; they weren't. Jet back! Or were they, perhaps? How did he know they weren't, by this time? Fossten the renegade Arisian... No use kidding himself; Fossten might have known as much about the Lens as Mentor himself, and might have developed an organization that even Mentor didn't know anything about. Or Mentor might be figuring that it would be good for what ailed a certain fat-headed Grey Lensman to have to dope this out for himself. QX.

He shot a call to Vice-Coordinator Maitland, who was now in complete charge of the office which Kinnison had temporarily abandoned.

'Cliff? Kim. Just gave birth to an idea.' He explained rapidly what the idea was. 'Maybe nothing in it, but we'd better get up on our toes and find out. You might suggest to the boys that they check up here and there, particularly around the rough spots. If any of them find any trace anywhere of off-color, sour, or even slightly rancid Lensmanship, with or without a Lens appearing in the picture, burn a hole in space getting it to me. QX?... Thanks.'

Viewed in this new perspective, Renwood of Antigan IV might have been neither a patriot nor a victim, but a saboteur. The tube could have been a prop, used deliberately to cap the mysterious climax. The four honest and devoted guards were the real casualties. Renwood – or whoever he was – having accomplished his object of undermining and destroying the whole planet's morale, might simply have gone elsewhere to continue his nefarious activities. It was fiendishly clever. That spectacularly theatrical finale was certainly one for the book. The whole thing, though, was very much of a piece in quality of workmanship with what he had done in becoming the Tyrant of Thrale. Far-fetched? No. He had already denied in his thoughts that the Boskonian operators were super-men. Conversely, he wasn't, either. He would have to admit that they might very well be as good as he was; to deny them the ability to do anything he himself could do would be sheer stupidity.

Where did that put him? On Radelix, by Klono's golden gills! A good-sized planet. Important enough, but not too much so. People human. Comparatively little hell being raised there – yet. Very few Lensmen, and Gerrond the top. Hm . . . m. Gerrond. Not too bright, as Lensmen went, and inclined to be a bit brass-hattish. To Radelix, by all means, next.

He went to Radelix, but not in the *Dauntless* and not in grey. He was a passenger aboard a luxury liner, a writer in search of local color for another saga of the space-ways. Sybly Whyte – one of the Patrol's most carefully-established figments – had a bullet-proof past. His omnivorous interest and his uninhibited nosiness were the natural attributes of his profession – everything is grist which comes to an author's mill.

Sybly Whyte, then, prowled about Radelix. Industriously and, to some observers, pointlessly. He and his red-leather notebook were apt to be seen anywhere at any time, day or night. He visited space-ports, he climbed through freighters, he lost small sums in playing various games of so-called chance in spacemen's dives. On the other hand, he truckled assiduously to the social elite and attended all functions into which he could wangle or could force his way. He made a pest of himself in the offices of politicians, bankers, merchant princes, tycoons of business and manufacture, and all other sorts of greats.

He was stopped one day in the outer office of an industrial potentate. 'Get out and stay out,' a peg-legged guard told him. 'The boss hasn't read any of your stuff, but I have, and neither of us wants to talk to you. Data, huh? What the hell do you need of data on atomic cats and bulldozers to write them damn space-operas of yours? Why don't you get a roustabout job on a freighter and learn something first-handed? Get yourself a space-tan instead of that imitation you got under a lamp; work some of that lard off your carcass!' Whyte was definitely fatter than Kinnison had been; and, somehow, softer; he peered owlishly through heavy lenses which, fortunately, did not interfere with his sense of perception. 'Then maybe some of your tripe will be half-fit to read – beat it!'

'Yes, sir. Thank you, sir; very much, sir.' Kinnison bobbed obsequiously and scurried out, writing industriously in his notebook the while. He had, however, found out what he wanted to know. The boss was nobody he wanted.

Nor was an eminent statesman whom he button-holed at a reception. 'I fail to see, sir, entirely, any point in your interviewing *me*,' that worthy informed him, frigidly. 'I am not, I am – uh – sure, suitable material for any opus upon which you may be at work.'

'Oh, you can't ever tell, sir,' Kinnison said. 'You see, I never know who or what is going to get into any of my stories until after I start to write it, and sometimes not even then.' The statesman glared and Kinnison retreated in disorder.

To stay in character Kinnison actually wrote a novel; it was later acclaimed as one of Sybly Whyte's best.

'Qadgop the Mercotan slithered flatly around the after-bulge of the tranship. One claw dug into the meters-thick armor of pure neutronium, then another. Its terrible xmex-like snout locked on. Its zymolosely polydactile tongue crunched out, crashed down, rasped across. *Slurp! Slurp!* At each abrasive stroke the groove in the tranship's plating deepened and Qadgop leered more fiercely. Fools! Did they think that the airlessness of absolute space, the heatlessness of absolute zero, the yieldlessness of absolute neutronium, could stop QADGOP THE MERCOTAN? And the stowaway, that human wench Cynthia, cowering in helpless terror just beyond this thin and fragile wall ...' Kinnison was taping verbosely along when his first real clue developed.

A yellow 'attention' light gleamed upon his visiphone panel, a subdued chime gave notice that a message of importance was about to be broadcast to the world. Kinnison-Whyte flipped his switch and the stern face of the provost-marshal appeared upon the screen.

'Attention, please,' the image spoke. 'Every citizen of Radelix is urged to be on the lookout for the source of certain inflammatory and subversive literature which is beginning to appear in various cities of this planet. Our officers cannot be everywhere at once; you citizens are. It is hoped that by the aid of your vigilance this threat to our planetary peace and security can be removed before it becomes really serious; that we can avoid the imposition of martial law.'

This message, while not of extreme or urgent import to most Radeligians, held for Kinnison a profound and unique meaning. He was right. He had deduced the thing one hundred percent. He knew what was going to happen next, and how; he knew that neither the law-enforcement officers of Radelix nor its massed citizenry could stop it. They could not even impede it. A force of Lensmen could stop it – but that would not get the Patrol anywhere unless they could capture or kill the beings really responsible for what was done. To alarm them would not do.

Whether or not he could do much of anything before the grand climax depended on a lot of factors. On what that climax was; who was threatened with what; whether or not the threatened one was actually a Boskonian. A great deal of investigation was indicated.

If the enemy were going to repeat, as seemed probable, the president would be the victim. If he, Kinnison, could not get the big shots lined up before the plot came to a head, he would have to let it develop right up to the point of disappearance; and for Whyte to appear at that time would be to attract undesirable attention. No – by that time he must already have been kicking around underfoot long enough to have become an unnoticeable fixture.

Wherefore he moved into quarters as close to the executive offices as he could possibly get; and in those quarters he worked openly and wordily at the bringing of the affair of Qadgop and the beautiful-but-dumb Cynthia to a satisfactory conclusion.

4
Nadreck of Palain VII at Work

In order to understand these and subsequent events it is necessary to cut back briefly some twenty-odd years, to the momentous interview upon chill, dark Onlo between monstrous Kandron and his superior in affairs Boskonian, the unspeakable Alcon, the Tyrant of Thrale. At almost the end of that interview, when Kandron had suggested the possibility that his own base had perhaps been vulnerable to Star A Star's insidious manipulations:

'Do you mean to admit that *you* may have been invaded and searched – tracelessly?' Alcon fairly shrieked the thought.

'Certainly,' Kandron replied, coldly. 'While I do not believe that it has been done, the possibility must be conceded. What science can devise science can circumvent. It is not Onlo and I who are their prime objectives, you must realize, but Thrale and you. Especially you.'

'You may be right. With no data whatever upon who or what Star A Star really is, with no tenable theory as to how he could have done what actually has been done, speculation is idle.' Thus Alcon ended the conversation and, almost immediately, went back to Thrale.

After the Tyrant's departure Kandron continued to think, and the more he thought the more uneasy he became. It was undoubtedly true that Alcon and Thrale were the Patrol's prime objectives. But, those objectives attained, was it reasonable to suppose that he and Onlo would be spared? It was not. Should he warn Alcon further? He should not. If the Tyrant, after all that had been said, could not see the danger he was in, he wasn't worth saving. If he preferred to stay and fight it out, that was his lookout. Kandron would take no chances with his own extremely valuable life.

Should he warn his own men? How could he? They were able and hardened fighters all; no possible warning could make them defend their fortresses and their lives any more efficiently than they were already prepared to do; nothing he could say would be of any use in preparing them for a threat whose basic nature, even, was completely unknown. Furthermore, this hypothetical invasion probably had not happened and very well might not happen at all, and to flee from an imaginary foe would not redound to his credit.

No. As a personage of large affairs, not limited to Onlo, he would be called elsewhere. He would stay elsewhere until after whatever was going to happen had happened. If nothing happened during the ensuing few weeks he would return from his official trip and all would be well.

He inspected Onlo thoroughly, he cautioned his officers repeatedly and insistently to keep alert against every conceivable emergency while he was so unavoidably absent. Then he departed, with a fleet of vessels manned by hand-picked crews, to a long-prepared and hitherto secret retreat.

From that safe place he watched, through the eyes and the instruments of his skilled observers, everything that occurred. Thrale fell, and Onlo. The Patrol triumphed. Then, knowing the full measure of the disaster and accepting it with the grim passivity so characteristic of his breed, Kandron broadcast certain signals and one of his – and Alcon's – superiors got in touch with him. He reported concisely. They conferred. He was given orders which were to keep him busy for over twenty Tellurian years.

He knew now that Onlo had been invaded, tracelessly, by some feat of mentality beyond comprehension and almost beyond belief. Onlo had fallen without any of its defenders having energized a single one of their gigantic engines of war. The fall of Thrale, and the manner of that fall's accomplishment, were plain enough. Human stuff. The work, undoubtedly,

40

of human Lensmen; perhaps the work of the human Lensman who was so frequently associated with Star A Star.

But Onlo! Kandron himself had set those snares along those intricately zig-zagged communications lines; he knew their capabilities. Kandron himself had installed Onlo's blocking and shielding screens; he knew their might. He knew, since no other path existed leading to Thrale, that those lines had been followed and those screens had been penetrated, and all without setting off a single alarm. Those things had actually happened. Hence Kandron set his stupendous mind to the task of envisaging what the being must be, mentally, who could do them; what the mind of this Star A Star – it could have been no one else – must in actuality be.

He succeeded. He deduced Nadreck of Palain VII, practically in toto; and for the Star A Star thus envisaged he set traps throughout both galaxies. They might or might not kill him. Killing him immediately, however, was not really of the essence; that matter could wait until he could give it his personal attention. The important thing was to see to it that Star A Star could never, by any possible chance, discover a true lead to any high Boskonian.

Sneeringly, gloatingly, Kandron issued orders; then flung himself with all his zeal and ability into the task of reorganizing the shattered fragments of the Boskonian Empire into a force capable of wrecking Civilization.

Thus it is not strange that for more than twenty years Nadreck of Palain VII made very little progress indeed. Time after time he grazed the hot edge of death. Indeed, it was only by the exertion of his every iota of skill, power, and callous efficiency that he managed to survive. He struck a few telling blows for Civilization, but most of the time he was strictly on the defensive. Every clue he followed, it seemed, led subtly into a trap; every course he pursued ended, always figuratively and all too often literally, in a cul-de-sac filled with semi-portable projectors all agog to blast him out of the ether.

Year by year he became more conscious of some imperceptible, indetectable, but potent foe, an individual enemy obstructing his every move and determined to make an end of him. And year by year, as material accumulated, it became more and more certain that the inimical entity was in fact Kandron, once of Onlo.

When Kit went into space, then, and Kinnison called Nadreck into consultation, the usually reticent and unloquacious Palainian was ready to talk. He told the Grey Lensman everything he knew and everything he deduced or suspected about the ex-Onlonian chieftain.

'Kandron of Onlo!' Kinnison exploded, so violently as to sear the sub-ether through which the thought passed. 'Holy Klono's gadolinium guts! And you can sit there on your spiny tokus and tell me Kandron got away from you back there? You knew it, and not only didn't do a damn thing about it yourself, but didn't even tell me or anybody else about it so we could do it? *What* a brain!'

'Certainly. Why do anything before action becomes necessary?' Nadreck was entirely unmoved by the Tellurian's passion. 'My powers are admittedly small, my intellect feeble. However, even to me it was clear then and it is clear now that Kandron was then of no importance. My assignment was to reduce Onlo. I reduced it. Whether or not Kandron was there at the time did not then have and cannot now have anything to do with that task. Kandron, personally, is another, an entirely distinct problem.'

Kinnison swore a blistering deep-space oath; then, by main strength, shut himself up. Nadreck wasn't human; there was no use even trying to judge him by human or near-human standards. He was fundamentally, incomprehensibly, and radically different. And it was just as well for humanity that he was. For if his hellishly able race had possessed the characteristically human abilities, in addition to their own, Civilization would of necessity have been basically Palainian instead of basically human, as it now is. 'QX, ace,' he growled, finally. 'Skip it.'

'But Kandron has been hampering my activities for years, and, now that you also have become interested in his operations, he has become a factor of which cognizance should be

42

taken,' Nadreck went imperturbably on. He could no more understand Kinnison's viewpoint than the Tellurian could understand his. 'With your permission, therefore, I shall find – and slay – this Kandron.'

'Go to it, little chum,' Kinnison sighed, bitingly – and uselessly. 'Clear ether.'

While this conference was taking place, Kandron reclined in a bitterly cold, completely unlighted room of his headquarters and indulged in a little gloating concerning the predicament in which he was keeping Nadreck of Palain VII, who was, in all probability, the once-dreaded Star A Star of the Galactic Patrol. It was true that the Lensman was still alive. He would probably, Kandron mused quite pleasurably, remain alive until he himself could find the time to attend to him in person. He was an able operator, but one presenting no real menace, now that he was known and understood. There were other things more pressing, just as there had been ever since the fall of Thrale. The revised Plan was going nicely, and as soon as he had resolved that human thing... The Ploorans had suggested... could it be possible, after all, that Nadreck of Palain was not he who had been known so long only as Star A Star? That the human factor was actually...?

Through the operation of some unknowable sense Kandron knew that it was time for his aide to be at hand to report upon those human affairs. He sent out a signal and another Onlonian scuttled in.

'That unknown human element,' Kandron radiated harshly. 'I assume that you are not reporting that it has been resolved?'

'Sorry, Supremacy, but your assumption is correct,' the creature radiated back, in no very conciliatory fashion. 'The trap at Antigan IV was set particularly for him; specifically to match the man whose mentality you computed and diagrammed for us. Was it too obvious, think you, Supremacy? Or perhaps not quite obvious enough? Or, the galaxy being large, is it perhaps that he simply did not learn of it in time? In the next attempt, what degree of obviousness should I employ and what degree of repetition is desirable?'

'The technique of the Antigan affair was flawless,' Kandron decided. 'He did not learn of it, as you suggest, or we should have caught him. He is a master workman, always concealed by his very obviousness until after he has done his work. Thus we can never, save by merest chance, catch him before the act; we must make him come to us. We must keep on trying until he does come to us. It is of no great moment, really, whether we catch him now or five years hence. This work must be done in any event – it is simply a fortunate coincidence that the necessary destruction of Civilization upon its own planets presents such a fine opportunity of trapping him.

'As to repeating the Antigan technique, we should not repeat it exactly – or, hold! It might be best to do just that. To repeat a process is of course the mark of an inferior mind; but if that human can be made to believe that our minds are inferior, so much the better. Keep on trying; report as instructed. Remember that he must be taken alive, so that we can take from his living brain the secrets we have not yet been able to learn. Forget, in the instant of leaving this room, everything about me and about any connection between us until I force recollection upon you. Go.'

The minion went, and Kandron set out to do more of the things which he could best do. He would have liked to take Nadreck's trail himself; he could catch and he could kill that evasive entity and the task would have been a pleasant one. He would have liked to supervise the trapping of that enigmatic human Lensman who might – or might not – be that frequently and copiously damned Star A Star. That, too, would be an eminently pleasant chore. There were, however, other matters more pressing by far. If the Great Plan were to succeed, and it absolutely must and would, every Boskonian must perform his assigned duties. Nadreck and his putative accomplice were side issues. Kandron's task was to set up and to direct certain psychoses and disorders; a ghastly train of mental ills of which he possessed such supreme mastery, and

44

which were surely and safely helping to destroy the foundation upon which Galactic Civilization rested. That part was his, and he would do it to the best of his ability. The other things, the personal and non-essential matters, could wait.

Kandron set out then, and traveled fast and far; and wherever he went there spread still further abroad the already widespread blight. A disgusting, a horrible blight with which no human physician or psychiatrist, apparently, could cope; one of, perhaps the worst of, the corrosive blights which had been eating so long at Civilization's vitals.

And L2 Nadreck, having decided to find and slay the ex-ruler of Onlo, went about it in his usual unhurried but eminently thorough fashion. He made no effort to locate him or to trace him personally. That would be bad – foolish. Worse, it would be inefficient. Worst, it would probably be impossible. No, he would find out where Kandron would be at some suitable future time, and wait for him there.

To that end Nadreck collected a vast mass of data concerning the occurrences and phenomena which the Big Four had discussed so thoroughly. He analyzed each item, sorting out those which bore the characteristic stamp of the arch-foe whom by now he had come to know so well. The internal evidence of Kandron's craftsmanship was unmistakable; and, not now to his surprise, Nadreck discerned that the number of the Onlonian's dark deeds was legion.

There was the affair of the Prime Minister of DeSilva III, who at a cabinet meeting shot and killed his sovereign and eleven chiefs of state before committing suicide. The president of Viridon; who, at his press conference, ran amuck with a scimitar snatched from a wall, hewed unsuspecting reporters to gory bits until overpowered, and then swallowed poison.

A variant of the theme, but still plainly Kandron's doing, was the interesting episode in which a Tellurian tycoon named Edmundson, while upon an ocean voyage, threw fifteen women passengers overboard, then leaped after them dressed only in a life-jacket stuffed with lead. Another out of the same whimsical mold was that of Dillway, the highly respected operations chief of Central Spaceways. That potentate called his secretaries one by one into his 60th floor office and unconcernedly tossed them, one by one, out of the window. He danced a jig on the coping before diving after them to the street.

A particularly juicy and entertaining bit, Nadreck thought, was the case of Narkor Base Hospital, in which four of the planet's most eminent surgeons decapitated every other person in the place – patients, nurses, orderlies, and all, with a fine disregard of age, sex, or condition – arranged the severed heads, each upright and each facing due north, upon the tiled floor to spell the word 'Revenge', and then hacked each other to death with scalpels.

These, and a thousand or more other vents of similar technique, Nadreck tabulated and subjected to statistical analysis. Scattered so widely throughout such a vast volume of space, they had created little or no general disturbance; indeed, they had scarcely been noticed by Civilization as a whole. Collected, they made a truly staggering, a revolting and appalling total. Nadreck, however, was inherently incapable of being staggered, revolted, or appalled. That repulsive summation, a thing which in its massed horror would have shaken to the core any being possessing any shred of sympathy or tenderness, was to Nadreck an interesting and not too difficult problem in psychology and mathematics.

He placed each episode in space and in time, correlating each with all of its fellows in a space-time matrix. He determined the locus of centers and derived the equations of its most probable motion. He extended it by extrapolation in accordance with that equation. Then, assuring himself that his margin of error was as small as he could make it, he set out for a planet which Kandron would most probably visit at a time far enough in the future to enable him to prepare to receive the Onlonian.

That planet, being inhabited by near-human beings, was warm, brightly sun-lit, and had an atmosphere rich in oxygen. Nadreck detested it, since his ideal of a planet was precisely the opposite. Fortunately, however, he would not have to land upon it until after Kandron's arrival – possibly not then – and the fact that his proposed quarry was, like himself, a frigid-blooded poison-breather, made the task of detection a simple one.

Nadreck set his indetectable speedster into a circular orbit around the planet, far enough out to be comfortable, and sent out course after course of delicate, extremely sensitive screen. Precision of pattern-analysis was of course needless. The probability was that all legitimate movement of personnel to and from the planet would be composed of warm-blooded oxygen-breathers; that any visitor not so classified would be Kandron. Any frigid-blooded visitor had at least to be investigated, hence his analytical screens had to be capable only of differentiation between the two types of beings as far apart as the galactic poles in practically every respect. Nadreck knew that no supervision would be necessary to perform such an open-and-shut separation as that; he would have nothing more to do until his electronic announcers should warn him of Kandron's approach – or until the passage of time should inform him that the Onlonian was not coming to this particular planet.

Being a mathematician, Nadreck knew that any datum secured by extrapolation is of doubtful value. He thus knew that the actual probability of Kandron's coming was less, by some indeterminable amount, than the mathematical one. Nevertheless, having done all that he could do, he waited with the monstrous, unhuman patience known only to such races as his.

Day by day, week by week, the speedster circled the planet and its big, hot sun; and as it circled, the lone voyager studied. He analyzed more data more precisely; he drew deeper and deeper upon his store of knowledge to determine what steps next to take in the event that this attempt should end, as so many previous ones had ended, in failure.

5

The Abduction of a President

Kinnison the author toiled manfully at his epic of space whenever he was under any sort of observation, and enough at other times to avert any suspicion. Indeed, he worked as much as Sybly Whyte, an advertisedly temperamental writer, had ever worked. Besides interviewing the high and the low, and taking notes everywhere, he attended authors' teas, at which he cursed his characters fluently and bitterly for their failure to cooperate with him. With short-haired women and long-haired men he bemoaned the perversity of a public which compelled them to prostitute the real genius of which each was the unique possessor. He sympathized particularly with a fat woman writer of whodunits, whose extremely unrealistic yet amazingly popular Grey Lensman hero had lived through ten full-length novels and twenty million copies.

Even though her real field was the drama, she wasn't writing the kind of detective tripe that most of these crank-turners ground out, she confided to Kinnison. She had known lots of Grey Lensmen *very* intimately, and *her* stories were drawn from real life in every particular!

Thus Kinnison remained in character; and thus he was enabled to work completely unnoticed at his real job of finding out what was going on, how the Boskonians were operating to ruin Radelix as they had ruined Antigan IV.

His first care was to investigate the planet's president. That took doing, but he did it. He examined that mind line by line and channel by channel, with no results whatever. No scars, no sign of tampering. Calling in assistance, he searched the president's past. Still no soap. Everything checked. Boring from within, then, was out. His first hypothesis was wrong; this invasion and this sabotage were being done from without. How?

Those first leaflets were followed by others, each batch more vitriolic in tone than the preceding one. Apparently they came from empty stratosphere; at least, no ships were to be detected in the neighborhood after any shower of the handbills had appeared. But that was not surprising. With its inertialess drive any space-ship could have been parsecs away before the papers touched atmosphere. Or they could have been bombed in from almost any distance. Or, as Kinnison thought most reasonable, they could have been simply dumped out of the mouth of a hyperspatial tube. In any event the method was immaterial. The results only were important; and those results, the Lensman discovered, were entirely disproportionate to the ostensible causes. The subversive literature had some effect, of course, but essentially it must be a blind. No possible tonnage of anonymous printing could cause that much sheer demoralization.

Crack-pot societies of all kinds sprang up everywhere, advocating everything from absolutism to anarchy. Queer cults arose, preaching free love, the imminent end of the world, and many other departures from the norm of thought. The Author's League, of course, was affected more than any other organization of its size, because of its relatively large content of strong and intensely opinionated minds. Instead of becoming one radical group it split into a dozen.

Kinnison joined one of those 'Down with Everything!' groups, not as a leader, but as a follower. Not too sheep-like a follower, but just inconspicuous enough to retain his invisibly average status; and from his place of concealment in the middle of the front row he studied the minds of each of his fellow anarchists. He watched those minds change, he found out who was doing the changing. When Kinnison's turn came he was all set for trouble. He expected to battle a powerful mentality. He would not have been overly surprised to encounter another mad Arisian, hiding behind a zone of hypnotic compulsion.

He expected anything, in fact, except what he found – which was a very ordinary Radeligian therapist. The guy was a clever enough operator, of course, but he could not work against even the feeblest opposition. Hence the Grey Lensman had no trouble at all, either in learning everything the fellow knew, or, upon leaving him, in implanting within his mind the knowledge that Sybly Whyte was now exactly the type of worker desired.

The trouble was that the therapist didn't know a thing. This not entirely unexpected development posed Kinnison three questions. Did the high-ups ever communicate with such small fry, or did they just give them one set of orders and cut them loose? Should he stay in this Radeligian's mind until he found out? If he was in control of the therapist when a big shot took over, did he have jets enough to keep from being found out? Risky business; better scout around first, anyway. He'd do a flit.

He drove his black speedster a million miles. He covered Radelix like a blanket, around the equator and from pole to pole. Everywhere he found the same state of things. The planet was literally riddled with the agitators; he found so many that he was forced to a black conclusion. There could be no connection or communication between such numbers of saboteurs and any real authority. They must have been given one set of do-or-die instructions – whether they did or died was immaterial. Experimentally, Kinnison had a few of the leaders taken into custody. Nothing happened.

Martial law was finally declared, but this measure succeeded only in driving the movement underground. What the subversive societies lost in numbers they more than made up in desperation and violence. Crime raged unchecked and uncheckable, murder became an every-day commonplace, insanity waxed rife. And Kinnison, knowing now that no channel to important prey would be opened until the climax, watched grimly while the rape of the planet went on.

President Thompson and Lensman Gerrond sent message after message to Prime Base and to Klovia, imploring help. The replies to these pleas were all alike. The matter had been referred to the galactic council and to the coordinator.

Everything that could be done was being done. Neither office could say anything else, except that, with the galaxy in such a disturbed condition, each planet must do its best to solve its own problems.

The thing built up toward its atrocious finale. Gerrond invited the president to a conference in a down-town hotel room, and there, eyes glancing from moment to moment at the dials of a complete little test-kit held open upon his lap:

'I have just had some startling news, Mr. Thompson,' Gerrond said, abruptly. 'Kinnison has been here on Radelix for weeks.'

'What? Kinnison? Where is he? Why didn't he ... ?'

'Yes, Kinnison. Kinnison of Klovia. The coordinator himself. I don't know where he is, or was. I didn't ask him.' The Lensman smiled fleetingly. 'One doesn't, you know. He discussed the situation with me at length. I'm still amazed...'

'Why doesn't he stop it, then?' the president demanded. 'Or can't he stop it?'

'That's what I've got to explain to you. He won't be able to do a thing, he says, until the last minute...'

'Why not? I tell you, if this thing can be stopped it's *got* to be stopped, and no matter what has to be done—'

'Just a minute!' Gerrond snapped. 'I know you're out of control – I don't like to see Radelix torn apart any better than you do – but you ought to know by this time that Galactic Coordinator Kimball Kinnison is in a better position to know what to do than any other man in the universe. Furthermore, his word is the last word. What he says, goes.'

'Of course,' Thompson apologized. 'I am overwrought... but to see our entire world pulled down around us, our institutions, the work of centuries, destroyed, millions of lives lost... all needlessly...'

'It won't come to that, he says, if we all do our parts. And you, sir, are very much in the picture.'

'I? How?'

'Are you familiar with what happened to Antigan IV?'

'Why, no. They had some trouble over there, I recall, but...'

'That's it. That's why this must go on. No planet cares particularly about what happens to any other planet, but Kinnison cares about them all as a whole. If this trouble is headed off now it will simply spread to other planets; if it is allowed to come to a climax there's a chance to put an end to the whole trouble, for good.'

'But what has that to do with me? What can I, personally, do?'

'Much. That last act at Antigan IV, the thing that made it a planet of maniacs, was the kidnapping of Planetary President Renwood. Murdered, supposedly, since no trace of him has been found.'

'Oh.' The older man's hands clenched, then loosened. 'I am willing . . . provided . . . is Kinnison fairly certain that my death will enable him . . .'

'It won't get that far, sir. He intends to stop it just before that. He and his associates – I don't know who they are – have been listing every enemy agent they can find, and they will all be taken care of at once. He believes that Boskone will publish in advance a definite time at which they will take you away from us. That was the way it went at Antigan.'

'Even from the Patrol?'

'From the main base itself. Coordinator Kinnison is pretty sure they can do it, except for something he can bring into play only at the last moment. Incidentally, that's why we're having this meeting here, with this detector he gave me. He's afraid this base is porous.'

'In that case . . . what can he . . .' The president fell silent.

'All I know is that we're to dress you in a certain suit of armor and have you in my private office a few minutes before the time they set. We and the guards leave the office at minus two minutes and walk down the corridor, just fast enough to be exactly in front of Room Twenty-Four at minus one. We're to rehearse it until our timing is perfect. I don't know what will happen then, but *something* will.'

Time passed; the Boskonian infiltration progressed according to plan. It appeared that Radelix was going in the same fashion in which Antigan IV had gone. Below the surface, however, there was one great difference. Every ship reaching Radelix brought at least one man who did not leave. Some of these visitors were tall and lithe, some were short and fat. Some were old, some were young. Some were pale, some were burned to the color of ancient leather by the fervent rays of space. They were alike only in the 'look of eagles' in their steady, quiet eyes. Each landed and went about his ostensible business, interesting himself not at all in any of the others.

Again the Boskonians declared their contempt of the Patrol by setting the exact time at which Planetary President Thompson was to be taken. Again the appointed hour was midnight.

Lieutenant-Admiral Lensman Gerrond was, as Kinnison had intimated frequently, somewhat of a brass hat. He did not, he simply could not, believe that his base was as pregnable as the coordinator had assumed it to be. Kinnison, knowing that all ordinary defenses would be useless, had not even mentioned them. Gerrond, unable to believe that his hitherto invincible and invulnerable weapons and defenses were all of a sudden useless, mustered them of his own volition.

All leaves had been cancelled. Every detector, every beam, every device of defense and offense was fully manned. Every man was keyed up and alert. And Gerrond, while apprehensive that something was about to happen which wasn't in the book, was pretty sure in his stout old war-dog's soul that he and his men had stuff enough.

At two minutes before midnight the armored president and his escorts left Gerrond's office. One minute later they were passing the door of the specified room. A bomb exploded shatteringly behind them, armored men rushed yelling out of a branch corridor in their rear. Everybody stopped and turned to look. So, the hidden Kinnison assured himself, did an unseen observer in an invisible, hovering, three-dimensional hyper-circle.

Kinnison threw the door open, flashed an explanatory thought at the president, yanked him into the room and into the midst of a corps of Lensmen armed with devices not usually encountered even in Patrol bases. The door snapped shut and Kinnison stood where Thompson had stood an instant before, clad in armor identical with that which the president had worn. The exchange had required less than one second.

'QX, Gerrond and you fellows!' Kinnison drove the thought. 'The president is safe – I'm taking over. Double time straight ahead – hipe! Get clear – give us a chance to use our stuff!'

The unarmored men broke into a run, and as they did so the door of Room Twenty-Four swung open and stayed open. Weapons erupted from other doors and from more branch corridors. The hyper-circle, which was in fact the terminus of a hyperspatial tube, began to thicken toward visibility.

It did not, however, materialize. Only by the intensest effort of vision could it be discerned as the sheerest wisp, more tenuous than fog. The men within the ship, if ship it was, were visible only as striations in air are visible, and no more to be made out in detail. Instead of a full materialization, the only thing that was or became solid was a dead-black thing which reached purposefully outward and downward toward Kinnison, a thing combined of tongs and coarse-meshed, heavy net.

Kinnison's DeLameters flamed at maximum intensity and minimum aperture. Useless. The stuff was dureum; that unbelievably dense and ultimately refractory synthetic which, saturated with pure force, is the only known substance which can exist as an actuality both in normal space and in that pseudo-space which composes the hyperspatial tube. The Lensman flicked on his neutralizer and shot away inertialess; but that maneuver, too, had been foreseen. The Boskonian engineers matched every move he made, within a split second after he made it; the tong-net closed.

Semi-portables flamed then – heavy stuff – but they might just as well have remained cold. Their beams could not cut the dureum linkages; they slid harmlessly *past* – not through – the wraith-like, figmental invaders at whom they were aimed. Kinnison was hauled aboard the Boskonian vessel; its structure and its furnishings and its crew becoming ever firmer and more substantial to his senses as he went from normal into pseudo space.

As the pseudo world became real, the reality of the base behind him thinned into unreality. In seconds it disappeared utterly, and Kinnison knew that to the senses of his fellow human beings he had simply vanished. This ship, though, was real enough. So were his captors.

The net opened, dumping the Lensman ignominiously to the floor. Tractor beams wrenched his blazing DeLameters out of his grasp – whether or not hands and arms came with them was entirely his own look-out. Tractors and pressors jerked him upright, slammed him against the steel wall of the room, held him motionless against it.

Furiously he launched his ultimately lethal weapon, the Worsel-designed, Thorndyke-built, mind-controlled projector of thought-borne vibrations which decomposed the molecules without which thought and life itself could not exist. Nothing happened. He explored, finding that even his sense of perception was stopped a full foot away from every part of every one of those humanoid bodies. He settled down then and thought. A great light dawned; a shock struck sickeningly home.

No such elaborate and super-powered preparations would have been made for the capture of any civilian. Presidents were old men, physically weak and with no extraordinary powers of mind. No – this whole chain of events had been according to plan – a high Boskonian's plan. Ruining a planet was, of course, a highly desirable thing in itself, but it could not have been the main feature.

Somebody with a real brain was out after the four Second-Stage Lensmen and he wasn't fooling. And if Nadreck, Worsel, Tregonsee and himself were all to disappear, the Patrol would know that it had been nudged. But jet back – which of the four other than himself would have taken that particular bait? Not one of them. Weren't they out after them, too? Sure they were – they must be. Oh, if he could only warn them – but after all, what good would it do? They had all warned each other repeatedly to watch out for traps; all four had been constantly on guard. What possible foresight could have avoided a snare set so perfectly to match every detail of a man's make-up?

But he wasn't licked yet. They had to know what he knew, how he had done what he had done, whether or not he had any superiors and who they were. Therefore they had had to take him alive, just as he had had to take various Boskonian chiefs. And they'd find out that as long as he was alive he'd be a dangerous buzz-saw to monkey with.

The captain, or whoever was in charge, would send for him; that was a foregone conclusion. He'd have to find out what he had caught; he'd have to make a report of some kind. And somebody would slip. One hundred percent vigilance was impossible, and Kinnison would be on his toes to take advantage of that slip, however slight it might be.

But the captors did not take Kinnison to the captain. Instead, accompanied by half a dozen unarmored men, that worthy came to Kinnison.

'Start talking, fellow, and talk fast,' the Boskonian directed crisply in the lingua franca of deep space as the armored soldiers strode out. 'I want to know who you are, what you are, what you've done, and everything about you and the Patrol. So talk – or do you want me to pull you apart with these tractors, armor and all?'

Kinnison paid no attention, but drove at the commander with his every mental force and weapon. Blocked. This ape too had a full-body, full-coverage screen.

There was a switch at the captain's hip, handy for fingertip control. If he could only move! It would be *so* easy to flip that switch! Or if he could throw something – or make one of those other fellows brush against him just right – or if the guy happened to sit down a little too close to the arm of a chair – or if there were a pet animal of any kind around – or a spider or a worm or even a gnat . . .

6
Tregonsee, Camilla, and 'X'

Second-Stage Lensman Tregonsee of Rigel IV did not rush madly out into space in quest of something or anything Boskonian in response to Kinnison's call. To hurry was not Tregonsee's way. He could move fast upon occasion, but before he would move at all he had to know exactly how, where, and why he should move.

He conferred with his three fellows, he furnished them with all the data he possessed, he helped integrate the totaled facts into one composite. That composite pleased the others well enough so that they went to work, each in his own fashion, but it did not please Tregonsee. He could not visualize any coherent whole from the available parts. Therefore, while Kinnison was investigating the fall of Antigan IV, Tregonsee was sitting – or rather, standing – still and thinking. He was still standing still and thinking when Kinnison went to Radelix.

Finally he called in an assistant to help him think. He had more respect for the opinions of Camilla Kinnison than for those of any other entity, outside of Arisia, of the two galaxies. He had helped train all five of the Kinnison children, and in Cam he had found a kindred soul. Possessing a truer sense of values than any of his fellows, he alone realized that the pupils had long since passed their tutors; and it is a measure of his quality that the realization brought into Tregonsee's tranquil soul no tinge of rancor, but only wonder. What those incredible Children of the Lens had he did not know, but he knew that they – particularly Camilla – had extraordinary gifts.

In the mind of this scarcely grown woman he perceived

depths which he could not plumb, extensions and vistas the meanings of which he could not even vaguely grasp. He did not try either to plumb the abysses or to survey the expanses; he made no slightest effort, ever, to take from any of the children anything which the child did not first offer to reveal. In his own mind he tried to classify theirs; but, realizing in the end that that task was and always would be beyond his power, he accepted the fact as calmly as he accepted the numberless others of Nature's inexplicable facts. Tregonsee came the closest of any Second-Stage Lensman to the real truth, but even he never did suspect the existence of the Eddorians.

Camilla, as quiet as her twin sister Constance was boisterous, parked her speedster in one of the capacious holds of the Rigellian's space-ship and joined him in the control room.

'You believe, I take it, that dad's logic is faulty, his deductions erroneous?' the girl thought, after a casual greeting. 'I'm not surprised. So do I. He jumped at conclusions. But then, he does that, you know.'

'Oh, I wouldn't say that, exactly. However, it seems to me,' Tregonsee replied carefully, 'that he did not have sufficient basis in fact to form any definite conclusion as to whether or not Renwood of Antigan was a Boskonian operative. It is that point which I wish to discuss with you first.'

Cam concentrated. 'I don't see that it makes any difference, fundamentally, whether he was or not,' she decided, finally. 'A difference in method only, not in motivation. Interesting, perhaps, but immaterial. It is virtually certain in either case that Kandron of Onlo or some other entity is the prime force and is the one who must be destroyed.'

'Of course, my dear, but that is only the first differential. How about the second, and the third? Method governs. Nadreck, concerning himself only with Kandron, tabulated and studied only the Kandronesque manifestations. He may – probably will – eliminate Kandron. It is by no means assured, however, that that step will be enough. In fact, from my preliminary study, I would risk a small wager that the larger and worse aspects would remain untouched. I would therefore suggest that we ignore, for the time being, Nadreck's findings and examine anew all the data available.'

'I wouldn't bet you a millo on that,' Camilla caught her lower lip between white, even teeth. 'Check. The probability is that Renwood was a loyal citizen. Let us consider every possible argument for and against that assumption . . .'

They went into contact of minds so close that the separate thoughts simply could not be resolved into terms of speech. They remained that way, not for the period of a few minutes which would have exhausted any ordinary brain, but for four solid hours; and at the end of that conference they had arrived at a few tentative conclusions.

Kinnison had said that there was no possibility of tracing a hyperspatial tube after it had ceased to exist. There were millions of planets in the two galaxies. There was an indefinite, quite possibly an infinite number of co-existent parallel spaces, into any one of which the tube might have led. Knowing these things, Kinnison had decided that the probability was infinitesimally small that any successful investigation could be made along those lines.

Tregonsee and Camilla, starting with the same facts, arrived at entirely different results. There were many spaces, true, but the inhabitants of any one space belonged to that space and would not be interested in the conquest or the permanent taking over of any other. Foreign spaces, then, need not be considered. Civilization had only one significant enemy; Boskonia. Boskonia, then, captained possibly by Kandron of Onlo, was the attacker. The tube itself could not be traced and there were millions of planets, yes, but those facts were not pertinent.

Why not? Because 'X', who might or might not be Kandron, was not operating from a fixed headquarters, receiving reports from subordinates who did the work. A rigid philosophical analysis, of which few other minds would have been capable, showed that 'X' was doing the work himself, and was moving from solar system to solar system to do it. Those mass psychoses in which entire garrisons went mad all at once, those mass hysterias in which vast groups of civilians went reasonlessly out of control, could not have been brought about by an ordinary mind. Of all Civilization, only Nadreck of Palain VII had the requisite ability; was it reasonable to suppose that Boskonia had many such minds? No. 'X' was either singular or a small integer.

Which? Could they decide the point? With some additional data, they could. Their linked minds went en rapport with Worsel, with Nadreck, with Kinnison, and with the Principal Statistician at Prime Base.

In addition to Nadreck's locus, they determined two more – one of all inimical manifestations, the other of those which Nadreck had not used in his computations. Their final exhaustive analysis showed that there were at least two, and very probably only two, prime intelligences directing those Boskonian activities. They made no attempt to identify either of them. They communicated to Nadreck their results and their conclusions.

'I am working on Kandron,' the Palainian replied, flatly. 'I made no assumptions as to whether or not there were other prime movers at work, since the point has no bearing. Your information is interesting, and may perhaps prove valuable, and I thank you for it – but my present assignment is to find and to kill Kandron of Onlo.'

Tregonsee and Camilla, then, set out to find 'X'; not any definite actual or deduced entity, but the perpetrator of certain closely related and highly characteristic phenomena, viz, mass psychoses and mass hysterias. Nor did they extrapolate. They visited the last few planets which had been affected, in the order in which the attacks occurred. They studied every phase of every situation. They worked slowly, but – they hoped and they believed – surely. Neither of them had any idea then that behind 'X' lay Ploor, and beyond Ploor, Eddore.

Having examined the planet latest to be stricken, they made no effort to pick out definitely the one next to be attacked. It might be any one of ten worlds, or possibly even twelve. Hence, neglecting entirely the mathematical and logical probabilities involved, they watched them all, each taking six. Each flitted from world to world, with senses alert to perceive the first sign of subversive activity. Tregonsee was a retired magnate, spending his declining years in seeing the galaxy. Camilla was a Tellurian business girl on vacation.

Young, beautiful, innocent-looking girls who traveled alone were, then as ever, regarded as fair game by the Don Juans of any given human world. Scarcely had Camilla registered at the Hotel Grande when a well-groomed, self-satisfied man-about-town made an approach.

'Hel-lo, beautiful! Remember me, don't you – old Tom Thomas? What say we split a bottle of fayalin, to renew old...' He broke off, for the red-headed eyeful's reaction was in no sense orthodox. She was not coldly unaware of his presence. She was neither coy nor angry, neither fearful nor scornful. She was only and vastly *amused*.

'You think, then, that I am human and desirable?' Her smile was devastating. 'Did you ever hear of the Canthrips of Ollenole?' She had never heard of them either, before that instant, but this small implied mendacity did not bother her.

'No... o, I can't say that I have.' The man, while very evidently taken aback by this new line of resistance, persevered. 'What kind of a brush-off do you think you're trying to give me?'

'Brush-off? See me as I am, you beast, and thank whatever gods you recognize that I am not hungry, having eaten just last night.' In his sight her green eyes darkened to a jetty black, the flecks of gold in them scintillated and began to emit sparks. Her hair turned into a mass of horribly clutching tentacles. Her teeth became fangs, her fingers talons, her strong, splendidly proportioned body a monstrosity out of hell's grisliest depths.

After a moment she allowed the frightful picture to fade back into her charming self, keeping the Romeo from fainting by the power of her will.

'Call the manager if you like. He has been watching and has seen nothing except that you are pale and sweating. I, a friend of yours, have been giving you some bad news, perhaps. Tell your stupid police all about me, if you wish to spend the next few weeks in a padded cell. I'll see you again in a day or two, I hope: I'll be hungry again by that time.' She walked away, serenely confident that the fellow would never willingly come within sight of her again.

She had not damaged his ego permanently – he was not a neurotic type – but she had given him a jolt that he'd never forget. Camilla Kinnison nor any of her sisters had anything to fear from any male or males infesting any planet or roaming any depths of space.

The expected and awaited trouble developed. Tregonsee and Camilla landed and began their hunt. The League for Planetary Purity, it appeared, was the primary focal point; hence the two attended a meeting of that crusading body. That was a mistake; Tregonsee should have stayed out in deep space, concealed behind a solid thought-screen.

For Camilla was an unknown. Furthermore, her mind was inherently stable at the third level of stress; no lesser mind could penetrate her screens or, having failed to do so, could recognize the fact of failure. Tregonsee, however, was known throughout all civilized space. He was not wearing his Lens, of course, but his very shape made him suspect. Worse, he could not hide from any mind as powerful as that of 'X' the fact that his mind was very decidedly not that of a retired Rigellian gentleman.

Thus Camilla had known that the procedure was a mistake. She intimated as much, but she could not sway the unswerving Tregonsee from his determined course without revealing things which must forever remain hidden from him. She acquiesced, therefore, but she knew what to expect.

Hence, when the invading intelligence blanketed the assemblage lightly, only to be withdrawn instantly upon detecting the emanations of a mind of real power, Cam had a bare moment of time in which to act. She synchronized with the intruding thought, began to analyze it and to trace it back to its source. She did not have time enough to succeed fully in either endeavor, but she did get a line. When the foreign influence vanished she shot a message to Tregonsee and they sped away.

Hurtling through space along the established line, Tregonsee's mind was a turmoil of thought; thoughts as plain as print to Camilla. She flushed uncomfortably – she could of course blush at will.

'I'm not half the super-woman you're picturing,' she said. That was true enough; no one this side of Arisia could have been. 'You're so famous, you know, and I'm not – while he was examining you I had a fraction of a second to work in. You didn't.'

'That may be true.' Although Tregonsee had no eyes, the girl knew that he was staring at her; scanning, but not intruding. She lowered her barriers so far that he thought they were completely down. 'You have, however, extraordinary and completely inexplicable powers . . . but, being the daughter of Kimball and Clarrissa Kinnison . . .'

'That's it, I think.' She paused, then, in a burst of girlish confidence, went on: 'I've got something, I really do think, but I don't know what it is or what to do with it. Maybe in fifty years or so I will.'

This also was close enough to the truth, and it did serve to restore to Tregonsee his wonted poise. 'Be that as it may, I will take your advice next time, if you will offer it.'

'Try and stop me – I love to give advice.' She laughed un-affectedly. 'It might not be any better next time.'

Then, further to quiet the shrewd Rigellian's suspicions, she strode over to the control panel and checked the course. Having done so, she fanned out detectors, centering upon that course, to the fullest range of their power. She swaggered a little when she speared with a CRX tracer a distant vessel in a highly satisfactory location. That act would cut her down to size in Tregonsee's mind.

'You think, then, that "X" is in that ship?' he asked quietly.

'Probably not.' She could not afford to act too dumb – she could fool a Second-Stage Lensman a little, but nobody could fool one much. 'It may, however, give us a lead.'

'It is practically certain that "X" is not in that vessel,'

Tregonsee thought. 'In fact, it may be a trap. We must, however, make the customary arrangements to take it into custody.'

Cam nodded and the Rigellian communications officers energized their long-range beams. Far ahead of the fleeing vessel, centering upon its line of flight, fast cruisers of the Galactic Patrol began to form a gigantic cup. Hours passed, and – a not unexpected circumstance – Tregonsee's super-dreadnought gained rapidly upon the supposed Boskonian.

The quarry did not swerve or dodge. Straight into the mouth of the cup it sped. Tractors and pressors reached out, locked on, and were neither repulsed nor cut. The strange ship did not go inert, did not put out a single course of screen, did not fire a beam. She did not reply to signals. Spy-rays combed her from needle nose to driving jets, searching every compartment. There was no sign of life aboard.

Spots of pink appeared upon Camilla's deliciously smooth cheeks, her eyes flashed. 'We've been had, Uncle Trig – *how* we've been had!' she exclaimed, and her chagrin was not all assumed. She had not quite anticipated such a complete fiasco as this.

'Score one for "X",' Tregonsee said. He not only seemed to be, but actually was, calm and unmoved. 'We will now go back and pick up where we left off.'

They did not discuss the thing at all, nor did they wonder how 'X' escaped them. After the fact, they both knew. There had been at least two vessels; at least one of them had been inherently indetectable and screened against thought. In one of these latter 'X' had taken a course at some indeterminable angle to the one which they had followed.

'X' was now at a safe distance.

'X' was nobody's fool.

7
Kathryn on Guard

Kathryn Kinnison, trim and taut in black glamorette, strolled into the breakfast nook humming a lilting song. Pausing before a full-length mirror, she adjusted her cocky little black toque at an even more piquant angle over her left eye. She made a couple of passes at her riot of curls and gazed at her reflected self in high approval as, putting both hands upon her smoothly rounded hips, she – 'wriggled' is the only possible term for it – in sheer joy of being alive.

'Kathryn...' Clarrissa Kinnison chided gently. 'Don't be exhibitionistic, dear.' Except in times of stress the Kinnison women used spoken language, 'to keep in practice', as they said.

'Why not? It's fun.' The tall girl bent over and kissed her mother upon the lobe of an ear. 'You're sweet, mums, you know that? You're the most *precious* thing – Ha! Bacon and eggs? Goody!'

The older woman watched half-enviously as her eldest daughter ate with the carefree abandon of one completely unconcerned about either digestion or figure. She had no more understood her children, even, than a hen can understand the brood of ducklings she has so unwittingly hatched out, and that comparison was more strikingly apt than Clarrissa Kinnison ever would know. She now knew, more than a little ruefully, that she never would understand them.

She had not protested openly at the rigor of the regime to which her son Christopher had been subjected from birth. That, she knew, was necessary. It was inconceivable that Kit should not be a Lensman, and for a man to become a Lensman he had to be given everything he could possibly take. She was deeply glad, however, that her four other babies had been girls. Her daughters were *not* going to be Lensmen. She, who had known so long and so heavily the weight of Lensman's Load, would see to that. Herself a womanly, feminine woman, she had fought with every resource at her command to make her girl babies grow up into replicas of herself. She had failed.

They simply would not play with dolls, nor play house with other little girls. Instead, they insisted upon 'intruding', as she considered it, upon Lensmen; preferably upon Second-Stage Lensmen, if any one of the four chanced to be anywhere within reach. Instead of with toys, they played with atomic engines and flitters; and, later, with speedsters and space-ships. Instead of primers, they read galactic encyclopedias. One of them might be at home, as now, or all of them; or none. She never did know what to expect.

But they were in no sense disloyal. They loved their mother with a depth of affection which no other mother, anywhere, has ever known. They tried their best to keep her from worrying about them. They kept in touch with her wherever they went – which might be at whim to Tellus or to Thrale or to Alsakan or to any unplumbed cranny of intergalactic space – and they informed her, apparently without reservation, as to everything they did. They loved their father and their brother and each other and themselves with the same whole-hearted fervor they bestowed upon her. They behaved always in exemplary fashion. None of them had ever shown or felt the slightest interest in any one of numerous boys and men; and this trait, if the truth is to be told, Clarrissa could understand least of all.

No. The only thing basically wrong with them was the fact, made abundantly clear since they first toddled, that they should not be and could not be subjected to any jot or tittle of any form of control, however applied.

Kathryn finished eating finally and gave her mother a bright, quick grin. 'Sorry, mums, you'll just have to give us up as hard cases, I guess.' Her fine eyes, so like Clarrissa's except in color, clouded as she went on: 'I *am* sorry, mother, really, that we can't be what you so want us to be. We've tried *so* hard, but we just can't. It's something here, and here.' She tapped one temple and prodded her midsection with a pink forefinger. 'Call it fatalism or anything you please, but I think we're slated to do a job of some kind, some day, even though none of us has any idea of what it's going to be.'

Clarrissa paled. 'I've been thinking just that for years, dear... I've been afraid to say it, or even to think it... You are Kim's children, and mine... If there ever was a perfect, a predestined marriage, it is ours... And Mentor said that our marriage was necessary...' She paused, and in that instant she almost perceived the truth. She was closer to it than she had ever been before or ever would be again. But that truth was far too vast for her mind to grasp. She went on: 'But I'd do it over again, Kathryn, knowing everything I know now. "Vast rewards", you know...'

'Of course you would,' Kat interrupted. 'Any girl would be a fool not to. The minute I meet a man like dad I'm going to marry him, if I have to scratch Kay's eyes out and snatch Cam and Con bald-headed to get him. But speaking of dad, just what do you think of l'affaire Radelix?'

Gone every trace of levity, both women stood up. Gold-flecked tawny eyes stared deeply into gold-flecked eyes of dark and velvety green.

'I don't know.' Clarrissa spoke slowly, meaningfully. 'Do you?'

'No. I wish I did.' Kathryn's was not the voice of a girl, but that of an avenging angel. 'As Kit says, I'd give four front teeth and my right leg to the knee joint to know who or what is back of that, but I don't. I feel very much in the mood to do a flit out that way.'

'Do you?' Clarrissa paused. 'I'm glad. I'd go myself, in spite of everything he says, except that I couldn't do anything... If that *should* be the job you were talking about... Oh, do anything you can, dear; *anything* to make sure he comes back to me!'

'Of course, mums.' Kathryn broke away almost by force from her mother's emotion. 'I don't think it is; at least, I haven't got any cosmic hunch to that effect. And don't worry; it puts wrinkles in the girlish complexion. I'll do just a little look-see, stick around long enough to find out what's what, and let you know all about it. Bye.'

At high velocity Kathryn drove her indetectable speedster to Radelix, and around and upon that planet she conducted invisible investigations. She learned a part of the true state of affairs, she deduced more of it, but she could not see, even dimly, the picture as a whole. This part, though, was clear enough.

A third-level operator, she did not have to be at the one apparent mouth of a hyperspatial tube in order to enter it; she knew that while communication was impossible either through such a tube from space to space or from the interior of the tube to either space, the quality of the tube was not the barrier. The interface was. Wherefore, knowing what to expect first and working diligently to solve the whole problem, she waited.

She watched Kinnison's abduction. There was nothing she could do about that. She could not interfere then without setting up repercussions which might very well shatter the entire structure of the Galactic Patrol. When the Boskonian ship had disappeared, however, she tapped the tube and followed it. Almost nose to tail she pressed it, tensely alert to do some helpful deed which could be ascribed to accident or to luck. For she knew starkly that Kinnison's present captors would not slip and that his every ability had been discounted in advance.

Thus she was ready, when Kinnison's attention concentrated on the switch controlling the Boskonian captain's thought-screen generator. There were no pets or spiders or worms, or even gnats, but the captain could sit down. Around his screen, then, she drove a solid beam of thought, on a channel which neither the pirate nor the Lensman knew existed. She took over in a trice the fellow's entire mind. He sat down, as Kinnison had so earnestly willed him to do, the merest fraction of an inch too close to the chair's arm. The switch-handle flipped

68

over and Kathryn snatched her mind away. She was sure that her father would think that bit of luck purely fortuitous. She was equally sure that the situation was safe, for a time at least, in Kinnison's highly capable hands. She slowed down, allowed the distance between the two vessels to increase. But she kept within range, for one or two more accidents might have to happen.

In the instant of the flicking of the switch the captain's mind became Kinnison's. He was going to issue orders, to take the ship over in an orderly way, but his first contact with the subjugated mind made him change his plans. Instead of uttering orders, the captain leaped out of the chair toward the beam-controllers.

And not an instant too soon. Others had seen what had happened, had heard that tell-tale click. All had been warned against that and many other contingencies. As the captain leaped one of his fellows drew a bullet-projector and calmly shot him through the head.

The shock of that bullet, the death of the mind in his own mind's grasp, jarred the Grey Lensman to the core. It was almost the same as though he himself had been killed. Nevertheless, by sheer force of will he held on, by sheer power of will he made that dead body take those last three steps and forced those dead hands to cut the master circuit of the beams which were holding him helpless.

Free, he leaped forward; but not alone. The others leaped, too, and for the same controls. Kinnison got there first – just barely first – and as he came he swung his armored fist.

What a dureum-inlaid glove, driven by all the brawn of Kimball Kinnison's mighty right arm and powerful torso backed by all the momentum of body- and armor-mass, will do to a human head met in direct central impact is nothing to detail here. Simply, that head splashed. Pivoting nimbly, considering his encumbering armor, he swung a terrific leg. His steel boot sank calf-deep into the abdomen of the foe next in line. Two more utterly irresistible blows disposed of two more of the Boskonians; the last two turned and, frantically,

69

ran. But the Lensman by that time had the juice back on; and when a man has been smashed against a bulkhead by the full power of a D2P pressor, all that remains to be done must be accomplished with a scraper and a sponge.

Kinnison picked up his DeLameters, reconnected them, and took stock. So far, so good. But there were other men aboard this heap – how many, he'd better find out – and at least some of them wore dureum-inlaid armor as capable as his own.

And in her speedster, concluding that this wasn't going to be so bad, after all, Kathryn glowed with pride in her father's prowess. She was no shrinking violet, this Third-Stage Lensman; she held no ruth whatever for Civilization's foes. She herself would have driven that beam as mercilessly as had the Grey Lensman. She could have told Kinnison what next to do; could even have inserted the knowledge stealthily into his mind; but, heroically, she refrained. She'd let him handle this in his own fashion as long as he possibly could.

The Grey Lensman sent his sense of perception abroad. Twenty more of them – the ship wasn't very big. Ten aft, armored. Six forward, also armored. Four, unarmored, in the control-room. That control-room was pure poison; he'd go aft first. He searched around . . . surely they'd have dureum space-axes? Oh yes, there they were. He hefted them, selected one of the right weight and balance. He strode down the companionway to the wardroom. He flung the door open and stepped inside.

His first care was to blast the communicator panels with his DeLameters. That would delay the mustering of reinforcements. The control room couldn't guess, at least for a time, that one man was setting out to capture their ship single-handed. His second, ignoring the beams of hand-weapons splashing refulgently from his screens, was to weld the steel door to the jamb. Then, sheathing his projectors, he swung up his axe and went grimly to work. He thought fleetingly of how nice it would be to have vanBuskirk, that dean of all axe-men, at his back; but he wasn't too old or too fat to swing a pretty mean axe himself. And, fortunately, these Boskonians, here in their quarters, didn't have axes. They were heavy, clumsy, and for emergency use only; they were not a part of the regular uniform, as with Valerians.

The first foe swung up his DeLameter involuntarily as Kinnison's axe swept down. When the curved blade, driven as viciously as the Lensman's strength could drive it, struck the ray-gun it did not even pause. Through it it sliced, the severed halves falling to the floor.

The dureum inlay of the glove held, and glove and axe smashed together against the helmet. The Boskonian went down with a crash; but, beyond a broken arm or some such trifle, he wasn't hurt much. And no armor that a man had to carry around could be made of solid dureum. Hence, Kinnison reversed his weapon and swung again, aiming carefully at a point between the inlay strips. The axe's wicked beak tore through steel and skull and brain, stopping only with the sharply ringing impact of dureum shaft against dureum stripping.

They were coming at him now, not only with DeLameters, but with whatever of steel bars and spanners and bludgeons they could find. QX – his armor could take oodles of that. They might dent it, but they couldn't possibly get through. Planting one boot solidly on his victim's helmet, he wrenched his axe out through flesh and bone and metal – no fear of breakage; not even a Valerian's full savage strength could break the helve of a space-axe – and struck again. And struck – and struck.

He fought his way to the door – two of the survivors were trying to unseal it and get away. They failed; and, in failing, died. A couple of the remaining enemies shrieked and ran in blind panic, and tried to hide; the others battled desperately on. But whether they ran or fought there was only one possible end, if the Patrolman were to survive. No enemy must or could be left alive behind him, to bring to bear upon his back some semi-portable weapon with whose energies his armor's screens could not cope.

When the grisly business was over Kinnison, panting, rested

71

briefly. This was the first real brawl he had been in for twenty years; and for a veteran – a white-collar man, a coordinator to boot – he hadn't done so bad, he thought. It was damned hard work and, while he was maybe a hair short of wind, he hadn't weakened a particle. To here, QX.

And lovely Kathryn, far enough back but not too far and reading imperceptibly his every thought, agreed with him enthusiastically. She did not have a father complex, but in common with her sisters she knew exactly what her father was. With equal exactitude she knew what other men were. Knowing them, and knowing however imperfectly herself, each of the Kinnison girls knew that it would be a physical and psychological impossibility for her to become even mildly interested in any man not at least her father's equal. They each had dreamed of a man who would be her own equal, physically and mentally, but it had not yet occurred to any of them that one such man already existed.

Kinnison cut the door away and again sent out his sense of perception. With it fanning out ahead of him he retraced his previous path. The apes in the control-room had done something; he didn't know just what. Two of them were tinkering with a communicator panel; probably the one to the ward-room. They probably thought the trouble was at their end. Or did they? Why hadn't they reconnoitered? He dismissed that problem as being of no pressing importance. The other two were doing something at another panel. What? He couldn't make head or tail of it – damn those full-coverage screens! And Nadreck's fancy drill, even if he had had one along, wouldn't work unless the screen were absolutely steady. Well, it didn't make much, if any, difference. They had called the men back from up forward, and here they came. He'd rather meet them in the corridor than in an open room, anyway, he could handle them a lot easier...

But tensely watching Kathryn gnawed her lip. Should she tell him, or control him, or not? No. She wouldn't – she couldn't – yet. Dad could figure out that pilot-room trap without her help ... and she herself, with all her power of brain, could not visualize with any degree of clarity the menace which was — which *must* be — at the tube's end or even now rushing along it to meet that Boskonian ship...

Kinnison met the oncoming six and vanquished them. By no means as easily as he had conquered the others, since they had been warned and since they also now bore space-axes, but just as finally. Kinnison did not consider it remarkable that he escaped practically unscratched — his armor was battered and dinged up, cut and torn, but he had only a couple of superficial wounds. He had met the enemy where they could come at him only one at a time; he was still the master of any weapon known to space warfare; it had been at no time evident that any outside influence was interfering with the normally rapid functioning of the Boskonians' minds.

He was full of confidence, full of fight, and far from spent when he faced about to consider what he should do about that control-room. There was plenty of stuff in there... tougher stuff than he had met up with so far...

Kathryn in her speedster gritted her teeth and clenched her hands into hard fists. This was bad — very, *very* bad — and it was going to get worse. Closing up fast, she uttered a bitter and exceedingly unladylike expletive.

Couldn't he see — couldn't the damn dumb darling *sense* — that he was apt to run out of time almost any minute now?

She fairly writhed in an agony of indecision; and indecision, in a Third-Stage Lensman, is a rare phenomenon indeed. She wanted intensely to take over, but if she did, was there any way this side of Palain's purple hells for her to cover up her tracks?

There was none... yet.

8
Black Lensmen

But Kinnison's mind, while slower than his daughter's and much less able, was sure. The four Boskonians in the control-room were screened against his every mental force and it was idle even to hope for another such lucky break as he had just had. They were armored by this time and they had both machine rifles and semi-portable projectors. They were entrenched; evidently intending to fight a delaying and defensive battle, knowing that if they could hold him off until the tube had been traversed, the Lensman would not have a chance. Armed with all they could use of the most powerful mobile weapons aboard and being four to one, they undoubtedly thought they could win easily enough.

Kinnison thought otherwise. Since he could not use his mind against them he would use whatever he could find, and this ship, having come upon such a mission, would be carrying plenty of weapons – and those four men certainly hadn't had time to tamper with them all. He might even find some negative-matter bombs.

Setting up a spy-ray block, he proceeded to rummage. They couldn't see him, and if any one of them had a sense of perception and cut his screen for even a fraction of a second to use it the battle would end right then. And if they decided to rush him, so much the better. They remained, however, forted up, as he had thought they would, and he rummaged in peace. Various death-dealing implements, invitingly set up, he ignored after one cursory glance into their interiors. He knew weapons – these had been fixed. He went on to the armory.

He did not find any negabombs, but he found plenty of untouched weapons like those now emplaced in the control-room. The rifles were beauties; high-caliber, water-cooled things, each with a heavy dureum shield-plate and a single-ply screen. Each had a beam, too, but machine-rifle beams weren't so hot. Conversely, the semi-portables had lots of screen, but very little dureum. Kinnison lugged one rifle and two semi-portables, by easy stages, into the room next to the control room; so placing them that the control panels would be well out of the line of fire.

What gave Kinnison his chance was the fact that the enemies' weapons were set to cover the door. Apparently they had not considered the possibility that the Lensman would attempt to flank them by blasting through an inch and a half of high-alloy steel. Kinnison did not know whether he could do it fast enough to mow them down from the side before they could reset their magnetic clamps, or not; but he'd give it the good old college try. It was bound to be a mighty near thing, and the Lensman grinned wolfishly behind the guard-plates of his helmet as he arranged his weapons to save every possible fractional second of time.

Aiming one at a spot some three feet above the floor, the other a little lower, Kinnison cut in the full power of his semis and left them on. He energized the rifle's beam – every little bit helped – set the defensive screens at 'full', and crouched down into the saddle behind the dureum shield. He had checked the feeds long since: he had plenty of rounds.

Two large spots and a small one smoked briefly, grew red. They turned bright red, then yellow, merged into one blinding spot. Metal melted, sluggishly at first, then thinly, then flaring, blowing out in raging coruscations of sparks as the fiercely-driven beams ate in. Through!

The first small opening appeared directly in line between the muzzle of Kinnison's rifle and one of the guns of the enemy, and in the moment of its appearance the Patrolman's weapon began its stuttering, shattering roar. The Boskonians had seen the hot spot on the wall, had known instantly what it meant, and were working frantically to swing their gun-mounts around so as to interpose their dureum shields and to bring their own rifles to bear. They had almost succeeded. Kinnison caught just the bulge of one suit of armor in his sights, but that was enough. The kinetic energy of the stream of metal tore him out of the saddle; he was literally riddled while still in air. Two savage bursts took care of the semi-portables and their operators – as has been intimated, the shields of the semis were not designed to withstand the type of artillery Kinnison was using.

That made it cannon to cannon, one to one; and the Lensman knew that those two identical rifles could hammer at each others' defenses for an hour without doing any serious damage. He had, however, one big advantage. Being closer to the bulkhead he could depress his line of fire more than could the Boskonian. He did so, aiming at the clamps, which were not built to take very much of that sort of punishment. One front clamp let go, then the other, and the Lensman knew what to do about the rear pair, which he could not reach. He directed his fire against the upper edge of the dureum plate. Under the awful thrust of that terrific storm of steel the useless front clamps lifted from the floor. The gun mount, restrained from sliding by the unbreakable grip of the rear clamps, reared up. Over it went, straight backward, exposing the gunner to the full blast of Kinnison's fire. That, definitely, was that.

Kathryn heaved a sigh of relief: as far as she could 'see', the tube was still empty. 'That's my Pop!' she applauded inaudibly to herself. 'Now,' she breathed, 'if the darling has just got jets enough to figure out that something may be coming at him down this tube – and sense enough to run back home before it can catch him!'

Kinnison had no suspicion that any danger to himself might lie within the tube. He had no desire, however, to land alone in an enemy ship in the exact center of an enemy base, and no intention whatever of doing so. Moreover, he had once come altogether too close to permanent immolation in a foreign space because of the discontinuance of a hyperspatial tube while he was in it, and once was once too many. Also, he had just got done leading with his chin, and once of that, too, was once too many. Therefore his sole thought was to get back into his own space as fast as he could get there, so as soon as the opposition was silenced he hurried into the control-room and reversed the vessel's drive.

Behind him, Kathryn flipped her speedster end for end and led the retreat. She left the tube before – 'before' is an extremely loose and inaccurate word in this connection, but it conveys the idea better than any other ordinary term – she got back to Base. She caused an officer to broadcast an 'evacuation' warning, then hung poised, watching intently. She knew that Kinnison could not leave the tube except at its terminus, hence would have to materialize inside the building itself. She had heard of what happened when two dense, hard solids attempted to occupy the same three-dimensional space at the same time; but to view that occurrence was not her purpose in lingering. She did not actually know whether there was anything in the tube or not; but she did know that if there were, and if it or they should follow her father out into normal space, even she would have need of every jet she could muster.

Kinnison, maneuvering his Boskonian cruiser to a halt just at the barest perceptible threshold of normal space, in the intermediate zone in which nothing except dureum was solid in either space or pseudo-space, had already given a great deal of thought to the problem of disembarkation. The ship was small, as space-ships go, but even so it was a lot bigger than any corridor of any ordinary structure. Those corridor walls and floor were thick and contained a lot of steel; the ship's walls were solid alloy. He had never seen metal materialize within metal and, frankly, he didn't want to be around, even inside G-P armor, when it happened. Also, there were a lot of explosives aboard, and atomic power plants, and the chance of touching off a loose atomic vortex within a few feet of himself was not one to be taken lightly.

He had already rigged a line to a master switch. Power off, with the ship's dureum cat-walk as close to the floor of the corridor as the dimensions of the tube permitted, he reversed the controls and poised himself for a running headlong dive. He could not feel Radeligian gravitation, of course, but he was pretty sure that he could jump far enough to get through the interface. He took a short run, jerked the line, and hurled himself through the space-ship's immaterial wall. The ship disappeared.

Going through that interface was more of a shock than the Lensman had anticipated. Even taken very slowly, as it customarily is, inter-dimensional acceleration brings malaise to which no one has ever become accustomed, and taking it so rapidly fairly turned Kinnison inside out. He was going to land with the rolling impact which constitutes perfect technique in such armored maneuvering. As it was, he never did know how he landed, except that he made a boiler-shop racket and brought up against the far wall of the corridor with a climactic clang. Beyond the addition of a few more bruises and contusions to his already abundant collection, however, he was not hurt.

As soon as he could collect himself he leaped to his feet and rapped out orders. 'Tractors – pressors – shears! Heavy stuff, to anchor, not to clamp! Hipe!' He knew what he was up against now, and if they'd only come back he'd yank them out of that blank tube so fast it'd break every blank blank one of their blank blank blank necks!

And Kathryn, still watching intently, smiled. Her dad was a pretty smart old duck, but he wasn't using his noggin now – he was cockeyed as Trenco's ether in even thinking they *might* come back. If anything at all erupted from that hyper-circle it would be something against which everything he was mustering would be precisely as effective as so much thin air. And she *still* had no concrete idea of what she so feared. It wouldn't be essentially physical, she was pretty sure. It would almost have to be mental. But who or what could possibly put it across? And how? And above all, what could she do about it if they did?

Eyes narrowed, brow furrowed in concentration, she thought as she had never thought before; and the harder she thought the more clouded the picture became. For the first time in her triumphant life she felt small – weak – impotent. It was in that hour that Kathryn Kinnison really grew up.

The tube vanished; she heaved a tremendous sigh of relief. They, whoever they were, having failed to bring Kinnison to them – this time – were not coming after him – this time. Not an important enough game to play to the end? No, that wasn't it. Maybe they weren't ready. But the next time...

Mentor the Arisian had told her bluntly, the last time she had seen him, to come to him again when she realized that she didn't know quite everything. Deep down, she had not expected that day ever to come. Now, however, it had. This escape – if it had been an escape – had taught her much.

'Mother!' She shot a call to distant Klovia. 'I'm on Radelix. Everything's on the green. Dad has just knocked a flock of Boskonians into an outside loop and come through QX. I've got to do a little flit, though, before I come home. Bye.'

Kinnison stood intermittent guard over the base for four days after the hyperspatial tube had disappeared before he gave up; before he did any very serious thinking about what he should do next.

Could he and should he keep on as Sybly Whyte? He could and he should, he decided. He hadn't been gone long enough for Whyte's absence to have been noticed; nothing whatever connected Whyte with Kinnison. If he really knew what he was doing a more specific alias might be better; but as long as he was merely smelling around, Whyte's was the best identity to use. He could go anywhere, do anything, ask anything of anybody, and all with a perfectly good excuse.

And as Sybly Whyte, then, for days that stretched into weeks, he roamed – finding, as he had feared, nothing whatever. It seemed as though all Boskonian activity of the type in which he was most interested had ceased with his return from the hyperspatial tube. Just what that meant he did not know. It was unthinkable that they had given up on him: much more probably they were hatching something new. And the frustration of inaction and the trying to figure out what was coming next was driving him not-so-slowly nuts.

Then, striking through the doldrums, came a call from Maitland.

'Kim? You told me to Lens you immediately about any off-color work. Don't know whether this is or not. The guy may be – probably is – crazy. Conklin, who reported him, couldn't decide. Neither can I, from Conklin's report. Do you want to send somebody special, take over yourself, or what?'

'I'll take over,' Kinnison decided instantly. If neither Conklin nor Maitland, Grey Lensmen both, could decide, there was no point in sending anyone else. 'Where and who?'

'Planet, Meneas II, not too far from where you are now. City, Meneateles; 116-3-29, 45-22-17. Place, Jack's Haven, a meteor-miner's hangout at the corner of Gold and Sapphire Streets. Person, a man called "Eddie".'

'Thanks, I'll check.' Maitland did not send, and Kinnison did not want, any additional information. Both knew that since the coordinator was going to investigate this thing himself, he should get his facts, and particularly his impressions, at first and unprejudiced hand.

To Meneas II, then, and to Jack's Haven, Sybly Whyte went, notebook very much in evidence. An ordinary enough space-dive Jack's turned out to be – higher-toned than that Radeligian space-dock saloon of Bominger's; much less flamboyant than notorious Miners' Rest on far Euphrosyne.

'I wish to interview a person named Eddie,' he announced, as he bought a bottle of wine. 'I have been informed that he has had deep-space adventures worthy of incorporation into one of my novels.'

'Eddie? Haw!' The barkeeper laughed raucously. 'That space-louse? Somebody's been kidding you, mister. He's nothing but a broken-down meteor-miner – you know what a space-louse is, don't you? – that we let clean cuspidors and do such-like odd jobs for his keep. We don't throw him out, like we do the others, because he's kind of funny in one way. Every hour or so he throws a fit, and that amuses people.'

Whyte's eager-beaver attitude did not change; his face reflected nothing of what Kinnison thought of this callous speech. For Kinnison did know exactly what a space-louse was. More, he knew what turned a man into one. Ex-meteor-miner himself, he knew what the awesome depths of space, the ever-present dangers, the privations, the solitude, the frustrations, did to any mind not adequately integrated. He knew that only the strong survived; that the many weak succumbed. From sickening memory he knew just what pitiful wrecks those many became. Nevertheless, and despite the fact that the information was not necessary:

'Where is this Eddie now?'

'That's him, over there in the corner. By the way he's acting, he'll have another fit pretty quick now.'

The shambling travesty of a man accepted avidly the invitation to table and downed at a gulp the proffered drink. Then, as though the mild potion had been a trigger, his wracked body tensed and his features began to writhe.

'Cateagles!' he screamed; eyes rolling, breath coming in hard, frantic gasps. 'Gangs of cateagles! Thousands! They're clawing me to bits! And the Lensman! He's sicking them on! *Ow!!* YOW!!!' He burst into unintelligible screams and threw himself to the floor. There, rolling convulsively over and over, he tried the impossible feat of covering simultaneously with his two claw-like hands his eyes, ears, nose, mouth, and throat.

Ignoring the crowding spectators, Kinnison invaded the helpless mind before him. He winced mentally as he scanned the whole atrocious enormity of what was there. Then, while Whyte busily scribbled notes, he shot a thought to distant Klovia.

'Cliff! I'm here in Jack's Haven, and I've got Eddie's data. What did you and Conklin make of it? You agree, of course, that the Lensman is the crux.'

'Definitely. Everything else is hop-happy space-drift. The fact that there are not – there *can't* be – any such Lensman as Eddie imagined makes him space-drift, too, in our opinion. We called you in on the millionth chance – sorry we sent you out on a false alarm, but you said we had to be sure.'

'You needn't be sorry.' Kinnison's thought was the grimmest

Clifford Maitland had ever felt. 'Eddie isn't an ordinary space-louse. You see, I know one thing that you and Conklin don't. You noticed the woman? Very faint, decidedly in the background?'

'Now that you mention her – yes. Too far in the background and too faint to be a key. Most every spaceman has a woman – or a lot of different ones – more or less on his mind all the time, you know. Immaterial, I'd say.'

'So would I, maybe, except for the fact that she isn't a woman at all, but a Lyranian . . .'

'A LYRANIAN!' Maitland interrupted. Kinnison could feel the racing of his assistant's thoughts. 'That complicates things . . . But how in Palain's purple hells, Kim, could Eddie ever have got to Lyrane – and if he did, how did he get away alive?'

'I don't know, Cliff.' Kinnison's mind, too, was working fast. 'But you haven't got all the dope yet. To cinch things, I know her personally – she's that airport manager who tried her damndest to kill me all the time I was on Lyrane II.'

'Hm . . . m . . . m.' Maitland tried to digest that undigestible bit. Tried, and failed. 'That would seem to make the Lensman real, too, then – real enough, at least, to investigate – much as I hate to think of the possibility of a Lensman going that far off the beam.' Maitland's convictions died hard. 'You'll handle this yourself, then?'

'Check. At least, I'll help. There may be people better qualified than I am. I'll get them at it. Thanks, Cliff – clear ether.'

He lined a thought to his wife; and after a short, warmly intimate contact, he told her the story.

'So you see, beautiful,' he concluded, 'your wish is coming true. I couldn't keep you out of this if I wanted to. So check with the girls, put on your Lens, shed your clothes, and go to work.'

'I'll do that.' Clarrissa laughed and her soaring spirit flooded his mind. 'Thanks, my dear.'

Then and only then did Kimball Kinnison, master therapist, pay any further attention to that which lay contorted upon the floor. But when Whyte folded up his notebook and left the place, the derelict was resting quietly; and in a space of time long enough so that the putative writer of space-opera would not be connected with the cure, those fits would end. Moreover, Eddie would return, whole, to the void; he would become what he had never before been – a successful meteor-miner.

Lensmen pay their debts; even to spiders and to worms.

9
An Arisian Education

Her adventure in the hyperspatial tube had taught Kathryn Kinnison much. Realizing her inadequacy and knowing what to do about it, she drove her speedster at high velocity to Arisia. Unlike the Second-Stage Lensmen, she did not even slow down as she approached the planet's barrier; but, as one sure of her welcome, merely threw out ahead of her an identifying thought.

'Ah, daughter Kathryn, again you are in time.' Was there, or was there not, a trace of emotion – of welcome, even of affection? – in that usually utterly emotionless thought? 'Land as usual.'

She neutralized her controls as she felt the mighty beams of the landing-engine take hold of her little ship. During previous visits she had questioned nothing – this time she was questioning *everything*. Was she landing, or not? Directing her every force inwardly, she probed her own mind to its profoundest depths. Definitely, she was her own mistress throughout – no conceivable mind could take *hers* over so tracelessly. As definitely, then, she was actually landing.

She landed. The ground on which she stepped was real. So was the automatic flyer – neither plane nor helicopter – which whisked her from the spaceport to her familiar destination, an unpretentious residence in the grounds of the immense hospital. The graveled walk, the flowering shrubs, and the indescribably sweet and pungent perfume were real; as were the tiny pain and the drop of blood which resulted when a needle-sharp thorn pierced her incautious finger.

84

Through automatically-opening doors she made her way into the familiar, comfortable, book-lined room which was Mentor's study. And there, at his big desk, unchanged, sat Mentor. A lot like her father, but older – much older. About ninety, she had always thought, even though he didn't look over sixty. This time, however, she drove a probe – and got the shock of her life. Her thought was stopped – cold – not by superior mental force, which she could have taken unmoved, but by a seemingly ordinary thought-screen, and her fast-disintegrating morale began visibly to crack.

'Is all this – are you – real, or not?' she burst out, finally. 'If it isn't, I'll go mad!'

'That which you have tested – and I – are real, for the moment and as you understand reality. Your mind in its present state of advancement cannot be deceived concerning such elementary matters.'

'But it all wasn't, before? Or don't you want to answer that?'

'Since the knowledge will affect your growth, I will answer. It was not. This is the first time that your speedster has landed physically upon Arisia.'

The girl shrank, appalled. 'You told me to come back when I found out that I didn't know it all,' she finally forced herself to say. 'I learned that in the tube; but I didn't realize until just now that I don't know *anything*. Is there any use, Mentor, in going on with me?' she concluded, bitterly.

'Much,' he assured her. 'Your development has been eminently satisfactory, and your present mental condition is both necessary and sufficient.'

Well, I'll be a spr . . .' Kathryn bit off the expletive and frowned. 'What were you doing to me before, then, when I thought I got everything?'

'Power of mind,' he informed her. 'Sheer power, and penetration, and control. Depth, and speed, and all the other factors with which you are already familiar.'

'But what was left? I know there is – lots of it – but I can't imagine what.'

'Scope,' Mentor replied, gravely. 'Each of those qualities and characteristics must be expanded to encompass the full sphere of thought. Neither words nor thoughts can give any adequate concept of what it means; a practically wide-open two-way will be necessary. This cannot be accomplished, daughter, in the adolescent confines of your present mind; therefore enter fully into mine.'

She did so: and after less than a minute of that awful contact slumped, inert and boneless, to the floor.

The Arisian, unchanged, unmoved, unmoving, gazed at her until finally she began to stir.

'That... father Mentor, that was...' She blinked, shook her head savagely, fought her way back to full consciousness. 'That was a shock.'

'It was,' he agreed. 'More so than you realize. Of all the entities of your Civilization, your brother and now you are the only ones it would not kill instantly. You now know what the word "scope" means, and are ready for your last treatment, in the course of which I shall take your mind as far along the road of knowledge as mine is capable of going.'

'But that would mean... you're implying... But my mind *can't* be superior to yours, Mentor! Nothing could be, *possibly* – it's sheerly, starkly unthinkable!'

'But true, daughter, nevertheless. While you are recovering your strength from that which was but the beginning of your education, I will explain certain matters previously obscure. You have long known, of course, that you five children are not like any others. You have always known many things without having learned them. You think upon all possible bands of thought. Your senses of perception, of sight, of hearing, of touch, are so perfectly merged into one sense that you perceive at will any possible manifestation upon any possible plane or dimension of vibration. Also, although this may not have occurred to you as extraordinary, since it is not obvious, you differ physically from your fellows in some important respects. You have never experienced the slightest symptom of physical illness; not even a headache or a decayed tooth. You do not really require sleep. Vaccinations and inoculations do not

86

"take". No pathogenic organism, however virulent; no poison, however potent ...'

'Stop, Mentor!' Kathryn gasped, turning white. 'I can't take it – you really mean, then, that we aren't human at all?'

'Before going into that I should give you something of background. Our Arisian visualizations foretold the rise and fall of galactic civilizations long before any such civilizations came into being. That of Atlantis, for instance. I was personally concerned in that, and could not stop its fall.' Mentor *was* showing emotion now; his thought was bleak and bitter.

'Not that I expected to stop it,' he resumed. 'It had been known for many cycles of time that the final abatement of the opposing force would necessitate the development of a race superior to ours in every respect.

'Blood lines were selected in each of the four strongest races of this that you know as the First Galaxy. Breeding programs were set up, to eliminate as many as possible of their weaknesses and to concentrate all of their strengths. From your knowledge of genetics you realize the magnitude of the task; you know that it would take much time uselessly to go into the details of its accomplishment. Your father and your mother were the penultimates of long – *very* long – lines of mating; their reproductive cells were such that in their fusion practically every gene carrying any trait of weakness was rejected. Conversely, you carry the genes of every trait of strength ever known to any member of your human race. Therefore, while in outward seeming you are human, in every factor of importance you are not; you are even less human than am I myself.'

'And just how human is that?' Kathryn flared, and again her most penetrant probe of force flattened out against the Arisian's screen.

'Later, daughter, not now. That knowledge will come at the end of your education, not at its beginning.'

'I was afraid so.' She stared at the Arisian, her eyes wide and hopeless; brimming, in spite of her efforts at control, with tears. 'You're a monster, and I am ... or am going to be – a worse one. A monster . . . and I'll have to live a million years . . . alone . . . why? *Why*, Mentor, did you have to do this to me?'

'Calm yourself, daughter. The shock, while severe, will pass. You have lost nothing, have gained much.'

'Gained? Bah!' The girl's thought was loaded with bitterness and scorn. 'I've lost my parents – I'll still be a girl long after they have died. I've lost every possibility of ever really living. I want love – and a husband – and children – and I can't have any of them, ever. Even without this, I've never seen a man I wanted, and now I can't ever love anybody. I don't *want* to live a million years, Mentor – especially alone!' The thought was a veritable wail of despair.

'The time has come to stop this muddy, childish thinking.' Mentor's thought, however, was only mildly reproving. 'Such a reaction is only natural, but your conclusions are entirely erroneous. One single clear thought will show you that you have no present psychic, intellectual, emotional, or physical need of a complement.'

'That's true . . .' wonderingly. 'But other girls of my age . . .'

'Exactly,' came Mentor's dry rejoinder. 'Thinking of yourself as an adult of *Homo Sapiens*, you were judging yourself by false standards. As a matter of fact, you are an adolescent, not an adult. In due time you will come to love a man, and he you, with a fervor and depth which you at present cannot even dimly understand.'

'But that still leaves my parents.' Kathryn felt much better. 'I can apparently age, of course, as easily as I can put on a hat . . . but I really do love them, you know, and it will simply break mother's heart to have all her daughters turn out to be – as she thinks – spinsters.'

'On that point, too, you may rest at ease. I am taking care of that. Kimball and Clarrissa both know, without knowing how they know it, that your life cycle is tremendously longer than theirs. They both know that they will not live to see their grandchildren. Be assured, daughter, that before they pass from this cycle of existence into the next – about which I know noth- ing – they shall know that all is to be supremely well with their line; even though, to Civilization at large, it shall apparently end with you Five.'

'End with us? What do you mean?'

'You have a destiny, the nature of which your mind is not yet qualified to receive. In due time the knowledge shall be yours. Suffice it now to say that the next forty or fifty years will be but a fleeting hour in the span of life which is to be yours. But time, at the moment, presses. You are now fully recovered and we must get on with this, your last period of study with me, at the end of which you will be able to bear the fullest, closest impact of my mind as easily as you have heretofore borne full contact with your sisters'. Let us proceed with the work.'

They did so. Kathryn took and survived those shattering treatments, one after another, emerging finally with a mind whose power and scope can no more be explained to any mind below the third level than can the general theory of relativity be explained to a chimpanzee.

'It was forced, not natural, yes,' the Arisian said, gravely, as the girl was about to leave. 'You are many millions of your years ahead of your natural time. You realize, however, the necessity of that forcing. You also realize that I can give you no more formal instruction. I will be with you or on call at all times; I will be of aid in crises; but in larger matters your further development is in your own hands.'

Kathryn shivered. 'I realize that, and it scares me clear through ... especially this coming conflict, at which you hint so vaguely. I wish you'd tell me at least *something* about it, so I can get ready for it!'

'Daughter, I can't.' For the first time in Kathryn's experience, Mentor the Arisian was unsure. 'It is certain that we have been on time; but since the Eddorians have minds of power little if any inferior to our own, there are many details which we cannot derive with certainty, and to advise you wrongly would be to do you irreparable harm. All I can say is that sufficient warning will be given by your learning, with no specific effort on your part and from some source other than myself, that there does in fact exist a planet named "Ploor" – a name which to you is now only a meaningless symbol. Go now, daughter Kathryn, and work.'

Kathryn went; knowing that the Arisian had said all that he would say. In truth, he had told her vastly more than she had expected him to divulge; and it chilled her to the marrow to think that she, who had always looked up to the Arisians as demi-gods of sorts, would from now on be expected to act as their equal – in some ways, perhaps, as their superior! As her speedster tore through space toward distant Klovia she wrestled with herself, trying to shake her new self down into a personality as well integrated as her old one had been. She had not quite succeeded when she felt a thought.

'Help! I am in difficulty with this, my ship. Will any entity receiving my call and possessing the tools of a mechanic please come to my assistance? Or, lacking such tools, possessing a vessel of power sufficient to tow mine to the place where I must immediately go?'

Kathryn was startled out of her introspective trance. That thought was on a terrifically high band; one so high that she knew of no race using it, so high that an ordinary human mind could not possibly have either sent or received it. Its phraseology, while peculiar, was utterly precise in definition – the mind behind it was certainly of precisionist grade. She acknowledged upon the stranger's wave, and sent out a locator. Good – he wasn't far away. She flashed toward the derelict, matched intrinsics at a safe distance, and began scanning, only to encounter a spy-ray block around the whole vessel! To her it was porous enough – but if the creature thought that his screen was tight, let him keep on thinking so. It was his move.

'Well, what are you waiting for?' The thought fairly snapped. 'Come close, so that I may bring you in.'

'Not yet,' Kathryn snapped back. 'Cut your block so that I can see what you are like. I carry equipment for many environments, but I must know what yours is and equip for it before I can come aboard. You will note that my screens are down.'

'Of course. Excuse me – I supposed that you were one of our own' – there came the thought of an unspellable and

90

unpronounceable name – 'since none of the lower orders can receive our thoughts direct. Can you equip yourself to come aboard with your tools?'

'Yes.' The stranger's light was fierce stuff; ninety-eight percent of its energy being beyond the visible. His lamps were beam-held atomics, nothing less: but there was very little gamma and few neutrons. She could handle it easily enough, she decided, as she finished donning her heat-armor and a helmet of practically opaque, diamond-hard plastic.

As she was wafted gently across the intervening space upon a pencil of force, Kathryn took her first good look at the precisionist himself – or herself. She – it – looked something like a Dhilian, she thought at first. There was a squat, powerful, elephantine body with its four stocky legs; the tremendous double shoulders and enormous arms; the domed, almost immobile head. But there the resemblance ended. There was only one head – the thinking head, and that one had no eyes and was not covered with bone. There was no feeding head – the thing could neither eat nor breathe. There was no trunk. And what a skin!

It was worse than a hide, really – worse even than a Martian's. The girl had never seen anything like it. It was incredibly thick, dry, pliable; filled minutely with cells of a liquid-gaseous something which she knew to be a more perfect insulator even than the fibres of the tegument itself.

'R-T-S-L-Q-P.' She classified the creature readily enough to six places, then stopped and wrinkled her forehead. 'Seventh place – that incredible skin – what? S? R? T? It would have to be R . . .'

'You have the requisite tools, I perceive,' the creature greeted Kathryn as she entered the central compartment of the strange speedster, no larger than her own. 'I can tell you what to do, if . . .'

'I know what to do.' She unbolted the cover, worked deftly with wrenches and cable and splicer and torch, and in ten minutes was done. 'It doesn't make sense that a person of your obvious intelligence, manifestly knowing enough to make such minor repairs yourself, would go so far from home, alone in such a small ship, without any tools. Burnouts and shorts are apt to happen any time, you know.'

'Not in the vessels of the . . .' Again Kathryn felt that unpronounceable symbol. She also felt the stranger stiffen in offended dignity. 'We of the higher orders, you should know, do not perform labor. We think. We direct. Others work, and do their work well, or suffer accordingly. This is the first time in nine full four-cycle periods that such a thing has happened, and it will be the last. The punishment which I shall mete out to the guilty mechanic will ensure that. I shall, at end, have his life.'

'Oh, come, now!' Kathryn protested. 'Surely it's no life-and-death mat . . .'

'Silence!' came curt command. 'It is intolerable that one of the lower orders should attempt to . . .'

'Silence yourself!' At the fierce power of the riposte the creature winced, physically and mentally. 'I did this bit of dirty work for you because you apparently couldn't do it for yourself. I did not object to the matter-of-course way you accepted it, because some races are made that way and can't help it. But if you insist on keeping yourself placed five rungs above me on any ladder you can think of, I'll stop being a lady – or even a good Girl Scout – and start doing things about it, and I'll start at any signal you care to call. Get ready, and say when!'

The stranger, taken fully aback, threw out a lightning tentacle of thought; a feeler which was stopped cold a full foot from the girl's radiant armor. This was a human female – or was it? It was not. No human being had ever had, or ever would have, a mind like that. Therefore:

'I have made a grave error,' the thing apologized handsomely, 'in thinking that you are not at least my equal. Will you grant me pardon, please?'

'Certainly – if you don't repeat it. But I still don't like the idea of your torturing a mechanic for a thing . . .' She thought intensely, lip caught between white teeth. 'Perhaps there's a way. Where are you going, and when do you want to get there?'

'To my home planet,' pointing out mentally its location in the galaxy. 'I must be there in two hundred G-P hours.'

'I see.' Kathryn nodded her head. 'You can – if you promise not to harm him. And I can tell whether you really mean it or not.'

'As I promise, so I do. But in case I do not promise?'

In that case you'll get there in about a hundred thousand G-P years, frozen stiff. For I shall fuse your Bergenholm down into a lump; then, after welding your ports to the shell, I'll mount a thought-screen generator outside, powered for seven hundred years. Promise, or that. Which?'

'I promise not to harm the mechanic in any way.' He surrendered stiffly, and made no protest at Kathryn's entrance into his mind to make sure that the promise would be kept.

Flushed by her easy conquest of a mind she would previously have been unable to touch, and engrossed in the problem of setting her own tremendously enlarged mind to rights, why should it have occurred to the girl that there was anything worthy of investigation concealed in the depths of that chance-met stranger's mentality?

Returning to her own speedster, she shed her armor and shot away; and it was just as well for her peace of mind that she was not aware of the tight-beamed thought even then speeding from the flitter so far behind her to dread and distant Ploor.

'... but it was very definitely not a human female. I could not touch it. It may very well have been one of the accursed Arisians themselves. But since I did nothing to arouse its suspicions, I got rid of it easily enough. Spread the warning!'

10
Constance Out-Worsels Worsel

While Kathryn Kinnison was working with her father in the hyperspatial tube and with Mentor of Arisia, and while Camilla and Tregonsee were sleuthing the inscrutable 'X', Constance was also at work. Although she lay flat on her back, not moving a muscle, she was working as she had never worked before. Long since she had put her indetectable speedster into the control of a director-by-chance. Now, knowing nothing and caring less of where she and her vessel might be or might go, physically completely relaxed, she drove her 'sensories' out to the full limit of their prodigious range and held them there for hour after hour. Worsel-like, she was not consciously listening for any particular thing; she was merely increasing her already incredibly vast store of knowledge. One hundred percent receptive, attached to and concerned with only the brain of her physical body, her mind sped at large; sampling, testing, analyzing, cataloguing every item with which its most tenuous fringe came in contact. Through thousands of solar systems that mind went; millions upon millions of entities either did or did not contribute something worthwhile.

Suddenly there came something that jarred her into physical movement: a burst of thought upon a band so high that it was practically always vacant. She shook herself, got up, lighted an Alsakanite cigarette, and made herself a pot of coffee.

'This is important, I think,' she mused. 'I'd better get to work on it while it's fresh.'

She sent out a thought tuned to Worsel, and was surprised when it went unanswered. She investigated: finding that the

Velantian's screens were full up and held hard – he was fighting Overlords so savagely that he had not felt her thought. Should she take a hand in this brawl? She should not, she decided, and grinned fleetingly. Her erstwhile tutor would need no help in that comparatively minor chore. She'd wait until he wasn't quite so busy.

'Worsel! Con calling. What goes on there, fellow old snake?' She finally launched her thought.

'As though you didn't know!' Worsel sent back. 'Been quite a while since I saw you – how about coming aboard?'

'Coming at max,' and she did.

Before entering the *Velan*, however, she put on a gravity damper, set at 980 centimeters. Strong, tough, and supple as she was she did not relish the thought of the atrocious accelerations used and enjoyed by Velantians everywhere.

'What did you make of that burst of thought?' she asked by way of greeting. 'Or were you having so much fun you missed it?'

'What burst?' Then, after Constance had explained, 'I was busy; but *not* having fun.'

'Somebody who didn't know you might believe that,' the girl derided. 'This thought was important, I think – much more so than dilly-dallying with Overlords, as you were doing. It was way up – on this band here.' She illustrated.

'So?' Worsel came as near to whistling as one of his inarticulate race could come. 'What are they like?'

'VWZY, to four places.' Con concentrated. 'Multi-legged. Not exactly carapaceous, but pretty nearly. Spiny, too, I believe. The world was cold, dismal, barren; but not frigid, but he – it – didn't seem exactly like an oxygen-breather – more like what a warm-blooded Palainian would perhaps look like, if you can imagine such a thing. Mentality very high – precisionist grade – no thought of cities as such. The sun was a typical yellow dwarf. Does any of this ring a bell in your mind?'

'No.' Worsel thought intensely for minutes. So did Constance. Neither had any idea – then – that the girl was describing the form assumed in their autumn by the dread inhabitants of the planet Ploor!

'This may indeed be important,' Worsel broke the mental silence. 'Shall we explore together?'

'We shall.' They tuned to the desired band. 'Give it plenty of shove, too – Go!'

Out and out and out the twinned receptors sped; to encounter a tenuous, weak, and utterly cryptic vibration. One touch – the merest possible contact – and it disappeared. It vanished before even Con's almost-instantaneous reaction could get more than a hint of directional alignment; and neither of the observers could read any part of it.

Both of these developments were starkly incredible, and Worsel's long body tightened convulsively, rock-hard, in the violence of the mental force now driving his exploring mind. Finding nothing, he finally relaxed.

'Any Lensmen, anywhere, can read and understand any thought, however garbled or scrambled, or however expressed,' he thought at Constance. 'Also, I have always been able to get an exact line on anything I could perceive, but all I know about this one is that it seemed to come mostly from somewhere over that way. Did you do any better?'

'Not much, if any.' If the thing was surprising to Worsel, it was sheerly astounding to his companion. She, knowing the measure of her power, thought to herself – not to the Velantian – 'Girl, file *this* one carefully away in the big black book!'

Slight as were the directional leads, the *Velan* tore along the indicated line at maximum blast. Day after day she sped, a wide-flung mental net out far ahead and out farther still on all sides. They did not find what they sought, but they did find – something.

'What is it?' Worsel demanded of the quivering telepath who had made the report.

'I don't know, sir. Not on that ultra-band, but well below it ... there. Not an Overlord, certainly, but something perhaps equally unfriendly.'

'An Eich!' Both Worsel and Con exclaimed the thought, and

the girl went on, 'It was practically certain that we couldn't get them all on Jarnevon, of course, but none have been reported before... where are they, anyway? Get me a chart, somebody... It's Novena IX... QX – tune up your heavy artillery, Worsel – it'd be nice if we could take the head man alive, but that's a little too much luck to expect.'

The Velantian, even though he had issued instantaneously the order to drive at full blast toward the indicated planet, was momentarily at a loss. Kinnison's daughter entertained no doubts as to the outcome of the encounter she was proposing – but she had never seen an Eich close up. He had. So had her father. Kinnison had come out a very poor second in that affair, and Worsel knew that he could have done no better, if as well. However, that had been upon Jarnevon, actually inside one of its strongest citadels, and neither he nor Kinnison had been prepared.

'What's the plan, Worsel?' Con demanded, vibrantly. 'How're you figuring on taking 'em?'

'Depends on how strong they are. If it's a long-established base, we'll simply have to report it to LaForge and go on about our business. If, as seems more probable because it hasn't been reported before, it's a new establishment – or possibly only a grounded space-ship so far – we'll go to work on them ourselves. We'll soon be close enough to find out.'

'QX,' and a fleeting grin passed over Con's vivacious face. For a long time she had been working with Mentor the Arisian, specifically to develop the ability to 'out-Worsel Worsel', and now was the best time she ever would have to put her hard schooling to test.

Hence, Master of Hallucination though he was, the Velantian had no hint of realization when his Klovian companion, working through a channel which he did not even know existed, took control of every compartment of his mind. Nor did the crew, in particular or en masse, suspect anything amiss when she performed the infinitely easier task of taking over theirs. Nor did the unlucky Eich, when the flying *Velan* had approached their planet closely enough to make it clear that their establishment was indeed a new one, being built around the nucleus of a Boskonian battleship. Except for their commanding officer they died then and there – and Con was to regret bitterly, later, that she had made this engagement such a one-girl affair.

The grounded battleship was a formidable fortress indeed. Under the fierce impact of its offensive beams the Velantians saw their very wall-shields flame violet. In return they saw their mighty secondary beams stopped cold by the Boskonian's inner screens, and had to bring into play the inconceivable energies of their primaries before the enemy's space-ship-fortress could be knocked out. And this much of the battle was real. Instrument- and recorder-tapes could be and were being doctored to fit; but spent primary shells could not be simulated. Nor was it thinkable that this superdreadnought and its incipient base should be allowed to survive.

Hence, after the dreadful primaries had quieted the Eich's main batteries and had reduced the ground-works to flaming pools of lava, needle-beamers went to work on every minor and secondary control board. Then, the great vessel definitely helpless as a fighting unit, Worsel and his hard-bitten crew thought that they went – thought-screened, full-armored, armed with semi-portables and DeLameters – joyously into the hand-to-hand combat which each craved. Worsel and two of his strongest henchmen attacked the armed and armored Boskonian captain. After a satisfyingly terrific struggle, in the course of which all three of the Velantians – and some others – were appropriately burned and wounded, they overpowered him and carried him bodily into the control-room of the *Velan*. This part of the episode, too, was real; as was the complete melting down of the Boskonian vessel which occurred while the transfer was being made.

Then, while Con was engaged in the exceedingly delicate task of withdrawing her mind from Worsel's without leaving any detectable trace that she had ever been in it, there happened the completely unexpected; the one thing for which she was utterly unprepared. The mind of the captive captain was wrenched from her control as palpably as a loosely-held stick is snatched from a physical hand; and at the same time there was hurled against her impenetrable barriers an attack which could not possibly have stemmed from any Eichian mind!

If her mind had been free, she could have coped with the situation, but it was not. She *had* to hold Worsel – she knew with cold certainty what would ensue if she did not. The crew? They could be blocked out temporarily – unlike the Velantian Lensman, no one of them could even suspect that he had been in a stasis unless it were long enough to be noticeable upon such timepieces as clocks. The procedure, however, occupied a millisecond or so of precious time; and a considerably longer interval was required to withdraw with the required traceless-ness from Worsel's mind. Thus, before she could do anything except protect herself and the Velantian from that surprisingly powerful invading intelligence, all trace of it disappeared and all that remained of their captive was a dead body.

Worsel and Constance stared at each other, wordless, for seconds. The Velantian had a completely and accurately detailed memory of everything that had happened up to that instant, the only matter not quite clear being the fact that their hard-won captive was dead; the girl's mind was racing to fabricate a bulletproof explanation of that startling fact. Worsel saved her the trouble.

'It is of course true,' he thought at her finally, 'that any mind of sufficient power can destroy by force of will alone the entity of flesh in which it resides. I never thought about this matter before in connection with the Eich, but no detail of the experience your father and I had with them on Jarnevon would support any contention that they do not have minds of the requisite power ... and today's battle, being purely physical, would not throw any light on the subject ... I wonder if a thing like that could be stopped? That is, if we had been on time ... ?'

'That's it, I think.' Con put on her most disarming, most engaging grin in preparation for the most outrageous series of lies of her long career. 'And I don't think it can be stopped – at

99

least I couldn't stop him. You see, I got into him a fraction of a second before you did, and in that instant, just like that,' in spite of the fact that Worsel could not hear, she snapped her fingers ringingly, 'faster even than that, he was gone. I didn't think of it until you brought it up, but you're right as can be – he killed himself to keep us from finding out whatever he knew.'

Worsel stared at her with six eyes now instead of one, gimlet probes which glanced imperceptibly off her shield. He was not consciously trying to break down her barriers – to his fullest perception they were already down; no barriers were there. He was not consciously trying to integrate or reintegrate any detail or phase of the episode just past – no iota of falsity had appeared at any point or instant. Nevertheless, deep down within those extra reaches that made Worsel of Velantia what he was, a vague disquiet refused to down. It was too ... too ... Worsel's consciousness could not supply the adjective.

Had it been too easy? Very decidedly it had not. His utterly worn-out, battered and wounded crew refuted that thought. So did his own body, slashed and burned, as well as did the litter of shells and the heaps of smoking slag which had once been an enemy stronghold.

Also, even though he had not theretofore thought that he and his crew possessed enough force to do what had just been done, it was starkly unthinkable that anyone, even an Arisian, could have helped him do anything without his knowledge. Particularly how could this girl, daughter of Kimball Kinnison although she was, possibly have stuff enough to play unperceived the part of guardian angel to him, Worsel of Velantia?

Least able of all the five Second-Stage Lensmen to appreciate what the Children of the Lens really were, he did not, then or ever, have any inkling of the real truth. But Constance, far behind her cheerfully innocent mask, shivered as she read exactly his disturbed and disturbing thoughts. For, conversely, an unresolved enigma would affect him more than it would any of his fellow L2's. He would work on it until he did resolve it, one way or another. This thing had to be settled, *now*. And there was a way – a good way.

'But I *did* help you, you big lug!' she stormed, stamping her booted foot in emphasis. 'I was in there every second, slugging away with everything I had. Didn't you even feel me, you dope?' She allowed a thought to become evident; widened her eyes in startled incredulity. 'You *didn't*!' she accused, hotly. 'You were reveling so repulsively in the thrill of body-to-body fighting, just like you were back there in that cavern of Overlords, that you couldn't have felt a thought if it was driven into you with a D2P pressor! Of *course* I helped you, you wigglesome clunker! If I hadn't been in there pitching, dulling their edges here and there at critical moments, you'd've had a hell of a time getting them at all! I'm going to flit right now, and I hope I *never* see you again as long as I live!'

This vicious counter-attack, completely mendacious though it was, fitted the facts so exactly that Worsel's inchoate doubts vanished. Moreover, he was even less well equipped than are human men to cope with the peculiarly feminine weapons Constance was using so effectively. Wherefore the Velantian capitulated, almost abjectly, and the girl allowed herself to be coaxed down from her high horse and to become her usual sunny and impish self.

But when the *Velan* was once more on course and she had retired to her cabin, it was not to sleep. Instead, she thought. Was this intellect of the same race as the one whose burst of thought she had caught such a short time before, or not? She could not decide – not enough data. The first thought had been unconscious and quite revealing; this one simply a lethal weapon, driven with a power the memory of which made her gasp again. They could, however, be the same: the mind with which she had been en rapport could very well be capable of generating the force she had felt. If they were the same, they were something that should be studied, intensively and at once; and she herself had kicked away her only chance to make that study. She had better tell somebody about this, even if it meant confessing her own bird-brained part, and get some competent advice. Who?

Kit? No. Not because he would smack her down – she *ought* to be smacked down! – but because his brain wasn't enough better than her own to do any good. In fact, it wasn't a bit better than hers.

Mentor? At the very thought she shuddered, mentally and physically. She would call him in, fast enough, regardless of consequences to herself, if it would do any good, but it wouldn't. She was starkly certain of that. He wouldn't smack her down, like Kit would, but he wouldn't help her, either. He'd just sit there and sneer at her while she stewed, hotter and hotter, in her own juice...

'In a childish, perverted, and grossly exaggerated way, daughter Constance, you are right,' the Arisian's thought rolled sonorously into her astounded mind. 'You got yourself into this: get yourself out. One promising fact, however, I perceive – although seldom and late, you at last begin really to think.'

In that hour Constance Kinnison grew up.

11
Nadreck Traps a Trapper

Any human or near-human Lensman would have been appalled by the sheer loneliness of Nadreck's long vigil. Almost any one of them would have cursed, fluently and bitterly, when the time came at which he was forced to concede that the being for whom he lay in wait was not going to visit that particular planet.

But utterly unhuman Nadreck was not lonely. In fact, there was no word in the vocabulary of his race even remotely resembling the term in definition, connotation, or implication. From his galaxy-wide study he had a dim, imperfect idea of what such an emotion or feeling might be, but he could not begin to understand it. Nor was he in the least disturbed by the fact that Kandron did not appear. Instead, he held his orbit until the minute arrived at which the mathematical probability became point nine nine nine that his proposed quarry was not going to appear. Then, as matter-of-factly as though he had merely taken half an hour out for lunch, he abandoned his position and set out upon the course so carefully planned for exactly this event.

The search for further clues was long and uneventful; but monstrously, unhumanly patient Nadreck stuck to it until he found one. True, it was so slight as to be practically non-existent – a mere fragment of a whisper of zwilnik instruction – but it bore Kandron's unmistakable imprint. The Palainian had expected no more. Kandron would not slip. Momentary leakages from faulty machines would have to occur from time to time, but Kandron's machines would not be at fault either often or long at a time.

Nadreck, however, had been ready. Course after course of the most delicate spotting screen ever devised had been out for weeks. So had tracers, radiation absorbers, and every other insidious locating device known to the science of the age. The standard detectors remained blank, of course – no more so than his own conveyance would that of the Onlonian be detectable by any ordinary instruments. And as the Palainian speedster shot away along the most probable course, some fifty delicate instruments in its bow began stabbing that entire region of space with a pattern of needles of force through which a Terrestrial barrel could not have floated untouched.

Thus the Boskonian craft – an inherently indetectable speedster – was located; and in that instant was speared by three modified CRX tracers. Nadreck then went inert and began to plot the other speedster's course. He soon learned that that course was unpredictable; that the vessel was being operated statistically, completely at random. This too, then, was a trap.

This knowledge disturbed Nadreck no more than had any more-or-less similar event of the previous twenty-odd years. He had realized fully that the leakage could as well have been deliberate as accidental. He had at no time underestimated Kandron's ability; the future alone would reveal whether or not Kandron would at any time underestimate his. He would follow through – there might be a way in which this particular trap could be used against its setter.

Leg after leg of meaningless course Nadreck followed, until there came about that which the Palainian knew would happen in time – the speedster held a straight course for more parsecs than six-sigma limits of probability could ascribe to pure randomness. Nadreck knew what that meant. The speedster was returning to its base for servicing, which was precisely the event for which he had been waiting. It was the base he wanted, not the speedster; and that base would never, under any conceivable conditions, emit any detectable quantity of traceable radiation. To its base, then, Nadreck followed the little space-ship, and to say that he was on the alert as he approached that base is a gross understatement indeed. He expected to set off at least one, and probably many blasts of force. That would almost certainly be necessary in order to secure sufficient information concerning the enemy's defensive screens. It was necessary – but when those blasts arrived Nadreck was elsewhere, calmly analyzing the data secured by his instruments during the brief contact which had triggered the Boskonian projectors into action.

So light, so fleeting, and so unorthodox had been Nadreck's touch that the personnel of the now doomed base could not have known with any certainty that any visitor had actually been there. If there had been, the logical supposition would have been that he and his vessel had been resolved into their component atoms. Nevertheless Nadreck waited – as has been shown, he was good at waiting – until the burst of extra vigilance set up by the occurrence would have subsided into ordinary watchfulness. Then he began to act.

At first this action was in ultra-slow motion. One millimeter per hour his drill advanced. Drill was synchronized precisely with screen, and so guarded as to give an alarm at a level of interference far below that necessary to energize any probable detector at the generators of the screen being attacked.

Through defense after defense Nadreck made his cautious, indetectable way into the dome. It was a small base, as such things go; manned, as expected, by escapees from Onlo. Scum, too, for the most part; creatures of even baser and more violent passions than those upon whom he had worked in Kandron's Onlonian stronghold. To keep those intractable entities in line during their brutally long tours of duty, a psychological therapist had been given authority second only to that of the base commander. That knowledge, and the fact that there was only one populated dome, made the Palainian come as close to grinning as one of his unsmiling race can.

The psychologist wore a multiplex thought-screen, of course, as did everyone else; but that did not bother Nadreck. Kinnison had opened such screens many times; not only by means of his own hands, but also at various times by the use of a dog's jaws, a spider's legs and mandibles, and even a worm's sinuous body. Wherefore, through the agency of a quasi-fourth-dimensional life form literally indescribable to three-dimensional man, Nadreck's ego was soon comfortably ensconced in the mind of the Onlonian.

That entity knew in detail every weakness of each of his personnel. It was his duty to watch those weaknesses, to keep them down, to condition each of his wards in such fashion that friction and strife would be minimized. Now, however, he proceeded to do exactly the opposite. One hated another. That hate became a searing obsession, requiring the concentration of every effort upon ways and means of destroying its objects. One feared another. That fear ate in, searing as it went, destroying every normality of outlook and of reason. Many were jealous of their superiors. This emotion, requiring as it does nothing except its own substance upon which to feed, became a fantastically spreading, caustically corrosive blight.

To name each ugly, noisome passion or trait resident in that dome is to call the complete roster of the vile; and calmly, mercilessly, unmovedly, ultra-efficiently, Nadreck manipulated them all. As though he were playing a Satanic organ he touched a nerve here, a synapse there, a channel somewhere else, bringing the whole group, with the lone exception of the commander, simultaneously to the point of explosion. Nor was any sign of this perfect work evident externally; for everyone there, having lived so long under the iron code of Boskonia, knew exactly the consequences of any infraction of that code.

The moment came when passion overmastered sense. One of the monsters stumbled, jostling another. That nudge became, in its recipient's seething mind, a lethal attack by his bitterest enemy. A forbidden projector flamed viciously: the offended one was sating his lust so insensately that he scarcely noticed the bolt that in turn rived away his own life. Detonated by this incident, the personnel of the base exploded as one. Blasters raved briefly; knives and swords bit and slashed; improvised bludgeons crashed against preselected targets; hard-taloned appendages gouged and tore. And Nadreck, who had long since withdrawn from the mind of the psychologist, timed with a stop-watch the duration of the whole grisly affair, from the instant of the first stumble to the death of the last Onlonian outside the commander's locked and armored sanctum. Ninety-eight and three-tenths seconds. Good – a nice job.

The commander, as soon as it was safe to do so, rushed out of his guarded room to investigate. Amazed, disgruntled, dismayed by the to him completely inexplicable phenomenon he had just witnessed, he fell an easy prey to the Palainian Lensman. Nadreck invaded his mind and explored it, channel by channel; finding – not entirely unexpectedly – that this Number One knew nothing whatever of interest.

Nadreck did not destroy the base. Instead, after setting up a small instrument in the commander's private office, he took that unfortunate wight aboard his speedster and drove off into space. He immobilized his captive, not by loading him with manacles, but by deftly severing a few essential nerve trunks. Then he really studied the Onlonian's mind – line by line, this time; almost cell by cell. A master – almost certainly Kandron himself – had operated here. There was not the slightest trace of tampering; no leads to or indications of what the activating stimulus would have to be; all that the fellow now knew was that it was his job to hold his base inviolate against any and every form of intrusion and to keep that speedster flitting around all over space on a director-by-chance as much as possible of the time, leaking slightly a certain signal now and then.

Even under this microscopic re-examination, he knew nothing whatever of Kandron; nothing of Onlo or of Thrale; nothing of any Boskonian organization, activity, or thing; and Nadreck, although baffled still, remained undisturbed. This trap, he thought, could almost certainly be used against the trapper. Until a certain call came through his relay in the base, he would investigate the planets of this system.

During the investigation a thought impinged upon his Lens

from Karen Kinnison, one of the very few warm-blooded beings for whom he had any real liking or respect.

'Busy, Nadreck?' she asked, as casually as though she had just left him.

'In large, yes. In detail and at the moment, no. Is there any small problem in which I can be of assistance?'

'Not small – big. I just got the funniest distress call I ever heard or heard of. On a high band – way, way up – there. Do you know of any race that thinks on that band?'

'I do not believe so.' He thought for a moment. 'Definitely, no.'

'Neither do I. It wasn't broadcast, either, but was directed at any member of a special race or tribe – very special. Classification, straight Z's to ten or twelve places, she – or it – seemed to be trying to specify.'

'A frigid race of extreme type, adapted to an environment having a temperature of approximately one degree absolute.'

'Yes. Like you, only more so.' Kay paused, trying to put into intelligible thought a picture inherently incapable of reception or recognition by her as yet strictly three-dimensional intelligence. 'Something like the Eich, too, but not much. Their visible aspect was obscure, fluid... amorphous... Indefinite?... skip it – I couldn't really perceive it, let alone describe it. I wish you had caught that thought.'

'I wish so, too – it is very interesting. But tell me – if the thought was directed, not broadcast, how could you have received it?'

'That's the funniest part of the whole thing.' Nadreck could feel the girl frown in concentration. 'It came at me from all sides at once – never felt anything like it. Naturally I started feeling around for the source – particularly since it was a distress signal – but before I could get even a general direction of the origin it... it... well, it didn't really disappear or really weaken, but something happened to it. I couldn't read it any more – and *that* really did throw me for a loss.' She paused, then went on. 'It didn't so much go away as go *down*, some way or other. Then it vanished completely, without really going anywhere. I'm not making myself clear – I simply can't – but have I given you enough leads so that you can make any sense at all out of any part of it?'

'I'm very sorry to say that I can not.'

Nor could he, ever, for excellent reasons. That girl had a mind whose power, scope, depth, and range she herself did not, could not even dimly understand; a mind to be fully comprehended only by an adult of her own third level. That mind had in fact received in toto a purely fourth-dimensional thought. If Nadreck had received it, he would have understood it and recognized it for what it was only because of his advanced Arisian training – no other Palainian could have done so – and it would have been sheerly unthinkable to him that any warmblooded and therefore strictly three-dimensional entity could by any possibility receive such a thought; or, having received it, could understand any part of it. Nevertheless, if he had really concentrated the full powers of his mind upon the girl's attempted description, he might very well have recognized in it the clearest possible three-dimensional delineation of such a thought; and from that point he could have gone on to a full understanding of the Children of the Lens.

However, he did not so concentrate. It was constitutionally impossible for him to devote real mental effort to any matter not immediately pertaining to the particular task in hand. Therefore neither he nor Karen Kinnison were to know until much later that she had been en rapport with one of Civilization's bitterest, most implacable foes; that she had seen with clairvoyant and telepathic accuracy the intrinsically three-dimensionally-indescribable form assumed in their winter by the horrid, the monstrous inhabitants of that viciously hostile world, the unspeakable planet Ploor!

'I was afraid you couldn't.' Kay's thought came clear. 'That makes it all the more important – important enough for you to drop whatever you're doing and join me in getting to the bottom of it, if you could be made to see it, which of course you can't.'

'I am about to take Kandron, and nothing in the Universe

can be as important as that,' Nadreck stated quietly, as a simple matter of fact. 'You have observed this that lies here?'

'Yes.' Karen, en rapport with Nadreck, was of course cognizant of the captive, but it had not occurred to her to mention this monster. When dealing with Nadreck she, against all the tenets of her sex, exhibited as little curiosity as did the coldly emotionless Lensman himself. 'Since you bid so obviously for the question, why are you keeping it alive – or rather, not dead?'

'Because he is my sure link to Kandron.' If Nadreck of Palain ever was known to gloat, it was then. 'He is Kandron's creature, placed by Kandron personally as an agency of my destruction. Kandron's brain alone holds the key compulsion which will restore his memories. At some future time – perhaps a second from now, perhaps a cycle of years – Kandron will use that key to learn how his minion fares. Kandron's thought will energize my re-transmitter in the dome; the compulsion will be forwarded to this still-living brain. The brain, however, will be in my speedster, not in that undamaged fortress. You now understand why I cannot stray far from this being's base; you should see that you should join me instead of me joining you.'

'No; not definite enough,' Karen countered decisively, 'I can't see myself passing up a thing like this for the opportunity of spending the next ten years floating around in an orbit, doing nothing. However, I check you to a certain extent – when and if anything really happens, shoot me a thought and I'll rally round.'

The linkage broke without formal *adieus*. Nadreck went his way. Karen went hers. She did not, however, go far along the way she had had in mind. She was still precisely nowhere in her quest when she felt a thought, of a type that only her brother or an Arisian could send. It was Kit.

'Hi, Kay!' A warm, brotherly contact. 'How'r'ya doing, sis – are you growing up?'

'Of *course* I'm grown up! What a question!'

'Don't get stiff, Kay, there's method in this. Got to be sure.'

All trace of levity gone, he probed her unmercifully. 'Not too bad, at that, for a kid. As dad would express it, if he could feel you this way, you're twenty-nine numbers Brinnell harder than a diamond drill. Plenty of jets for this job, and by the time the real one comes, you'll probably be ready.'

'Cut the rigmarole, Kit!' she snapped, and hurled a vicious bolt of her own. If Kit did not counter it as easily as he had handled her earlier efforts, he did not reveal the fact. 'What job? What d'you think you're talking about? I'm on a job now that I wouldn't drop for Nadreck, and I don't think I'll drop it for you.'

'You'll have to.' Kit's thought was grim. 'Mother is going to have to go to work on Lyrane II. The probability is pretty bad that there is or will be something there that she can't handle. Remote control is out, or I'd do it myself, but I can't work on Lyrane II in person. Here's the whole picture – look it over. You can see, sis, that you're elected, so hop to it.'

'I won't!' she stormed. 'I can't – I'm too busy. How about asking Con, or Kat, or Cam?'

'They don't fit the picture,' he explained patiently – for him. 'In this case hardness is indicated, as you can see for yourself.'

'Hardness, phooey!' she jeered. 'To handle Ladora of Lyrane? She thinks she's a hard-boiled egg, I know, but ...'

'Listen, you bird-brained knot-head!' Kit cut in, venomously. 'You're fogging the issue deliberately – stop it! I spread you the whole picture – you know as well as I do that while there's nothing definite as yet, the thing needs covering and you're the one to cover it. But no – just because I'm the one to suggest to or ask anything of you, you've always got to go into that damned mulish act of yours ...'

'Be silent, children, and attend!' Both flushed violently as Mentor came between them. 'Some of the weaker thinkers here are beginning to despair of you, but my visualization of your development is still clear. To mold such characters as yours sufficiently, and yet not too much, is a delicate task indeed; but one which must and shall be done. Christopher, come to me at once, in person. Karen, I would suggest that you go to Lyrane and do there whatever you find necessary to do.'

'I won't – I've *still* got this job here to do!' Karen defied even the ancient Arisian sage.

'That, daughter, can and should wait. I tell you solemnly, as a fact, that if you do not go to Lyrane you will never get the faintest clue to that which you now seek.'

12
Kalonia Becomes of Interest

Christopher Kinnison drove toward Arisia, seething. Why couldn't those damned sisters of his have sense to match their brains – or why couldn't he have had some brothers? Especially – right now – Kay. If she had the sense of a Zabriskan fontema she'd know that this job was *important* and would snap into it, instead of wild-goose-chasing all over space. If he were Mentor he'd straighten her out. He had decided to straighten her out once himself, and he grinned wryly to himself at the memory of what had happened. What Mentor had done to him, before he even got started, was really rugged. What he would like to do, next time he got within reach of her, was to shake her until her teeth rattled.

Or would he? Uh-uh. By no stretch of the imagination could he picture himself hurting any one of them. They were swell kids – in fact, the finest people he had ever known. He had rough-housed and wrestled with them plenty of times, of course – he liked it, and so did they. He could handle any one of them – he surveyed without his usual complacence his two-hundred-plus pounds of meat, bone, and gristle – he ought to be able to, since he outweighed them by fifty or sixty pounds; but it wasn't easy. Worse than Valerians – just like taking on a combination of boa constrictor and cateagle – and when Kat and Con ganged up on him that time they mauled him to a pulp in nothing flat.

But jet back! Weight wasn't it, except maybe among themselves. He had never met a Valerian yet whose shoulders he couldn't pin flat to the mat in a hundred seconds, and the smallest of them outweighed him two to one. Conversely, although he had never thought of it before, what his sisters had taken from him, without even a bruise, would have broken any ordinary women up into masses of compound fractures. They were – they must be – made of different stuff.

His thoughts took a new tack. The kids were special in another way, too, he had noticed lately, without paying it any particular attention. It might tie in. They didn't *feel* like other girls. After dancing with one of them, other girls felt like robots made out of putty. Their flesh *was* different. It was firmer, finer, infinitely more responsive. Each individual cell seemed to be endowed with a flashing, sparkling life; a life which, inter-linking with that of one of his own cells, made their bodies as intimately one as were their perfectly synchronized minds.

But what did all this have to do with their lack of sense? QX, they were nice people. QX, he couldn't beat their brains out, either physically or mentally. But damn it all, there ought to be *some* way of driving some ordinary common sense through their fine-grained, thick, hard, tough skulls!

Thus it was that Kit approached Arisia in a decidedly mixed frame of mind. He shot through the barrier without slowing down and without notification. Inerting his ship, he fought her into an orbit around the planet. The shape of the orbit was immaterial, as long as its every inch was inside Arisia's inner-most screen. For young Kinnison knew precisely what those screens were and exactly what they were for. He knew that distance of itself meant nothing – Mentor could give anyone either basic or advanced treatments just as well from a distance of a thousand million parsecs as at hand to hand. The reason for the screens and for the personal visits was the existence of the Eddorians, who had minds probably as capable as the Arisians' own. And throughout all the infinite reaches of the macro-cosmic Universe, only within these highly special screens was there *certainty* of privacy from the spying senses of the ultimate foe.

'The time has come, Christopher, for the last treatment I

am able to give you,' Mentor announced without preamble, as soon as Kit had checked his orbit.

'Oh – so soon? I thought you were pulling me in to pin my ears back for fighting with Kay – the dim-wit!'

'That, while a minor matter, is worthy of passing mention, since it is illustrative of the difficulties inherent in the project of developing, without over-controlling, such minds as yours. En route here, you made a masterly summation of the situation, with one outstanding omission.'

'Huh? What omission? I covered it like a blanket!'

'You assumed throughout, and still assume, as you always do in dealing with your sisters, that you are unassailably right; that your conclusion is the only tenable one; that they are always wrong.'

'But damn it, they *are*! That's why you sent Kay to Lyrane!'

'In these conflicts with your sisters, you have been right in approximately half of the cases,' Mentor informed him.

'But how about their fights with each other?'

'Do you know of any such?'

'Why . . . uh . . . can't say that I do.' Kit's surprise was plain. 'But since they fight with me so much, they must . . .'

'That does not follow, and for a very good reason. We may as well discuss that reason now, as it is a necessary part of the education which you are about to receive. You already know that your sisters are very different, each from the other. Know now, youth, that each was specifically developed to be so completely different that there is no possible point which could be made an issue between any two of them.'

'Ungh . . . um . . .' It took some time for Kit to digest that news. 'Then where do I come in that they *all* fight with me at the drop of a hat?'

'That, too, while regrettable, is inevitable. Each of your sisters, as you may have suspected, is to play a tremendous part in that which is to come. The Lensmen, we of Arisia, all will contribute, but upon you Children of the Lens – especially upon the girls – will fall the greater share of the load. Your individual task will be that of coordinating the whole; a duty which no Arisian is or ever can be qualified to perform. You will have to direct the efforts of your sisters; re-enforcing every heavily-attacked point with your own incomparable force and drive; keeping them smoothly in mesh and in place. As a side issue, you will also have to coordinate the feebler efforts of us of Arisia, the Lensmen, the Patrol, and whatever other minor forces we may be able to employ.'

'Holy – Klono's – claws!' Kit was gasping like a fish. 'Just where, Mentor, do you figure I'm going to pick up the jets to swing *that* load? And as to coordinating the kids – that's out. I'd make just one suggestion to any one of them and she'd forget all about the battle and tear into me – no, I'll take that back. The stickier the going, the closer they rally round.'

'Right. It will always be so. Now, youth, that you have these facts, explain these matters to me, as a sort of preliminary exercise.'

'I think I see.' Kit thought intensely. 'The kids don't fight with each other because they don't overlap. They fight with me because my central field overlaps them all. They have no occasion to fight with anybody else, nor have I, because with anybody else our viewpoint is always right and the other fellow knows it – except for Palainians and such, who think along different lines than we do. Thus, Kay never fights with Nadreck. When he goes off the beam, she simply ignores him and goes on about her business. But with them and me ... we'll have to learn to arbitrate, or something, I suppose ...' His thought trailed off.

'Manifestations of adolescence; with adulthood, now coming fast, they will pass. Let us get on with the work.'

'But wait a minute!' Kit protested. 'About this coordinator thing. I can't do it. I'm too much of a kid – I won't be ready for a job like that for a thousand years!'

'You must be ready.' Mentor's thought was inexorable. 'And, when the time comes, you shall be. Now, youth, come fully into my mind.'

There is no use repeating in detail the progress of an Arisian super-education, especially since the most accurate possible description of the most important of those details would be intrinsically meaningless. When, finally, Kit was ready to leave Arisia, he looked much older and more mature than before; he felt immensely older than he looked. The concluding conversation of that visit, however, is worth recording.

'You now know, Christopher,' Mentor mused, 'what you children are and how you came to be. You are the accomplishment of long lifetimes of work. It is with profound satisfaction that I now perceive clearly that those lifetimes have not been spent in vain.'

'Yours, you mean.' Kit was embarrassed, but one point still bothered him. 'Dad met and married mother, yes, but how about the others? Tregonsee, Worsel, and Nadreck? They and the corresponding females – don't take that literally for Nadreck, of course – were also penultimates, of lines as long as ours. You Arisians decided that the human stock was best, so none of the other Second-Stage Lensmen ever met their complements. Not that it could make any difference to them, of course, but I should think that three of your fellow students wouldn't feel so good.'

'Ah, youth, I am very glad indeed that you mention the point.' The Arisian's thought was positively gleeful. 'You have at no time, then, detected anything peculiar about this that you know as Mentor of Arisia?'

'Why, of course not. How could I? Or, rather, why should I?'

'Any lapse on our part, however slight, from practically perfect synchronization would have revealed to such a mentality as yours that I whom you know as Mentor am not an individual, but four. While we each worked as individuals upon all of the experimental lines, whenever we dealt with any one of the penultimates or ultimates we did so as a fusion. This was necessary, not only for your fullest possible development, but also to be sure that each of us had complete data upon every minute facet of the truth. While it was in no sense important to the work itself to keep you in ignorance of Mentor's plurality, the fact that we could keep you ignorant of it, particularly now that you have become adult, showed that our work was being done in a really workman-like fashion.'

Kit whistled; a long, low whistle which was tribute enough to those who knew what it meant. He knew what he meant, but there were not enough words or thoughts to express it.

'But you're going to keep on being Mentor, aren't you?' he asked.

'I am. The real task, as you know, lies ahead.'

'QX. You say I'm adult. I'm not. You imply that I'm more than several notches above you in qualifications. I could laugh myself silly about that one, if it wasn't so serious. Why, any one of you Arisians has forgotten more than I know, and could tie me up into bow-knots!'

'There are elements of truth in your thought. That you can now be called adult, however, does not mean that you have attained your full power; only that you are able to use effectively the powers you have and are able to acquire other and larger powers.'

'But what *are* those powers?' Kit demanded. 'You've hinted on that same theme a thousand times, and I don't know what you mean any better than I did before!'

'You must develop your own powers.' Mentor's thought was as final as Fate. 'Your mind is potentially far abler than mine. You will in time come to know my mind in full; I never will be able to know yours. For the lesser, but full mind to attempt to instruct in methodology the greater, although emptier one, is to set that greater mind in an undersized mold and thus to do it irreparable harm. You have the abilities and the powers. You will have to develop them yourself, by the perfection of techniques concerning which I can give you no instructions whatever.'

'But surely you can give me some kind of a hint!' Kit pleaded. 'I'm just a kid, I tell you – I don't even know how or where to begin!'

Under Kit's startled mental gaze, Mentor split suddenly into four parts, laced together by a pattern of thoughts so intricate and so rapid as to be unrecognizable. The parts fused and again Mentor spoke.

'I can point the way in only the broadest, most general terms. It has been decided, however, that I can give you one hint – or, more properly, one illustration. The surest test of knowledge known to us is the visualization of the Cosmic All. All science is, as you know, one. The true key to power lies in the knowledge of the underlying reasons for the succession of events. If it is pure causation – that is, if any given state of things follows as an inevitable consequence because of the state existing an infinitesimal instant before – then the entire course of the macro-cosmic universe was set for the duration of all eternity in the instant of its coming into being. This well-known concept, the stumbling-block upon which many early thinkers came to grief, we now know to be false. On the other hand, if pure randomness were to govern, natural laws as we know them could not exist. Thus neither pure causation nor pure randomness alone can govern the succession of events.

'The truth, then, must lie somewhere in between. In the macro-cosmos, causation prevails; in the micro-, randomness; both in accord with the mathematical laws of probability, It is in the region between them – the intermediate zone, or the interface, so to speak – that the greatest problems lie. The test of validity of any theory, as you know, is the accuracy of the predictions which are made possible by its use, and our greatest thinkers have shown that the completeness and fidelity of any visualization of the Cosmic All are linear functions of the clarity of definition of the components of that interface. Full knowledge of that indeterminate zone would mean infinite power and a statistically perfect visualization. None of these things, however, will ever be realized; for the acquirement of that full knowledge would require infinite time.

'That is all I can tell you. It will, properly studied, be enough. I have built within you a solid foundation; yours alone is the task of erecting upon that foundation a structure strong enough to withstand the forces which will be thrown against it.

'It is perhaps natural, in view of what you have recently

gone through, that you should regard the problem of the Eddorians as one of insuperable difficulty. Actually, however, it is not, as you will perceive when you have spent a few weeks in reintegrating yourself. You must not, you shall not, and in my clear visualization you do not, fail.'

Communication ceased. Kit made his way groggily to his control board, went free, and lined out for Klovia. For a guy whose education was supposed to be complete, he felt remarkably like a total loss with no insurance. He had asked for advice and had got – what? A dissertation on philosophy, mathematics, and physics – good enough stuff, probably, if he could see what Mentor was driving at, but not of much immediate use. He did have a brainful of new stuff, though – didn't know yet what half of it was – he'd better be getting it licked into shape. He'd 'sleep' on it.

He did so, and as he lay quiescent in his bunk the tiny pieces of an incredibly complex jig-saw puzzle began to click into place. The ordinary zwilniks – all the small fry fitted in well enough. The Overlords of Delgon. The Kalonians ... hm ... he'd better check with dad on that angle. The Eich – under control. Kandron of Onlo, ditto. 'X' was in safe hands; Cam had already been alerted to watch her step. Some planet named Ploor – what in all the purple hells of Palain had Mentor meant by that crack? Anyway, that piece didn't fit anywhere – yet. That left Eddore – and at the thought a series of cold waves raced up and down the young Lensman's spine. Nevertheless, Eddore was his oyster – his, and nobody else's. Mentor had made that plain enough. Everything the Arisians had done for umpteen skillions of years had been aimed at the Eddorians. They had picked him out to emcee the show – and how could a man coordinate an attack against something he knew nothing about? And the only way to get acquainted with Eddore and its denizens was to go there. Should he call in the kids? He should not. Each of them had her hands full of her own job; that of developing her own full self. He had his; and the more he studied the question, the clearer it became that the first number on the program of his self-development was – would *have* to be – a single-handed expedition against the key planet of Civilization's top-ranking foes.

He sprang out of his bunk, changed his vessel's course, and lined out a thought to his father.

'Dad? Kit. Been flitting around out Arisia way, and picked up an idea I want to pass along to you. It's about Kalonians. What do you know about them?'

'They're blue . . .'

'I don't mean that.'

'I know you don't. There were Helmuth, Jalte, Prellin, Crowninshield . . . all I can think of at the moment. Big operators, son, and smart hombres, if I do say so myself as shouldn't; but they're all ancient history . . . hold it! Maybe I know of a modern one, too – Eddie's Lensman. The only part of that picture that was sharp was the Lens, since Eddie was never analytically interested in any of the hundreds of types of people he met, but there was something about that Lensman . . . I'll bring him back and focus him as sharply as I can . . . there.' Both men studied the blurred statue posed in the Grey Lensman's mind. 'Wouldn't you say he could be a Kalonian?'

'Check. I wouldn't want to say much more than that. But about that Lens – did you really examine it? It *is* sharp – under the circumstances, of course, it would be.'

'Certainly! Wrong in every respect – rhythm, chroma, context, and aura. Definitely not Arisian; therefore Boskonian. That's the point – that's what I was afraid of, you know.'

'Double check. And that point ties in tight with the one that made me call you just now, that everybody, including you and me, seems to have missed. I've been searching my memory for five hours – you know what my memory is like – and I have heard of exactly two other Kalonians. They were big operators, too. I have never heard of the planet itself. To me it is a startling fact that the sum total of my information on Kalonia, reliable or otherwise, is that it produced seven big-shot zwilniks; six of them before I was born. Period.'

Kit felt his father's jaw drop.

'No, I don't remember of hearing anything about the planet, either,' the older man finally replied. 'But I'll bet I can get you all the information you want in fifteen minutes.'

'Credits to millos it'll be a lot nearer fifteen days. You can find it sometime, though, if anybody can – that's why I'm taking it up with you. While I don't want to seem to be giving a Grey Lensman orders' – that jocular introduction had come to be a sort of ritual in the Kinnison family – 'I would very diffidently suggest that there might be some connection between that completely unnoticed planet and some of the things we don't know about Boskonia.'

'Diffident! You?' The Grey Lensman laughed deeply. 'Like a hydride bomb! I'll start a search of Kalonia right away. As to your credits-to-millos-fifteen-days thing, I'd be ashamed to take your money. You don't know our librarians or our system. Ten millos, even money, that we get operational data in less than five G-P days from right now. Want it?'

'I'll say so. I'll wear that cento on my tunic as a medal of victory over the Grey Lensman. I *do* know the size of these here two galaxies!'

'QX – it's a bet. I'll Lens you when we get the dope. In the meantime, Kit, remember that you're my favorite son.'

'Well, you're not so bad, yourself. Any time I want mother to divorce you so as to change fathers for me I'll suggest it to her.' What a terrific, what a tremendous meaning was heterodyned upon that seemingly light exchange! 'Clear ether, dad!'

'Clear ether, son!'

13
Clarrissa Takes Her L-2 Work

Thousands of years were to pass before Christopher Kinnison could develop the ability to visualize, from the contemplation of one fact or artifact, the entire Universe to which it belonged. He could not even plan in detail his one-man invasion of Eddore until he could integrate all available data concerning the planet Kalonia into his visualization of the Boskonian Empire. One unknown, Ploor, blurred his picture badly enough; two such completely unknown factors made visualization, even in broad, impossible.

Anyway, he decided, he had one more job to do before he tackled the key planet of the enemy; and now, while he was waiting for the dope on Kalonia, would be the best time to do it. Wherefore he sent out a thought to his mother.

'Hi, First Lady of the Universe! 'Tis thy first-born who wouldst fain converse with thee. Art pressly engaged in matters of moment or import?'

'Art not, Kit.' Clarrissa's characteristic chuckle was as infectious, as full of the joy of life, as ever. 'Not that it would make any difference – but methinks I detect an undertone of seriosity beneath thy persiflage. Spill it.'

'Let's make it a rendezvous, instead,' he suggested. 'We're fairly close, I think – closer than we've been for a long time. Where are you, exactly?'

'Oh! Can we? Wonderful!' She marked her location and velocity in his mind. She made no effort to conceal her joy at the idea of a personal meeting. She never had tried and she never would try to make him put first matters other than first.

She had not expected to see him again, physically, until this war was over. But if she could...!

'QX. Hold your course and speed; I'll be seeing you in eighty-three minutes. In the meantime, it'll be just as well if we don't communicate, even by Lens...'

'Why, son?'

'Nothing definite – just a hunch, is all. Bye, gorgeous!'

The two speedsters approached each other – inerted – matched intrinsics – went free – flashed into contact – sped away together upon Clarissa's original course.

'Hi, mums!' Kit spoke into a visiphone. 'I should of course come to you, but it might be better if you come in here – I've got some special rigs set up here that I don't want to leave. QX?' He snapped on one of the special rigs as he spoke – a device which he himself had built and installed; the generator of the most efficient thought-screen then known.

'Why, of course!' She came, and was swept off her feet in the exuberance of her tall son's embrace; a greeting which she returned with equal fervor.

'It's nice, mother, seeing you again.' Words, or thoughts even, were *so* inadequate! Kit's voice was a trifle rough; his eyes were not completely dry.

'Uh-huh. It *is* nice,' she agreed, snuggling her spectacular head even more firmly into the curve of his shoulder. 'Mental contact is better than nothing, of course, but *this* is perfect!'

'Just as much a menace to navigation as ever, aren't you?' He held her at arm's length and shook his head in mock disapproval. 'Do you think it's quite right for one woman to have so much of everything when all the others have so little of anything?'

'Honestly, I don't.' She and Kit had always been exceptionally close; now her love for and her pride in this splendid creature, her son and her first-born, simply would not be denied. 'You're joking, I know, but that strikes too deep for comfort. I wake up in the night to wonder why, of all the women in existence, I should be so lucky, especially in my husband and children... QX, skip it.' Kit was shying away – she should have known better than to try in words even to skirt the profound depths of sentiment which both she and he knew so well were there.

'Get back onto the beam, gorgeous, you know what I meant. Look at yourself in the mirror some day – or do you, perchance?'

'Once in a while – maybe twice.' She giggled unaffectedly. 'You don't think all this charm and glamor comes without effort, do you? But maybe you'd better get back onto the beam yourself – you didn't come all these parsecs out of your way to say pretty things to your mother – even though I admit they've built up my ego no end.'

'On target, dead center.' Kit had been grinning, but he sobered quickly. 'I wanted to talk to you about Lyrane and the job you're figuring on doing out there.'

'Why?' she demanded. 'Do you know anything about it?'

'Unfortunately, I don't.' Kit's black frown of concentration reminded her forcibly of his father's characteristic scowl. 'Guesses – suspicions – theories – not even good hunches. But I thought ... I wondered ...' He paused, embarrassed as a schoolboy, then went on with a rush: 'Would you mind it too much if I went into something pretty personal?'

'You know I wouldn't, son.' In contrast to Kit's usual clarity and precision of thought, the question was highly ambiguous, but Clarissa covered both angles. 'I can conceive of no subject, event, action, or thing, in either my life or yours, too intimate or too personal to discuss with you in full. Can you?'

'No, I can't – but this is different. As a woman, you're tops – the finest and best that ever lived.' This statement, made with all the matter-of-factness of stating that a triangle had three corners, thrilled Clarissa through and through. 'As a Grey Lensman you're over the rest of them like a cirrus cloud. But you should rate full Second-Stage, and ... well, you may run up against something too hot to handle, some day, and I ... that is, you ...'

'You mean that I don't measure up?' she asked, quietly. 'I know very well I don't, and admitting an evident fact should not hurt my feelings a bit. Don't interrupt, please,' as Kit began to protest. 'In fact, it is sheerest effrontery – it has always bothered me terribly, Kit – to be classed as a Lensman at all, considering what splendid men they all are and what each one of them had to go through to earn his Lens, to say nothing of a Release. You know as well as I do that I've never done a single thing to earn or to deserve it. It was handed to me on a silver platter. I'm not worthy of it, Kit, and all the real Lensmen know I'm not. They must know it, Kit – they *must* feel that way!'

'Did you ever express yourself in exactly that way before, to anybody? You didn't, I know.' Kit stopped sweating; this was going to be easier than he had feared.

'I couldn't, Kit, it was too deep; but as I said, I can talk *anything* over with you.'

'QX. We can settle that fast enough if you'll answer just one question. Do you honestly believe that you would have been given the Lens if you were not absolutely worthy of it? Perfectly – in every minute particular?'

'Why, I never thought of it that way ... probably not ... no, certainly not.' Clarrissa's somber mien lightened markedly. 'But I still don't see how or why ...'

'Clear enough,' Kit interrupted. 'You were born with what the rest of them had to work so hard for – with stuff that no other woman, anywhere, ever had.'

'Except the girls, of course,' Clarrissa corrected, half absently.

'Except the kids,' he concurred. It could do no harm to agree with his mother's statement of a self-evident fact. 'You can take it from me, as one who *knows* that the other Lensmen know you've got plenty of jets. They know very well that the Arisians wouldn't make a Lens for anybody who hasn't got what it takes. And so, very neatly, we've stripped ship for the action I came over here to see you about. It isn't a case of you not measuring up, because you do, in every respect. It's simply that you're short a few jets that you ought by rights to have. You really are a Second-Stage Lensman – you know that, mums – but you never went to Arisia for your L2 work. I hate to see you blast off without full equipment into what may prove to be a big-time job; especially when you're so eminently able to take it. Mentor could give you the works in a few hours. Why don't you flit for Arisia right now, or let me take you there?'

'No – NO!' Clarrissa backed away, shaking her head emphatically. 'Never! I couldn't, Kit, ever – not *possibly*!'

'Why not?' Kit was amazed. 'Why, mother, you're actually shaking!'

'I know I am – I can't help it. That's why. He's the only thing in the entire Universe that I'm really afraid of. I can talk *about* him without quite getting goose-bumps all over me, but the mere thought of actually being with him simply scares me into shivering, quivering fits – no less.'

'I see . . . it might very well work that way, at that. Does dad know it?'

'Yes – or, that is, he knows I'm afraid of him, but he doesn't know it the way you do – it simply doesn't register in true color. Kim can't conceive of me being either a coward or a cry-baby. And I don't want him to, either, Kit, so please don't tell him, ever.'

'I won't – he'd fry me to a cinder in my own grease if I did. Frankly, I can't see any part of your self-portrait, either. As a matter of cold fact, you are so obviously neither a coward nor a cry-baby . . . well, that's about the silliest crack you ever made. What you've really got, mums, is a fixation, and if it can't be removed . . .'

'It can't,' she declared flatly. 'I've tried that, now and then, ever since before you were born. Whatever it is, it's a permanent installation and it's really deep. I've known all along that Kim didn't give me the whole business – he couldn't – and I've tried again and again to make myself go to Arisia, or at least to call Mentor about it, but I can't do it, Kit – I simply *can't*!'

'I understand.' Kit nodded. He did understand, now. What she felt was not, in essence and at bottom, fear at all. It was worse than fear, and deeper. It was true revulsion; the basic, fundamental, sub-conscious, sex-based reaction of an intensely vital human female against a mental monstrosity who had not had a sexual thought for countless thousands of her years. She could neither analyze nor understand her feeling; but it was as immutable, as ineradicable, and as old as the surging tide of life itself.

'But there's another way, just as good – probably better, as far as you're concerned. You aren't afraid of me, are you?'

'What a *question*! Of course I'm not ... why, do you mean *you* ...' Her expressive eyes widened. 'You children – especially you – are far beyond us ... as of course you should be ... but *can* you, Kit? Really?'

Kit keyed a part of his mind to an ultra-high level. 'I know the techniques, Mentor, but the first question is, should I do it?'

'You should, youth. The time has come when it is necessary.'

'Second – I've never done anything like this before, and she's my own mother. If I make one slip I'll never forgive myself. Will you stand by and see that I don't slip? And stand guard?'

'I will stand by and stand guard.'

'I really can, mums.' Kit answered her question with no perceptible pause. 'That is, if you're willing to put everything you've got into it. Just letting me into your mind isn't enough. You'll have to sweat blood – you'll think you've been run through a hammer-mill and spread out on a Delgonian torture screen to dry.'

'Don't worry about that, Kit.' All the passionate intensity of Clarrissa's being was in her vibrant voice. 'If you just knew how utterly I've been longing for it – I'll work; and whatever you give me I can take.'

'I'm sure of that. And, not to work under false pretenses, I'd better tell you how I know. Mentor showed me what to do and told me to do it.'

'*Mentor!*'

'Mentor,' Kit agreed. 'He knew that it was a psychological impossibility for you to work with him, and that you could and would work with me. So he appointed me a committee of one.'

Clarrissa was reacting to this news as it was inevitable that she should react; and to give her time to steady down he went on:

'Mentor also knew, and so do you and I, that even though you are afraid of him, you know what he is and what he means to Civilization. I had to tell you this so you'd know, without any tinge of doubt, that I'm not a half-baked kid setting out to do a man's job of work.'

'Jet back, Kit! I may have thought a lot of different things about you at times, but "half-baked" was never one of them. That's your own thinking, not mine.'

'I wouldn't wonder.' Kit grinned wryly. 'My ego could stand some stiffening right now. This isn't going to be funny. You're too fine a woman, and I think too much of you, to enjoy the prospect of mauling you around so unmercifully.'

'Why, Kit!' Her mood was changing fast. Her old-time, impish smile came back in force. 'You aren't weakening, surely? Shall I hold your hand?'

'Uh-huh – cold feet,' he admitted. 'It might be a smart idea, at that, holding hands. Physical linkage. Well, I'm as ready as I ever will be, I guess – whenever you are, say so. And you'd better sit down before you fall down.'

'QX, Kit – come in.'

Kit came; and at the first terrific surge of his mind within hers the Red Lensman caught her breath, stiffened in every muscle, and all but screamed in agony. Kit's fingers needed their strength as her hands clutched his and closed in a veritable spasm. She had thought that she knew what to expect; but the reality was different – much different. She had suffered before. On Lyrane II, although she had never told anyone of it, she had been burned and wounded and beaten. She had borne five children. This was as though every poignant experience of her past had been rolled into one, raised to the nth power, and stabbed relentlessly into the deepest, tenderest, most sensitive centers of her being.

And Kit, boring in and in and in, knew exactly what to do; and, now that he had started, he proceeded unflinchingly and with exact precision to do what had to be done. He opened up her mind as she had never dreamed it possible for a mind to open. He separated the tiny, jammed compartments, each completely from every other. He showed her how to make room for this tremendous expansion and watched her do it, against the shrieking protests of every cell and fiber of her body and of her brain. He drilled new channels everywhere, establishing an inconceivably complex system of communication lines of infinite conductivity. He knew just what he was doing to her, since the same thing had been done to him so recently, but he kept on relentlessly until the job was done. Completely done.

Then, working together, they sorted and labeled and classified and catalogued. They checked and double-checked. Finally she knew, and Kit knew that she knew, every hitherto unplumbed recess of her mind and every individual cell of her brain. Every iota of every quality and characteristic, every scrap of knowledge she had ever acquired or ever would acquire, would be at her command instantaneously and effortlessly. Then, and only then, did Kit withdraw his mind from hers.

'Did you say that I was short just a *few* jets, Kit?' She got up groggily and mopped her face; upon which her few freckles stood out surprisingly dark upon a background of white. 'I'm a wreck – I'd better go and...'

'As you were for just a sec – I'll break out a bottle of fayalin. This rates a celebration of sorts, don't you think?'

'Very much so.' As she sipped the pungently aromatic red liquid her color began to come back. 'No wonder I felt as though I were missing something all these years. Thanks, Kit. I really appreciate it. You're a...'

'Seal it, mums.' He picked her up and squeezed her, hard. He scarcely noticed her sweat-streaked face and disheveled hair, but she did.

'Good Heavens, Kit, I'm a perfect *hag*!' she exclaimed. 'I've *got* to go and put on a new face!'

'QX. I don't feel quite so fresh, myself. What I need, though, is a good, thick steak. Join me?'

'Uh-uh. How can you even think of *eating*, at a time like this?'

'Same way you can think of war-paint and feathers, I suppose. Different people, different reactions. QX, I'll be in there and see you in fifteen or twenty minutes. Flit!'

She left, and Kit heaved an almost explosive sigh of relief. Mighty good thing she hadn't asked too many questions – if she had become really curious, he would have had a horrible time keeping her away from the fact that that kind of work never had been done and never would be done outside of solid Arisian screen. He ate, cleaned up, ran a comb through his hair, and, when his mother was ready, crossed over into her speedster.

'Whee – whee-yu!' Kit whistled descriptively. '*What* a seven-sector call-out! Just who do you think you're going to knock out of the ether on Lyrane Two?'

'Nobody at all.' Clarrissa laughed. 'This is all for you, son – and maybe a little bit for me, too.'

'I'm stunned. You're a blinding flash and a deafening report. But I've got to do a flit, gorgeous. So clear . . .'

'Wait a minute – you *can't* go yet! I've got questions to ask you about these new networks and things. How do I handle them?'

'Sorry – you've got to develop your own techniques. You know that already.'

'In a way. I thought maybe, though, I could wheedle you into helping me a little. I should have known better – but tell me, all Lensman don't have minds like this, do they?'

'I'll say they don't. They're all like yours was before, but not as good. Except the other L2's, of course – dad, Worsel, Tregonsee, and Nadreck. Theirs are more or less like yours is now; but you've got a lot of stuff they haven't.'

'Huh?' she demanded. 'Such as?'

'Way down – there.' He showed her. 'You worked all that stuff yourself. I only showed you how, without getting in too close.'

'Why? Oh, I see – you would. Life force. I would have lots of that, of course.' She did not blush, but Kit did.

'Life force' was a pitifully inadequate term indeed for that which Civilization's only Lensman-mother had in such measure, but they both knew what it was. Kit ducked.

'You can always tell all about a Lensman by looking at his Lens; it's the wiring diagram of his total mind. You've studied dad's of course.'

'Yes. Three times as big as the ordinary ones – or mine – and much finer and brighter. But *mine* isn't, Kit?'

'It *wasn't*, you mean. Look at it now.'

She opened a drawer, reached in, and stared; her eyes and mouth becoming three round O's of astonishment. She had never seen that Lens before, or anything like it. It was three times as big as hers, seven times as fine and as intricate, and ten times as bright.

'Why, this isn't mine!' she gasped. 'But it *must* be ...'

'Sneeze, beautiful,' Kit advised. 'Cobwebs. You aren't thinking a lick. Your mind changed, so your Lens had to. See?'

'Of course – I wasn't thinking; that's a fact. Let me look at *your* Lens, Kit – you never seem to wear it – I haven't seen it since you graduated.'

'Sure. Why not?' He reached into a pocket. 'I take after you, that way; neither of us gets any kick out of throwing his weight around.'

His Lens flamed upon his wrist. It was larger in diameter than Clarrissa's, and thicker. Its texture was finer; its colors were brighter, harsher, and seemed, somehow, *solider*. Both studied both Lenses for a moment, then Kit seized his mother's hand, brought their wrists together, and stared.

'That's it,' he breathed. 'That's it ... That's IT, just as sure as Klono has got teeth and claws.'

'What's it? What do you see?' she demanded.

'I see how and why I got the way I am – and if the kids had Lenses theirs would be the same. Remember dad's? Look at your dominants – notice that every one of them is duplicated in mine. Blank them out of mine, and see what you've got left – pure Kimball Kinnison, with just enough extras thrown in to make me an individual instead of a carbon copy. Hm . . . hm . . . credits to millos this is what comes of having Lensmen on both sides of the family. No wonder we're freaks! Don't know whether I'm in favor of it or not – I don't think they should produce any more Lady Lensmen, do you? Maybe that's why they never did.'

'Don't try to be funny,' she reproved; but her dimples were again in evidence. 'If it would result in more people like you and your sisters, I'd be very much in favor of it; but, some way or other, I doubt it. I know you're squirming to go, so I won't hold you any longer. What you just found out about Lenses is fascinating. For the rest of it . . . well . . . thanks, son, and clear ether.'

'Clear ether, mother. This is the worst part of being together, leaving so quick. I'll see you again, though, soon and often. If you get stuck, yell, and one of the kids or I – or all of us – will be with you in a split second.'

He gave her a quick, hard hug; kissed her enthusiastically, and left. He did not tell her, and she never did find out, that his 'discovery' of one of the secrets of the Lens was made to keep her from asking questions which he could not answer.

The Red Lensman was afraid that she would not have time to put her new mind in order before reaching Lyrane II; but, being naturally a good housekeeper, she did. More, so rapidly and easily did her mind now work, she had time to review and to analyze every phase of her previous activities upon that planet and to lay out in broad her first lines of action. She wouldn't put on the screws at first, she decided. She would let them think that she didn't have any more jets than before. Helen was nice, but a good many of the others, especially that airport manager, were simply quadruply-distilled vixens. She'd take it easy at first, but she'd be very sure that she didn't get into any such jams as last time.

She coasted down through Lyrane's stratosphere and poised high above the city she remembered so well.

'Helen of Lyrane!' she sent out a sharp, clear thought. 'That is not your name, I know, but we did not learn any other...'

She broke off, every nerve taut. Was that, or was it not, Helen's thought; cut off, wiped out by a guardian block before it could take shape?

'Who are you, stranger, and what do you want?' the thought came, almost instantly, from a person seated at the desk which had been Helen's.

Clarrissa glanced at the sender and thought that she recognized the face. Her new channels functioned instantaneously; she remembered every detail.

'Lensman Clarrissa, formerly of Sol III. Unattached. I remember you, Ladora, although you were only a child when I was here. Do you remember me?

'Yes. I repeat, what do you want?' The memory did not decrease Ladora's hostility.

'I would like to speak to the former Elder Person, if I may.'

'You may not. It is no longer with us. Leave at once, or we will shoot you down.'

'Think again, Ladora.' Clarrissa held her tone even and calm. 'Surely your memory is not so short that you have forgotten the *Dauntless* and its capabilities.'

'I remember. You may take up with me whatever it is that you wish to discuss with my predecessor.'

'You are familiar with the Boskonian invasion of years ago. It is suspected that they are planning new and galaxy-wide outrages, and that this planet is in some way involved. I have come here to investigate the situation.'

'We will conduct our own investigations,' Ladora declared, curtly. 'We insist that you and all other foreigners stay away from this planet.'

'*You* investigate a galactic condition?' In spite of herself, Clarrissa almost let the connotations of that question become perceptible. 'If you give me permission I will land alone. If you do not, I shall call the *Dauntless* and we will land in force. Take your choice.'

'Land alone, then, if you must land.' Ladora yielded seethingly. 'Land at City Airport.'

'Under those guns? No, thanks; I am neither invulnerable nor immortal. I land where I please.'

She landed. During her previous visit she had had a hard enough time getting any help from these pig-headed matriarchs, but this time she encountered a non-cooperation so utterly fanatical that it put her completely at a loss. None of them tried to harm her in any way; but not one of them would have anything to do with her. Every thought, even the friendliest, was stopped by a full-coverage block; no acknowledgment, even, was ever made.

'I can crack those blocks easily enough, if I want to,' she declared, one bad evening, to her mirror, 'and if they keep this up very much longer, by Klono's emerald-filled gizzard, I will!'

14
Kinnison-Thyron, Drug Runner

When Kimball Kinnison received his son's call he was in Ultra Prime, the Patrol's stupendous Klovian base, about to enter his ship. He stopped for a moment; practically in mid-stride. While nothing was to be read in his expression or in his eyes, the lieutenant to whom he had been talking had been an interested, if completely uninformed, witness to many such Lensed conferences and knew that they were usually important. He was therefore not surprised when the Lensman turned around and headed for an exit.

'Put her back, please. I won't be going out for a while, after all,' Kinnison explained, briefly. 'Don't know exactly how long.'

A fast flitter took him to the hundred-story pile of stainless steel and glass which was the coordinator's office. He strode along a corridor, through an unmarked door.

'Hi, Phyllis – the boss in?'

'Why, Coordinator Kinnison! Yes, sir . . . no, I mean . . .' His startled secretary touched a button and a door opened; the door of his private office.

'Hi, Kim – back so soon?' Vice-Coordinator Maitland also showed surprise as he got up from the massive desk and shook hands cordially. 'Good! Taking over?'

'Emphatically no. Hardly started yet. Just dropped in to use your plate, if you've got a free high-power wave. QX?'

'Certainly. If not, you can free one fast enough.'

'Communications.' Kinnison touched a stud. 'Will you please get me Thrale? Library One; Principal Librarian Nadine Ernley. Plate to plate.'

This request was surprising enough to the informed. Since the coordinator practically never dealt personally with anyone except Lensmen, and usually Unattached Lensmen at that, it was a rare event indeed for him to use any ordinary channels of communication. And as the linkage was completed, subdued murmurs and sundry squeals gave evidence of the intense excitement at the other end of the line.

'Mrs. Ernley will be on in one moment, sir.' The operator's business was done. Her crisp, clear-cut voice ceased, but the background noise increased markedly.

'Sh ... sh ... sh! It's the Grey Lensman, himself!' Everywhere upon Klovia, Tellus, and Thrale, and in many localities of many other planets, the words 'Grey Lensman', without sur-name, had only one meaning.

'Not the *Grey Lensman*!'

'It can't be!'

'It *is*, really – I know him – I actually *met* him once!'

'Let *me* look – just a peek!'

'Sh ... sh! He'll *hear* you!'

'Switch on the vision. If we've got a moment, let's get acquainted,' Kinnison suggested, and upon his plate there burst into view a bevy of excitedly embarrassed blondes, brun-ettes, and redheads. 'Hi, Madge! Sorry I don't know the rest of you, but I'll make it a point to meet you all – before long, I think. Don't go away.' The head of the library was coming on the run. 'You're all in on this. Hi, Nadine! Long time no see. Remember that bunch of squirrel food you rounded up for me?'

'I remember, sir.' What a question! As though Nadine Ernley, née Hostetter, could ever forget her share in that famous meet-ing of the fifty-three greatest scientific minds of all Civilization! 'I'm sorry that I was out in the stacks when you called.'

'QX – we all have to work sometime, I suppose. What I'm calling about is that I've got a mighty big job for you and those smart girls of yours. Something like that other one, only a lot more so. I want all the information you can dig up about a planet named Kalonia, just as fast as you can possibly get it.

What makes it extra tough is that I have never even heard of the planet itself and don't know of anyone who has. There may be a million other names for it, on a million other planets, but we don't know any of them. Here's all I know.' He summarized; concluding: 'If you can get it for me in less than four point nine five G-P days from now I'll bring you, Nadine, a Manarkan star-drop; and you can have each of your girls go down to Brenleer's and pick out a wrist-watch, or whatever else she likes, and I'll have it engraved for her "In appreciation, Kimball Kinnison". This job is important – my son Kit bet me ten millos that we can't do it that fast.'

'Ten *millos!*' Four or five of the girls gasped as one.

'Fact,' he assured them, gravely. 'So whenever you get the dope, tell Communications – no, you listen while I tell them myself. Communications, all along the line, come in!' They came. 'I expect one of these librarians to call me, plate to plate, within the next few days. When she does, no matter what time of day or night it is, and no matter what I or anyone else happen to be doing, that call will have the right-of-way over any other business in the Universe. Cut!' The plates went dead, and in Library One:

'But he was joking, surely!'

'Ten *millos* – and a star-drop – why, there aren't more than a dozen of them on all Thrale!'

'Wrist-watches – or something – from the Grey Lensman!'

'Be quiet, everybody!' Madge exclaimed. 'I see now. That's the way Nadine got *her* watch, that she always brags about so insufferably and that makes everybody's eyes turn green. But I don't understand that silly ten millo bet . . . do you, Nadine?'

'I think so. He does the nicest things – things that nobody else would think of. You've all seen Red Lensman's Chit, in Brenleer's.' This was a statement, not a question. They all had, with what emotions they all knew. 'How would you like to have that one-cento piece, in a thousand-credit frame, here in our main hall, with the legend "won from Christopher Kinnison for Kimball Kinnison by . . ." and our names? He's got something like that in mind, I'm sure.'

The ensuing clamor indicated that they liked the idea.

'He knew we would; and he knew that doing it this way would make us dig like we never dug before. He'll give us the watches and things anyway, of course, but we won't get that one-cento piece unless we win it. So let's get to work. Take everything out of the machines, finished or not. Madge, you might start by interviewing Lanion and the other – no, I'd better do that myself, since you are more familiar with the encyclopedia than I am. Run the whole English block, starting with K, and follow up any leads, however slight, that you can find. Betty, you can analyze for synonyms, starting with the Thralian equivalent of Kalonia and spreading out to the other Boskonian planets. Put half a dozen techs on it, with transformers. Frances, you can study Prellin and Bronseca. Joan, Leona, Edna – Jalte, Helmuth, and Crowninshield. Beth, as our best linguist, you can do us the most good by sensitizing a tech to the sound of Kalonia in each of all the languages you know or that the rest of us can find, and running and re-running all the transcripts we have of Boskonian meetings. How many of us are left? Not enough ... we'll have to spread ourselves thin on this list of Boskonian planets ...'

Thus Principal Librarian Ernley organized a search beside which the proverbial one of finding a needle in a haystack would have been as simple as locating a football in a bushel basket. And she and her girls worked. *How* they worked! And thus, in four days and three hours, Kinnison's crash-priority person-to-person call came through. Kalonia was no longer a planet of mystery.

'Fine work, girls! Put it on a tape and I'll pick it up.'

He then left Klovia – precipitately. Since Kit was not within rendezvous distance, he instructed his son – after giving him the high points of what he had learned – to forward one one-cento piece to Brenleer of Thrale, personal delivery. He told Brenleer what to do with it upon arrival. He landed. He bestowed the star-drop; one of Cartiff's collection of fine gems. He met the girls, and gave each one her self-chosen reward. He departed.

Out in open space, he ran the tape, and sat still, scowling

blackly. It was no wonder that Kalonia had remained unknown to Civilization for over twenty years. There was a lot of information on that tape – and all of it stunk – but it had been assembled, one unimportant bit at a time, from the more than eight hundred million cards of Thrale's Boskonian Archives; and all the really significant items had been found on vocal transcriptions which had never before been played.

Civilization in general had assumed that Thrale had housed the top echelons of the Boskonian Empire, and that the continuing inimical activity had been due solely to momentum. Kinnison and his friends had had their doubts, but they had not been able to find any iota of evidence that any higher authority had ever issued any orders to Thrale. The Grey Lensman now knew, however, that Thrale had never been the top. Nor was Kalonia. The information on this tape, by its paucity, its brevity, its incidental and casual nature, made that fact startlingly clear. Thrale and Kalonia were not in the same ladder. Neither gave the other any orders – in fact, they had surprisingly little to do with each other. While Thrale formerly directed the activities of a half-million or so planets – and Kalonia apparently still did much the same – their fields of action had not overlapped at any point.

His conquest of Thrale, hailed so widely as such a triumph, had got him precisely nowhere in the solution of the real problem. It might be possible for him to conquer Kalonia in a similar fashion, but what would it get him? Nothing. There would be no more leads upward from Kalonia than there had been from Thrale. How in all of Noshabkeming's variegated and iridescent hells was he going to work this out?

A complete analysis revealed only one possible method of procedure. In one of the transcriptions – made twenty-one years ago and unsealed for the first time by Beth, the librarian-linguist – one of the speakers had mentioned casually that the new Kalonian Lensmen seemed to be doing a good job, and a couple of the others had agreed with him. That was all. It might, however, be enough; since it made it highly probable that Eddie's Lensman was in fact a Kalonian, and since even a Black Lensman would certainly know where he got his Lens. At the thought of trying to visit the Boskonian equivalent of Arisia he flinched, but only momentarily. Invasion, or even physical approach, would of course be impossible; but any planet, even Arisia itself, could be destroyed. If it could be found, that planet would be destroyed. He had to find it – that was probably what Mentor had been wanting him to do all the time! But how?

In his various previous enterprises against Boskonia he had been a gentleman of leisure, a dock-walloper, a meteor-miner, and many other things. None of his already established aliases would fit on Kalonia; and besides, it was very poor technique to repeat himself, especially at this high level of opposition. To warrant appearance on Kalonia at all, he would have to be an operator of some kind – not too small, but not big enough so that an adequate background could not be synthesized in not too long a time. A zwilnik – an actual drug-runner with a really worth-while cargo – would be the best bet.

His course of action decided, the Grey Lensman started making calls. He first called Kit, with whom he held a long conversation. He called the captain of his battleship-yacht, the *Dauntless*, and gave him many and explicit orders. He called Vice-Coordinator Maitland, and various other Unattached Lensmen who had plenty of weight in Narcotics, Public Relations, Criminal Investigation, Navigation, Homicide, and many other apparently totally unrelated establishments of the Galactic Patrol. Finally, after ten solid hours of mind-racking labor, he ate a tremendous meal and told Clarrissa – he called her last of all – that he was going to go to bed and sleep for one whole G-P week.

Thus it was that the name of Bradlow Thyron began to obtrude itself above the threshold of Galactic consciousness. For seven or eight years that name had been below the middle of the Patrol's long, black list of the wanted; now it was well up toward the top. That notorious zwilnik and his villainous crew had been chased from one side of the First Galaxy to the other. For a few months it had been supposed that they had been blown out of the ether. Now, however, it was known definitely that he was operating in the Second Galaxy, and he and every one of his cutthroat gang – fiends who had blasted thousands of lives with noxious wares – were wanted for piracy, drug-mongering, and first-degree murder. From the Patrol's standpoint, the hunting was very poor. G-P planetographers have charted only a small percentage of the planets of the Second Galaxy; and only a few of those are peopled by the adherents of Civilization.

Therefore it required some time, but finally there came the message for which Kinnison was so impatiently waiting. A Boskonian pretty-big-shot and drug-master named Harkleroy, on the planet Phlestyn II, city, Nelto, coordinates so-and-so, fitted his specifications to a 'T'; a middle-sized operator neither too close to nor too far away from Kalonia. And Kinnison, having long since learned the lingua franca of the region from a local meteor-miner, was ready to act.

First, he made sure that the mighty *Dauntless* would be where he wanted her when he needed her. Then, seated at his speedster's communicator, he put through regular channels to call to the Boskonian.

'Harkleroy? I've got a proposition you'll be interested in. Where and when do you want to see me?'

'What makes you think I want to see you at all?' a voice snarled, and the plate showed a gross, vicious face. 'Who are you, scum?'

'Who I am is nobody's business – and if you don't clamp a baffle on that damn mouth of yours I'll come down there and shove a glop-skinner's glove so far down your throat you can sit on it.'

At the first defiant word the zwilnik began visibly to swell; but in a matter of seconds he recognized Bradlow Thyron, and Kinnison knew that he did. That pirate could, and would be expected to, talk back to anybody.

'I didn't recognize you at first.' Harkleroy almost apologized. 'We might do some business, at that. What have you got?'

'Cocaine, heroin, bentlam, hashish, nitrolabe – most

anything a warm-blooded oxygen-breather would want. The prize, though, is two kilograms of clear-quill thionite.'

'Thionite – two kilograms!' The Phlestan's eyes gleamed. 'Where and how did you get it?'

'I asked the Lensman on Trenco to make it for me, special, and he did.'

'So you won't talk, huh?' Kinnison could see Harkleroy's brain work. Thyron could be made to talk, later. 'We can maybe do business at that. Come down here right away.'

'I'll do that, but listen!' and the Lensman's eyes burned into the zwilnik's. 'I know what you're figuring on, and I'm telling you right now not to try it if you want to keep on living. You know this ain't the first planet I ever landed on, and if you've got a brain you know that a lot of smarter guys than you are have tried monkey business on me – and I'm still here. So watch your step!'

The Lensman landed, and made his way to Harkleroy's inner office in what seemed to be an ordinary enough, if somewhat over-size, suit of light space-armor. But it was no more ordinary than it was light. It was a power-house, built of dureum a quarter of an inch thick. Kinnison was not walking in it; he was merely the engineer of a battery of two-thousand-horsepower motors. Unaided, he could not have lifted one leg of that armor off the ground.

As he had expected, everyone he encountered wore a thought-screen; nor was he surprised at being halted by a blaring loudspeaker in the hall, since the zwilnik's searchbeams were being stopped four feet away from his armor.

'Halt! Cut your screens or we'll blast you where you stand!'

'Yeah? Act your age, Harkleroy. I told you I had something up my sleeve besides my arm, and I meant it. Either I come as I am or I flit somewhere else, to do business with somebody who wants this stuff bad enough to act like half a man. 'Smatter – afraid you ain't got blasters enough in there to handle me?'

This taunt bit deep, and the visitor was allowed to proceed. As he entered the private office, however, he saw that Harkleroy's hand was poised near a switch, whose closing would signal a score or more of concealed gunners to burn him down. They supposed that the stuff was either on his person or in his speedster just outside. Time was short.

'I abase myself – that's the formula you insist on, ain't it?' Kinnison sneered, without bending his head a millimeter.

Harkleroy's finger touched the stud.

'*Dauntless!* Come down!' Kinnison snapped out the order.

Hand, stud, and a part of the desk disappeared in the flare of Kinnison's beam. Wall-ports opened; projectors and machine rifles erupted vibratory and solid destruction. Kinnison leaped toward the desk; the attack slowing down and stopping as he neared and seized the Boskonian. One fierce, short blast reduced the thought-screen generator to blobs of fused metal. Harkleroy screamed to his gunners to resume fire, but before bullet or beam took the zwilnik's life, Kinnison learned what he most wanted to know.

The ape did know something about Black Lensmen. He didn't know where the Lenses came from, but he did know how the men were chosen. More, he knew a Lensman personally – one Melasnikov, who had his office in Cadsil, on Kalonia III itself.

Kinnison turned and ran – the alarm had been given and they were bringing up stuff too heavy for even his armor to handle. But the *Dauntless* was landing already; smashing to rubble five city blocks in the process. She settled; and as the dureum-clad Grey Lensman began to fight his way out of Harkleroy's fortress, Major Peter vanBuskirk and a full battalion of Valerians, armed with space-axes and semiportables, began to hew and to blast their way in.

15
Thyron Follows a Lead

Inch by inch, foot by foot, Kinnison fought his way back along the corpse-littered corridor. Under the ravening force of the attackers' beams his defensive screens flared into pyrotechnic splendor, but they did not go down. Fierce-driven metallic slugs spanged and whanged against the unyielding dureum of his armor; but that, too, held. Dureum is incredibly massive, unbelievably tough, unimaginably hard – against these qualities and against the thousands of horsepower driving that veritable tank and energizing its screen the zwilniks might just as well have been shining flashlights at him and throwing confetti. His immediate opponents could not touch him, but the Boskonians were bringing up reserves that he didn't like a little bit; mobile projectors with whose energies even those screens could not cope.

He had, however, one great advantage over his enemies. He had the sense of perception; they did not. He could see them, but they could not see him. All he had to do was to keep at least one opaque wall between them until he was securely behind the mobile screens, powered by the stupendous generators of the *Dauntless*, which vanBuskirk and his Valerians were so earnestly urging toward him. If a door was handy in the moment of need, he used it. If not he went through a wall.

The Valerians were fighting furiously and were coming fast. Those two words, when applied to members of that race, mean something starkly incredible to anyone who has never seen Valerians in action. They average something less than seven feet in height; something over four hundred pounds in weight;

and are muscled, boned, and sinewed against a normal gravitational force of almost three times that of Earth. VanBuskirk's weakest warrior could do, in full armor, a standing high jump of fourteen feet against one Tellurian gravity; he could handle himself and the thirty-pound monstrosity which was his space-axe with a blinding speed and a devastating efficiency literally appalling to contemplate. They are the deadliest hand-to-hand fighters ever known; and, unbelievable as it may seem to any really highly advanced intelligence, they did and still do fairly revel in that form of combat.

The Valerian tide reached the battling Grey Lensman; closed around him.

'Hi ... you little ... Tellurian ... wart!' Major Peter van-Buskirk boomed this friendly thought, a yell of pure joy, in cadence with the blows of his utterly irresistible weapon. His rhythm broke – his frightful axe was stuck. Not even dureum-inlaid armor could bar the inward course of those furiously-driven beaks; but sometimes it made it fairly difficult to get them out. The giant pulled, twisted – put one red-splashed boot on a battered breastplate – bent his mighty back – heaved viciously. The weapon came free with a snap that would have broken any ordinary man's arms, but the Valerian's thought rolled smoothly on: 'Ain't we got fun?'

'Ho, Bus, you big Valerian baboon!' Kinnison thought back in kind. 'Thought maybe we'd need you and your gang – thanks a million. But back now, and fast!'

Although the Valerians did not like to retreat, after even a successful operation, they knew how to do it. Hence in a matter of minutes all the survivors – and the losses had been surprisingly small – were back inside the *Dauntless*.

'You picked up my speedster, Frank.' It was a statement, not a question, directed at the young Lensman sitting at the 'big board'.

'Of course, sir. They're massing fast, but without any hostile demonstration, as you said they would.' He nodded unconcernedly at a plate, which showed the sky dotted with warlike shapes.

'No maulers?'

'None detectable as yet, sir.'

'QX. Original orders stand. At detection of one mauler, execute Operation Able. Tell everybody that while the announcement of Operation Able will put me out of control instantly and automatically, until such announcement I will give instructions. What they'll be like I haven't the foggiest notion. It depends on what his nibs upstairs decides to do – it's his move next.'

As though the last phrase were a cue, a burst of noise rattled from the speaker – of which only the words 'Bradlow Thyron' were intelligible to the un-Lensed members of the crew. That name, however, explained why they were not being attacked – yet. Kalonia had heard much of that intransigent and obdurate pirate and of the fabulous prowess of his ship; and Kinnison was pretty sure that they were much more interested in his ship than in him.

'I can't understand you!' The Grey Lensman barked, in the polyglot language he had so lately learned. 'Talk pidgin!'

'Very well. I see that you are indeed Bradlow Thyron, as we were informed. What do you mean by this outrageous attack? Surrender! Disarm your men, take off their armor, and march them out of your vessel, or we will blast you as you lie there – Vice-Admiral Mendonai speaking!'

'I abase myself.' Kinnison-Thyron did not sneer – exactly – and he did incline his stubborn head perhaps the sixteenth part of an inch; but he made no move to comply with the orders so summarily issued. Instead:

'What the hell kind of planet is this, anyway?' he demanded, hotly. 'I come here to see this louse Harkleroy because a friend of mine tells me he's a big shot and interested enough in my line so we can do a lot of business. I give the lug fair warning, too – tell him plain I've been around plenty and if he tries to give me the works I'll rub him out like a pencil mark. So what happens? In spite of what I just tell him he tries dirty work and I knock hell out of him, which he certainly has got coming to him. Then you and your flock of little tin boats come barging in like I'd busted a law or something. Who do you think you are, anyway? What license you got to stick your beak into private business?'

'Ah, I had not heard that version.' Vision came on; the face upon the plate was typically Kalonian – blue, cold, cruel, and keen. 'Harkleroy was warned, you say? Definitely?'

'Plenty definitely. Ask any of the zwilniks in that private office of his. They're mostly alive and they all must of heard it.'

The plate fogged, the speaker again gave out gibberish. The Lensman knew, however, that the commander of the forces above them was indeed questioning the dead zwilnik's guards. They knew that Kinnison's story was being corroborated in full.

'You interest me.' The Boskonian's language again became intelligible to the group at large. 'We will forget Harkleroy – stupidity brings its own reward and the property damage is of no present concern. From what I have been able to learn of you, you have never belonged to that so-called Civilization. I know for a fact that you are not, and never have been, one of us. How have you been able to survive? And why do you work alone?'

'"How" is easy enough – by keeping one jump ahead of the other guy, like I did with your pal here, and by being smart enough to have good engineers put into my ship everything that any other one ever had and everything they could dream up besides. As to "why", that's simple, too. I don't trust nobody. If nobody knows what I'm going to do, nobody's going to stick a knife into me when I ain't looking – see? So far, it's paid off big. I'm still around and still healthy. Them that trusted other guys ain't.'

'I see. Crude, but graphic. The more I study you, the more convinced I become that you make a worthwhile addition to our force . . .'

'No deal, Mendonai,' Kinnison interrupted, shaking his unkempt head positively. 'I never yet took no orders from no damn boss, and I ain't going to.'

'You misunderstand me, Thyron.' The zwilnik was queerly

148

patient and much too forbearing. Kinnison's insulting omission of his title should have touched him off like a rocket. 'I was not thinking of you in any minor capacity, but as an ally. An entirely independent ally, working with us in certain mutually advantageous undertakings.'

'Such as?' Kinnison allowed himself to betray his first sign of interest. 'You may be talking sense now, brother, but what's in it for me? Believe me, there's got to be plenty.'

'There will be plenty. With the ability you have already shown, and with our vast resources back of you, you will take more every week than you have been taking in a year.'

'Yeah? People like you just love to do things like that for people like me. What do *you* figure on getting out of it?' Kinnison wondered, and Lensed a sharp thought to his junior at the board.

'On your toes, Frank. He's stalling for something, and I'm betting it's maulers.'

'None detectable yet, sir.'

'We stand to gain, of course,' the pirate admitted, smoothly. 'For instance, there are certain features of your vessel which might – just possibly, you will observe, and speaking only to mention an example – be of interest to our naval designers. Also, we have heard that you have an unusually hot battery of primary beams. You might tell me about some of those things now; or at least re-focus your plate so that I can see something besides your not unattractive face.'

'I might not, too. What I've got here is my own business, and stays mine.'

'Is that what we are to expect from you in the way of co-operation?' The commander's voice was still low and level, but now bore a chill of deadly menace.

'Cooperation, hell!' The cutthroat chief was unimpressed. 'I'll maybe tell you a thing or two – eat out of your dish – after I get good and sold on your proposition, whatever it is, but not one damn second sooner!'

The commander glared. 'I weary of this. You probably are

not worth the trouble, after all. I might as well blast you out now as later. You know that I can, of course, as well as I do.'

'Do I?' Kinnison did sneer, this time. 'Act your age, pal. As I told that fool Harkleroy, this ain't the first planet I ever sat down on, and it won't be the last. And don't call no maulers,' as the Boskonian officer's hand moved almost imperceptibly toward a row of buttons. 'If you do, I start blasting as soon as we spot one on our plates, and they're full out right now.'

'*You* would start blasting?' The zwilnik's surprise was plain, but the hand stopped its motion.

'Yeah – me. Them heaps you got up there don't bother me a bit, but maulers I can't handle, and I ain't afraid to tell you so because you probably know it already. I can't stop you from calling 'em, if you want to, but bend both ears to this – I can out-run 'em and I'll guarantee that you personally won't be alive to see me run. Why? Because your ship will be the first one I'll whiff on the way out. And if the rest of your junkers stick around long enough to try to stop me I'll whiff twenty-five or thirty more before your maulers get close enough so I'll have to do a flit. Now, if your brains are made out of the same kind of thick, blue mud as Harkleroy's, start something!'

This was an impasse. Kinnison knew what he wanted the other to do, but he could not give him a suggestion, or even a hint, without tipping his hand. The officer, quite evidently, was in a quandary. He did not want to open fire upon this tremendous, this fabulous ship. Even if he could destroy it, such a course would be unthinkable – unless, indeed, the very act of destruction would brand as false rumor the tales of invincibility and invulnerability which had heralded its coming, and thus would operate in his favor at the court-martial so sure to be called. He was very much afraid, however, that those rumors were not false – a view which was supported very strongly both by Thyron's undisguised contempt for the Boskonian warships threatening him and by his equally frank declaration of his intention to avoid engagement with any craft of really superior force. Finally, however, the Boskonian perceived one thing that did not quite fit.

'If you are as good as you claim to be, why aren't you blasting right now?' he asked, skeptically.

'Because I don't *want* to, that's why. Use your head, pal.' This was better. Mendonai had shifted the conversation into a line upon which the Lensman could do a bit of steering. 'I had to leave the First Galaxy because it got too hot for me, and I got no connections at all, yet, here in the Second. You folks need certain kinds of stuff that I've got and I need other kinds, that you've got. So we could do a nice business, if you wanted to. Like I told you, that's why I come to see Harkleroy. I'd like to do business with some of you people, but I just got bit pretty bad, and I've got to have some kind of solid guarantee that you mean business, and no monkey business, before I take a chance again. See?'

'I see. The idea is good, but the execution may prove difficult. I could give you my word, which I assure you has never been broken.'

'Don't make me laugh,' Kinnison snorted. 'Would you take mine?'

'The case is different. I would not. Your point, however, is well taken. How about the protection of a high court of law? I will bring you an unalterable writ from any court you say.'

'Uh-uh,' the Grey Lensman dissented. 'There never was no court yet that didn't take orders from the big shots who keep the fat cats fat, and lawyers are the crookedest damn crooks in the universe. You'll have to do better than that, pal.'

'Well, then, how about a Lensman? You know about Lensmen, don't you?'

'A Lensman!' Kinnison gasped. He shook his head violently. 'Are you completely nuts, or do you think I am? I *do* know Lensmen, cully – a Lensman chased me from Alsakan to Vandemar once, and if I hadn't had a dose of hell's own luck he'd of got me. Lensmen chased me out of the First Galaxy – why the hell else do you think I'm here? Use your brain, mister; use your brain!'

'You're thinking of Civilization's Lensmen; particularly of Grey Lensmen.' Mendonai was enjoying Thyron's passion.

'Ours are different – entirely different. They have as much power, or more, but don't use it the same way. They work with us right along. In fact, they've been bumping Grey Lensmen off right and left lately.'

'You mean he could open up, for instance, your mind and mine, so we could see the other guy wasn't figuring on running in no stacked decks? And he'd sort of referee this business we got on the fire? Do you know one yourself, personally?'

'He could, and would, do all that. Yes, I know one personally. His name is Melasnikov, and his office is on Three, just a short flit from here. He may not be there at the moment, but he'll come in if I call. How about it – shall I call him now?'

'Don't work up a sweat. Sounds like it might work, if we can figure the approach. I don't suppose you and him would come out to me in space?'

'Hardly. You wouldn't expect us to, would you?'

'It wouldn't be very bright of you to. And since I want to do business, I guess I got to meet you part way. How'd this be? You pull your ships out of range. My ship takes station right over your Lensman's office. I go down in my speedster, like I did here, and go inside to meet him and you. I wear my armor – and when I say it's real armor I ain't just snapping my choppers, neither.'

'I can see only one slight flaw.' The Boskonian was really trying to work out a mutually satisfactory solution. 'The Lensman will open our minds to you in proof, however, that we will have no intention of bringing up our maulers or other heavy stuff while we're in conference.'

'Right then you'll find out you hadn't better, too.' Kinnison grinned wolfishly.

'What do you mean?' Mendonai demanded.

'I've got enough super-atomic bombs aboard to blow this planet to hellangone and the boys'll drop 'em all the second you make a queer move. I've got to take a little chance to start doing business, but it's a damn small one, 'cause if I go you go too, pal. You and your Lensman and your fleet and everything alive on your whole damn planet. And your bosses still won't get any dope on what makes this ship of mine tick the way she does. So I'm betting you won't make that kind of a swap.'

'I certainly would not.' Hard as he was, Mendonai was shaken. 'Your suggested method of procedure is satisfactory.'

'QX. Are you ready to flit?'

'We are ready.'

'Call your Lensman, then, and lead the way. Boys, take her upstairs!'

16
Red Lensman in Grey

Karen Kinnison was worried. She, who had always been so sure of herself, had for weeks been conscious of a gradually increasing – what was it, anyway? Not exactly a loss of control... a *change*... a something that manifested itself in increasingly numerous fits of senseless – sheerly idiotic – stubbornness. And always and only it was directed at – of all the people in the universe! – her brother. She got along with her sisters perfectly; their tiny tiffs barely rippled the surface of any of their minds. But any time her path of action crossed Kit's, it seemed, the profoundest depths of her being flared into opposition like exploding duodec. Worse than senseless and idiotic, it was inexplicable, for the feeling which the Five had for each other was much deeper than that felt by ordinary brothers and sisters.

She didn't want to fight with Kit. She *liked* the guy! She liked to feel his mind en rapport with hers, just as she liked to dance with him; their bodies as completely in accord as were their minds. No change of step or motion, however suddenly conceived and executed or however bizarre, had ever succeeded in taking the other by surprise or in marring by a millimeter the effortless precision of their performance. She could do things with Kit that would tie any other man into knots and break half his bones. All other men were lumps. Kit was so far ahead of any other man in existence that there was simply no comparison. If she were Kit she would give her a going-over that would... or could even he...

At the thought she turned cold inside. He could not. Even

Kit, with all his tremendous power, would hit that solid wall and bounce. Well, there was one – not a man, but an entity – who could. He might kill her, but even that would be better than to allow the continued growth within her mind of this monstrosity which she could neither control nor understand. Where was she, and where was Lyrane, and where was Arisia? Good – not too far off line. She would stop off at Arisia en route.

She did so, and made her way to Mentor's office on the hospital grounds. She told her story.

'Fighting with Kit was bad enough,' she concluded, 'but when I start defying *you*, Mentor, it's high time that something was done about it. Why didn't Kit ever knock me into a log-arithmic spiral? Why didn't you work me over? You called Kit in, with the distinct implication that he needed more education – why didn't you pull me in here, too, and pound some sense into me?'

'Concerning you, Christopher had definite instructions, which he obeyed. I did not touch you for the same reason that I did not order you to come to me; neither course would have been of any use. Your mind, daughter Karen, is unique. One of its prime characteristics – the one, in fact, which is to make you an all-important player in the drama which is to come – is a yieldlessness very nearly absolute. Your mind might, just conceivably, be broken; but it cannot be coerced by any imaginable external force, however applied. Thus it was inevitable from the first that nothing could be done about the untoward manifestations of this characteristic until you yourself should recognize the fact that your development was not complete. It would be idle for me to say that during adolescence you have not been more than a trifle trying. I was not speaking idly when I said that the development of you Five has been a tremendous task. It is with equal seriousness, however, that I now tell you that the reward is commensurate with the magnitude of the undertaking. It is impossible to express the satisfaction I feel – the fulfillment, the completion, the justification – as you children come, one by one, each in his proper time, for final instruction.'

'Oh – you mean, then, that there's nothing really the matter with me?' Hard as she was, Karen trembled as her awful tension eased. 'That I was *supposed* to act that way? And I can tell Kit, right away?'

'No need. Your brother has known that it was a passing phase; he shall know very shortly that it has passed. It is not that you were "supposed" to act as you acted. You could not help it. Nor could your brother, nor I. From now on, however, you shall be completely the mistress of your own mind. Come fully, daughter Karen, into mine.'

She did so, and in a matter of time her 'formal education' was complete.

'There is one thing that I don't quite understand...' she began, just before she boarded her speedster.

'Consider it, and I am sure that you will,' Mentor assured her. 'Explain it, whatever it is, to me.'

'QX – I'll try. It's about Fossten and dad.' Karen cogitated. 'Fossten was, of course, Gharlane – your making dad believe him to be an insane Arisian was a masterpiece. I see, of course, how you did that – principally by making Fossten's "real" shape exactly like the one he saw of you on Arisia. But his physical actions as Fossten...'

'Go on, daughter. I am sure that your visualization will be sound.'

'While acting as Fossten he had to act as a Thralian would have acted,' she decided with a rush. 'He was watched everywhere he went, and knew it. To display his real power would have been disastrous. Just like you Arisians, they have to follow the pattern to avoid setting up an inferiority complex that would ruin everything for them. Gharlane's actions as Fossten, then, were constrained. Just as they were when he was Grey Roger, so long ago – except that then he did make a point of unhuman longevity, deliberately to put an insoluble problem up to First Lensman Samms and his men. Just as you – you *must* have . . . you *did* coach Virgil Samms, Mentor, and some of you Arisians *were* there, as men!'

'We were. We lived and wrought as men and seemed to die as men.'

'But you weren't Virgil Samms, please!' Karen almost begged. 'Not that it would break me if you were, but I'd much rather you hadn't been.'

'No, none of us was Samms,' Mentor assured her. 'Nor Cleveland, nor Rodebush, nor Costigan, nor even Clio Marsden. We worked with – "coached", as you express it – those persons and others from time to time in certain small matters, but we were at no time integral with any of them. One of us was, however, Nels Bergenholm. The full inertialess space-drive became necessary at that time, and it would have been poor technique to have had either Rodebush or Cleveland develop so suddenly the ability to perfect the device as Bergenholm did perfect it.'

'QX. Bergenholm isn't important – he was just an inventor. To get back to the subject of Fossten: when he was there on the flagship with dad, and in position to throw his full weight around, it was too late – you Arisians were on the job. You'll have to take it from there, though; I'm out beyond my depth.'

'Because you lack data. In those last minutes Gharlane knew that Kimball Kinnison was neither alone nor unprotected. He called for help, but help did not come. He was isolated; no one of his fellows received his call. Nor could he escape from the form of flesh he was then energizing. I myself saw to that.' Karen had never before felt the Arisian display emotion, but his thought was grim and cold. 'From that form, which your father never did perceive, Gharlane of Eddore passed into the next plane of existence.'

Karen shivered. 'It served him right . . . That clears everything up, I think. But are you *sure*, Mentor' – wistfully – 'that you can't, or rather shouldn't, teach me any more than you have? It's . . . I feel . . . well, "incompetent" is putting it very mildly indeed.'

'To a mind of such power and scope as yours, in its present

state of development, such a feeling is inevitable. Nor can anyone except yourself do anything about it. Cold comfort, perhaps, but it is the stark truth that from now on your development is your own task. Yours alone. As I have already told Christopher and Kathryn, and will very shortly tell Camilla and Constance, you have had your last Arisian treatment. I will be on call to any of you at any instant of any day, to aid you or to guide you or to re-enforce you at need; but of formal instruction there can be no more.'

Karen left Arisia and drove for Lyrane, her thoughts in a turmoil. The time was too short by far; she deliberately cut her vessel's speed and took a long detour so that the vast and chaotic library of her mind could be reduced to some semblance of order before she landed.

She reached Lyrane II, and there, again to all outward seeming a happy, carefree girl, she hugged her mother rapturously.

'You're the most *wonderful* thing, mums!' Karen exclaimed. 'It's simply marvelous, seeing you again in the flesh . . .'

'Now why bring *that* up?' Clarrissa had – just barely – become accustomed to working undraped, in the Lyranian fashion.

'I didn't mean it that way at all, and you know I didn't,' Kay snickered. 'Shame on you – fishing for compliments, and at your age, too!' Ignoring the older woman's attempt at protest she went on: 'All kidding aside, mums, you're a mighty smart-looking hunk of woman. I approve of you exceedingly much. In fact, we're a keen pair and I like both of us. I've got one advantage over you, of course, in that I never did care whether I had any clothes on or not. How are you doing?'

'Not so well – of course, though, I haven't been here very long.' Forgetting her undressedness, Clarrissa frowned. 'I haven't found Helen, and I haven't found out yet why she retired. I can't quite decide whether to put pressure on now, or wait a while longer. Ladora, the new Elder Person, is . . . that is, I don't know . . . Oh, here she comes now. I'm glad – I want you to meet her.'

If Ladora was glad to see Karen, however, she did not show

it. Instead, for an inappreciable instant of time which was nevertheless sufficient for the acquirement of much information, each studied the other. Like Helen, the former queen, Ladora was tall, beautifully proportioned, flawless of skin and feature, hard and fine. But so, and in most respects even more so, to Ladora's astonishment and quickly-mounting wrath, was this pink-tanned stranger. Practically instantaneously, therefore, the Lyranian hurled a vicious mental bolt; only to get the surprise of her life.

She hadn't found out yet what this strange near-person, Clarrissa of Sol III, had in the way of equipment, but from the meek way she acted, it couldn't be much. So Clarrissa's offspring, younger and less experienced, would be easy enough prey.

But Ladora's bolt, the heaviest she could send, did not pierce even the outermost fringes of her intended victim's defenses, and so vicious was the almost simultaneous counter-thrust that it went through the Lyranian's hard-held block in nothing flat. Inside her brain it wrought such hellishly poignant punishment that the matriarch, forgetting everything, tried only and madly to scream. She could not. She could not move a muscle of her face or of her body. She could not even fall. And the one brief glimpse she had into the stranger's mind showed it to be such a blaze of incandescent fury that she, who had never feared in the slightest any living creature, knew now in full measure what fear was.

'I'd like to give that alleged brain of yours a good going over, just for fun.' Karen forced her emotion to subside to a mere seething rage, and Ladora watched her do it. 'But since this whole stinking planet is my mother's dish, not mine, she'd blast me to a cinder – she's done it before – if I dip in.' She cooled still more – visibly. 'At that, I don't suppose you're too bad an egg, in your own poisonous way – you just don't know any better. So maybe I'd better warn you, you poor fool, since you haven't got sense enough to see it, that you're playing with an atomic vortex when you push her around like you've been doing. Just a very little more of it and she'll get mad, like I did a second ago except more so, and you'll wish to Klono you'd never been born. She won't make a sign until she blows her top, but I'm telling you she's as much harder and tougher than I am as she is older, and what she does to people she gets mad at I wouldn't want to watch happen again, even to a snake. She'll pick you up, curl you into a circle, pull off your arms, shove your feet down your throat, and roll you across that field there like a hoop. After that I don't know what she'll do – depends on how much pressure she develops before she goes off. One thing, though; she's always sorry afterwards. Why, she even attends the funerals, sometimes, and insists on paying all the expenses!'

With which outrageous thought she kissed Clarrissa an enthusiastic goodbye. 'Told you I couldn't stay a minute – got to do a flit – "see a man about a dog", you know – came a million parsecs to squeeze you, mums, but it was worth it – clear ether!'

She was gone, and it was a dewy-eyed and rapt mother, not a Lensman, who turned to the still completely disorganized Lyranian. Clarrissa had perceived nothing whatever of what had happened; Karen had very carefully seen to that.

'My daughter,' Clarrissa mused, as much to herself as to Ladora. 'One of four. The four dearest, finest, sweetest girls that ever lived. I often wonder how a woman of my limitations, of my faults, could possibly have borne such children.'

And Ladora of Lyrane, humorless and literal as all Lyranians are, took those thoughts at their face value and correlated their every connotation and implication with what she herself had perceived in that 'dear, sweet' daughter's mind; with what that daughter had done and had said. The nature and quality of this hellish near-person's 'limitations' and 'faults' became eminently clear; and as she perceived what she thought was the truth, the Lyranian literally cringed.

'As you know, I have been in doubt as to whether or not to support you actively, as you wish,' Ladora offered, as the two walked across the field, toward the line of ground-cars. 'On the one hand, the certainty that the safety, and perhaps the very existence, of my race will be at hazard. On the other, the possibility that you are right in saying that the situation will continue to deteriorate if we do nothing. The decision has not been an easy one to make.' Ladora was no longer aloof. She was just plain scared. She had been talking against time, and hoping that the help for which she had long since called would arrive in time. 'I have touched only the outer surface of your mind. Will you allow me, without offense, to test its inner quality before deciding definitely?' In the instant of asking, Ladora sent out a full-driven probe.

'I will not.' Ladora's beam struck a barrier which seemed to her exactly like Karen's. None of her race had developed anything like it. She had never seen ... yes, she had, too – years ago, when she was a child, that time in the assembly hall – that utterly hated male, Kinnison of Tellus! Tellus – Sol III! Clarrissa of Sol III, then, wasn't a near-person at all, but a *female* – Kinnison's kind of female – and a creature who was physically a person, but mentally that inconceivable monstrosity, a *female*, might be anything and might do *anything*! Ladora temporized.

'Excuse me; I did not mean to intrude against your will,' she apologized, smoothly enough. 'Since your attitude makes it extremely difficult for me to cooperate with you, I can make no promises as yet. What is it that you wish to know first?'

'I wish to interview your predecessor, the person we called Helen.' Strangely refreshed, in a sense galvanized by the brief personal visit with her dynamic daughter, it was no longer Mrs. Kimball Kinnison who faced the Lyranian queen. Instead, it was the Red Lensman; a full-powered Second-Stage Lensman who had finally decided that, since appeals to reason, logic, and common sense had no perceptible effect upon this stiff-necked near-woman, the time had come to bear down. 'Furthermore, I intend to interview her now, and not at some such indefinite future time as your whim may see fit to allow.'

Ladora sent out a final desperate call for help and mustered her every force against the interloper. Fast and strong as her mind was, however, the Red Lensman's was faster and stronger.

The Lyranian's defensive structure was wrecked in the instant of its building, the frantically struggling mind was taken over in toto. Help arrived – uselessly; since although Clarrissa's newly enlarged mind had not been put to warlike use, it was brilliantly keen and ultimately sure. Nor, in time of stress, did the softer side of her nature operate to stay mind or hand. While carrying Lensman's Load she contained no more of ruth for Civilization's foes than did abysmally frigid Nadreck himself.

Head thrown back, taut and tense, gold-flecked tawny eyes flashing, she stood there for a moment and took on her shield everything those belligerent persons could send. More, she returned it in kind, plus; and under those withering blasts of force more than one of her attackers died. Then, still holding her block, she and her unwilling captive raced across the field toward the line of peculiar little fabric-and-wire machines that were still the last word in Lyranian air-transport.

Clarrissa knew that the Lyranians had no modern offensive or defensive weapons. They did, however, have some fairly good artillery at the airport; and she hoped fervently as she ran that she could put out jets enough to spoil aim and fuzing – luckily, they hadn't developed proximity fuzes yet! – of whatever ack-ack they could bring to bear on her crate during the few minutes she would have to use it. Fortunately, there was no artillery at the small, unimportant airport on which her speedster lay.

'Here we are. We'll take this tripe – it's the fastest thing here!'

Clarrissa could operate the triplane, of course – any knowledge or ability that Ladora had ever had was now and permanently the Lensman's. She started the queer engines; and as the powerful little plane screamed into the air, hanging from its props, she devoted what of her mind she could spare to the problem of anti-aircraft fire. She could not handle all the guncrews; but she could and did control the most important members of most of them. Thus, nearly all the shells either went wide or exploded too soon. Since she knew every point of aim of the few guns with whose operations she could not interfere, she avoided their missiles by not being at any one of those points at the predetermined instant of functioning.

Thus plane and passengers escaped unscratched; and in a matter of minutes arrived at their destination. The Lyranians there had been alerted, of course; but they were few in number and they had not been informed that it would take physical force, not mental, to keep that red-headed pseudo-person from boarding her outlandish ship of space.

In a few more minutes, then, Clarrissa and her captive were high in the stratosphere. Clarrissa sat Ladora down – hard – in a seat and fastened the safety straps.

'Stay in that seat and keep your thoughts to yourself,' she directed, curtly. 'If you don't, you'll never again either move or think in this life.' She opened a sliding door, put on a couple of wisps of Manarkan glamorette, reached for a dress, and paused. Eyes glowing, she gazed hungrily at a suit of plain grey leather; a costume which she had not as yet so much as tried on. Should she wear it, or not?

She could work efficiently – at service maximum, really – in ordinary clothes. Ditto, although she didn't like to, unclothed. In Grey, though, she could hit absolute max if she had to. Nor had there ever been any question of right involved; the only barrier had been her own hyper-sensitivity.

For over twenty years she herself had been the only one to deny her right. What license, she was wont to ask, did an imitation or synthetic or amateur or 'Red' Lensman have to wear the garb which meant so much to so many? Over those years, however, it had become increasingly widely known that hers was one of the five finest and most powerful minds in the entire Grey Legion; and when Coordinator Kinnison recalled her to active duty in Unattached status, that Legion passed by unanimous vote a resolution asking her to join them in Grey. Psychics all, they knew that nothing less would suffice; that if there was any trace of resentment or of antagonism or of feelings that she did not intrinsically belong, she would never don the uniform which every adherent of Civilization so revered and for which, deep down, she had always so intensely longed.

The Legion had sent her these Greys. Kit had convinced her that she did actually deserve them.

She really should wear them. She would.

She put them on, thrilling to the core as she did so, and made the quick little gesture she had seen Kim make so many times. Grey Seal. No one, however accustomed, has ever donned or ever will don unmoved the plain grey leather of the Unattached Lensman of the Galactic Patrol.

Hands on hips, she studied herself minutely and approvingly, both in the mirror and by means of her vastly more efficient sense of perception. She wriggled a little, and giggled inwardly as she remembered deploring as 'exhibitionistic' this same conduct in her oldest daughter.

The Greys fitted her perfectly. A bit revealing, perhaps, but her figure was still good – very good, as a matter of fact. Not a speck of dirt or tarnish. Her DeLameters were fully charged. Her tremendous Lens flamed brilliantly upon her wrist. She looked – and felt – ready. She could hit absolute max in a fraction of a micro-second. If she had to get really tough, she would. She sent out a call.

'Helen of Lyrane! I know they've got you around here somewhere, and if any of your guards try to screen out *this* thought I'll burn their brains out. Clarrissa of Sol III calling. Come in, Helen!'

'Clarrissa!' This time there was no interference. A world of welcome was in every nuance of the thought. 'Where are you?'

'High up, at...' Clarrissa gave her position. 'I'm in my speedster, so can get to anywhere on the planet in minutes. More important, where are you? And why?'

'In jail, in my own apartment.' Queens should have palaces, but Lyrane's ruler did not. Everything was strictly utilitarian. 'The tower on the corner, remember? On the top floor? "Why" it is too long to go into now – I'd better tell you as much as possible of what you should know, while there's still time.'

'Time? Are you in danger?'

'Yes. Ladora would have killed me long ago if it had dared. My following grows less daily, the Boskonians stronger. The guards have already summoned help. They are coming now, to take me.'

'That's what *they* think!' Clarrissa had already reached the scene. She had exactly the velocity she wanted. She slanted downward in a screaming dive. 'Can you tell whether they're limbering up any ack-ack around there?'

'I don't believe so – I don't feel any such thoughts.'

'QX. Get away from the window.' If they hadn't started already they never would; the Red Lensman was deadly sure of that.

She came within range – her range – of the guns. She was in time. Several gunners were running toward their stations. None of them arrived. The speedster leveled off and stuck its hard, sharp nose into and almost through the indicated room; reenforced concrete, steel bars, and glass showering abroad as it did so. The port snapped open. As Helen leaped in, Clarrissa practically threw Ladora out.

'Bring Ladora back!' Helen demanded. 'I shall have its life!'

'Nix!' Clarrissa snapped. 'I know everything she does. We've other fish to fry, my dear.'

The massive door clanged shut. The speedster darted forward, straight through the solid concrete wall. Clarrissa's vessel, solidly built of beryllium alloys, had been designed to take brutal punishment. She took it.

Out in open space, Clarrissa went free, leaving the artificial gravity at normal. Helen stood up, took Clarrissa's hand, and shook it gravely and strongly; a gesture at which the Red Lensman almost choked.

Helen of Lyrane had changed even less than had the Earth-woman. She was still six feet tall; erect, taut, springy, and poised. She didn't weigh a pound more than the one-eighty she had scaled twenty-odd years ago. Her vivid auburn hair showed not one strand of grey. Her eyes were as clear and as proud; her skin almost as fine and firm.

'You are, then, alone?' In spite of her control, Helen's thought showed relief.

'Yes. My hus... Kimball Kinnison is very busy elsewhere.'

Clarrissa understood perfectly. Helen, after twenty years of thinking things over, really liked her; but she still simply couldn't stand a male, not even Kim; any more than Clarrissa could ever adapt herself to the Lyranian habit of using the neuter pronoun 'it' when referring to one of themselves. She couldn't. Anybody who ever got one glimpse of Helen would simply have to think of her as *she*! But enough of this woolgathering – which had taken perhaps one millisecond of time.

'There's nothing to keep us from working together perfectly,' Clarrissa's thought flashed on. 'Ladora didn't know much, and you do. So tell me all about things, so we can decide where to begin!'

17
Nadreck vs. Kandron

When Kandron called his minion in that small and nameless base to learn whether or not he had succeeded in trapping the Palainian Lensman, Nadreck's relay station functioned so perfectly, and Nadreck was so completely in charge of his captive's mind, that the caller could feel nothing out of the ordinary. Ultra-suspicious though Kandron was, there was nothing whatever to indicate that anything had changed at that base since he had last called its commander. That individual's subconscious mind reacted properly to the key stimulus. The conscious mind took over, remembered, and answered properly a series of trick questions.

These things occurred because the minion was still alive. His ego, the pattern and matrix of his personality, was still in existence and had not been changed. What Kandron did not and could not suspect was that that ego was no longer in control of mind, brain, or body; that it was utterly unable, of its own volition, either to think any iota of independent thought or to stimulate any single physical cell. The Onlonian's ego was present – just barely present – but that was all. It was Nadreck who, using that ego as a guide and, in a sense, as a helplessly impotent transformer, received the call. Nadreck made those exactly correct replies. Nadreck was now ready to render a detailed and fully documented – and completely mendacious – report upon his own destruction!

Nadreck's special tracers were already out, determining line and intensity. Strippers and analyzers were busily at work on the fringes of the beam, dissecting out, isolating, and identifying each of the many scraps of extraneous thought accompanying the main beam. These side-thoughts, in fact, were Nadreck's prime concern. The Second-Stage Lensman had learned that no being – except possibly an Arisian – could narrow a beam of thought down to one single, pure sequence. Of the four, however, only Nadreck recognized in those side-bands a rich field; only he had designed and developed mechanisms with which to work that field.

The stronger and clearer the mind, the fewer and less complete were the extraneous fragments of thought; but Nadreck knew that even Kandron's brain would carry quite a few such non-germane accompaniments, and from each of those bits he could reconstruct an entire sequence as accurately as a competent paleontologist reconstructs a prehistoric animal from one fossilized piece of bone.

Thus Nadreck was completely ready when the harshly domineering Kandron asked his first real question.

'I do not suppose that you have succeeded in killing the Lensman?'

'Yes, Your Supremacy, I have.' Nadreck could feel Kandron's start of surprise; could perceive without his instruments Kandron's fleeting thoughts of the hundreds of unsuccessful previous attempts upon his life. It was clear that the Onlonian was not at all credulous.

'Report in detail!' Kandron ordered.

Nadreck did so, adhering rigidly to the truth up to the moment in which his probes of force had touched off the Boskonian alarms. Then:

'Spy-ray photographs taken at the instant of alarm show an indetectable speedster, with one, and only one occupant, as Your Supremacy anticipated. A careful study of all the pictures taken of that occupant shows: first, that he was definitely alive at that time, and was neither a projection nor an artificial mechanism; and second, that his physical measurements agree in every particular with the specifications furnished by Your Supremacy as being those of Nadreck of Palain VII.

'Since Your Supremacy personally computed and supervised

the placement of those projectors,' Nadreck went smoothly on, 'you know that the possibility is vanishingly small that any material thing, free or inert, could have escaped destruction. As a check, I took seven hundred twenty nine samples of the circumambient space, statistically at random, for analysis. After appropriate allowances for the exactly-observed elapsed times of sampling, diffusion of droplets and molecular and atomic aggregates, temperatures, pressures, and all other factors known or assumed to be operating, I determined that there had been present in the center of action of our beams a mass of approximately four thousand six hundred seventy eight point zero one metric tons. This value, Your Supremacy will note, is in close agreement with the most efficient mass of an indetectable speedster designed for long distance work.'

That figure was in fact closer than close. It was an almost exact statement of the actual mass of Nadreck's ship.

'Exact composition?' Kandron demanded.

Nadreck recited a rapid-fire string of elements and figures. They, too, were correct within the experimental error of a very good analyst. The base commander had not known them, but it was well within the bounds of possibility that the insidious Kandron would. He did. He was now practically certain that his ablest and bitterest enemy had been destroyed at last, but there were still a few lingering shreds of doubt.

'Let me look over your work,' Kandron directed.

'Yes, Your Supremacy.' Nadreck the Thorough was ready for even that extreme test. Through the eyes of the ultimately enslaved monstrosity Kandron checked and rechecked Nadreck's pictures, Nadreck's charts and diagrams, Nadreck's more than four hundred pages of mathematical, physical, and chemical notes and determinations; all without finding a single flaw.

In the end Kandron was ready to believe that Nadreck had in fact ceased to exist. However, he himself had not done the work. There was no corpse. If he himself had killed the Palainian, if he himself had actually felt the Lensman's life depart in the grasp of his own tentacles; then, and only then, would he have *known* that Nadreck was dead. As it was, even though the work had been done in exact accordance with his own instructions, there remained an infinitesimal uncertainty. Wherefore:

'Shift your field of operations to cover X-174, Y-240, Z-16. Do not relax your vigilance in the slightest because of what has happened.' He considered briefly the idea of allowing the underling to call him, in case anything happened, but decided against it. 'Are the men standing up?'

'Yes, Your Supremacy, they are in very good shape indeed.'

And so on. 'Yes, Your Supremacy, the psychologist is doing a very fine job. Yes, Your Supremacy... yes... yes... yes...'

Very shortly after the characteristically Kandronesque ending of that interview, Nadreck had learned everything he needed to know. He knew where Kandron was and what he was doing. He knew much of what Kandron had done during the preceding twenty years; and, since he himself figured prominently in many of those sequences, they constituted invaluable checks upon the validity of his other reconstructions. He knew the construction, the armament, and the various ingenious mechanisms, including the locks, of Kandron's vessel; he knew more than any other outsider had ever known of Kandron's private life. He knew where Kandron was going next, and what he was going to do there. He knew in broad what Kandron intended to do during the coming century.

Thus well informed, Nadreck set his speedster into a course toward the planet of Civilization which was Kandron's next objective. He did not hurry; it was no part of his plan to interfere in any way in the horrible program of planet-wide madness and slaughter which Kandron had in mind. It simply did not occur to him to try to save the planet as well as to kill the Onlonian; Nadreck, being Nadreck, took without doubt or question the safest and surest course.

Nadreck knew that Kandron would set his vessel into an orbit around the planet, and that he would take a small boat – a flitter – for the one personal visit necessary to establish his lines of communication and control. Vessel and flitter would be alike indetectable, of course; but Nadreck found the one easily enough and knew when the other left its mother-ship. Then, using his lightest, stealthiest spy-rays, the Palainian set about the exceedingly delicate business of boarding the Boskonian craft.

That undertaking could be made a story in its own right, for Kandron did not leave his ship unguarded. However, merely by thinking about his own safety, Kandron had all unwittingly given away the keys to his supposedly impregnable fortress. While Kandron was wondering whether or not the Lensman was really dead, and especially after he had been convinced that he most probably was, the Onlonian's thoughts had touched fleetingly upon a multitude of closely-related subjects. Would it be safe to abandon some of the more onerous precautions he had always taken, and which had served him so well for so many years? And as he thought of them, each one of his safeguards flashed at least partially into view; and for Nadreck, any significant part was as good as the whole. Kandron's protective devices, therefore, did not protect. Projectors, designed to flame out against intruders, remained cold. Ports opened; and as Nadreck touched sundry buttons various invisible beams, whose breaking would have produced unpleasant results, ceased to exist. In short, Nadreck knew all the answers. If he had not been coldly certain that his information was complete, he would not have acted at all.

After entry, his first care was to send out spotting devices which would give warning in case Kandron should return unexpectedly soon. Then, working in the service-spaces behind instrument-boards and panels, in junction boxes, and in various other out-of-the-way places, he cut into lead after lead, ran wire after wire, and installed item after item of apparatus and equipment upon which he had been at work for weeks. He finished his work undisturbed. He checked and rechecked the circuits, making absolutely certain that every major one of the vessel's controlling leads ran to or through at least one of the things he had just installed. With painstaking nicety he obliterated every visible sign of his visit. He departed as carefully as he had come; restoring to full efficiency as he went each one of Kandron's burglar-alarms.

Kandron returned, entered his ship as usual, stored his flitter, and extended a tentacular member toward the row of switches on his panel.

'Don't touch anything, Kandron,' he was advised by a thought as cold and as deadly as any one of his own; and upon the Onlonian equivalent of a visiplate there appeared the one likeness which he least expected and least desired to perceive.

'Nadreck of Palain VII – Star A Star – THE Lensman!' The Onlonian was physically and motionally incapable of gasping, but the idea is appropriate. 'You have, then, wired and mined this ship.'

There was a subdued clicking of relays. The Bergenholm came up to speed, the speedster spun about and darted away under a couple of kilodynes of drive.

'I am Nadreck of Palain VII, yes. One of the group of Lensmen whose collective activities you have ascribed to Star A Star and *the* Lensman. Your ship is, as you have deduced, mined. The only reason you did not die as you entered it is that I wish to be really certain, and not merely statistically so, that it is Kandron of Onlo, not someone else, who dies.'

'That unutterable fool!' Kandron quivered in helpless rage. 'Oh, that I had taken the time and killed you myself!'

'If you had done your own work, the techniques I used here could not have been employed, and you might have been in no danger at the present moment,' Nadreck admitted, equably enough. 'My powers are small, my intellect feeble, and what might have been has no present bearing. I am inclined, however, to question the validity of your conclusions, due to the known fact that you have been directing a campaign against me for over twenty years without success; whereas I have succeeded against you in less than half a year ... My analysis is now complete. You may now touch any control you please. By the way, you do not deny that you are Kandron of Onlo, do you?'

Neither of those monstrous beings mentioned or even

thought of mercy. In neither of their languages was there any word for or concept of such a thing.

'That would be idle. You know my pattern as well as I know yours . . . I cannot understand how you got through that . . .'

'It is not necessary that you should. Do you wish to close one of those switches or shall I?'

Kandron had been thinking for minutes, studying every aspect of his predicament. Knowing Nadreck, he knew just how desperate the situation was. There was, however, one very small chance – just one. The way he had come was clear. That was the *only* clear way. Wherefore, to gain an extra instant of time, he reached out toward a switch; but even while he was reaching he put every ounce of his tremendous strength into a leap which hurled him across the room toward his flitter.

No luck. One of Nadreck's minor tentacles was already curled around a switch, tensed and ready. Kandron was still in air when a relay snapped shut and four canisters of duodec detonated as one. Duocecaplylatomate, that frightful detonant whose violence is exceeded only by that of nuclear disintegration!

There was an appalling flash of viciously white light, which expanded in milliseconds into an enormous globe of incandescent gas. Cooling and darkening as it expanded rapidly into the near-vacuum of interplanetary space, the gases and vapors soon became invisible. Through and throughout the entire volume of volatilization Nadreck drove analyzers and detectors, until he knew positively that no particle of material substance larger in diameter than five microns remained of either Kandron or his space-ship. He then called the Grey Lensman.

'Kinnison? Nadreck of Palain VII calling, to report that my assignment has been completed. I have destroyed Kandron of Onlo.'

'Good! Fine business, ace! What kind of a picture did you get? He must have known something about the higher echelons – or did he? Was he just another dead end?'

'I did not go into that.'

'Huh? Why not?' Kinnison demanded, exasperation in every line of his thought.

'Because it was not included in the project,' Nadreck explained, patiently. 'You already know that one must concentrate in order to work efficiently. To secure the requisite minimum of information it was necessary to steer his thoughts into one, and only one, set of channels. There were some foreign side-bands, of course, and it may be that some of them touched upon this new subject which you have now, too late, introduced . . . no, there were no such.'

'Damnation!' Kinnison exploded; then by main strength shut himself up. 'QX, ace; skip it. But listen, my spiny and murderous friend. Get this – engrave it in big type right on the topside inside of your thick skull – what we want is INFORMATION, not mere liquidation. Next time you get hold of such a big shot as Kandron must have been, don't kill him until either: first, you get some leads as to who or what the real head of the outfit is; or, second, you make sure that he doesn't know. Then kill him all you want to, but FIND OUT WHAT HE KNOWS FIRST. Have I made myself clear this time?'

'You have, and as coordinator your instructions should and will govern. I point out, however, that the introduction of a multiplicity of objectives into a problem not only destroys its unity, but also increases markedly both the time necessary for, and the actual personal danger involved in, its solution.'

'So what?' Kinnison countered, as evenly as he could. 'That way, we may be able to get the answer some day. Your way, we never will. But the thing's done – there's no use yapping and yowling about it now. Have you any ideas as to what you should do next?'

'No. Whatever you wish, that I shall try to do.'

'I'll check with the others.' He did so, receiving no helpful ideas until he consulted his wife.

'Hi, Kim, my dear!' came Clarrissa's buoyant thought; and, after a brief but intense greeting: 'Glad you called. Nothing definite enough yet to report to you officially, but there are indications that Lyrane IX may be an important . . .'

174

'Nine?' Kinnison interrupted. 'Not Eight again?'

'Nine,' she confirmed. 'A new item. So I may be doing a flit over there one of these days.'

'Uh-uh,' he denied. 'Lyrane Nine would be none of your business. Stay away from it.'

'Says who?' she demanded. 'We went into this once before, Kim, about you telling me what I could and couldn't do.'

'Yeah, and I came out second best.' Kinnison grinned. 'But now, as coordinator, I make suggestions to even Second-Stage Lensmen, and they follow them – or else. I therefore suggest officially that you stay away from Lyrane IX on the grounds that since it is colder than a Palainian's heart, it is definitely not your problem, but Nadreck's. And I'm adding this – if you don't behave yourself I'll come over there and administer appropriate physical persuasion.'

'Come on over – that'd be fun!' Clarrissa giggled, then sobered quickly. 'But seriously, you win, I guess – this time. You'll keep me informed?'

'I'll do that. Clear ether, Cris!' and he turned back to the Palainian.

'. . . so you see this is your problem. Go to it, little chum.'

'I go, Kinnison.'

18
Camilla Kinnison, Detector

For hours Camilla and Tregonsee wrestled separately and fruitlessly with the problem of the elusive 'X'. Then, after she had studied the Rigellian's mind in a fashion which he could neither detect nor employ, Camilla broke the mental silence.

'Uncle Trig, my conclusions frighten me. Can you conceive of the possibility that it was contact with *my* mind, not yours, that made "X" run away?'

'That is the only tenable conclusion. I know the power of my own mind, but I have never been able to guess at the capabilities of yours. I fear that I, at least, underestimated our opponent.'

'I know I did, and I was terribly wrong. I shouldn't have tried to fool you, either, even a little bit. There are some things about me that I just *can't* show to most people, but you are different – you're *such* a wonderful person!'

'Thanks, Camilla, for your trust.' Understandingly, he did not go on to say that he would keep on being worthy of it. 'I accept the fact that you five, being children of two Second-Stage Lensmen, are basically beyond my comprehension. There are indications that you do not as yet thoroughly understand yourself. You have, however, decided upon a course of action.'

'Oh – I'm *so* relieved! Yes, I have. But before we go into that, I haven't been able to solve the problem of "X". More, I have proved that I cannot solve it without more data. Therefore, you can't either. Check?'

'I had not reached that conclusion, but I accept your statement as truth.'

'One of those uncommon powers of mine, to which you referred a while ago, is a wide range of perception, from large masses down to extremely tiny components. Another, or perhaps a part of the same one, is that, after resolving and analyzing these fine details, I can build up a logical and coherent whole by processes of interpolation and extrapolation.'

'I can believe that such things would be possible to such a mind as yours must be. Go on.'

'Well, that is how I know that I underestimated Mr. "X". Whoever or whatever he is, I am completely unable to resolve the structure of his thought. I gave you all I got of it. Look at it again, please – hard. What can you make of it now?'

'It is exactly the same as it was before; a fragment of a simple and plain introductory thought to an audience. That is all.'

'That's all I can see, too, and that's what surprises me so.' The hitherto imperturbable and serene Camilla got up and began to pace the floor. 'That thought is apparently absolutely solid; and since that is a definitely impossible condition, the truth is that its structure is so fine that I cannot resolve it into its component units. This shows that I am not nearly as competent as I thought I was. When you and dad and the others reached that point, you each went to Arisia. I've decided to do the same thing.'

'That decision seems eminently sound.'

'Thanks, Uncle Trig – that was what I hoped you'd say. I've never been there, you know, and the idea scared me a little. Clear ether!'

There is no need to go into detail as to Camilla's bout with Mentor. Her mind, like Karen's, had had to mature of itself before any treatment could be really effective; but, once mature, she took as much in one session as Kathryn had taken in all her many. She had not suggested that the Rigellian accompany her to Arisia; they both knew that he had already received all he could take. Upon her return she greeted him casually as though she had been gone only a matter of hours.

'What Mentor did to me, Uncle Trig, shouldn't have been

done to a Delgonian catlat. It doesn't show too much, though, I hope – does it?'

'Not at all.' He scanned her narrowly, both physically and mentally. 'I can perceive no change in gross. In fine, however, you have changed. You have developed.'

'Yes, more than I would have believed possible. I can't do much with my present very poor transcription of that thought, since the all-important fine detail is missing. We'll have to intercept another one. I'll get it *all*, this time.'

'But you did something with this one, I am sure. There must have been some developable features – a sort of latent-image effect?'

'A little. Practically infinitesimal compared to what was really there. Physically, his classification to four places is TUUV; quite a bit like the Nevians, you notice. His home planet is big, and practically covered with liquid. No real cities, just groups of half-submerged, temporary structures. Mentality very high, but we knew that already. Normally, he thinks upon a very short wave, so short that he was then working at the very bottom of his range. His sun is a fairly hot main-sequence star, of spectral class somewhere around F, and it's probably more or less variable, because there was quite a distinct implication of change. But that's normal enough, isn't it?'

Within the limits imposed by the amount and kind of data available, Camilla's observations and analyses had been perfect, her reconstruction flawless. She did not then have any idea, however, that 'X' was in fact a spring-form Plooran. More, she did not even know that such a planet as Ploor existed, except for Mentor's one mention of it.

'Of course. Peoples of planets of variable suns think that such suns are the only kind fit to have planets. You cannot reconstruct the nature of the change?'

'No. Worse, I can't find even a hint of where his planet is in space – but then, I probably couldn't, anyway, even with a whole, fresh thought to study.'

'Probably not. "Rigel Four" would be an utterly meaningless thought to anyone ignorant of Rigel; and, except when making a conscious effort, as in directing strangers, I never think of its location in terms of galactic coordinates. I suppose that the location of a home planet is always taken for granted. That would seem to leave us just about where we were before in our search for "X", except for your implied ability to intercept another of his thoughts, almost at will. Explain, please.'

'Not *my* ability – ours.' Camilla smiled, confidently. 'I couldn't do it alone, neither could you, but between us it won't be too difficult. You, with your utterly calm, utterly unshakable certainty, can drive a thought to any corner of the universe. You can fix and hold it steady on any indicated atom. I can't do that, or anything like it, but with my present ability to detect and to analyze I'm not afraid of missing "X" if we can come within parsecs of him. So my idea is a sort of piggy-back hunting trip; you to take me for a ride, mentally, very much as Worsel takes Con, physically. That would work, don't you think?'

'Perfectly, I am sure.' The stolid Rigellian was immensely pleased. 'Link your mind with mine, then, and we will set out. If you have no better plan of action mapped out, I would suggest starting at the point where we lost him and working outward, covering an expanding sphere.'

'You know best. I'll stick to you wherever you go.'

Tregonsee launched his thought; a thought which, at a velocity not to be measured even in multiples of that of light, generated the surface of a continuously enlarging sphere of space. And with that thought, a very part of it, sped Camilla's incomprehensibly delicate, instantaneously reactive detector web. The Rigellian, with his unhuman perseverance, would have surveyed total space had it been necessary; and the now adult Camilla would have stayed with him. However, the patient pair did not have to comb all of space. In a matter of hours the girl's almost infinitely tenuous detector touched, with infinitesimal power and for an inappreciable instant of time, the exact thought-structure to which it had been so carefully attuned.

'Halt!' she flashed, and Tregonsee's mighty superdread-nought shot away along the indicated line at maximum blast.

'You are not now thinking at him, of course, but how sure are you that he did not feel your detector?' Tregonsee asked.

'Positive,' the girl replied. 'I couldn't even feel it myself until after a million-fold amplification. It was just a web, you know, not nearly solid enough for an analyzer or a recorder. I didn't touch his mind at all. However, when we get close enough to work efficiently, which will be in about five days, we will have to touch him. Assuming that he is as sensitive as we are, he will feel us; hence we will have to work fast and according to some definite plan. What are your ideas as to technique?'

'I may offer a suggestion or two, later, but I resign leadership to you. You already have made plans, have you not?'

'Only a framework; we'll have to work out the details together. Since we agree that it was my mind that he did not like, you will have to make the first contact.'

'Of course. But since the action of thought is so nearly instantaneous, are you sure that you will be able to protect yourself in case he overcomes me at that first contact?' If the Rigellian gave any thought at all to his own fate in such a case, no trace of it was evident.

'My screens are good. I am fairly certain that I could protect both of us, but it might slow me down a trifle; and even an instant's delay might keep me from getting the information we want. It would be better, I think, to call Kit in. Or, better yet, Kay. She can stop a super-atomic bomb. With Kay covering us, we will both be free to work.'

Again they went into a union of minds; considering, weighing, analyzing, rejecting, and – a few times – accepting. And finally, well within the five-day time limit, they had drawn up a completely detailed plan of action.

How uselessly that time was spent! For that action, instead of progressing according to their carefully worked-out plan, was ended almost in the instant of its beginning.

According to plan, Tregonsee tuned his mind to 'X's' pattern as soon as they had come within working range. He reached out as delicately as he could, and his best was very fine work indeed. He might just as well have struck with all his power, for at first touch of the fringe, extremely light and entirely innocuous though it was, the stranger's barriers flared into being and there came back instantly a mental bolt of such vicious intensity that it would have gone through Tregonsee's hardest-held block as though no barrier had been there. But that bolt did not strike Tregonsee's shield. Instead, it struck Karen Kinnison's, which has already been described.

It did not exactly bounce, nor did it cling, nor did it linger, even for a microsecond, to do battle as expected. It simply vanished; as though that minute interval of time had been sufficient for the enemy to have recovered from the shock of encountering a completely unexpected resistance, to have analyzed the texture of the shield, to have deduced from that analysis the full capabilities of its owner and operator, to have decided that he did not care to have any dealings with the entity so deduced, and finally, as he no doubt supposed, to have begun to retreat in good order.

His retreat, however, was not in good order. He did not escape, this time. This time, as she had declared that she would be, Camilla was ready for anything – literally anything. Everything she had – and she had plenty – was on the trips; tense, taut, and poised. Knowing that Karen, the Ultimate of Defense, was on guard, she was wholly free to hurl her every force on the instant. Scarcely had the leading element of her probe touched the stranger's screens, however, when those screens, 'X' himself, his vessel and any others that might have been accompanying it, and everything tangible in nearby space, all disappeared at once in the inconceivably violent, the ultimately cataclysmic detonation of a super-atomic bomb.

It may not, perhaps, be generally known that the 'completely liberating' or 'super-atomic' bomb liberates one hundred percent of the component energy of its total mass in approximately sixty nine hundredths of one microsecond. Its violence and destructiveness thus differ, both in degree and in kind, from those of the earlier type, which liberated only the energy of nuclear fission, very much as the radiation of S-Doradus differs from that of Earth's moon. Its mass attains, and holds for an appreciable length of time, a temperature to be measured only in millions of Centigrade degrees; which fact accounts in large part for its utterly incredible vehemence.

Nothing inert in its entire sphere of primary action can even begin to move out of the way before being reduced to its subatomic constituents and thus contributing in some measure to the cataclysm. Nothing is or becomes visible until the secondary stage begins; until the frightful globe has expanded to a diameter of thousands of yards and by this expansion has cooled down to a point at which some of its radiation lies in the visible violet. And as for lethal radiation – there are radiations and they are lethal.

The conflict with 'X' had occupied approximately two milliseconds of actual time. The expansion had been progressing for a second or two when Karen lowered her shield.

'Well, that finished that,' she commented. 'I'd better get back on the job. Did you find out what you want to know, Cam, or not?'

'I got a little in the moment before the explosion. Not much.' Camilla was deep in study. 'It's going to be quite a job of reconstruction. One thing of interest to you, though, is that this "X" had quit sabotage temporarily and was on his way to Lyrane IX, where he had some important . . .'

'Nine?' Karen asked sharply. 'Not Eight? I've been watching Eight, you know – I haven't even thought of Nine.'

'Nine, definitely. The thought was clear. You might give it a scan once in a while. How is mother doing?'

'She's doing a grand job, and that Helen is quite an operator, too. I'm not doing much – just a touch here and there – I'll see what I can see on Nine. I'm not the scanner or detector you are, though, you know – maybe you'd better come over here too. Suppose?'

'I think so – don't you, Uncle Trig?' Tregonsee did. 'We can do some exploring as we come, but since I have no definite patterns for web work, we may not be able to do much until we get close. Clear ether, Kay!'

'The fine structure is there, and I can resolve it and analyze it,' Camilla informed Tregonsee, after a few hours of intense concentration. 'There are quite a few clear extraneous sequences, instead of the blurred latent images we had before, but there's still no indication of the location of his home planet. I can see his physical classification to ten places instead of four, more detail as to the sun's variation, the seasons, their habits, and so on. Things that seem mostly to be of very little importance, as far as we're concerned. I learned one fact, though, that is new and important. According to my reconstruction, his business on Lyrane IX was the induction of Boskonian Lensmen – *Black* Lensmen, Tregonsee, just as father suspected!'

'In that case, he must have been the Boskonian counterpart of an Arisian, and hence one of the highest echelon. I am very glad indeed that you and Karen relieved me of the necessity of trying to handle him myself . . . your father will be very glad to know that we have at last and in fact reached the top . . .'

Camilla was paying attention to the Rigellian's cogitations with only a fraction of her mind; most of it being engaged in a private conversation with her brother.

'. . . so you see, Kit, he was under a sub-conscious compulsion. He *had* to destroy himself, his ship, and everything in it, in the very instant of attack by any mind definitely superior to his own. Therefore he couldn't have been an Eddorian, possibly, but merely another intermediate, and I haven't been of much help.'

'Sure you have, Cam! You got a lot of information, and some mighty good leads to Lyrane IX and what goes on there. I'm on my way to Eddore now; and by working down from there and up from Lyrane IX we can't go wrong. Clear ether, sis!'

19
The Hell-Hole in Space

Constance Kinnison did not waste much time in idle recriminations, even at herself. Realizing at last that she was still not fully competent, and being able to define exactly what she lacked, she went to Arisia for final treatment. She took that treatment and emerged from it, as her brother and sisters had emerged, a completely integrated personality.

She had something of everything the others had, of course, as did they all; but her dominants, the characteristics which had operated to make Worsel her favorite Second-Stage Lensman, were much like those of the Velantian. Her mind, like his, was quick and facile, yet of extraordinary power and range. She did not have much of her father's flat, driving urge or of his indomitable will to do; she was the least able of all the Five to exert long-sustained extreme effort. Her top, however, was vastly higher than theirs. Her armament was almost entirely offensive: she was far and away the deadliest fighter of them all. She only of them all had more than a trace of pure killer instinct; and when roused to full fighting pitch her mental bolts were weapons of as starkly incomprehensible an effectiveness as the sphere of primary action of a super-atomic bomb.

As soon as Constance had left the *Velan*, remarking that she was going to Arisia to take her medicine, Worsel called a staff meeting to discuss in detail the matter of the 'Hell-Hole in Space'.

That conference was neither long nor heated; it was unanimously agreed that the phenomenon was – *must* be – simply another undiscovered cavern of Overlords.

In view of the fact that Worsel and his crew had been hunting down and killing Overlords for more than twenty years, the only logical course of action was for them to deal similarly with one more, perhaps the only remaining large group of their hereditary foes. Nor did any doubt of their ability to do so enter any one of the Velantian's minds.

How wrong they were!

They did not have to search for the 'Hell-Hole'. Long since, to stop its dreadful toll, a spherical cordon of robot guard-ships had been posted to warn all traffic away from the outer fringes of its influence. Since they merely warned against, but could not physically prohibit, entry into the dangerous space. Worsel did not pay any attention to the guard-ships or to their signals as the *Velan* went through the warning web. His plans were, he thought, well laid. His ship was free. Its speed, by Velantian standards, was very low. Each member of his crew wore a full-coverage thought-screen; a similar and vastly more powerful screen would surround the whole vessel if one of Worsel's minor members were either to tighten or to relax its grip upon a spring-mounted control. Worsel was, he thought, ready for anything.

But the 'Hell-Hole in Space' was not a cavern of Overlords. No sun, no planet, nothing material existed within that spherical volume of space. But *something* was there. Slow as was the *Velan*'s pace, it was still too fast by far; for in a matter of seconds, through the supposedly impervious thought-screens, there came an attack of utterly malignant ferocity; an assault which tore at Worsel's mind in a fashion he had never imagined possible; a poignant, rending, unbearably crescendo force whose violence seemed to double with every mile of distance.

The *Velan*'s all-encompassing screen snapped on – uselessly. Its tremendous power was as unopposed as were the lesser powers of the personal shields; that highly inimical thought was coming past, not through, the barriers. An Arisian, or one of the Children of the Lens, would have been able to perceive and to block that band; no one of lesser mental stature could.

Strong and fast as Worsel was, mentally and physically, he

acted just barely in time. All his resistance and all his strength had to be called into play to maintain his mind's control over his body; to enable him to spin his ship end for end and to kick her drive up to maximum blast. To his surprise, his agony decreased with distance as rapidly as it had built up; disappearing entirely as the *Velan* reached the web she had crossed such a short time before.

Groggy, sick, and shaken, hanging slackly from his bars, the Velantian Lensman was roused to action by the mental and physical frenzy of his crew. Ten of them had died in the Hell-Hole; six more were torn to bits before their commander could muster enough force to stop their insane rioting. Then Master Therapist Worsel went to work; and one by one he brought the survivors back. They remembered; but he made those memories bearable.

He then called Kinnison. '... but there didn't seem to be anything personal about it, as one would expect from an Overlord,' he concluded his brief report. 'It did not concentrate on us, reach for us, or follow us as we left. Its intensity seemed to vary only with distance – perhaps inversely as distance squared; it might very well have been radiated from a center. While it is nothing like anything I ever felt before, I still think it must be an Overlord – maybe a sort of Second-Stage Overlord, just as you and I are Second-Stage Lensmen. He's too strong for me now, just as they used to be too strong for us before we met you. By the same reasoning, however, I'm pretty sure that if you can come over here, you and I together could figure out a way of taking him. How about it?'

'Mighty interesting, and I'd like to, but I'm right in the middle of a job,' Kinnison replied, and went on to explain rapidly what he, as Bradlow Thyron, had done and what he still had to do. 'As soon as I can get away I'll come over. In the meantime, chum, keep away from there. Do a flit – find something else to keep you amused until I can join you.'

Worsel set out, and after a few days – or weeks? Idle time means practically nothing to a Velantian – a sharply-Lensed thought drove in.

'Help! A Lensman calling help! Line this thought and come fast...' The message ended as sharply as it had begun; in a flare of agony which, Worsel knew, meant that that Lensman, whoever he was, had died.

Since the thought, although broadcast, had come in strong and clear, Worsel knew that its sender had been close by. While the time had been very short indeed, he had been able to get a line of sorts. Into that line he whirled the *Velan*'s sharp prow and along it she hurtled at the literally inconceivable pace of her maximum drive. As the Grey Lensman had often remarked, the Velantian superdreadnought had more legs than a centipede, and now she was using them all. In minutes, then, the scene of battle grew large upon her plates.

The Patrol ship, hopelessly outclassed, could last only minutes longer. Her screens were down; her very wall-shield was dead. Red pock-marks sprang into being along her sides as the Boskonian needle-beamers wiped out her few remaining controls. Then, as the helplessly raging Worsel looked on, his brain seething with unutterable Velantian profanity, the enemy prepared to board; a course of action which, Worsel could see, was changed abruptly by the fact – and perhaps as well by the terrific velocity – of his own unswerving approach. The conquered Patrol cruiser disappeared in a blaze of detonating duodec; the conqueror devoted his every jet to the task of running away; strewing his path as he did so with sundry items of solid and explosive destruction. Such things, however, whether inert or free, were old and simple stuff to the *Velan*'s war-wise crew. Their spotters and detectors were full out, as was also a forefan of annihilating and disintegrating beams.

Thus none of the Boskonian's missiles touched the *Velan*, nor, with all his speed, could he escape. Few indeed were the ships of space able to step it, parsec for parsec, with Worsel's mighty craft, and this luckless pirate vessel was not one of them. Up and up the *Velan* rushed; second by second the intervening distance lessened. Tractors shot out, locked on, and pulled briefly with all the force of their stupendous generators.

Briefly, but long enough. As Worsel had anticipated, that

savage yank had, in the fraction of a second required for the Boskonian commander to recognize and to cut the tractors, been enough to bring the two inertialess warcraft almost screen to screen.

'Primaries! Blast!' Worsel hurled the thought even before his tractors snapped. He was in no mood for a long-drawn-out engagement. He *might* be able to win with his secondaries, his needles, his tremendously powerful short-range stuff, and his other ordinary offensive weapons; but he was taking no chances.

One! Two! Three! The three courses of Boskonian defensive screen scarcely winked as each, locally overloaded, flared through the visible into the black and went down.

Crash! The stubborn fabric of the wall-shield offered little more resistance before it, too, went down, exposing the bare metal of the Boskonian hull – and, as is well known, any conceivable material substance simply vanishes at the touch of such fields of force as those.

Driving projectors carved away and main batteries silenced, Worsel's needle-beamers proceeded systematically to riddle every control panel and every lifeboat, to make of the immense space-rover a completely helpless hulk.

'Hold!' An observer flashed the thought. 'Number Eight slip is empty – Number Eight lifeboat got away!'

'Damnation!' Worsel, at the head of his armed and armored storming party, as furiously eager as they to come to grips with the enemy, paused briefly. 'Trace it – or can you?'

'I did. My tracers can hold it for fifteen minutes, perhaps twenty. No longer than twenty.'

Worsel thought intensely. Which had first call, ship or lifeboat? The ship, he decided. Its resources were vastly greater; most of its personnel were probably unharmed. Given any time at all, they might be able to jury-rig a primary, and that would be bad – very bad. Besides, there were more people here; and even if, as was distinctly possible, the Boskonian captain had abandoned his vessel and his crew in an attempt to save his own life, there was plenty of time.

'Hold that lifeboat,' he instructed the observer. 'Ten minutes is all we need here.'

And it was. The Boskonians – barrel-bodied, blocky-limbed monstrosities resembling human beings about as much as they did the Velantians – wore armor, possessed hand-weapons of power, and fought viciously. They had even managed to rig a few semi-portable projectors, but none of these was allowed a single blast. Spy-ray observers were alert, and needle-beam operators; hence the fighting was all at hand to hand, with hand-weapons only. For, while the Velantians to a man lusted to kill, they had had it drilled into them for twenty years that the search for information came first; the pleasure of killing, second.

Worsel himself went straight for the Boskonian officer in command. That wight had a couple of guards with him, but they did not matter – needle-ray men took care of them. He also had a pair of heavy blasters, which he held steadily on the Velantian. Worsel paused momentarily; then, finding his screens adequate, he slammed the control-room door shut with a flick of his tail and launched himself, straight and level at his foe, with an acceleration of ten gravities. The Boskonian tried to dodge but could not. The frightful impact did not kill him, but it hurt him, badly. Worsel, on the other hand, was scarcely jarred. Hard, tough, and durable, Velantians are accustomed from birth to knockings-about which would pulverize human bones.

Worsel batted the Boskonian's guns away with two terrific blows of an armored paw, noting as he did so that violent contact with a steel wall didn't do their interior mechanisms a bit of good. Then, after cutting off both his enemy's screens and his own, he batted the Boskonian's helmet; at first experimentally, then with all his power. Unfortunately, however, it held. So did the thought-screen, and there were no external controls. That armor, damn it, was good stuff!

Leaping to the ceiling, he blasted his whole mass straight down upon the breastplate, striking it so hard this time that he hurt his head. Still no use. He wedged himself between two heavy braces, flipped a loop of tail around the Boskonian's feet, and heaved. The armored form flew across the room, struck the heavy steel wall, bounced, and dropped. The bulges of the armor were flattened by the force of the collision, the wall was dented – but the thought-screen still held!

Worsel was running out of time, fast. He couldn't treat the thing very much rougher without killing him, if he wasn't dead already. He couldn't take him aboard; he *had* to cut that screen here and now! He could see how the armor was put together; but, armored as he was, he could not take it apart. And, since the whole ship was empty of air, he could not open his own.

Or could he? He could. He could breathe space long enough to do what had to be done. He cut off his air, loosened a plate enough to release four or five hands, and, paying no attention to his laboring lungs, set furiously to work. He tore open the Boskonian's armor, snapped off his thought-screen. The creature wasn't quite dead yet – good! He didn't know a damn thing, though, nor did any member of his crew . . . but . . . a ground-gripper – a big shot – had got away. Who, or what was he?

'Tell me!' Worsel demanded, with the full power of mind and Lens, even while he was exploring with all his skill and speed. 'TELL ME!'

But the Boskonian was dying fast. The ungentle treatment, and now the lack of air, were taking toll. His patterns were disintegrating by the second, faster and faster. Meaningless blurs, which, under Worsel's vicious probing, condensed into something which seemed to be a Lens.

A Lensman? Impossible – starkly unthinkable! But jet back – hadn't Kim intimated a while back that there might be such things as Black Lensmen?

But Worsel himself wasn't feeling so good. He was only half conscious. Red, black, and purple spots were dancing in front of every one of his eyes. He sealed his suit, turned on his air, gasped, and staggered. Two of the nearest Velantians, both of whom had been en rapport with him throughout, came running to his aid; arriving just as he recovered full control.

'Back to the *Velan*, everybody!' he ordered. 'No time for any more fun – we've got to get that lifeboat!' Then, as soon as he had been obeyed: 'Bomb that hulk... Good! Flit!'

Overtaking the lifeboat did not take long. Spearing it with a tractor and yanking it alongside required only seconds. For all his haste, Worsel found in it only a something that looked as though it once might have been a Delgonian Lensman. It had blown itself apart. Because of its reptilian tenacity of life, however, it was not quite dead: its Lens still showed an occasional flicker of light and its disintegrating mind was not yet entirely devoid of patterns. Worsel studied that mind until all trace of life had vanished. Then he called Kinnison.

'...so you see I guessed wrong. The Lens was too dim to read, but he must have been a Black Lensman. The only readable thought in his mind was an extremely fuzzy one of the planet Lyrane Nine. I hate to have hashed the job up so; especially since I had one chance in two of guessing right.'

'Well, no use squawking now...' Kinnison paused in thought. 'Besides, he could have done it anyway, and would have. You haven't done too badly, at that. You found a Black Lensman who isn't a Kalonian, and you've got confirmation of Boskonian interest in Lyrane Nine. What more do you want? Stick around fairly close to the Hell-Hole, Slim, and as soon as I can make it, I'll join you there.'

20
Kinnison and the Black Lensman

'Boys, take her upstairs,' Kinnison-Thyron ordered, and the tremendous raider – actually the *Dauntless* in disguise – floated serenely upward to a station immediately astern of Mendonai's flagship. All three courses of multi-ply defensive screen were out, as were full-coverage spy-ray blocks and thought-screens.

As the fleet blasted in tight formation for Kalonia III, Boskonian experts tested the *Dauntless'* defenses thoroughly, and found them bottle-tight. No intrusion was possible. The only open channel was to Thyron's plate, which was so villainously fogged that nothing could be seen except Thyron's face. Convinced at last of that fact, Mendonai sat back and seethed quietly; his pervasive Kalonian blueness pointing up his grim and vicious mood.

He had never, in all his life, been insulted so outrageously. Was there anything – *anything!* – he could do about it? There was not. Thyron, personally, he could not touch – yet – and the fact that the outlaw had so brazenly and so nonchalantly placed his vessel in the exact center of the Boskonian fleet made it pellucidly clear to any Boskonian mind that he had nothing whatever to fear from that fleet.

Wherefore the Kalonian seethed, and his minions stepped ever more softly and followed with ever-increasing punctilio the rigid Boskonian code. For the grapevine carries news swiftly; by this time the whole fleet knew that His Nibs had been taking a God-awful kicking around, and the first guy who gave him an excuse to blow his stack would be lucky if he only got skinned alive.

As the fleet spread out for inert maneuvering above the Kalonian atmosphere, Kinnison turned again to the young Lensman.

'One last word, Frank. I'm sure everything's covered – a lot of smart people worked on this problem. Nevertheless, something may happen, so I'll send you the data as fast as I get it. Remember what I told you before – if I get the dope we need, I'm expendable and it'll be your job to get it back to Base. No heroics. Is that clear?'

'Yes, sir.' The young Lensman gulped. 'I hope, though, that it doesn't . . .'

'So do I,' Kinnison grinned as he climbed into his highly special dureum armor, 'and the chances are a million to one that it won't. That's why I'm going down there.'

In their respective speedsters Kinnison and Mendonai made the long drop to ground, and side by side they went into the office of Black Lensman Melasnikov. That worthy, too, wore heavy armor; but he did not have a mechanical thought-screen. With his terrific power of mind, he did not need one. Thyron, of course, did; a fact of which Melasnikov became instantly aware.

'Release your screen,' he directed, bruskly.

'Not yet, pal – don't be so hasty,' Thyron advised. 'Some things about this here hook-up don't exactly click. We got a little talking to do before I open up.'

'No talk, worm. Talk, especially your talk, is meaningless. From you I want, and will have, the truth, and not talk. CUT THOSE SCREENS!'

And lovely Kathryn, in her speedster not too far away, straightened up and sent out a call.

'Kit – Kay – Cam – Con . . . are you free?' They were, for the moment. 'Stand by, please, all of you. I'm pretty sure something is going to happen. Dad can handle this Melasnikov easily enough, if none of the higher-ups step in, but they probably will. Their Lensmen are probably important enough to rate protection. Check?'

'Check.'

'So, as soon as dad begins to get the best of the argument, the protector will step in,' Kathryn continued, 'and whether I can handle him alone or not depends on how high a higher up they send in. So I'd like to have you all stand by for a minute or two, just in case.'

How different was Kathryn's attitude now than it had been in the hyperspatial tube! And how well for Civilization that it was!

'Hold it, kids, I've got a thought,' Kit suggested. 'We've never done any teamwork since we learned how to handle heavy stuff, and we'll have to get in some practice sometime. What say we link up on this?'

'Oh yes!' 'Let's do!' 'Take over, Kit!' Three approvals came as one, and:

'QX, Kit,' came Kathryn's less enthusiastic concurrence, a moment later. Naturally enough, she would rather do it alone if she could; but she had to admit that her brother's plan was the better.

Kit laid out the matrix and the four girls came in. There was a brief moment of snuggling and fitting; then each of the Five caught his breath in awe. This was new – brand new. Each had thought himself complete and full; each had supposed that much practice and at least some give-and-take would be necessary before they could work efficiently as a group. But this! This was the supposedly ultimately unattainable – perfection itself! This was UNITY: full; round; complete. No practice was or ever would be necessary. Not one micro-micro-second of doubt or of uncertainty would or ever could exist. This was the UNIT, a thing for which there are no words in any written or spoken language, a thing theretofore undreamed-of save as a purely theoretical concept in an unthinkably ancient, four-ply Arisian brain.

'U-m-n-g-n-k.' Kit swallowed a lump as big as his fist. 'This, kids, is really . . .'

'Ah, children, you have done it.' Mentor's thought rolled smoothly in. 'You now understand why I could not attempt to describe the Unit to any one of you. This is the culminating moment of my life – of our lives, we may now say. For the first time in more years than you can understand, we are at last sure that our lives have not been lived in vain. But attend – that for which you are waiting will soon be here.'

'What is it?' 'Who?' 'Tell us how to . . .'

'We cannot.' Four separate Arisians smiled as one; a wash of ineffable blessing and benediction suffused the Five. 'We who made the Unit possible are almost completely ignorant of the details of its higher functions. But that it will need no help from our lesser minds is certain; it is the most powerful and the most nearly perfect creation this universe has ever seen.'

The Arisian vanished; and, even before Kimball Kinnison had released his screen, a cryptic, utterly untraceable and all-pervasive foreign thought came in.

To aid the Black Lensman? To study this disturbing new element? Or merely to observe? Or what? The only certainty was that that thought was coldly, clearly, and highly inimical to all Civilization.

Again everything happened at once. Karen's impenetrable block flared into being – not instantly, but instantaneously. Constance assembled and hurled, in the same lack of time, a mental bolt of whose size and power she had never been capable. Camilla, the detector-scanner, synchronized with the attacking thought and steered. And Kathryn and Kit, with all the force, all the will, and all the drive of human heredity, got behind it and pushed.

Nor was this, any of it, conscious individual effort. The children of the Lens were not now five, but one. This was the Unit at work; doing its first job. It is literally impossible to describe what happened; but each of the Five knew that one would-be Protector, wherever he had been in space or whenever in time, would never think again. Seconds passed. The Unit held tense, awaiting the riposte. No riposte came.

'Fine work, kids!' Kit broke the linkage and each girl felt hard, brotherly pats on her back. 'That's all there is to this one,

I guess – must have been only one guard on duty. You're good eggs, and I like you – *How* we can operate now!'

'But it was too easy, Kit!' Kathryn protested. 'Too easy by far for it to have been an Eddorian. We aren't that good. Why, I could have handled him alone . . . I think,' she added hastily, as she realized that she, although an essential part of the Unit, had as yet no real understanding of what that Unit really was.

'You *hope*, you mean!' Constance jeered. 'If that bolt was as big and as hot as I'm afraid it was, anything it hit would have looked easy. Why didn't you slow us down, Kit? You're supposed to be the Big Brain, you know. As it was, we haven't the faintest idea of what happened. Who was he, anyway?'

'Didn't have time,' Kit grinned. 'Everything got out of hand. All of us were sort of inebriated by the exuberance of our own enthusiasm, I guess. Now that we know what our speed is, though, we can slow down next time – if we want to. As for your last question, Con, you're asking the wrong guy. Was it Eddorian, Cam, or not?'

'What difference does it make?' Karen asked.

'On the practical side, none. For the completion of the picture, maybe a lot. Come in, Cam.'

'It was not an Eddorian,' Camilla decided. 'It was not of Arisian, or even near-Arisian, grade. Sorry to say it, Kit, but it was another member of that high-thinking race you've already got down on Page One of your little black book.'

'I thought it might be. The missing link between Kalonia and Eddore. Credits to millos it's that dopey planet Ploor Mentor was yowling about. Oh DAMN!'

'Why the capital damn?' asked Constance, brightly. 'Let's link up and let the Unit find it and knock hell out of it. That'd be fun.'

'Act your age, baby,' Kit advised. 'Ploor is taboo – you know that as well as I do. Mentor told us all not to try to investigate it – that we'd learn of it in time, so we probably will. I told him a while back I was going to hunt it up myself, and he told me if I did he'd tie both my legs around my neck in a lovers' knot, or words to that effect. Sometimes I'd like to half-brain the old buzzard, but everything he has said so far has dead-centered the beam. We'll just have to take it, and try to like it.'

Kinnison was eminently willing to cut this thought-screen, since he could not work through it to do what had to be done here. Nor was he over-confident. He knew that he could handle the Black Lensman – *any* Black Lensman – but he also knew enough of mental phenomena in general and of Lensmanship in particular to realize that Melasnikov might very well have within call reserves about whom he, Kinnison, could know nothing. He knew that he had lied outrageously to young Frank in regard to the odds applicable to this enterprise; that instead of a million to one, the actuality was one to one, or even less.

Nevertheless, he was well content. He had neither lied nor exaggerated in saying that he himself was expendable. That was why Frank and the *Dauntless* were upstairs now. Getting the dope and getting it back to Base were what mattered. Nothing else did.

He was coldly certain that he could get all the information that Melasnikov had, once he had engaged the Kalonian Lensman mind to mind. No Boskonian power or thing, he was convinced, could treat him rough enough or kill him fast enough to keep him from doing that. And he could and would shoot the stuff along to Frank as fast as he got it. And he stood an even – almost even, anyway – chance of getting away afterward. If he could, QX. If he couldn't . . . well, that would have to be QX, too.

Kinnison flipped his switch and there ensued a conflict of wills that made the sub-ether boil. The Kalonian was one of the strongest, hardest, and ablest individuals of his hellishly capable race; and the fact that he believed implicitly in his own complete invulnerability operated to double and to quadruple his naturally tremendous strength.

On the other hand, Kimball Kinnison was a Second-Stage Lensman of the Galactic Patrol.

Back and back, then, inch by inch and foot by foot, the

Black Lensman's defensive zone was forced; back to and down into his own mind. And there, appallingly enough, Kinnison found almost nothing of value.

No knowledge of the higher reaches of the Boskonian organization; no hint that any real organization of Black Lensmen existed; only the peculiarly disturbing fact that he had picked up his Lens on Lyrane IX. And 'picked up' was literal. He had not seen, nor heard, nor had any dealings of any kind with anyone while he was there.

Since both armored figures stood motionless, no sign of the tremendous actuality of their mental battle was evident. Thus the Boskonians were not surprised to hear their Black Lensman speak.

'Very well, Thyron, you have passed this preliminary examination. I know all that I now need to know. I will accompany you to your vessel, to complete my investigation there. Lead the way.'

Kinnison did so, and as the speedster came to rest inside the *Dauntless* the Black Lensman addressed Vice-Admiral Mendonai via plate.

'I am taking Bradlow Thyron and his ship to the spaceyards on Four, where a really comprehensive study of it can be made. Return to and complete your original assignment.'

'I abase myself, Your Supremacy, but . . . but I . . . I *discovered* that ship!' Mendonai protested.

'Granted,' the Black Lensman sneered. 'You will be given full credit in my report for what you have done. The fact of discovery, however, does not excuse your present conduct. Go – and consider yourself fortunate that, because of that service, I forbear from disciplining you for your intolerable insubordination.'

'I abase myself, Your Supremacy. I go.' He really did abase himself, this time, and the fleet disappeared.

Then, the mighty *Dauntless* safely away from Kalonia and on her course to rendezvous with the *Velan*, Kinnison again went over his captive's mind; line by line and almost cell by cell. It was still the same. It was still Lyrane IX and it still didn't make any kind of sense. Since Boskonians were certainly not supermen, and hence could not possibly have developed their own Lenses, it followed that they must have obtained them from the Boskonian counterpart of Arisia. Hence, Lyrane IX must be IT – a conclusion which was certainly fallacious. Ridiculous – preposterous – utterly untenable: Lyrane IX never had been, was not, and never would be the home of any Boskonian super-race. Nevertheless, it was a definite fact that Melasnikov had got his Lens there. Also, if he had ever had any special training, such as any Lensman must have had, he didn't have any memory of it. Nor did he carry any scars of surgery. What a hash! How could *anybody* make any sense out of such a mess as that?

Ever-watchful Kathryn, eyes narrowed now in concentration, could have told him, but she did not. Her visualization was beginning to clear up. Lyrane was out. So was Ploor. The Lenses originated on Eddore; that was certain. The fact that their training was subconscious weakened the Black Lensman in precisely the characteristics requisite for ultimate strength – although probably neither the Eddorians nor the Ploorans, with their warped, Boskonian sense of values, realized it. The Black Lensmen would never constitute a serious problem. QX.

Kinnison, having attended to the unpleasant but necessary job of resolving Melasnikov into his component atoms, turned to his Lensman-aide.

'Hold everything, Frank, until I get back. This won't take long.'

Nor did it, although the outcome was not at all what the Grey Lensman had expected.

Kinnison and Worsel, in an inert speedster, crossed the Hell-Hole's barrier web at a speed of only miles per hour, and then slowed down. The ship was backing in on her brakes, with everything set to hurl her forward under full free drive should either Lensman flick a finger. Kinnison could feel nothing, even though, being en rapport with Worsel, he knew that his friend was soon suffering intensely.

'Let's flit,' the Grey Lensman suggested, and threw on the drive. 'I probed my limit, and couldn't touch or feel a thing. Had enough, didn't you?'

'More than enough – I couldn't have taken much more.'

Each boarded his ship; and as the *Dauntless* and the *Velan* tore through space toward far Lyrane, Kinnison paced his room, scowling in black abstraction. Nor would a mind-reader have found his thoughts either cogent or informative.

'Lyrane Nine... *Lyrane* Nine... Lyrane *Nine*... *LYRANE NINE*... and something I can't feel or sense or perceive that kills anybody and everybody else... KLONO'S tungsten TEETH and CURVING CARBALLOY CLAWS!!!'

21
The Red Lensman on Lyrane

Helen's story was short and bitter. Human or near-human Boskonians came to Lyrane II and spread insidious propaganda all over the planet. Lyranian matriarchy should abandon its policy of isolationism. Matriarchs were the highest type of life. Matriarchy was the most perfect of all existing forms of government – why keep on confining it to one small planet, when it should by rights be ruling the entire galaxy? The way things were, there was only one Elder Person; all other Lyranians, even though better qualified than the then incumbent, were nothing... and so on. Whereas, if things were as they should be, each individual Lyranian person could be and would be the Elder Person of a planet at least, and perhaps of an entire solar system... and so on. And the visitors, who, they insisted, were no more males than the Lyranian persons were females, would teach them. They would be amazed at how easily, under Boskonian guidance, this program could be put into effect.

Helen fought the intruders with everything she had. She despised the males of her own race; she detested those of all others. Believing hers to be the only existing matriarchal race, especially since neither Kinnison nor the Boskonians seemed to know of any other, she was sure that any prolonged contact with other cultures would result, not in the triumph of matriarchy, but in its fall. She not only voiced these beliefs as she held them – violently – but also acted upon them in the same fashion.

Because of the ingrained matriarchially conservative habit

of Lyranian thought, particularly among the older persons, Helen found it comparatively easy to stamp out the visible manifestations; and, being in no sense a sophisticate, she thought the whole matter settled. Instead, she merely drove the movement underground, where it grew tremendously. The young, of course, rebellious as always against the hidebound, mossbacked, and reactionary older generation, joined the sub-terranean New Deal in droves. Nor was the older generation solid. In fact, it was riddled by the defection of many thousands who could not expect to attain any outstanding place in the world as it was and who believed that the Boskonians' glittering forecasts would come true.

Disaffection spread, then, rapidly and unobserved; culminat-ing in the carefully-planned uprising which made Helen an ex-queen and put her under restraint to await a farcical trial and death.

'I see.' Clarrissa caught her lower lip between her teeth. 'Very unfunny... You didn't mention or think of any of your persons as ringleaders... peculiar that you couldn't catch them, with your telepathy... no, natural enough, at that... but there's one I want very much to get hold of. Don't know whether she was really a leader, or not, but she was mixed up in some way with a Boskonian Lensman. I never did know her name. She was the wom— the person who managed your airport here when Kim and I were...'

'Cleonie? Why, I never thought... but it might have, at that... yes, as I look back...'

'Yes, hindsight *is* a lot more accurate than foresight,' the Red Lensman grinned. 'I've noticed that myself, lots of times.'

'It *did!* It *was* a leader!' Helen declared, furiously. 'I shall have its life, too, the damned, jealous cat – the blood-sucking, back-biting *louse!*'

'She's all of that, in more ways than you know,' Clarrissa agreed, grimly, and spread in the Lyranian's mind the story of Eddie the derelict. 'So you see that Cleonie has got to be our starting-point. Have you any idea of where we can find her?'

'I haven't seen or heard anything of Cleonie lately.' Helen paused in thought. 'If, though, as I am now almost certain, it was one of the prime movers behind this brainless brat Ladora, it wouldn't dare leave the planet for very long at a time. As to how to find it, I don't quite know... Anybody would be apt to shoot me on sight... would you dare fly this funny plane of yours down close to a few of our cities?'

'Certainly. I don't know of anything around here that my screens and fields can't stop. Why?'

'Because I know of several places where Cleonie might be, and if I can get fairly close to them, I can find it in spite of anything it can do to hide itself from me. But I don't want to get you into too much trouble, and I don't want to get killed myself, either, now that you have rescued me – at least, until after I have killed Cleonie and Ladora.'

'QX. What are you waiting for? Which way, Helen?'

'Back to the city first, for several reasons. Cleonie probably is not there, but we must make sure. Also, I want my guns...'

'Guns? No. DeLameters are better. I have several spares.' In one fleeting mental contact Clarrissa taught the Lyranian all there was to know about DeLameters. And that feat impressed Helen even more than did the nature and power of the weapon.

'What a mind!' she exclaimed. 'You didn't have any such equipment as that, the last time I saw you. Or were you – no, you weren't hiding it.'

'You're right; I have developed considerably since then. But about guns – what do you want of one?'

'To kill that nitwit Ladora on sight, and that snake Cleonie, too, as soon as you get done with it.'

'But why guns? Why not the mental force you always used?'

'Except by surprise, I couldn't,' Helen admitted, frankly. 'All adult persons are of practically equal mental strength. But speaking of strength, I marvel that a craft as small as this should be able to ward off the attack of one of those tremendous Boskonian ships of space...'

'But she *can't!* What made you think she could?'

'Your own statement – or were you thinking of purely Lyranian dangers, not realizing that Ladora of course called Cleonie as soon as you showed your teeth, and that Cleonie as surely called the Lensman or some other Boskonian? And that they must have ships of war not too far away?'

'Heavens, no! It never occurred to me!'

Clarrissa thought briefly. It wouldn't do any good to call Kim. Both the *Dauntless* and the *Velan* were coming as fast as they could, but it would be a day or so yet before they arrived. Besides, he would tell her to lay off, which was exactly what she was not going to do. She turned her thought back to the matriarch.

'Two of our best ships are coming, and I hope they get here first. In the meantime, we'll just have to work fast and keep our detectors full out. Anyway, Cleonie won't know that I'm looking for her – I haven't even mentioned her to anyone except you.'

'No?' pessimistically. 'Cleonie knows that *I* am looking for it, and since it knows by now that I am with you, it would think that both of us were hunting it even if we weren't. But we are nearly close enough now; I must concentrate. Fly around quite low over the city, please.'

'QX. I'll tune in with you too. "Two heads", you know.' Clarrissa learned Cleonie's pattern, tuned to it, and combed the city while Helen was getting ready.

'She isn't here, unless she's behind one of those thought-screens,' the Red Lensman remarked. 'Can you tell?'

'Thought-screens! The Boskonians had a few of them, but none of us ever did. How can you find them? Where are they?'

'One there – two over there. They stick out like big black spots on a white screen. Can't you see them? I supposed your scanners were the same as mine, but apparently they aren't. Take a quick peek at them with the spy – you work it like so. If they've got spy-ray blocks up, too, we'll have to go down there and blast.'

'Politicians only,' Helen reported, after a moment's manipulation of the suddenly familiar instrument. 'They need killing, of course, on general principles, but perhaps we shouldn't take time for that now. The next place to look is a few degrees east of north of here.'

Cleonie was not, however, in that city. Nor in the next, nor the next. But the speedster's detector screens remained blank and the two allies, so much alike physically, so different mentally, continued their hunt. There was opposition, of course – all that the planet afforded – but Clarrissa's Second-Stage mind took care of the few items of offense which her speedster's defenses could not handle.

Finally two things happened almost at once. Clarrissa found Cleonie, and Helen saw a dim and fuzzy white spot upon the lower left-hand corner of the detector plate.

'Can't be ours,' the Red Lensman decided instantly. 'Almost exactly the wrong direction. Boskonians. Ten minutes – twelve at most – before we have to flit. Time enough – I hope – if we work fast.'

She shot downward, going inert and matching intrinsics at a lack of altitude which would have been suicidal for any ordinary pilot. She rammed her beryllium-bronze torpedo through the first-floor wall of a forbidding, almost window-less building – its many stories of massive construction, she knew, would help no end against the heavy stuff so sure to come. Then, while every hitherto-hidden offensive arm of the Boskone-coached Lyranians converged, screaming through the air and crashing and clanking along the city's streets, Clarrissa probed and probed and probed. Cleonie had locked herself into a veritable dungeon cell in the deepest sub-basement of the structure. She was wearing a thought-screen, too, but she had been releasing it, for an instant at a time, to see what was going on. One of those instants was enough – that screen would never work again. She had been prepared to kill herself at need; but her full-charged weapons emptied themselves futilely against a massive lock and she threw her vial of poison across the corridor and into an empty cell.

So far, so good; but how to get her out of there? Physical approach was out of the question. There must be somebody around, somewhere, with keys, or hack-saws, or sledge-hammers, or something. Ha – oxyacetylene torches! Very much against their wills, two Lyranian mechanics trundled a dolly along a corridor, into an elevator. The elevator went down four levels; the artisans began to burn away a barrier of thick steel bars.

By this time the whole building was rocking to the detonation of high explosive. Much more of that kind of stuff and she would be trapped by the sheer mass of the rubble. She was handling six jackass-stubborn people already and that Boskonian warship was coming fast; she did not quite know whether she was going to get away with this or not.

But somehow, from the unplumbed and unplumbable depths which made her what she so uniquely was, the Red Lensman drew more and ever more power. Kinnison, who had once made heavy going of handling two-and-a-fraction Lensman, guessed, but never did learn from her, what his beloved wife really did that day.

Even Helen, only a few feet away, could not understand what was happening. Left parsecs behind long since, the Lyranian could not help in any particular, but could only stand and wonder. She knew that this queerly powerful Lens-bearing Earth-person – white-faced, sweating, strung to the very snapping-point as she sat motionless at her board – was exerting some terrible, some tremendous force. She knew that the heaviest of the circling bombers sheered away and crashed. She knew that certain mobile projectors, a few blocks away, did not come any closer. She knew that Cleonie, against every iota of her mulish Lyranian will, was coming toward the speedster. She knew that many persons, who wished intensely to bar Cleonie's progress or to shoot her down, were physically unable to act. She had no faint idea, however, of how such work could possibly be done.

Cleonie came aboard and Clarrissa snapped out of her trance. The speedster nudged and blasted its way out of the wrecked stronghold, then tore a hole through protesting air into open space. Clarrissa shook her head, wiped her face, studied a tiny dot in the corner of the plate opposite the one now showing clearly the Boskonian warship, and set her controls.

'We'll make it – I think,' she announced. 'Even though we're indetectable, they of course know our line, and they're so much faster that they'll be able to find us on their visuals before long. On the other hand, they must be detecting our ships now, and my guess is that they won't dare follow us long enough to do us any harm. Keep an eye on things, Helen, while I find out what Cleonie really knows. And while I think of it, what's your real name? It isn't polite to keep on calling you by a name that you never even heard of until you met us.'

'Helen,' the Lyranian made surprising answer. 'I liked it, so I adopted it – officially.'

'Oh... That's a compliment, really, to both Kim and me. Thanks.'

The Red Lensman then turned her attention to her captive, and as mind fitted itself precisely to mind her eyes began to gleam in gratified delight. Cleonie was a real find; this seemingly unimportant Lyranian knew a lot – an immense lot – about things that no adherent of the Patrol had ever heard before. And she, Clarrissa Kinnison, would be the first of all the Grey Lensmen to learn of them! Therefore, taking her time now, she allowed every detail of the queer but fascinating picture-story-history to imprint itself upon her mind.

And Karen and Camilla, together in Tregonsee's ship, glanced at each other and exchanged flashing thoughts. Should they interfere? They hadn't had to so far, but it began to look as though they might have to, now – it would wreck their mother's mind, if she could understand. She probably could not understand it, any more than Cleonie could – but even if she could, she had so much more inherent stability, even than dad, that she might be able to take it, at that. Nor would she ever leak, even to dad – and he, bless his tremendous boots, was not the type to pry. Maybe, though, just to be on the safe side, it would be better to screen the stuff, and to edit it a little if necessary.

The two girls synchronized their minds all imperceptibly with their mother's and Cleonie's, and 'listened'.

The time was in the unthinkably distant past; the location was unthinkably remote in space. A huge planet circled slowly about a cooling sun. Its atmosphere was not air; its liquid was not water. Both were noxious; composed in large part of compounds known to man only in his chemical laboratories.

Yet life was there; a race which was even then ancient. Not sexual, this race. Not androgynous, nor hermaphroditic, but absolutely sexless. Except for the many who died by physical or mental violence, its members lived endlessly: after hundreds of thousands of years each being, having reached his capacity to live and to learn, divided into two individuals; each of which, although possessing in toto the parent's memories, knowledges, skills, and powers, had also a renewed and increased capacity.

And, since life was, there had been competition. Competition for power. Knowledge was desirable only insofar as it contributed to power. Power for the individual – the group – the city. Wars raged – *what* wars! – and internecine strifes which lasted while planets came into being, grew old, and died. And finally, to the survivors, there came peace. Since they could not kill each other, they combined their powers and hurled them outward – together they would dominate and rule solar systems – regions – the Galaxy itself – the entire macrocosmic universe!

More and more they used their minds, to bring across gulfs of space and to enslave other races, to labor under their direction. By nature and by choice they were bound to their own planet; few indeed were the planets upon which their race could possibly live. Thus, then, they lived and ruled by proxy, through echelon after echelon of underlings, an ever-increasing number of worlds.

Although they had long since learned that their asexuality was practically unique, that sexual life dominated the universe, this knowledge served only to stiffen their determination not only to rule the universe, but also to change its way of life to conform with their own. They were still seeking a better proxy race; the more nearly asexual a race, the better. The Kalonians, whose women had only one function in life – the production of men – approached that ideal.

Now these creatures had learned of the matriarchs of Lyrane. That they were physically females meant nothing; to the Eddorians one sex was just as good – or as bad – as any other. The Lyranians were strong; not tainted by the weaknesses which seemed to characterize all races believing in even near-equality of the sexes. Lyranian science had been trying for centuries to do away with the necessity for males; in a few more generations, with some help, that goal could be achieved and the perfect proxy race would have been developed.

This story was not obtained in any such straightforward fashion as it is presented here. It was dim, murky, confused. Cleonie never had understood it. Clarrissa understood it somewhat better: that unnamed and as yet unknown race was the highest of Boskone, and the place of the Kalonians in the Boskonian scheme was at long last clear.

'I am giving you this story,' the Kalonian Lensman told Cleonie coldly, 'not of my own free will but because I must. I hate you as much as you hate me. What I would like to do to you, you may imagine. Nevertheless, so that your race may have its chance, I am to take you on a trip and, if possible, make a Lensman out of you. Come with me.' And, urged by her jealousy of Helen, her seething ambition, and probably, if the truth were to be known, by an Eddorian mind, Cleonie went.

There is no need to dwell at length upon the horrors, the atrocities, of that trip; of which the matter of Eddie the meteor-miner was only a very minor episode. It will suffice to say that Cleonie was very good Boskonian material; that she learned fast and passed all tests successfully.

'That's all,' the Black Lensman informed her then, 'and I'm glad to see the last of you. You'll get a message when to hop over to Nine and pick up your Lens. Flit – and I hope the first

Grey Lensman you meet rams his Lens down your throat and turns you inside out.'

'The same to you, brother, and soon,' Cleonie sneered. 'Or, better, when my race supplants yours as Proxies of Power, I shall give myself the pleasure of doing just that to you.'

'Clarrissa! Clarrissa! Pay attention, please!' The Red Lensman came to herself with a start – Helen had been thinking at her, with increasing power, for seconds. The *Velan*'s image filled half the plate.

In minutes, then, Clarrissa and her party were in Kinnison's private quarters in the *Dauntless*. There had been warm mental greetings; physical demonstrations would come later. Worsel broke in.

'Excuse it, Kim, but seconds count. Better we split, don't you think? You find out what the score around here is, from Clarrissa, and take steps, and I'll chase that damn Boskonian. He's flitting – fast.'

'QX, Slim,' and the *Velan* disappeared.

'You remember Helen, of course, Kim.' Kinnison bent his head, flipping a quick grin at his wife, who had spoken aloud. The Lyranian, trying to unbend, half-offered her hand, but when he did not take it she withdrew it as enthusiastically as she had twenty years before. 'And this is Cleonie, the . . . the wench I've been telling you about. You knew her before.'

'Yeah. She hasn't changed much, either – still as unbarbered a mess as ever. If you've got what you want, Cris, we'd better . . .'

'Kimball Kinnison, I demand Cleonie's life!' came Helen's vibrant thought. She had snatched one of Clarrissa's DeLameters and was swinging it into line when she was caught and held as though in a vise.

'Sorry, Toots,' The Grey Lensman's thought was more than a little grim. 'Nice little girls don't play so rough. 'Scuse me, Cris, for dipping into your dish. Take over.'

'Do you really mean that, Kim?'

'Yes. It's your meat – slice it as thick or as thin as you please.'

'Even to letting her go?'

'Check. What else could you *do*? In a lifeboat – I'll even show the jade how to run it.'

'Oh ... Kim ...'

'Quartermaster! Kinnison. Please check Number Twelve lifeboat and break it out. I am loaning it to Cleonie of Lyrane II.'

22
Kit Invades Eddore; and—

Kit had decided long since that it was his job to scout the planet Eddore. His alone. He had told several people that he was en route there, and in a sense he had been, but he was not hurrying. Once he started *that* job, he would have to see it through with absolutely undisturbed attention, and there had been altogether too many other things popping up. Now, however, his visualization showed a couple of weeks of free time, and that would be enough. He wasn't sure whether he was grown-up enough yet to do a man's job of work or not, and Mentor wouldn't tell him. This was the best way to find out. If so, QX. If not, he would back off, wait and try again later.

The kids had wanted to go along, of course.

'Come on, Kit, don't be a pig!' Constance started what developed into the last violent argument of their long lives. 'Let's gang up on it – think what a grand work-out that would be for the Unit!'

'Uh-uh, Con. Sorry, but it isn't in the cards, any more than it was the last time we discussed it,' he began, reasonably enough.

'We didn't agree to it then,' Kay cut in, stormily, 'and I for one am not going to agree to it now. You don't have to do it today. In fact, later on would be better. Anyway, Kit, I'm telling you right now that if you go in, we all go, as individuals if not as the Unit.'

'Act your age, Kay,' he advised. 'Get conscious. This is one of the two places in the universe that can't be worked from a distance, and by the time you could get here I'll have the job done. So what difference does it make whether you agree or not? I'm going in now and I'm going in alone. Pick *that* one out of your pearly teeth!'

That stopped Karen, cold – they all knew that even she would not endanger the enterprise by staging a useless demonstration against Eddore's defensive screens – but there were other arguments. Later, he was to come to see that his sisters had some right upon their side, but he could not see it then. None of their ideas would hold air, he declared, and his temper wore thinner and thinner.

'No, Cam – NO! You know as well as I do that we can't all be spared at once, either now or at any time in the near-enough future. Kay's full of pickles, and you all know it. Right now is the best time I'll ever have . . .

'Seal it, Kat – you can't be that dumb! Taking the Unit in would blow things wide open. There isn't a chance that I can get in, even alone, without touching *something* off. I, alone, won't be giving too much away, but the Unit would be a flare-lit tip-off and all hell would be out for noon. Or are you actually nit-witted enough to think, all Arisia to the contrary, that we're ready for the grand show-down? . . .

'Hold it, all of you! Pipe down!' he snorted, finally. 'Have I got to bash in your skulls to make you understand that I can't coordinate an attack against something without even the foggiest idea of what it is? Use your brains, kids – *please* use your brains!'

He finally won them over, even Karen; and while his speed-ster covered the last leg of the flight he completed his analysis.

He had all the information he could get – in fact, all that was available – and it was pitifully meager and confusingly contradictory in detail. He knew the Arisians, each of them, personally; and had studied, jointly and severally, the Arisian visualizations of the ultimate foe. He knew the Lyranian impression of the Plooran version of the story of Eddore . . . Ploor! Merely a name. A symbol which Mentor had always kept rigorously apart from any Boskonian actuality . . . Ploor *must* be the missing link between Kalonia and Eddore . . . and he knew practically everything about it except the two really important facts – whether or not it really was that link, and where, within eleven thousand million parsecs, it was in space!

He and his sisters had done their best. So had many librarians; who had found, not at all to his surprise, that no scrap of information or conjecture concerning Eddore or the Eddorians was to be found in any library, however comprehensive or exclusive.

Thus he had guesses, hypotheses, theories, and visualizations galore; but none of them agreed and not one of them was convincing. He had no real facts whatever. Mentor had informed him, equably enough, that such a state of affairs was inevitable because of the known power of the Eddorian mind. That state, however, did not make Kit Kinnison any too happy as he approached dread and dreaded Eddore. He was in altogether too much of a dither as to what, actually, to expect.

As he neared the boundary of the star-cluster within which Eddore lay, he cut his velocity to a crawl. An outer screen, he knew, surrounded the whole cluster. How many intermediate protective layers existed, where they were, or what they were like, nobody knew. That information was only a small part of what he had to have.

His far-flung detector web, at practically zero power, touched the barrier without giving alarm and stopped. His speedster stopped. Everything stopped.

Christopher Kinnison, the matrix and the key element of the Unit, had tools and equipment about which even Mentor of Arisia knew nothing in detail; about which, it was hoped and believed, the Eddorians were completely in ignorance. He reached deep into the storehouse-toolbox of his mind, arranged his selections in order, and went to work.

He built up his detector web, one infinitesimal increment at a time, until he could just perceive the structure of the barrier. He made no attempt to analyze it, knowing that any fabric or structure solid enough to perform such an operation would certainly touch off an alarm. Analysis could come later, after he had found out whether the generator of this outer screen was a machine or a living brain.

He felt his way along the barrier; slowly – carefully. He completely outlined one section, studying the fashion in which the joints were made and how it must be supported and operated. With the utmost nicety of which he was capable he synchronized a probe with the almost impossibly complex structure of the thing and slid it along a feederbeam into the generator station. A mechanism – they didn't waste live Eddorians, then, any more than the Arisians did, on outer defenses. QX.

A precisely-tuned blanket surrounded his speedster – a blanket which merged imperceptibly into, and in effect became an integral part of, the barrier itself. The blanket thinned over half of the speedster. The speedster crept forward. The barrier – unchanged, unaffected – was *behind* the speedster. Man and vessel were through!

Kit breathed deeply in relief and rested. This didn't prove much, of course. Nadreck had done practically the same thing in getting Kandron – except that the Palainian would never be able to analyze or to synthesize such screens as these. The real test would come later; but this had been mighty good practice.

The real test came with the fifth, the innermost screen. The others, while of ever-increasing sensitivity, complexity, and power, were all generated mechanically, and hence posed problems differing only in degree, and not in kind, from that of the first. The fifth problem, however, involving a living and highly capable brain, differed in both degree and kind from the others. The Eddorian would be sensitive to form and to shape, as well as to interference. Bulges were out, unless he could do something about the Eddorian – and the speedster couldn't go through a screen without making a bulge.

Furthermore, this zone had visual and electromagnetic detectors, so spaced as not to let a microbe through. There were fortresses, maulers, battleships, and their attendant lesser craft. There were projectors, and mines, and automatic torpedoes with super-atomic warheads, and other such things.

Were these things completely dependent upon the Eddorian guardian, or not?

They were not. The officers – Kalonians for the most part – would go into action at the guardian's signal, of course; but they could at need act without instructions. A nice set-up – a mighty hard nut to crack! He would have to use zones of compulsion. Nothing else would do.

Picking out the biggest fortress in the neighborhood, with its correspondingly large field of coverage, he insinuated his mind into that of one observing officer after another. When he left, a few minutes later, he knew that none of those officers would initiate any action in response to the alarms which he would so soon set off. They were alive, fully conscious, alert; and would have resented bitterly any suggestion that they were not completely normal in every respect. Nevertheless, whatever colors the lights flashed, whatever pictures the plates revealed, whatever noises blared from the speakers, in their consciousnesses would be only blankness and silence. Nor would recorder tapes reveal later what had occurred. An instrument cannot register fluctuations when its movable member is controlled by a couple of steady fingers.

Then the Eddorian. To take over his whole mind was, Kit knew, beyond his present power. A partial zone, though, could be set up – and young Kinnison's mind had been developed specifically to perform the theretofore impossible. Thus the guardian, without suspecting it, suffered an attack of partial blindness which lasted for the fraction of a second necessary for the speedster to flash through the screen. And there was no recorder to worry about. Eddorians, never sleeping and never relaxing their vigilance, had no doubt whatever of their own capabilities and needed no checks upon their own performances.

Christopher Kinnison, Child of the Lens, was inside Eddore's innermost defensive sphere. For countless cycles of time the Arisians had been working toward and looking forward to the chain of events of which this was the first link. Nor would he have much time here: he would have known that even if Mentor had not so stressed the point. As long as he did nothing he was safe; but as soon as he started sniffing around he would be open to detection and some Eddorian would climb his frame in mighty short order. Then blast and lock on – he might get something, or a lot, or nothing at all. Then – win, lose, or draw – he had to get away. Strictly under his own power, against an unknown number of the most powerful and the most ruthless entities ever to live. The Arisian couldn't get in here to help him, and neither could the kids. Nobody could. It was strictly and solely up to him.

For more than a moment his spirit failed. The odds against him were far too long. The load was too heavy; he didn't have half enough jets to swing it. Just how did a guy as smart as Mentor figure it that he, a dumb, green kid, stood a Zabriskan fontema's chance against all Eddore?

He was scared, scared to the core of his being; scared as he never had been before and never would be again. His mouth felt dry, his tongue cottony. His fingers shook, even as he doubled them into fists to steady them. To the very end of his long life he remembered the fabric and the texture of that fear; remembered how it made him decide to turn back, before it was too late to retrace his way as unobserved as he had come.

Well, why not? Who would care, and what matter? The Arisians? Nuts! It was all their fault, sending him in half-ready. His parents? They wouldn't know what the score was, and wouldn't care. They'd be on his side, no matter what_happened. The kids? ... The *kids*! ... Oh-oh – THE KIDS!

They'd tried to talk him out of coming in alone. They'd fought like wildcats to make him take them along. He'd smacked 'em down. Now, if he sneaked back with his tail between his legs, how'd they take it? What'd they do? What would they *think*? Then, later, after he had loused everything up and let the Arisians and the Patrol and all Civilization get knocked out – then what? The kids would know exactly how and why it had happened. He couldn't defend himself, even if he tried, and he wouldn't try. Did he have any idea how much sheer, vitriolic, corrosive contempt those four red-headed sisters of his could generate? Or, even if they didn't – or as a follow-up – their condescending, sisterly pity would be a thousand million times worse. And what would he think of himself? No soap. It was out. Definitely. The Eddorians could kill him only once. QX.

He drove straight downward, noting as he did so that his senses were clear, his hands steady, his tongue normally moist. He was still scared, but he was no longer paralysed.

Low enough, he let his every perceptive sense roam abroad – and became instantly too busy to worry about anything. There was an immense amount of new stuff here – if he could only be granted time enough to get it all!

He wasn't. In a second or so, it seemed, his interference was detected and an Eddorian came in to investigate. Kit threw everything he had, and in the brief moment before the completely surprised denizen died, the young Klovian learned more of the real truth of Eddore and of the whole Boskonian Empire than all the Arisians had ever found out. In that one flash of ultimately intimate fusion, he *knew* Eddorian history, practically in toto. He knew the enemies' culture; he knew how they behaved, and why. He knew their ideals and their ideologies. He knew a great deal about their organization; their systems of offense and of defense. He knew their strengths and, more important, their weaknesses. He knew exactly how, if Civilization were to triumph at all, its victory must be achieved.

This seems – or rather, it is – incredible. It is, however, simple truth. Under such stresses as those, an Eddorian mind can yield, and the mind of such a one as Christopher Kinnison can absorb, an incredible amount of knowledge in an incredibly brief interval of time.

Kit, already seated at his controls, cut in his every course of thought-screen. They would help a little in what was coming, but not much – no mechanical screen then known to Civilization could block third-level thought. He kicked in full drive toward the one small area in which he and his speedster would not encounter either beams or bombs – the fortress whose observers would not perceive that anything was amiss.

He did not fear physical pursuit, since his speedster was the fastest thing in space.

For a second or so it was not so bad. Another Eddorian came in, suspicious and on guard. Kit blasted him down – learning still more in the process – but he could not prevent him from radiating a frantic and highly revealing call for help. And although the Eddorians could scarcely realize that such an astonishing thing as physical invasion had actually happened, that fact neither slowed them down nor made their anger less violent.

When Kit flashed past his friendly fortress he was taking about all he could handle, and more and more Eddorians were piling on. At the fourth screen it was worse; at the third he reached what he was sure was his absolute ceiling. Nevertheless, from some hitherto unsuspected profundity of his being, he managed to draw enough reserve force to endure that hellish punishment for a little while longer.

Hang on, Kit, hang on! Only two more screens to go. Maybe only one. Maybe less. Living Eddorian brains, and not mechanical generators, are now handling all the screens, of course; but if the Arisians' visualization is worth a tinker's damn, they must have that first screen knocked down by this time and must be working on the second. Hang on, Kit, and keep on slugging!

And grimly; doggedly; toward the end sheerly desperately: Christopher Kinnison, eldest Child of the Lens, hung on and slugged.

23
—Escapes With His Life

If the historian has succeeded in his attempt to describe the characters and abilities concerned, it is not necessary to enlarge upon what Kit went through in escaping Eddore. If he has not succeeded, enlargement would be useless. Therefore it is enough to say that the young Lensman, by dint of calling up and putting out everything he had, hung on long enough and slugged his way through.

Arisia had acted precisely on time. The Eddorian guardians had scarcely taken over the first screen when it was overwhelmed by a tremendous wave of Arisian thought. It is to be remembered, however, that this was not the first time that the massed might of Arisia had been thrown against Eddore's defenses, and the Eddorians had learned much, during the intervening years, from their exhaustive analyses of the offensive and defensive techniques of the Arisians. Thus the Arisian drive was practically stopped at the second zone of defense as Kit approached it. The screen was wavering, shifting; yielding stubbornly wherever it must and springing back into place whenever it could.

Under a tremendous concentration of Arisian force the screen weakened in a limited area directly ahead of the hurtling speedster. A few beams lashed out aimlessly, uselessly – if the Eddorians could not hold their main screens proof against the power of the Arisian attack, how could they protect such minor things as gunners' minds? The little ship flashed through the weakened barrier and into the center of a sphere of impenetrable, impermeable Arisian thought.

At the shock of the sudden ending of his terrific battle –
the instantaneous transition from supreme to zero effort – Kit
fainted in his control chair. He lay slumped, inert, in a stupor
which changed gradually into a deep and natural sleep. And as
the sleeping man in his inertialess speedster traversed space at
full touring blast, that peculiar sphere of force still enveloped
and still protected him.

Kit finally began to come to. His first foggy thought was
that he was hungry – then, wide awake and remembering, he
grabbed his levers.

'Rest quietly, youth, and eat your fill,' a grave, resonant
pseudo-voice assured him. 'Everything is exactly as it should
be.'

'Hi, Ment ... well, well, if it isn't my old chum Eukonidor!
Hi, young fellow! What's the good word? And what's the big
idea of letting – or making – me sleep for a week when there's
work to do?'

'Your part of the work, at least for the immediate present,
is done; and, let me say, very well done.'

'Thanks ... but ...' Kit broke off, flushing darkly.

'Do not reproach yourself, youth, nor us. Consider, please,
and recite, the manufacture of a fine tool of ultimate quality.'

'The correct alloy. Hot working – perhaps cold, too. Forging
– heating – quenching – drawing ...'

'Enough, youth. Think you that the steel, if sentient, would
enjoy those treatments? While you did not enjoy them, you are
able to appreciate their necessity. You are now a finished tool,
forged and tempered.'

'Oh ... you may have something there, at that. But as to
ultimate quality, don't make me laugh.' There was no nuance
of merriment in Kit's thought. 'You can't square that with
cowardice.'

'Nor is there need. The term ultimate was used advisedly,
and still stands. It does not mean or imply, however, a state
of perfection, since that condition is unattainable. I am not
advising you to try to forget; nor am I attempting to force
forgetfulness upon you, since your mind cannot now be coerced

by any force at my command. Be assured that nothing that occurred should irk you; for the simple truth is, that although stressed as no other mind has ever before been stressed, you did not yield. Instead, you secured and retained information which we of Arisia have never been able to obtain; information which will in fact be the means of preserving your Civilization.'

'I can't believe ... that is, it doesn't seem ...' Kit, knowing that he was thinking muddily and foolishly, paused and pulled himself together. Overwhelming, almost paralyzing as that information was, it must be true. It *was* true!

'Yes, youth, it is the truth. While we of Arisia have at various times made ambiguous statements, to lead certain Lensmen and others to arrive at erroneous conclusions, you know that we do not lie.'

'Yes, I know that.' Kit plumbed the Arisian's mind. 'It sort of knocks me out of my orbit – that's an awfully big bite to swallow at one gulp, you know.'

'It is. That is one reason I am here, to convince you of the truth, which you would not otherwise believe fully. Also to see to it that your rest, without which you might have taken hurt, was not disturbed; as well as to make sure that you were not permanently damaged by the Eddorians.'

'I wasn't ... at least, I don't think so ... was I?'

'You were not.'

'Good. I was wondering ... Mentor will be tied up for a while, of course, so I'll ask you ... They must have got a sort of pattern of me, in spite of all I could do, and they'll be camping on my trail from now on. So I suppose I'll have to keep a solid block up all the time?'

'They will not, Christopher, and you need not. Guided by those whom you know as Mentor, I myself am to see to that. But time presses – I must rejoin my fellows.'

'One more question first. You've been trying to sell me a bill of goods I'd certainly like to buy. But damn it, Eukonidor, the kids will know that I showed a streak of yellow a meter wide. What will *they think*?'

'Is *that* all?' Eukonidor's thought was almost a laugh. 'They will make that eminently plain in a moment.'

The Arisian's presence vanished, as did his sphere of force, and four clamoring thoughts came jamming in.

'Oh, Kit, we're *so* glad!' 'We *tried* to help, but they wouldn't let us!' 'They smacked us down!' '*Honestly,* Kit!' '*Oh,* if we'd *only* been in there, too!'

'Hold it, everybody! Jet back!' This was Con, Kit knew, but an entirely new Con. 'Scan him, Cam, as you never scanned anything before. If they burned out even one cell of his mind I'm going to hunt Mentor up right now and kick his cursed teeth out one by one!'

'And listen, Kit!' This was an equally strange Kathryn; blazing with fury and yet suffusing his mind with a more than sisterly tenderness, a surpassing richness. 'If we'd had the faintest idea of what they were doing to you, all the Arisians and all the Eddorians and all the devils in all the hells of the macrocosmic Universe couldn't have kept us away. You *must* believe that, Kit – or can you, quite?'

'Of course, sis – you don't have to prove an axiom. Seal it, all of you. You're swell people – absolute tops. But I . . . you . . . that is . . .' He broke off and marshaled his thoughts.

He knew that they knew, in every minute particular, everything that had occurred. Yet to a girl they thought he was wonderful; their common thought was that they should have been in there, too: taking what he took; giving what he gave!

'What I don't get is that you're trying to blame yourselves for what happened to me, when you were on the dead center of the beam all the time. You *couldn't* have been in there, kids; it would have blown the whole works higher than up. You knew that then, and you know it even better now. You also know that I flew the yellow flag. Didn't that even *register?*'

'Oh, *that!*' Practically identical thoughts of complete dismissal came in unison, and Karen followed through:

'Since you knew exactly what to expect, we marvel that you ever managed to go in at all – no one else could have possibly.

Or, once in, and seeing what was really there, that you didn't flit right out again. Believe me, brother of mine, you qualify!'

Kit choked. This was too much; but it made him feel good all over. These kids ... the universe's best ...

As he thought, a partial block came unconsciously into being. For not one of those gorgeous, those utterly splendid creatures suspected, even now, that which he so surely knew – that each one of them was very shortly to be wrought and tempered as he himself had been. And, worse, he would have to stand aside and watch them, one by one, walk into it. Was there anything he could do to ward off, or even to soften, what was coming to them? There was not. With his present power, he could step in, of course – at what awful cost to Civilization only he, Christopher Kinnison, of all Civilization, really knew. No. That was out. Definitely. He could come in afterward to ease their hurts, as each had come to him, but that was all ... and there was a difference. They hadn't known about it in advance. It was tough ...

Could he do *anything*?

He could not.

And on clammy, noisome Eddore, the Arisian attackers having been beaten off and normality restored, a meeting of the Highest Command was held. No two of those entities were alike in form; some were changing from one horrible shape into another; all were starkly, indescribably monstrous. All were concentrating upon the problem which had been so suddenly thrust upon them; each of them thought at and with each of the others. To do justice to the complexity or the cogency of the maze of intertwined thoughts is impossible; the best that can be done is to pick out a high point here and there.

'This explains the Star A Star whom the Ploorans and the Kalonians so fear.'

'And the failure of our operator on Thrale, and its fall.'

'Also our recent quite serious reverses.'

'Those stupid – those utterly brainless underlings!'

'We should have been called in at the start!'

'Could you analyze, or even perceive, its pattern save in small part?'

'No.'

'Nor could I; an astounding and highly revealing circumstance.'

'An Arisian; or, rather, an Arisian development, certainly. No other entity of Civilization could possibly do what was done here. Nor could any Arisian as we know them.'

'They have developed something very recently which we had not visualized . . .'

'Kinnison's son? Bah! Think they to deceive us by the old device of energizing a form of ordinary flesh?'

'Kinnison – his son – Nadreck – Worsel – Tregonsee – what matters it?'

'Or, as we now know, the completely imaginary Star A Star.'

'We must revise our thinking,' an authoritatively composite mind decided. 'We must revise our theory and our plan. It may be possible that this new development will necessitate immediate, instead of later, action. If we had had a competent race of proxies, none of this would have happened, as we would have been kept informed. To correct a situation which may become grave, as well as to acquire fullest and latest information, we must attend the conference which is now being held on Ploor.'

They did so. With no perceptible lapse of time or mode of transit, the Eddorian mind was in an assembly room upon that now flooded world. Resembling Nevians as much as any other race with which man is familiar, the now amphibious Ploorans lolled upon padded benches and argued heatedly. They were discussing, upon a lower level, much of the same material which the Eddorians had been considering so shortly before.

Star A Star. Kinnison had been captured easily enough, but had, almost immediately, escaped from an escape-proof trap. Another trap was set, but would it take him? Would it hold him if it did? Kinnison was – *must* be – Star A Star. No, he could not be, there had been too many unrelated and simultaneous occurrences. Kinnison, Nadreck, Clarrissa, Worsel, Tregonsee, even Kinnison's young son, had all shown intermittent flashes of inexplicable power. Kinnison most of all. It was a fact worthy of note that the beginning of the long series of Boskonian set-backs coincided with Kinnison's appearance among the Lensmen.

The situation was bad. Not irreparable, by any means, but grave. The fault lay with the Eich, and perhaps with Kandron of Onlo. Such stupidity! Such incompetence! Those lower-echelon operators should have had brains enough to have reported the matter to Ploor before the situation got completely out of hand. But they didn't; hence this mess. None of them, however, expressed a thought that the present situation was already one with which they themselves could not cope; nor suggested that it be referred to Eddore before it should become too hot for even the Masters to handle.

'Fools! Imbeciles! We, the Masters, although through no foresight or design of yours, are already here. Know now that you have been and still are yourselves guilty of the same conduct which you are so violently condemning in others.' Neither Eddorians nor Ploorans realized that that deficiency was inherent in the Boskonian Scheme of Things, or that it stemmed from the organization's very top. 'Sheer stupidity! Gross overconfidence! Those are the reasons for our recent reverses!'

'But, Masters,' a Plooran argued, 'now that we have taken over, we are winning steadily. Civilization is rapidly going to pieces. In a few more years we will have smashed it flat.'

'That is precisely what they wish you to think. They have been and are playing for time. Your bungling and mis-management have already given them sufficient time to develop an object or an entity able to penetrate our screens; so that Eddore suffered the disgrace of an actual physical invasion. It was brief, to be sure, and unsuccessful, but it was an invasion, none the less – the first in our long history.'

'But, Masters...'

'Silence! We are not here to indulge in recriminations, but to determine facts. Since you do not know Eddore's location in space, it is a certainty that you did not, either wittingly or otherwise, furnish that information. That in turn makes it clear who, basically, the invader was...'

'Star A Star?' A wave of questions swept the group.

'One name serves as well as another for what is almost certainly an Arisian entity or device. It is enough for you to know that it is something with which your massed minds would be completely unable to deal. To the best of your knowledge, have you been invaded, either physically or mentally?'

'We have not, Masters; and it is unbelievable that...'

'Is it so?' The Masters sneered. 'Neither our screens nor our Eddorian guardsmen gave any alarm. We learned of the Arisian's presence only when he attempted to probe our very minds, at Eddore's very surface. Are your screens and minds, then, so much better than ours?'

'We erred, Masters. We abase ourselves. What do you wish us to do?'

'That is better. You will be informed, as soon as certain details have been worked out. Although nothing is established by the fact that you know of no occurrences here on Ploor, the probability is that you are still unknown and unsuspected. Nevertheless, one of us is now taking over control of the trap which you set for Kinnison, in the belief that he is Star A Star.'

'Belief, Masters? It is certain that he is Star A Star!'

'In essence, yes. In exactness, no. Kinnison is, in all probability, merely a puppet through whom an Arisian works at times. If *you* take Kinnison in that trap, however, the entity you call Star A Star will assuredly kill you all.'

'But, Masters...'

'Again, fools, silence!' The thought dripped vitriol. 'Remember how easily Kinnison escaped from you? It was the supremely clever move of not following through and destroying you then that obscured the truth. You are completely powerless against the one you call Star A Star. Against any lesser force, however – and the probability is great that only such forces, if any, will be sent against you – you should be able to win. Are you ready?'

'We are ready, Masters.' At last the Ploorans were upon

familiar ground. 'Since ordinary weapons will be useless against us, they will not attempt to use them; especially since they have developed three extraordinary and supposedly irresistible weapons of attack. First; projectiles composed of negative matter, particularly those of planetary anti-mass. Second; loose planets, driven inertialess, but inerted at the point at which their intrinsic velocities render collision unavoidable. Third, and worst; the sunbeam. These gave us some trouble, particularly the last, but the problems were solved and if any one of the three, or all of them, are used against us, disaster for the Galactic Patrol is assured.

'Nor did we stop there. Our psychologists, working with our engineers, after having analyzed exhaustively the capabilities of the so-called Second-Stage Lensmen, developed countermeasures against every super-weapon which they will be able to develop during the next century.'

'Such as?' The Masters were unimpressed.

'The most probable one is an extension of the sunbeam principle, to operate from a distant sun; or, preferably, a nova. We are now installing fields and grids by the use of which we, not the Patrol, will direct that beam.'

'Interesting – if true. Spread in our minds the details of all that you have foreseen and the fashions in which you have safeguarded yourselves.'

It was a long operation, even at the speed of thought. At the end the Eddorians were unconvinced, skeptical, and pessimistic.

'We can visualize several other things which the forces of Civilization may be able to develop well within the century,' the Master mind said, coldly. 'We will assemble data concerning a few of them for your study. In the meantime, hold yourselves in readiness to act, as we shall issue final orders very shortly.'

'Yes, Masters,' and the Eddorians went back to their home planet as effortlessly as they had left it. There they concluded their conference.

'. . . It is clear that Kinnison will enter that trap. He cannot do otherwise. Kinnison's protector, whoever or whatever he or it may be, may or may not enter it with him. It may or may not be taken with him. Whether or not the new Arisian figment is taken, Kimball Kinnison must die. He is the very keystone of the Galactic Patrol. At his death, as we will advertise it to have come about, the Patrol will fall apart. The Arisians, themselves unknown to the rank and file, will be forced to try to rebuild it around another puppet; but neither his son nor any other man will ever be able to take Kinnison's place in the esteem of the hero-worshipping, undisciplined mob which is Civilization. Hence the importance of your project. You, personally, will supervise the operation of the trap. You, personally, will kill him.'

'With one exception, I agree with everything said. I am not at all certain that death is the answer. One way or another, however, I shall deal effectively with Kinnison.'

'Deal with? We said kill!'

'I heard you. I still say that mere death may not be adequate. I shall consider the matter at length, and shall submit in due course my conclusions and recommendations, for your consideration and approval.'

Although none of the Eddorians knew it, their pessimism in regard to the ability of the Ploorans to defend their planet against the assaults of Second-Stage Lensmen was even then being justified. Kimball Kinnison, after pacing the floor for hours, called his son.

'Kit, I've been working on a thing for months, and I don't know whether I've got a workable solution at last, or not. It may depend entirely on you. Before I go into it, though, when we find Boskonia's top planet we've got to blow it out of the ether, and nothing we've used before will work. Check?'

'Check, on both.' Kit thought soberly for minutes. 'Also, it should be faster than anything we have.'

'My thought exactly. I've got something, I think, but nobody except old Cardynge and Mentor of Arisia...'

'Hold it, dad, while I do a bit of spying and put out some coverage... QX, go ahead.'

'Nobody except those two knew anything about the mathematics involved. Even Sir Austin knew only enough to be able to understand Mentor's directions – he didn't do any of the deep stuff himself. Nobody in the present Conference of Scientists could even begin to handle it. It's that foreign space, you know, that we called the Nth space, where that hyperspatial tube dumped us that time. You've been doing a lot of work with some of the Arisians on that sort of stuff – suppose you could get them to help you compute a tube to take a ship there and back?'

'Hm ... m. Let me think a second. Yes, I can. When do you need it?'

'Today – or even yesterday.'

'Too fast. It'll take a couple of days, but it'll be ready for you long before you can get your ship ready and get your gang and the stuff for your gadget aboard her.'

'That won't take so long, son. Same ship we rode before. She's still in commission, you know – *Space Laboratory Twelve*, her name is now. Special generators, tools, instruments, everything. We'll be ready in two days.'

They were, and Kit smiled as he greeted Lieutenant-Admiral LaVerne Thorndyke, Principal Technician, and the other surviving members of his father's original crew.

'*What* a tonnage of brass!' Kit said to Kim, later. 'Heaviest load I ever saw on one ship. One sure thing, though, they earned it. You must have been able to pick *men*, too, in those days.'

'What d'ya mean, "those days", you disrespectful young ape? I can still pick *men*, son!' Kim grinned back at Kit, but sobered quickly. 'There's more to this than meets the eye. They went through the strain once, and know what it means. They can take it, and just about all of them will come back. With a crew of kids, twenty percent would be a high estimate.'

As soon as the vessel was outside the system, Kit got another surprise. Even though those men were studded with brass and were, by a boy's standard, *old*, they were not passengers. In their old *Dauntless* and well away from port, they gleefully threw off their full-dress regalia. Each donned the uniform of his status of twenty-odd years back and went to work. The members of the regular crew, young as all regular space crewmen are, did not know at first whether they liked the idea of working watch-and-watch with so much braid or not; but they soon found out that they did. Those men were men.

It is an iron-clad rule of space, however, that operating pilots must be young. Master Pilot Henry Henderson cursed that ruling sulphurously, even while he watched with a proud, if somewhat jaundiced eye, the smooth performance of Henry Junior at his own old board.

They approached their destination – cut the jets – felt for the vortex – found it – cut in the special generators. Then, as the fields of the ship reacted against those of the tube, every man aboard felt a malaise to which no being has ever become accustomed. Most men become immune rather quickly to seasickness, to airsickness, and even to spacesickness. Inter-dimensional acceleration, however, is something else. It is different – just how different cannot be explained to anyone who has never experienced it.

The almost unbearable acceleration ceased. They were in the tube. Every plate showed blank; everywhere there was the same drab and featureless grey. There was neither light nor darkness; there was simply and indescribably – nothing whatever, not even empty space.

Kit threw a switch. There was wrenching, twisting, shock, followed by a deceleration exactly as sickening as the accel-eration had been. It ceased. They were in that enigmatic Nth space which each of the older men remembered so well; in which so many of their 'natural laws' did not hold. Time still raced, stopped, or ran backward, seemingly at whim; inert bodies had intrinsic velocities far above that of light – and so on. Each of those men, about to be marooned of his own choice in this utterly hostile environment, drew a deep breath and squared his shoulders as he prepared to disembark.

'That's computation, Kit!' Kinnison applauded, after one glance into a plate. 'That's the same planet we worked on before, right there. All our machines and stuff, untouched. If you'd figured it any closer it'd have been a collision course. Are you dead sure, Kit, that everything's QX?'

'Dead sure, dad.'

'QX. Well, fellows, I'd like to stay here with you, and so would Kit, but we've got chores to do. I don't have to tell you to be careful, but I'm going to, anyway. BE CAREFUL! And as soon as you get done, come back home just as fast as Klono will let you. Clear ether, fellows!'

'Clear ether, Kim!'

Lensman father and Lensman son boarded their speedster and left. They traversed the tube and emerged into normal space. All without a word.

'Kit,' the older man ground out, finally. 'This gives me the colly wobblies, no less. Suppose some of them – or all of them – get killed out there? Is it worth it? I know it's my own idea, but will we need it badly enough to take such a chance?'

'We will, dad. Mentor says so.'

And that was that.

24
The Conference Solves a Problem

Kit wanted to get back to normal space as soon as possible, in order to help his sisters pull themselves together, just as they had helped him. Think as he would, he had not been able to find any flaw in any of them; but he knew that Mentor would; and he stood aside and watched while Mentor did.

Kinnison had to get back because he had a lot of business, all of it pressing. Finally, however, he took time to call a conference of all the Second-Stage Lensmen and his children; a conference which, bizarrely enough, was to be held in person and not via Lens.

'Not strictly necessary, of course,' the Grey Lensman half-apologized to his son as their speedsters approached the *Dauntless*. 'I still think it was a good idea, though, especially since we were all so close to Lyrane anyway.'

'So do I. It's been mighty long since we were all together.'

They boarded. Clarrissa met Kinnison head-on just inside the portal. The girls hung back a bit, with a trace, almost, of diffidence; even while Kit was attempting the physically impossible feat of embracing all four of them at once.

By common consent the Five used only their eyes. Nothing showed. Nevertheless, the girls blushed vividly and Kit's face twisted into a dry, wry grin.

'It was good for what ailed us, though, at that – I guess.' Kit did not seem at all positive. 'Mentor, the lug, told me no less than six times that I had arrived – or at least made statements which I interpreted as meaning that. And Eukonidor told me I was a "finished tool", whatever that means. Personally, I think they were sitting back and wondering how long it was going to take us to realize that we never could be half as good as we used to think we were. Suppose?'

'Something like that, probably. We've shivered more than once, wondering whether we're finished products *yet* or not.'

'We've learned – I hope.' Karen, hard as she was, did shiver, physically. 'If we aren't, it'll be... p-s-s-t – dad's starting the meeting!'

'...so settle down, all of you, and we'll get going.'

What a group! Tregonsee of Rigel IV – stolid, solid, blocky, immobile; looking as little as possible like one of the profoundest thinkers Civilisation had ever produced – did not move. Worsel, the ultra-sensitive yet utterly implacable Velantian, curled out three or four eyes and looked on languidly while Constance kicked a few coils of his tail into a comfortable chaise lounge, reclined unconcernedly in the seat thus made, and lighted an Alsakanite cigarette. Clarrissa Kinnison, radiant in her Greys and looking scarcely older than her daughters, sat beside Kathryn, each with an arm around the other. Karen and Camilla, neither of whom could ordinarily be described by the adjective 'cuddlesome', were on a davenport with Kit, snuggling as close to him as they could get. And in the farthest corner the heavily-armored, heavily-insulated space-suit which contained Nadreck of Palain VII chilled the atmosphere for yards around.

'QX?' Kinnison began. 'We'll take Nadreck first, since he isn't any too happy here, and let him flit – he'll keep in touch from outside after he leaves. Report, please, Nadreck.'

'I have explored Lyrane IX *thoroughly*.' Nadreck made the statement and paused. When he used such a thought at all, it meant much. When he emphasized it, which no one there had ever before known him to do, it meant that he had examined the planet practically atom by atom. 'There was no life of the level of intelligence in which we are interested to be found on, beneath, or above its surface. I could find no evidence that such life has ever been there, either as permanent dwellers or as occasional visitors.'

'When Nadreck settles anything as definitely as that, it stays settled,' Kinnison remarked as soon as the Palainian had left. 'I'll report next. You all know what I did about Kalonia, and so on. The only significant fact that I've been able to find – the only lead to the Boskonian higher-ups – is that Black Lensman Melasnikov got his Lens on Lyrane IX. There were no traces of mental surgery. I can see two, and only two, alternatives. Either there was mental surgery which I could not detect, or there were visitors to Lyrane IX who left no traces of their visits. More reports may enable us to decide. Worsel?'

The other Second-Stage Lensmen reported in turn. Each had uncovered leads to Lyrane IX, but Worsel and Tregonsee, who had also studied that planet with care, agreed with Nadreck that there was nothing to be found there.

'Kit?' Kinnison asked then. 'How about you and the girls?'

'We believe that Lyrane IX was visited by beings having sufficient power of mind to leave no traces whatever as to who they were or where they came from. We also believe that there was no surgery, but an infinitely finer kind of work – an indetectable subconscious compulsion – done on the minds of the Black Lensmen and others who came into physical contact with the Boskonians. These opinions are based upon experiences which we five have had and upon deductions we have made. If we are right, Lyrane is actually, as well as apparently, a dead end and should be abandoned. Furthermore, we believe that the Black Lensmen have not been and cannot become important.'

The coordinator was surprised, but after Kit and his sisters had detailed their findings and their deductions, he turned to the Rigellian.

'What next, then, Tregonsee?'

'After Lyrane IX, it seems to me that the two most promising subjects are those entities who think upon such a high band, and the phenomenon which has been called "The Hell-Hole in Space". Of the two, I preferred the first until Camilla's researches showed that the available data could not be reconciled with the postulate that the life-forms of her reconstruction were identical with those reported to you as coordinator. This data, however, was scanty and casual. While we are here, therefore, I suggest that we review this matter much more carefully, in the hope that additional information will enable us to come to a definite conclusion, one way or the other. Since it was her research, Camilla will lead.'

'First, a question,' Camilla began. 'Imagine a sun so variable that it periodically covers practically the entire possible range. It has a planet whose atmosphere, liquid, and distance are such that its surface temperature varies from approximately two hundred degrees Centigrade in midsummer to about five degrees absolute in midwinter. In the spring its surface is almost completely submerged. There are terrible winds and storms in the spring, summer, and fall; but the fall storms are the worst. Has anyone here ever heard of such a planet having an intelligent life-form able to maintain a continuing existence through such varied environments by radical changes in its physical body?'

A silence ensued, which Nadreck finally broke.

'I know of two such planets. Near Palain there is an extremely variable sun, two of whose planets support life. All of the higher life-forms, the highest of which are quite intelligent, undergo regular and radical changes, not only of form, but of organization.'

'Thanks, Nadreck. That will perhaps make my story believable. From the thoughts of one of the entities in question, I reconstructed such a solar system. More, that entity himself belonged to just such a race. It was *such* a nice reconstruction,' Camilla went on, plaintively, 'and it fitted all those other life-forms so beautifully, especially Kat's "four-cycle periods". And to prove it, Kat – put up your block, now – you never told anybody the classification of your pet to more than seven places, did you, or even thought about it?'

'No.' Kathryn's mind, since the moment of warning, had been unreadable.

'Take the seven, RTSL and so on. The next three were S-T-R. Check?'

'Check.'

'But that makes it *solid*, sis!' Kit exclaimed.

'That's what I thought, for a minute – that we had Boskone at last. However, when Tregonsee and I first felt "X", long before you met yours, Kat, his classification was TUUV. That would fit in well enough as a spring form, with Kat's as the summer form. What ruins it, though, is that when he killed himself, just a little while ago and long after a summer form could possibly exist – to say nothing of a spring form – his classification was *still* TUUV. To ten places it was TUUVWYXXWT.'

'Well, go on,' Kinnison suggested. 'What do you make of it?'

'The obvious explanation is that one or all of those entities were planted or primed – not specifically for us, probably, since we are relatively unknown, but for any competent observer. If so, they don't mean a thing.' Camilla was not now over-estimating her own powers or underestimating those of Boskonia. 'There are a few other things, less obvious, leading to the same conclusion. Tregonsee is not ready to believe any of them, however, and neither am I. Assuming that our data was not biased, we must also account for the fact that the locations in space were . . .'

'Just a minute, Cam, before you leave the classifications,' Constance interrupted. 'I'm guarded – what was my friend's, to ten places?'

'VWZYTXSYZY,' Camilla replied, unhesitatingly.

'Right; and I don't believe it was planted, either, so there . . .'

'Let me in a second!' Kit demanded. 'I didn't know you were on that band at all. I got that RTSL thing even before I graduated . . .'

'Huh? What RTSL?' Cam broke in, sharply.

'My fault,' Kinnison put in then. 'Skipped my mind entirely, when she asked me for the dope. None of us thought any of this stuff important until just now, you know. Tell her, Kit.'

Kit repeated his story, concluding:

'Beyond four places was pretty dim, but Q P arms and legs – Dhilian, eh? – would fit, and so would an R-type hide. Both Kat's and mine, then, could very well have been summer

237

forms, one of their years apart. The thing I felt was on its own planet, and it *died* there, and credits to millos the thought I got wasn't primed. And the location . . .'

'Brake down, Kit,' Camilla instructed. 'Let's settle this thing of timing first. I've got a theory, but I want some ideas from the rest of you.'

'Maybe something like this?' Clarrissa asked, after a few minutes of silence. 'In many forms which metamorphose completely the change depends on temperature. No change takes place as long as the temperature stays constant. Your TUUV could have been flitting around in a space-ship at constant temperature. Could this apply here, Cam, do you think?'

'*Could* it?' Kinnison exclaimed. 'That's it, Cris, for all the tea in China!'

'That was my theory,' Camilla said, still dubiously, 'but there is no proof that it applies. Nadreck, do you know whether or not it applies to your neighbors?'

'Unfortunately, I do not; but I can find out – by experiment if necessary.'

'It might be a good idea,' Kinnison suggested. 'Go on, Cam.'

'Assuming its truth, there is still left the problem of location, which Kit has just made infinitely worse than it was before. Con's and mine were so indefinite that they might possibly have been reconciled with any precisely-known coordinates; but yours, Kit, is almost as definite as Kat's, and cannot possibly be made to agree with it. After all, you know, there are many planets peopled by races similar to ten places. And if there are four different races, none of them can be the one we want.'

'I don't believe it,' Kit argued. 'Not that thing on that peculiar band. I'm sure enough of my dope so that I want to cross-question Kat on hers. QX, Kat?'

'Surely, Kit. Any questions you like.'

'Those minds both had plenty of jets – how do you know he wasn't lying to you? Did you drive in to see? Are you sure even that you saw his real shape?'

'Certainly I'm sure of his shape!' Kathryn snapped. 'If

there had been any zones of compulsion around, I would have known it and got suspicious right then.'

'Maybe, and maybe not,' Kit disagreed. 'That might depend, you know, on how good the guy was who was putting out the zone.'

'Nuts!' Kathryn snorted, inelegantly. 'But as to his telling the truth about his home planet ... um ... I'm not sure of that, no. I didn't check his channels. I was thinking about other things then.' The Five knew that she had just left Mentor. 'But why should he want to lie about a thing like that – he would have, though, at that. Good Boskonian technique.'

'Sure. In your official capacity of coordinator, dad, what do you think?'

'The probability is that all those four forms of life belong on one planet. Your location must be wrong, Kat – he gave you the wrong galaxy, even. Too close to Trenco, too – Tregonsee and I both know that region like a book and no such variable is anywhere near there. We've got to find out all about that planet – and fast. Worsel, will you please get the charts of Kit's region? Kit, will you check with the planetographers of Klovia as to the variable stars anywhere near where you want them, and how many planets they've got? I'll call Tellus.'

The charts were studied, and in due time the reports of the planetographers were received. The Klovian scientists reported that there were four long-period variables in the designated volume of space, gave the spatial coordinates and catalogue numbers of each, and all available data concerning their planets. The Tellurians reported only three, in considerably less detail; but they had named each sun and each planet.

'Which one did they leave out?' Kinnison wondered audibly as he fitted the two transparencies together. 'This one they call Artonon, no planets. Dunlie, two planets, Abab and Dunster. Descriptions, and so on. Rontieff, one planet that they don't know anything about except the name they have given it. Silly-sounding names – suppose they assemble them by grabbing letters at random? – Ploor ...'

PLOOR! At last! Only their instantaneous speed of reaction

enabled the Five to conceal from the linkage the shrieked thought of what Ploor really meant. After a flashing exchange of thought, Kit smoothly took charge of the conference.

'The planet Ploor should be investigated first, I think,' he resumed communication with the group as though his attention had not wavered. 'It is the planet nearest the most probable point of origin of that thought-burst. Also, the period of the variable and the planet's distance seem to fit our observations and deductions better than any of the others. Any arguments?'

No arguments. They all agreed. Kinnison, however, demanded action; direct and fast.

'We'll investigate it!' he exclaimed. 'With the *Dauntless*, the Z_9M_9Z, and Grand Fleet; and with our very special knick-knack as an ace up our sleeve!'

'Just a minute, dad!' Kit protested. 'If, as some of this material seems to indicate, the Ploorans actually are the top echelon of Boskonia, even that array may not be enough.'

'You may be right – probably are. What, then? What do you say, Tregonsee?'

'Fleet action, yes,' the Rigellian agreed. 'Also, as you implied, but did not clearly state, independent but correlated action by us five Second-Stage Lensmen, with our various skills. I would suggest, however, that your children be put first – very definitely first – in command.'

'We object – we haven't got jets enough to . . .'

'Over-ruled!' Kinnison did not have to think to make that decision. He knew. 'Any other objections? . . . Approved. I'll call Cliff Maitland right now, then, and get things going.'

That call, however, was never sent; for at that moment the mind of Mentor of Arisia flooded the group.

'Children, attend! This intrusion is necessary because a matter has come up which will permit of no delay. Boskonia is now launching the attack which has been in preparation for over twenty years. Arisia is to be the first point of attack. Kinnison, Tregonsee, Worsel, and Nadreck will take immediate steps to assemble the Grand Fleet of the Galactic Patrol in defense. I will confer at length with the younger Kinnisons.

'The Eddorians, as you know,' Mentor went on to the Children of the Lens, 'believe primarily in the efficacy of physical, material force. While they possess minds of real power, they use them principally as tools in the development of more and ever more efficient mechanical devices. We of Arisia, on the other hand, believe in the superiority of the mind. A fully competent mind would have no need of material devices, since it could control all material substance directly. While we have made some progress toward that end, and you will make more in the cycles to come, Civilization is, and for some time will be, dependent upon physical things. Hence the Galactic Patrol and its Grand Fleet.

'The Eddorians have succeeded finally in inventing a mechanical generator able to block our most penetrant thoughts. They believe implicitly that their vessels, so protected, will be able to destroy our planet. They may believe that the destruction of our planet would so weaken us that they would be able to destroy us. It is assumed that you children have deduced that neither we nor the Eddorians can be slain by physical force?'

'Yes – the clincher being that no suggestion was made about giving Eddore a planet from Nth space.'

'We Arisians, as you know, have been aiding Nature in the development of minds much abler than our own. While your minds have not yet attained their full powers, you will be able to use the Patrol and its resources to defend Arisia and to destroy the Boskonian fleet. That we cannot do it ourselves is implicit in what I have said.'

'But that means . . . this is the big show, then, that you have been hinting at so long?'

'Far from it. An important engagement, of course, but only preliminary to the real test, which will come when we invade Eddore. Do you agree with us that if Arisia were to be destroyed now, it would be difficult to repair the damage done to the morale of the Galactic Patrol?'

'Difficult? It would be impossible!'

'Not necessarily. We have considered the matter at length,

however, and have decided that a Boskonian success at this time would not be for the good of Civilization.'

'I'll say it wouldn't – that's a masterpiece of understatement if there ever was one! Also, a successful defense of Arisia would be about the best thing that the Patrol could possibly do for itself.'

'Exactly so. Go then, children, and work to that end.'

'But how, Mentor – *how?*'

'Again I tell you that I do not know. You have powers – individually, collectively, and as the Unit – about which I know little or nothing. *Use them!*'

25
The Defense of Arisia

The 'Big Noise' – socially the *Directrix*, technically the Z_9M_9Z – floated through space at the center of a hollow sphere of maulers packed almost screen to screen. She was the Brain. She had been built around the seventeen million cubic feet of unobstructed space which comprised her 'tank' – the three-dimensional chart in which varicolored lights, stationary and moving, represented the positions and motions of solar systems, ships, loose planets, negaspheres, and all other objects and items in which Grand Fleet Operations was, or might become, interested. Completely encircling the tank's more than two thousand feet of circumference was the Rigellian-manned, multi-million-plug board; a crew and a board capable of handling efficiently more than a million combat units.

In the 'reducer', the comparatively tiny ten-foot tank set into an alcove, there were condensed the continuously-changing major features of the main chart, so that one man could comprehend and direct the board strategy of the engagement.

Instead of Port Admiral Haynes, who had conned that reducer and issued general orders during the only previous experience of the Z_9M_9Z in serious warfare, Kimball Kinnison was now in supreme command. Instead of Kinnison and Worsel, who had formerly handled the big tank and the board, there were Clarrissa, Worsel, Tregonsee, and the Children of the Lens. There also, in a built-in, thoroughly competent refrigerator, was Nadreck. Port Admiral Raoul LaForge and Vice-Coordinator Clifford Maitland were just coming aboard.

Might he need anybody else, Kinnison wondered. Couldn't

think of anybody – he had just about the whole top echelon of Civilization. Cliff and Laf weren't L2's, of course, but they were mighty good men... besides, he *liked* them! Too bad the fourth officer of their class couldn't be there, too... gallant Wiedel Holmberg, killed in action... at that, three out of four was a high average – mighty high...

'Hi, Cliff – Hi, Laf!' 'Hi, Kim!'

The three old friends shook hands cordially, then the two newcomers stared for minutes into the maze of lights flashing and winking in the tremendous space-chart.

'Glad I don't have to try to make sense out of that,' LaForge commented, finally. 'Looks a lot different in battle harness than on practice cruises. You want me on that forward wall there, you said?'

'Yes. You can see it plainer down in the reducer. The white star is Arisia. The yellows, all marked, are suns and other fixed points, such as the markers along the arbitrary rim of the galaxy, running from there to there. Reds will be Boskonians when they get close enough to show. Greens are ours. Up in the big tank everything is identified, but down here there's no room for details – each green light marks the location of a whole operating fleet. That block of green circles, there, is your command. It's about eighty parsecs deep and covers everything within two hours – say a hundred and fifty parsecs – of the line between Arisia and the Second Galaxy. Pretty loose now, of course, but you can tighten it up and shift it as you please as soon as some reds show up. You'll have a Rigellian talker – here he is now – when you want anything done, think at him and he'll give it to the right panel on the board. QX?'

'I think so. I'll practice a bit.'

'Now you, Cliff. These green crosses, half-way between the forward wall and Arisia, are yours. You won't have quite as much depth as Laf, but a wider coverage. The green tetra-hedrons are mine. They blanket Arisia, you notice, and fill the space out to the second wall.'

'Do you think you and I will have anything to do?' Maitland asked, waving a hand at LaForge's tremendous barrier.

'I wish I could hope not, but I can't. They're going to throw everything they've got at us.'

For weeks Grand Fleet drilled, maneuvered, and practiced. All space within ten parsecs of Arisia was divided into cubes, each of which was given a reference number. Fleets were so placed that any point in that space could be reached by at least one fleet in thirty seconds or less of elapsed time.

Drill went on until, finally, it happened. Constance, on guard at the moment, perceived the slight 'curdling' of space which presages the appearance of the terminus of a hyperspatial tube and gave the alarm. Kit, the girls, and all the Arisians responded instantly – all knew that this was to be a thing which not even the Five could handle unaided.

Not one, or a hundred, or a thousand, but at least two hundred thousand of those tubes erupted, practically at once. Kit could alert and instruct ten Rigellian operators every second, and so could each of his sisters; but since every tube within striking distance of Arisia had to be guarded or plugged within thirty seconds of its appearance, it is seen that the Arisians did practically all of the spotting and placing during those first literally incredible two or three minutes.

If the Boskonians could have emerged from a tube's terminus in the moment of its appearance, it is quite probable that nothing could have saved Arisia. As it was, however, the enemy required seconds, or sometimes even whole minutes, to traverse their tubes, which gave the defenders much valuable time.

Upon arriving at the tube's end, the fleet laced itself, by means of tractors and pressors, into a rigid although inertialess structure. Then, if there was time, and because the theory was that the pirates would probably send a negasphere through first, with an intrinsic velocity aimed at Arisia, a suitably-equipped loose planet was tossed into 'this end' of the tube. Since they might send a loose or an armed planet through first, however, the fleet admiral usually threw a negasphere in, too.

What happened when planet met negasphere, in the unknown medium which makes up the 'interior' of a hyperspatial tube, is not surely known. Several highly abstruse mathematical treatises and many volumes of rather gruesome fiction have been written upon the subject – none of which, however, has any bearing here.

If the Patrol fleet did not get there first, the succession of events was different; the degree of difference depending upon how much time the enemy had had. If, as sometimes happened, a fleet was coming through it was met by a super-atomic bomb and by the concentrated fire of every primary projector that the englobing task force could bring to bear; with consequences upon which it is neither necessary or desirable to dwell. If a planet had emerged, it was met by a negasphere...

Have you ever seen a negasphere strike a planet?

The negasphere is built of negative matter. This material – or, rather, anti-material – is in every respect the exact opposite of the everyday matter of normal space. Instead of electrons, it has positrons. To it a push, however violent, is a pull; a pull is a push. When negative matter strikes positive, then, there is no collision in the usual sense of the word. One electron and one positron neutralize each other and disappear; giving rise to two quanta of extremely hard radiation.

Thus, when the spherical hyper-plane which was the aspect of the negasphere tended to occupy the same three-dimensional space in which the loose planet already was, there was no actual collision. Instead, the materials of both simply vanished, along the surface of what should have been a contact, in a gigantically crescendo burst of pure, raw energy. The atoms and the molecules of the planet's substance disappeared; the physically incomprehensible texture of the negasphere's anti-mass changed into that of normal space. And all circumambient space was flooded with inconceivably lethal radiation; so intensely lethal that any being not adequately shielded from it died before he had time to realize that he was being burned.

Gravitation, of course, was unaffected; and the rapid disappearance of the planet's mass set up unbalanced forces of tremendous magnitude. The hot, dense, pseudo-liquid magma tended to erupt as the sphere of nothingness devoured so rapidly the planet's substance, but not a particle of it could move. Instead, it vanished. Mountains fell, crashingly. Oceans poured. Earth-cracks appeared; miles wide, tens of miles deep, hundreds of miles long. The world heaved... shuddered... disintegrated... vanished.

The shock attack upon Arisia itself, which in the Eddorian mind had been mathematically certain to succeed, was over in approximately six minutes. Kinnison, Maitland, and LaForge, fuming at their stations, had done nothing at all. The Boskonians had probably thrown everything they could; the probability was vanishingly small that that particular attack was to be or could be resumed. Nevertheless a host of Kinnison's task forces remained on guard and a detail of Arisians still scanned all nearby space.

'What shall I do next, Kit?' Camilla asked. 'Help Connie crack that screen?'

Kit glanced at his youngest sister, who was stretched out flat, every muscle rigidly tense in an extremity of effort.

'No,' he decided. 'If she can't crack it alone, all four of us couldn't help her much. Besides, I don't believe she can break it. It's a mechanical, you know, powered by atomic-motored generators. My guess is that it'll have to be *solved*, not cracked, and the solution will take time. When she comes down off that peak, Kay, you might tell her so, and both of you start solving it. The rest of us have another job. The Boskonian moppers-up are coming in force, and there isn't a chance that either we or the Arisians can derive the counter-formula of that screen in less than a week. Therefore the rest of this battle will have to be fought out on conventional lines. We can do the most good, I think, by spotting the Boskonians into the big tank – our scouts aren't locating five percent of them – for the L_2's to pass on to dad and the rest of the top brass so they can run this battle the way it ought to be run. You'll do the spotting, Cam, of course; Kat and I will do the pushing. And if you thought that Tregonsee took you for a ride...! It'll work, don't you think?'

'Of *course* it'll work!'

Thus, apparently as though by magic, red lights winked into being throughout a third of the volume of the immense tank; and the three master strategists, informed of what was being done, heaved tremendous sighs of relief. They now had real control. They knew, not only the positions of their own task-forces, but also, and exactly, the position of *every* task-force of the enemy. More, by merely forming in his mind the desire for the information, any one of the three could know, with no appreciable lapse of time, the exact composition and the exact strength of any individual fleet, flotilla, or squadron!

Kit and his two sisters stood close-grouped, motionless; heads bent and almost touching, arms interlocked. Kinnison perceived with surprise that Lenses, as big and as bright as Kit's own, flamed upon his daughters' wrists; a surprise which changed to awe as the very air around those three red-bronze-auburn heads began to thicken, to pulsate, and to glow with that indefinable, indescribable polychromatic effulgence so uniquely characteristic of the Lens of the Galactic Patrol. But there was work to do, and Kinnison did it.

Since the $Z9M9Z$ was now working as not even the most optimistic of her planners and designers had dared to hope, the war could now be fought strategically; that is, with the object of doing the enemy as much harm as possible with the irreducible minimum of risk. It was not sporting. It was not clubby. There was nothing whatever of chivalry. There was no thought whatever of giving the enemy a break. It was massacre – it was murder – it was war.

It was not ship to ship. No, nor fleet to fleet. Instead, ten or twenty Patrol task-forces, under sure pilotage, dashed out to englobe at extreme range one fleet of the Boskonians. Then, before the opposing admiral could assemble a picture of what was going on, his entire command became the center of impact of hundreds or even thousands of super-atomic bombs, as well as the focus of an immensely greater number of scarcely less ravaging primary beams. Not a ship nor a scout nor a lifeboat of the englobed fleet escaped, ever. In fact, few indeed were the blobs, or even droplets, of hard alloy or of dureum which remained merely liquefied or which, later, were able to condense.

Fleet by fleet the Boskonians were blown out of the ether; one by one the red lights in the tank and in the reducer winked out. And finally the slaughter was done.

Kit and his two now Lensless sisters unlaced themselves. Karen and Constance came up for air, announcing that they knew how to work the problem Kit had handed them, but that it would take time. Clarrissa, white and shaken by what she had driven herself to do, looked and felt sick. So did Kinnison; nor had either of the other two commanders derived any pleasure from the engagement. Tregonsee deplored it. Of all the Lensed personnel, only Worsel had enjoyed himself. He liked to kill enemies, at close range or far, and he could not understand or sympathize with squeamishness. Nadreck, of course, had neither liked nor disliked any part of the whole affair; to him his part had been merely another task, to be performed with the smallest outlay of physical and mental effort consistent with good workmanship.

'What next?' Kinnison asked then, of the group at large. 'I say the Ploorans. They're not like these poor devils were – they probably sent them in. *They've* got it coming!'

'They certainly have!'

'Ploor!'

'By all means Ploor!'

'But how about Arisia here?' Maitland asked.

'Under control,' Kinnison replied. 'We'll leave a heavy guard and a spare tank – the Arisians will do the rest.'

As soon as the tremendous fleet had shaken itself down into the course for Ploor, all seven of the Kinnisons retired to a small dining room and ate a festive meal. They drank after-dinner coffee. Most of them smoked. They discussed, for a long time and not very quietly, the matter of the Hell-Hole in Space. Finally:

'I know it's a trap, as well as you do.' Kinnison got up from the table, rammed his hands into his breeches' pockets, and paced the floor. 'It's got T - R - A - P painted all over it, in billposter letters seventeen meters high. So what? Since I'm the only one who can, I've got to go in, if it's still there after we knock Ploor off. And it'll still be there, for all the tea in China. All the Ploorans aren't on Ploor.'

Four young Kinnisons flashed thoughts at Kathryn, who frowned and bit her lip. She had hit that hole with everything she had, and simply bounced. She had been able to block the radiation, of course, but such solid barriers had been necessary that she had blinded herself by her own screens. That it was Eddorian there could be no doubt... warned by her own activities in the other tube – Plooran of course – and dad would be worth taking in more ways than one...

'I can't say that I'm any keener about going in than any of you are about having me do it,' the big Lensman went on, 'but unless some of you can figure out a reason for my *not* going in that isn't fuller of holes than a sponge, I'm going to tackle it just as soon after we blow Ploor apart as I can possibly get there.'

And Kathryn, his self-appointed guardian, knew that nothing could stop him. Nor did anyone there, even Clarrissa, try to stop him. Lensmen all, they knew that he had to go in.

To the Five, the situation was not too serious. Kinnison would come through unhurt. The Eddorians could take him, of course. But whether or not they could do anything to him after they got him would depend on what the Kinnison kids would be doing in the meantime – and that would be plenty. They couldn't delay his entry into the tube very much without making a smell, but they could and would hurry Arisia up. And even if, as seemed probable, he was already in the tube when Arisia was ready for the big push, a lot could be done at the other end. Those amoeboid monstrosities would be fighting for their own precious lives, this time, not for the lives of slaves; and the Five promised each other grimly that the Eddorians would have too much else to worry about to waste any time on Kimball Kinnison.

Clarrissa Kinnison, however, fought the hardest and bitterest battle of her life. She loved Kim with a depth and a fervor which very few women, anywhere, have ever been able to feel. She knew with a sick, cold certainty, knew with every fibre of her being and with every cell of her brain, that if he went into that trap he would die in it. Nevertheless, she would have to let him go in. More, and worse, she would have to send him in – to his death – with a smile. She could not ask him not to go in. She could not even suggest again that there was any possibility that he need not go in. He had to go in. He *had* to . . .

And if Lensman's Load was heavy on him, on her it was almost unbearable. His part was vastly the easier. He would only have to die; she would have to live. She would have to keep on living – without Kim – living a lifetime of deaths, one after another. And she would have to hold her block and smile, not only with her face, but with her whole mind. She could be scared, of course, apprehensive, as he himself was; she could wish with all her strength for his safe return: but if he suspected the thousandth part of what she really felt it would break his heart. Nor would it do a bit of good. However broken-hearted at her rebellion against the inflexible Code of the Lens, he would still go in. Being Kimball Kinnison, he could not do anything else.

As soon as she could, Clarrissa went to a distant room and turned on a full-coverage block. She lay down, buried her face in the pillow, clenched her fists, and fought.

Was there any way – any *possible* way – that she could die instead? None. It was not that simple.

She would have to let him go . . .

With a SMILE . . .

Not gladly, but proudly and willingly . . . for the good of the Patrol . . .

DAMN THE PATROL!

Clarrissa Kinnison gritted her teeth and writhed.

She would simply *have* to let him go into that ghastly trap – go to his absolutely sure and certain death – without showing one white feather, either to her husband or to her children.

Her husband, her Kim, would have to die... and she would
– *have* – to – *live*...

She got up, smiled experimentally, and snapped off the
block. Then, actually smiling and apparently confident, she
strolled down the corridor.

Such is Lensman's Load.

26
The Battle of Ploor

Twenty-odd years before, when the then *Dauntless* and her crew were thrown out of a hyperspatial tube and into that highly enigmatic Nth space, LaVerne Thorndyke had been Chief Technician. Mentor of Arisia found them, and put into the mind of Sir Austin Cardynge, mathematician extraordinary, the knowledge of how to find the way back to normal space. Thorndyke, working under nerve-shattering difficulties, had been in charge of building the machines which were to enable the vessel to return to her home space. He built them. She returned.

He was now again in charge, and every man of his present crew had been a member of his former one. He did not command the space-ship or her regular crew, of course, but they did not count. Not one of those kids would be allowed to set foot on the fantastically dangerous planet to which the inertia-less *Space Laboratory Twelve* was anchored.

Older, leaner, greyer, he was now, even more than then, Civilization's Past Master of Mechanism. If anything could be built, 'Thorny' Thorndyke could build it. If it couldn't be built, he could build something just as good.

He lined his crew up for inspection; men who, although many of them had as much rank and had had as many years of as much authority as their present boss, had been working for days to forget as completely as possible their executive positions and responsibilities. Each man wore not one, but three, personal neutralizers; one inside and two outside of his space-suit. Thorndyke, walking down the line, applied his test-kit to each individual neutralizer. He then tested his own. QX – all were at max.

'Fellows,' he said then, 'you all remember what it was like last time. This is going to be the same, except more so and for a longer time. How we did it before without any casualties I'll never know. If we can do it again it'll be a major miracle, no less. Before, all we had to do was to build a couple of small generators and some controls out of stuff native to the planet, and we didn't find that any too easy a job. This time, for a starter, we've got to build a Bergenholm big enough to free the whole planet; after which we install the Bergs, tube-generators, atomic blasts, and other stuff we brought along.

'But that native Berg is going to be a Class A Prime headache, and until we get it running it's going to be hell on wheels. The only way we can get away with it is to check and re-check every thing and every step. Check, check, double-check; then go back and double-check again.

'Remember that the fundamental characteristics of this Nth space are such that inert matter can travel faster than light; and remember, every second of the time, that our intrinsic velocity is something like fifteen lights relative to anything solid in this space. I want every one of you to picture himself going inert accidentally. You might take a tangent course or higher – but you might not, too. And it wouldn't only kill the one who did it. It wouldn't only spoil our record. It could very easily kill us all and make a crater full of boiling metal out of our whole installation. So BE CAREFUL! Also bear in mind that one piece, however small, of this planet's material, accidentally brought aboard, might wreck the *Dauntless*. Any questions?'

'If the fundamental characteristics – constants – of this space are so different, how do you know that the stuff will work here?'

'Well, the stuff we built here before worked. The Arisians told Kit Kinnison that two of the fundamentals, mass and length, are about normal. Time is a lot different, so that we can't compute power-to-mass ratios and so on, but we'll have enough power, anyway, to get any speed we can use.'

'I see. We miss the really fancy stuff?'

'Yes. Well, the quicker we get started the quicker we'll get done. Let's go.'

The planet was airless, waterless, desolate; a chaotic jumble of huge and jagged fragments of various metals in a non-metallic continuous phase. It was as though some playful child-giant of space had poured dipperfuls of silver, of iron, of copper, and of other granulated pure metals into a tank of something else – and then, tired of play, had thrown the whole mess away!

Neither the metals nor the non-metallic substances were either hot or cold. They had no apparent temperature, to thermometers or to the 'feelers' of the suits. The machines which these men had built so long before had not changed in any particular. They still functioned perfectly; no spot of rust or corrosion or erosion marred any part. This, at least, was good news.

Inertialess machines, extravagantly equipped with devices to keep them inertialess, were taken 'ashore'; nor were any of these ever to be returned to the ship. Kinnison had ordered and reiterated that no unnecessary chances were to be taken of getting any particle of Nth-space stuff aboard *Space Laboratory Twelve*, and none were taken.

Since men cannot work indefinitely in space-suits, each man had periodically to be relieved; but each such relief amounted almost to an operation. Before he left the planet his suit was scrubbed, rinsed, and dried. In the vessel's airlock it was air-blasted again before the outer port was closed. He unshelled in the lock and left his suit there – everything which had come into contact with Nth-space matter either would be left on the planet's surface or would be jettisoned before the vessel was again inerted. Unnecessary precautions? Perhaps – but Thorndyke and his crew returned unharmed to normal space in undamaged ships.

Finally the Bergenholm was done; by dint of what improvisation, substitutions and artifice only 'Thorny' Thorndyke ever knew; at what strain and cost was evidenced by the gaunt bodies and haggard faces of his overworked and underslept crew. To those experts and particularly to Thorndyke, the thing was not a good job. It was not quiet, nor smooth. It was not in balance, statically, dynamically, or electrically. The Chief Technician, to whom a meter-jump of one and a half thousandths had always been a matter of grave concern, swore feelingly in all the planetary languages he knew when he saw what those meters were doing.

He scowled morosely. There might have been poorer machines built sometime, somewhere, he supposed – but damned if he had ever seen any!

But the improvised Berg ran, and kept on running. The planet became inertialess and remained that way. For hours, then, Thorndyke climbed over and around and through the Brobdingnagian fabrication, testing and checking the operation of every part. Finally he climbed down and reported to his waiting crew.

'QX, fellows, a nice job. A hell of a good job, in fact, considering – even though we all know that it isn't what any of us would call a good machine. Part of that meter-jump, of course, is due to the fact that nothing about the heap is true or balanced, but most of it must be due to this cockeyed ether. Anyway, none of it is due to the usual causes – loose bars and faulty insulation. So my best guess is that she'll keep on doing her stuff while we do ours. One sure thing, she isn't going to fall apart, even under that ungodly knocking; and I don't *think* she'll shake herself off of the planet.'

After Thorndyke's somewhat less than enthusiastic approval of his brain-child, the adventurers into that fantastic region attacked the second phase of their project. The planetary Bergenholm was landed and set up. Its meters jumped, too, but the engineers were no longer worried about that. *That* machine would run indefinitely. Pits were dug. Atomic blasts and other engines were installed; as were many exceedingly complex instruments and mechanisms. A few tons of foreign matter on the planet's surface would now make no difference; but there was no relaxation of the extreme precautions against the transfer of any matter whatever from the planet to the space-ship.

When the job was done, but before the clean-up, Thorndyke called his crew into conference.

'Fellows, I know just what a God-awful shellacking you've been taking. We all feel as though we'd been on a Delgonian clambake. Nevertheless, I've got to tell you something. Kinnison said that if we could get this one fixed up without too much trouble, it'd be a mighty good idea to have two of them. What do you say? Did we have too much trouble?'

He got exactly the reaction he had expected.

'Lead us to it!'

'Pick out the one you want!'

'Trouble? Hell, no! If this scrap-heap we built held together this long, she'll run for years. We can tow her on a tractor-pressor combo, match intrinsics with clamp-on drivers, and mount her anywhere!'

Another metal-studded, barren, lifeless world was therefore found and prepared; and no real argument arose until Thorndyke broached the matter of selecting the two men who were to stay with him and Henderson in the two lifeboats which were to remain for a time near the two loose planets after *Space Laboratory Twelve* had returned to normal space. Everybody wanted to stay. Each one *was* going to stay, too, by all the gods of space, if he had to pull rank to do it!

'Hold it!' Thorndyke commanded. 'We'll do the same as we did before, then, by drawing lots. Quartermaster Allerdyce...'

'Not by a damn sight!' Uhlenhuth, formerly Atomic Technician 1/c, objected vigorously, and was supported by several others. 'He's too clever with his fingers – look what he did to the original draw! We're not squawking about that one, you understand – a little fixing was QX back there – but *this* one's got to be on the level.'

'Now that you mention it, I do remember hearing about the laws of chance being jimmied a bit.' Thorndyke grinned broadly. 'So you hold the pot yourself, Uhly, and Hank and I will each pull out one name.'

So it was. Henderson drew Uhlenhuth, to that burly admiral's loud delight, and Thorndyke drew Nelson, the erstwhile chief communications officer. The two lifeboats disembarked, each near one of the newly 'loosened' planets. Two men would stay on or near each of those planets, to be sure that all the machinery functioned perfectly. They would stay there until the atomic blasts went into action and it became clear that the Arisians would need no help in navigating those tremendous globes through Nth space to the points at which two hyper-spatial tubes were soon to appear.

Long before the advance scouts of Grand Fleet were within surveying distance of Ploor, Kit and his sisters had spread a completely detailed chart of its defenses in the tactical tank. A white star represented Ploor's sun; a white sphere the planet itself; white Ryerson string-lights marked a portion of the planetary orbit. Points of white light, practically all of which were connected to the white sphere by red string-lights, marked the directions of neighboring stars and the existence of sunbeams, installed and ready. Pink globes were loose planets; purple ones negaspheres; red points of light were, as before, Boskonian task-force fleets. Blues were mobile fortresses; bands of canary yellow and amber luminescence showed the locations and emplacements of sunbeam grids and deflectors.

Layer after layer of pinks, purples, and blues almost hid the brilliant white sphere from sight. More layers of the same colors, not quite as dense, surrounded the entire solar system. Yellow and amber bands were everywhere.

Kinnison studied the thing briefly, whistling unmelodiously through his teeth. The picture was familiar enough, since it duplicated in practically every respect the chart of the neighborhood of the Patrol's own Ultra Prime, around Klovia. Those defenses simply could not be cracked by any concentration possible of any mobile devices theretofore employed in war.

'Just about what we expected,' Kinnison thought to the group at large. 'Some new stuff, but not much. What I want to know, Kit and the rest of you, is there anything there that looks as though it was supposed to handle our new baby? Don't see anything, myself.'

'There is not,' Kit stated, definitely. 'We looked. There couldn't be, anyway. It can't be handled. Looking backwards at it, they may be able to reconstruct how it was done, but in advance? No. Even Mentor couldn't – he had to call in a fellow who has studied ultra-high mathematics for Klono-only-knows-how-many-millions of years to compute the resultant vectors.'

Kit's use of the word 'they', which of course meant Ploorans to everyone except his sisters, concealed his knowledge of the fact that the Eddorians had taken over the defense of Ploor. Eddorians were handling those screens. Eddorians were directing and correlating those far-flung task-forces, with a precision which Kinnison soon noticed.

'Much smoother work than I ever saw them do before,' he commented. 'Suppose they have developed a *Z9M9Z*?'

'Could be. They copied everything else you invented, why not that?' Again the highly ambiguous 'they'. 'No sign of it around Arisia, though – but maybe they didn't think they'd need it there.'

'Or, more likely, they didn't want to risk it so far from home. We can tell better after the mopping-up starts – if the widget performs as per specs . . . but if your dope is right, this is about close enough. You might tip the boys off, and I'll call Mentor.' Kinnison could not reach Nth space, but it was no secret that Kit could.

The terminus of one of the Patrol's hyperspatial tubes erupted into space close to Ploor. That such phenomena were expected was evident – a Boskonian fleet moved promptly and smoothly to englobe it. But this was an Arisian tube; computed, installed, and handled by Arisians. It would be in existence only three seconds; and anything the fleet could do, even if it got there in nothing flat, would make no difference.

To the observers in the *Z9M9Z* those three seconds stretched endlessly. What would happen when that utterly foreign planet, with its absolutely impossible intrinsic velocity of over fifteen times that of light, erupted into normal space and went inert? Nobody, not even the Arisians, knew.

Everybody there had seen pictures of what happened when the insignificant mass of a space-ship, traveling at only a hundredth of the velocity of light, collided with a planetoid. That was bad enough. This projectile, however, had a mass of about eight times ten to the twenty-first power – an eight followed by twenty-one zeroes – metric tons; would tend to travel fifteen hundred times as fast; and kinetic energy equals mass times velocity squared.

There seemed to be a theoretical possibility, since the mass would instantaneously become some higher order of infinity, that all the matter in normal space would coalesce with it in zero time; but Mentor had assured Kit that operators would come into effect to prevent such an occurrence, and that untoward events would be limited to a radius of ten or fifteen parsecs. Mentor could solve the problem in detail; but since the solution would require some two hundred Klovian years and the event was due to occur in two weeks . . .

'How about the big computer at Ultra Prime?' Kinnison had asked, innocently. 'You know how fast that works.'

'Roughly two thousand years – if it could take that kind of math, which it can't,' Kit had replied, and the subject had been dropped.

Finally, it happened. What happened? Even after the fact none of the observers knew; nor did any except the L_3's ever find out. The fuses of all the recorder and analyser circuits blew at once. Needles jumped instantly to maximum and wrapped themselves around their stops. Charts and ultra-photographic films showed only straight or curved lines running from the origin to and through the limits in zero time. Ploor and everything around it disappeared in an utterly indescribable and completely incomprehensible blast of pure, wild, raw, uncontrolled and uncontrollable energy. The infinitesimal fraction of that energy which was visible, heterodyned upon the ultra as it was and screened as it was, blazed so savagely upon the plates that it seared the eyes.

And if the events caused by the planet aimed at Ploor were indescribable, what can be said of those initiated by the one directed against Ploor's sun?

When the heat generated in the interior of a sun becomes greater than its effective surface is able to radiate, that surface expands. If the expansion is not fast enough, a more or less insignificant amount of the sun's material explodes, thus enlarging by force the radiant surface to whatever extent is necessary to restore equilibrium. Thus come into being the ordinary novae; suns which may for a few days or for a few weeks radiate energy at a rate a few hundreds of thousands of times greater than normal. Since ordinary novae can be produced at will by the collision of a planet with a sun, the scientists of the Patrol had long since completed their studies of all the phenomena involved.

The mechanisms of super-novae, however, remained obscure. No adequate instrumentation had been developed to study conclusively the occasional super-nova which occurred naturally. No super-nova had ever been produced artificially – with all its resources of mass, atomic energy, cosmic energy, and sunbeams, Civilization could neither assemble nor concentrate enough power.

At the impact of the second loose planet, accompanied by the excess energy of its impossible and unattainable intrinsic velocity, Ploor's sun became a super-nova. How deeply the intruding thing penetrated, how much of the sun's mass exploded, never was and perhaps never will be determined. The violence of the explosion was such, however, that Klovian astronomers reported – a few years later – that it was radiating energy at the rate of some five hundred and fifty million suns.

Thus no attempt will be made to describe what happened when the planet from Nth space struck the Boskonians' sun. It was indescribability cubed.

27

Kinnison Trapped

The Boskonian fleets defending Ploor were not all destroyed, of course. The vessels were inertialess. None of the phenomena accompanying the coming into being of the super-nova were propagated at a velocity above that of light; a speed which to any space-ship is scarcely a crawl.

The survivors were, however, disorganized. They had lost their morale when Ploor was wiped out in such a spectacularly nerve-shattering fashion. Also, they had lost practically all of their high command; for the bosses, instead of riding the ether as did the Patrol commanders, remained in their supposedly secure headquarters and directed matters from afar. Mentor and his fellows had removed from this plane of existence the Eddorians who had been present in the flesh on Ploor. The Arisians had cut all communication between Eddore and the remnants of the Boskonian defensive force.

Grand Fleet, then, moved in for the kill; and for a time the action near Arisia was repeated. Following definite flight-and-course orders from the Z_9M_9Z, ten or more Patrol fleets would make short hops. At the end of those assigned courses they would discover that they had englobed a task-force of the enemy. Bomb and beam!

Over and over – flit, bomb, and beam!

One Boskonian high officer, however, had both the time and the authority to act. A full thousand fleets massed together, their heaviest units outward, packed together screen to screen in a close-order globe of defense.

'According to Haynes, that was good strategy in the old

days,' Kinnison commented, 'but it's no good against loose planets and negaspheres.'

Six loose planets were so placed and so released that their inert masses would crash together at the center of the Boskonian globe; then, a few minutes later, ten negaspheres of high anti-mass were similarly launched. After those sixteen missiles had done their work and the resultant had attained an equilibrium of sorts, there was very little mopping-up to do.

The Boskonian observers were competent. The Boskonian commanders now knew that they had no chance whatever of success; that to stay was to be annihilated; that the only possibility of life lay in flight. Therefore each remaining Boskonian vice-admiral, after perhaps a moment of consultation with a few others, ordered his fleet to drive at maximum blast for his home planet.

'No use chasing them individually, is there, Kit?' Kinnison asked, when it became clear in the tank that the real battle was over; that all resistance had ended. 'They can't do anything, and this kind of killing makes me sick at the stomach. Besides, I've got something else to do.'

'No. Me, too. So have I.' Kit agreed with his father in full.

As soon as the last Boskonian fleet was beyond detector range Grand Fleet broke up, its component fleets setting out for their respective worlds.

'The Hell-Hole is still there, Kit,' the Grey Lensman said soberly. 'If Ploor was the top – I'm beginning to think there *is* no top – it leads either to an automatic mechanism set up by the Ploorans or to Ploorans who are still alive somewhere. If Ploor wasn't the top, this seems to be the only lead we have. In either case I've got to take it. Check?'

'Well, I . . .' Kit tried to duck, but couldn't. 'Yes, dad, I'm afraid it's check.'

Two big hands met and gripped: and Kinnison went to take leave of his wife.

There is no need to go into detail as to what those two said or did. He knew that he was going into danger; that he might not return. That is, he knew empirically or academically, as a non-germane sort of fact, that he might die. He did not, however, really believe so. No man really believes, ever, that any given event will kill him.

Kinnison expected to be captured, imprisoned, questioned, tortured. He could understand all of those things, and he did not like any one of them. That he was more than a trifle afraid and that he hated to leave her now more than he ever had before were both natural enough – he had nothing whatever to hide from her.

She, on the other hand, knew starkly that he would never come back. She knew that he would die in that trap. She knew that she would have to live a lifetime of emptiness, alone. Hence she had much to conceal from him. She must be just as scared and as apprehensive as he was, but no more; just as anxious for their continued happiness as he was, but no more; just as intensely loving, but no more and in exactly the same sense. Here lay the test. She must kiss him goodbye as though he were going into mere danger. She *must not* give way to the almost irresistible urge to act in accordance with what she so starkly, chillingly knew to be the truth, that she would never . . . *never* . . . NEVER kiss her Kim again!

She succeeded. It is a measure of the Red Lensman's quality that she did not weaken, even when her husband approached the boundary of the Hell-Hole and sent what she knew would be his last message.

'Here it is – about a second now. Don't worry – I'll be back shortly. Clear ether, Cris!'

'Of *course* you will, dear. Clear ether, Kim!'

His speedster did not mount any special generators, nor were any needed. He and his ship were sucked into that trap as though it had been a maelstrom.

He felt again the commingled agonies of inter-dimensional acceleration. He perceived again the formless, textureless, space-less void of blankly grey nothingness which was the three-dimensionally-impossible substance of the tube. A moment later, he felt a new and different acceleration – he was speeding up *inside the tube*! Then, very shortly, he felt nothing at all. Startled, he tried to jump up to investigate, and discovered that he could not move. Even by the utmost exertion of his will he could not stir a finger or an eyelid. He was completely immobilized. Nor could he feel. His body was as devoid of sensation as though it belonged to somebody else. Worse, for his heart was not beating. He was not breathing. He could not see. It was as though his every nerve, motor and sensory, voluntary and involuntary, had been separately anaesthetized. He could still think, but that was all. His sense of perception still worked.

He wondered whether he was still accelerating or not, and tried to find out. He could not. He could not determine whether he was moving or stationary. There were no reference points. Every infinitesimal volume of that enigmatic greyness was like each and every other.

Mathematically, perhaps, he was not moving at all; since he was in a continuum in which mass, length and time, and hence inertia and inertialessness, velocity and acceleration, are meaningless terms.

He was outside of space and beyond time. Effectively, however, he was moving; moving with an acceleration which nothing material had ever before approached. He and his vessel were being driven along that tube by every watt of power generable by one entire Eddorian atomic power plant. His velocity, long since unthinkable, became incalculable.

All things end: even Eddorian atomic power was not infinite. At the very peak of power and pace, then, all the force, all the momentum, all the kinetic energy of the speedster's mass and velocity were concentrated in and applied to Kinnison's physical body. He sensed something, and tried to flinch, but could not. In a fleeting instant of what he thought was time he went *past*, not through, his clothing and his Lens; *past*, not through, his armor; and *past*, not through, the hard beryllium-alloy structure of his vessel. He even went past but not through the N-dimensional interface of the hyperspatial tube.

This, although Kinnison did not know it, was the Eddorian's climactic effort. He had taken his prisoner as far as he could possibly reach: then, assembling and concentrating all available power, he had given him a catapultic shove into the absolutely unknown and utterly unknowable. The Eddorian did not know any vector of the Lensman's naked flight; he did not care where he went. He did not know and could not compute or even guess at his victim's probable destination.

In what his spacehound's time sense told him was one second, Kinnison passed exactly two hundred million foreign spaces. He did not know how he knew the precise number, but he did. Hence, in the Patrol's measured cadence, he began to count groups of spaces of one hundred million each. After a few days, his velocity decreased to such a value that he could count groups of single millions. Then thousands – hundreds – tens – until finally he could perceive the salient features of each space before it was blotted out by the next.

How could this be? He wondered, but not foggily; his mind was as clear and as strong as it had ever been. Spaces were coexistent, not spread out like this. In the fourth dimension they were flat together, like pages in a book, except thinner. This was all wrong. It was impossible. Since it could not happen, it was not happening. He had not been and could not be drugged. Therefore some Plooran must have him in a zone of compulsion. *What* a zone! *What* an operator the ape must be!

It was, however, real – all of it. What Kinnison did not know, then or ever, was that he was actually outside the boundaries of space; actually beyond the confines of time. He was going past, not through, those spaces and those times.

He was now in each space long enough to study it in some detail. He was an immense distance above this one; at such a distance that he could perceive many globular super-universes; each of which in turn was composed of billions of lenticular galaxies.

Another one. Closer now, galaxies only; the familiar random masses whose apparent lack of symmetrical grouping is due to the limitations of Civilization's observers. He was still going too fast to stop.

In the next space Kinnison found himself within the limits of a solar system and tried with all the force of his mind to get in touch with some intelligent entity upon one – any one – of its planets. Before he could succeed, that system vanished and he was dropping, from a height of a few thousand kilometers, toward the surface of a warm and verdant world, so much like Tellus that he thought for an instant he must have circumnavigated total space. The aspect, the ice-caps, the cloud-effects, were identical. The oceans, however, while similar, were different; as were the continents. The mountains were larger and rougher and harder.

He was falling much too fast. A free fall from infinity wouldn't give him *this* much speed!

This whole affair was, as he had decided once before, absolutely impossible. It was simply preposterous to believe that a naked man, especially one without blood-circulation or breath, could still be alive after spending as many weeks in open space as he had just spent. He *knew* that he was alive. Therefore none of this was happening; even though, as surely as he knew that he was alive, he knew that he was falling.

'Jet back, Lensman!' he thought viciously to himself; tried to shout it aloud.

For this could be deadly stuff, if he let himself believe it. If he believed that he was falling from any such height he would die in the instant of landing. He would not actually crash; his body would not move from wherever it was that it was. Nevertheless the shock of that wholly imaginary crash would kill him just as dead and just as instantaneously as though all his flesh had been actually smashed into a crimson smear upon one of the neighboring mountain's huge, flat rocks.

'Pretty close, my bright young Plooran friend, but you didn't quite ring the bell,' he thought savagely, trying with all the power of his mind to break through the zone of compulsion. 'So I'm telling you something right now. If you want to kill me you'll have to do it physically, and you haven't got jets enough to swing the load. You might as well cut your zone, because this kind of stuff has been pulled on me by experts, and it hasn't worked yet.'

He was apparently falling, feet downward, toward an open, grassy mountain meadow, surrounded by forests, through which meandered a small stream. He was so close now that he could perceive the individual blades of grass in the meadow and the small fishes in the stream; and he was still apparently at terminal velocity.

Without his years of spacehound's training in inertialess maneuvering, he might have died even before he landed, but speed as speed did not affect him at all. He was used to instantaneous stops from light-speeds. The only thing that worried him was the matter of inertia. Was he inert or free?

He declared to himself that he was free. Or, rather, that he had been, was, and would continue to be motionless. It was physically, mathematically, intrinsically impossible that any of this stuff had actually occurred. It was all compulsion, pure and simple, and he – Kimball Kinnison, Grey Lensman – would not let it get him down. He clenched his mental teeth upon that belief and held it doggedly. One bare foot struck the tip of a blade of grass and his entire body came to a shockless halt. He grinned in relief – this was what he had wanted, but had not quite dared wholly to expect. There followed immediately, however, other events which he had not expected at all.

His halt was less than momentary; in the instant of its accomplishment he began to fall normally the remaining eight or ten inches to the ground. Automatically he sprung his space-trained knees, to take the otherwise disconcerting jar; automatically his left hand snapped up to the place where his controls should have been. *Legs and arms worked!*

He could see with his eyes. He could feel with his skin. He was drawing a breath, the first time he had breathed since leaving normal space. Nor was it an unduly deep breath – he felt no lack of oxygen. His heart was beating as normally as though it had never missed a beat. He was not unusually hungry or thirsty. But all that stuff could wait – where was that damned Plooran?

Kinnison had landed in complete readiness for strife. There were no rocks or clubs handy, but he had his fists, feet, and teeth; and they would do until he could find or make something better. But there was nothing to fight. Drive his sense of perception as he would, he could find nothing larger or more intelligent than a deer.

The farther this thing went along the less sense it made. A compulsion, to be any good at all, ought to be logical and coherent. It should fit into every corner and cranny of the subject's experience and knowledge. This one didn't fit anything or anywhere. It didn't even come close. Yet technically, it was a marvelous job. He couldn't detect a trace of it. This grass looked and felt real. The pebbles hurt his tender feet enough to make him wince as he walked to the water's edge. He drank deeply. The water, real or not, was cold, clear, and eminently satisfying.

'Listen, you misguided ape!' he thought probingly. 'You might as well open up now as later whatever you've got in mind. If this performance is supposed to be non-fiction, it's a flat bust. If it's supposed to be science-fiction, it isn't much better. If it's space-opera, even, you've violating all the fundamentals. I've written better stuff – Qadgop and Cynthia were a lot more convincing.' He waited a moment, then went on:

'Who ever heard of the intrepid hero of a space-opera as big as this one started out to be getting stranded on a completely Earth-like planet and then have nothing happen? No action at all? How about a couple of indescribable monsters of super-human strength and agility, for me to tear apart with my steel-thewed fingers?'

He glanced around expectantly. No monsters appeared.

'Well, then, how about a damsel for me to rescue from a fate worse than death? Better make it two of them – safety in numbers, you know – a blonde and a brunette. No redheads.'

He waited again.

'QX, sport, no women. Suits me perfectly. But I hope you haven't forgotten about the tasty viands. I can eat fish if I have to, but if you want to keep your hero happy let's see you lay down here, on a platter, a one-kilogram steak, three centimeters thick, medium rare, fried in Tellurian butter and smothered in Venerian superla mushrooms.'

No steak appeared, and the Grey Lensman recalled and studied intensively every detail of what had apparently happened. It *still* could not have occurred. He could not have imagined it. It could not have been compulsion or hypnosis. None of it made any kind of sense.

As a matter of plain fact, however, Kinnison's first and most positive conclusion was wrong. His memories were factual records of actual events and things. He would eat well during his stay upon that nameless planet, but he would have to procure his own food. Nothing would attack him, or even annoy him. For the Eddorian's *binding* – this is perhaps as good a word for it as any, since 'geas' implies a curse – was such that the Grey Lensman could return to space and time only under such conditions and to such an environment as would not do him any iota of physical harm. He must continue alive and in good health for at least fifty more of his years.

And Clarrissa Kinnison, tense and strained, waited in her room for the instant of her husband's death. They two were one, with a oneness no other man and woman had ever known. If one died, from any cause whatever, the other would feel it.

She waited. Five minutes – ten – fifteen – half an hour – an hour. She began to relax. Her fists unclenched, her shallow breathing grew deeper.

Two hours. Kim was *still alive*! A wave of happy, buoyant relief swept through her; her eyes flashed and sparkled. If they hadn't been able to kill him in two hours they never could. Her Kim had plenty of jets.

Even the top minds of Boskonia could not kill her Kim!

28
The Battle of Eddore

The Arisians and the Children of the Lens had known that Eddore must be attacked as soon as possible after the fall of Ploor. They were fairly certain that the interspatial use of planets as projectiles was new; but they were completely certain that the Eddorians would be able to deduce in a short time the principles and the concepts, the fundamental equations, and the essential operators involved in the process. They would find Nth space or one like it in one day; certainly not more than two. Their slaves would duplicate the weapon in approximately three weeks. Shortly thereafter both Ultra Prime and Prime Base, both Klovia and Tellus, would be blown out of the ether. So would Arisia – perhaps Arisia would go first. The Eddorians would probably not be able to aim such planets as accurately as the Arisians had, but they would keep on trying and they would learn fast.

This weapon was the sheer ultimate in destructiveness. No defense against it was possible. There was no theory which applied to it or which could be stretched to cover it. Even the Arisian Masters of Mathematics had not as yet been able to invent symbologies and techniques to handle the quantities and magnitudes involved when those interloping masses of foreign matter struck normal space.

Thus Kit did not have to follow up his announced intention of making the Arisians hurry. They did not hurry, of course, but they did not lose or waste a minute. Each Arisian, from the youngest watchman up to the oldest philosopher, tuned a part of his mind to Mentor, another part to some one of the millions of Lensmen upon his list, and flashed a message.

'Lensmen, attend – keep your mind sensitized to this, the pattern of Mentor of Arisia, who will speak to you as soon as all have been alerted.'

That message went throughout the First Galaxy, throughout intergalactic space, and throughout what part of the Second Galaxy had felt the touch of Civilization. It went to Alsakan and Vandemar and Klovia, to Thrale and Tellus and Rigel IV, to Mars and Velantia and Palain VII, to Medon and Venus and Centralia. It went to flitters, battleships, and loose planets. It went to asteroids and moonlets, to planets large and small. It went to newly graduated Lensmen and to Lensmen long since retired; to Lensmen at work and at play. It went to every First-Stage Lensman of the Galactic Patrol.

Wherever the message went, turmoil followed. Lensmen everywhere flashed questions at other Lensmen.

'What do you make of it, Fred?'

'Did you get the same thing I did?'

'*Mentor!* Grinning Noshabkeming, what's up?'

'Damfino. Must be big, though, for Mentor to be handling it.'

'*Big!* It's immense! Who ever heard of Arisia stepping in before?'

'*Big!* Colossal! Mentor never talked twice to anybody except the L2's before, did he?'

Millions of Lensed questions flooded every base and every office of the Patrol. Nobody, not even the vice-coordinator, knew a thing.

'You might as well stop sending in questions as to what this is all about, because none of us knows any more about it than you do,' Maitland finally sent out a general message. 'Apparently everybody with a Lens is getting the same thought, no more and no less. All I can say is that it must be a Class A Prime emergency, and everyone who is not actually tied up in a life and death matter will please drop everything and stand by.'

Mentor wanted, and had to have, high tension. He got it.

Tension mounted higher and higher as eventless hours passed and as, for the first time in history, Patrol business slowed down almost to a stop.

And in a small cruiser, manned by four red-headed girls and one red-headed youth, tension was also building up. The problem of the mechanical screens had long since been solved. Atomic powered counter-generators were in place, ready at the touch of a button to neutralize the mechanically-generated screens of the enemy and thus to make the engagement a mind-to-mind combat. They were as close to Eddore's star-cluster as they could be without giving alarm. They had had nothing to do for hours except wait. They were probably keyed up higher than any other five Lensmen in all of space.

Kit, son of his father, was pacing the floor, chain-smoking. Constance was alternately getting up and sitting down – up – down – up. She, too, was smoking; or, rather, she was lighting cigarettes and throwing them away. Kathryn was sitting, stiffly still, manufacturing Lenses which, starting at her wrists, raced up both bare arms to her shoulders and disappeared. Karen was meticulously sticking holes in a piece of blank paper with a pin, making an intricate and meaningless design. Only Camilla made any pretense of calmness, and it was as transparent as glass. She was pretending to read a novel; but instead of absorbing its full content at the rate of one glance per page, she had read half of it word by word and still had no idea of what the story was about.

'Are you ready, children?' Mentor's thought came in at last.

'Ready!' Without knowing how they got there, the Five found themselves standing in the middle of the room, packed tight.

'Oh, Kit, I'm shaking like a torso-tosser!' Constance wailed. 'I just *know* I'm going to louse up this whole damn war!'

'QX, baby, we're all in the same fix. Can't you hear my teeth chatter? Doesn't mean a thing. Good teams – champions – all feel the same way before a big game starts . . . and this is the biggest game ever . . . steady down, kids. We'll be QX as soon as the whistle blows – I hope . . .'

'*P-s-s-t!*' Kathryn hissed. 'Listen!'

'Lensmen of the Galactic Patrol!' Mentor's resonant pseudo-voice filled all space. 'I, Mentor of Arisia, am calling upon you because of a crisis in which no lesser force can be of use. You have been informed upon the matter of Ploor. It is true that Ploor has been destroyed; that the Ploorans, physically, are no more. You of the Lens, however, already know dimly that the physical is not the all. Know now that there is a residuum of non-material malignancy against which all the physical weapons of all the universes would be completely impotent. That evil effluvium, intrinsically vicious, is implacably opposed to every basic concept and idea of your Patrol. It has been on the move ever since the destruction of the planet Ploor. Unaided, we of Arisia are not strong enough to handle it, but the massed and directed force of your collective mind will be able to destroy it completely. If you wish me to do so, I will supervise the work of so directing your mental force as to encompass the complete destruction of this menace, which I tell you most solemnly is the last weapon of power with which Boskonia will be able to threaten Civilization. Lensmen of the Galactic Patrol, met as one for the first time in Civilization's long history, what is your wish?'

A tremendous wave of thought, expressed in millions of variant phraseologies, made the wish of the Lensmen very clear indeed. They did not know how such a thing could be done, but they were supremely eager to have Mentor of Arisia lead them against the Boskonians, whoever and wherever they might be.

'Your verdict is unanimous, as I had hoped and believed that it would be. It is well. The part of each of you will be simple, but not easy. You will all of you, individually, think of two things, and of only two. First, of your love for and your pride in and your loyalty to your Patrol. Second, of the clear fact that Civilization must and shall triumph over Boskonia. Think these thoughts, each of you with all the strength that in him lies.

'You need not consciously direct those thoughts. Being attuned to my pattern, the force will flow at my direction. As

274

it passes from you, you will replenish it, each according to his strength. You will find it the hardest labor you have ever performed, but it will be of permanent harm to none and it will not be of long duration. Are you ready?'

'WE ARE READY!' The crescendo roar of thought bulged the galaxy to its poles.

'Children – strike!'

The generators flared into action – the mechanical screens collapsed – the Unit struck. The outermost mental screen went down. The Unit struck again, almost instantly. Down went the second. The third. The fourth.

It was that flawless Unit, not Camilla, who detected and analyzed and precisely located the Eddorian guardsmen handling each of those far-flung screens. It was the Unit, not Kathryn and Kit, who drilled the pilot hole through each Eddorian's hard-held block and enlarged it into a working orifice. It was the Unit, not Karen, whose impenetrable shield held stubbornly every circular mil of advantage gained in making such ingress. It was the Unit, not Constance, who assembled and drove home the blasts of mental force in which the Eddorians died. No time whatever was lost in consultation or decision. Action was not only instantaneous, but simultaneous with perception. The Children of the Lens were not now five, but one. The UNIT.

'Come in, Mentor!' Kit snapped then. 'All you Arisians and all the Lensmen. Nothing specialized – just a general slam at the whole screen. This fifth screen is the works – they've got twenty minds on it instead of one, and they're top-notchers. Best strategy now is for us five to lay off for a second or two and show 'em what we've got in the line of defense, while the rest of you fellows give 'em hell!'

Arisia and the massed Lensmen struck; a tidal wave of such tremendous weight and power that under its impact the fifth screen sagged flat against the planet's surface. Any one Lensman's power was small, of course, in comparison with that of any Eddorian; but every available Lensman of the Galactic Patrol was giving, each according to his strength, and the

275

output of one Lensman, multiplied by the countless millions which was the number of Lensmen then at work, made itself tellingly felt.

Countless? Yes. Only Mentor ever knew how many minds contributed to that stupendous flood of force. Bear in mind that in the First Galaxy alone there are over one hundred thousand million suns: that each sun has, on the average, something over one and thirty seven hundredths planets inhabited by intelligent life: that about one-half of these planets then adhered to Civilization; and that Tellus, an average planet, graduates approximately one hundred Lensmen every year.

'So far, Kit, so good,' Constance panted. Although she was no longer trembling, she was still highly excited. 'But I don't know how many more shots like that I've – we've – got left in the locker.'

'You're doing fine, Connie,' Camilla soothed.

'Sure you are, baby. You've got plenty of jets,' Kit agreed. Except in moments of supreme stress these personal, individual exchanges of by-thoughts did not interfere with the smooth functioning of the Unit. 'Fine work, all of you, kids. I thought we'd get over the shakes as soon as...'

'Watch it!' Camilla snapped. 'Here comes the shockwave. Brace yourself, Kay. Hold us together, Kit!'

The wave came. Everything that the Eddorians could send. The Unit's barrier did not waver. After a full second of it – a time comparable to days of saturation atomic bombing in ordinary warfare – Karen, who had been standing stiff and still, began to relax.

'This is too, *too* easy,' she declared. 'Who's helping me? I can't feel anything, but I simply *know* I haven't got this much stuff. You, Cam – or is it all of you?' Not one of the Five was as yet thoroughly familiar with the operating characteristics of the Unit.

'All of us, more or less, but mostly Kit,' Camilla decided after a moment's thought. 'He's as solid as an inert planet.'

'Not me,' Kit denied, vigorously. 'Must be you other kids. Feels to me like Kat, mostly. All I'm doing is just sort of leaning up against you a little – just in case. I haven't done a thing so far.'

'Oh, no? Sure not!' Kathryn giggled, an infectious chuckle inherited or copied directly from her mother. 'We know it, Kit. You wouldn't think of doing anything, even if you could. Just the same, we're mighty glad you're here, chum!'

'QX, kids, seal the chatter. We've had time to learn that they can't crack us, and so have they, so let's get to work.'

Since the Unit was now under continuous attack, its technique would have to be entirely different from that used previously. Its barrier must vanish for an infinitesimal period of time, during which it must simultaneously detect and blast. Or, rather, the blast would have to be directed in mid-flight, while the Unit's own block was open. Nor could that block be open for more than the barest fractional millimicro-second before or after the passage of the bolt. It is true that the bolt compared with the power of the Unit very much as the steady pressure of burning propellant powder compares with the disruptive force of detonating duodec: even so it would have wrought much damage to the minds of the Five had any of it been allowed to reach them.

Also, like parachute-jumping, this technique could not be practiced. Since the timing had to be so nearly absolute, the first two shots missed their targets completely; but the Unit learned fast. Eddorian after Eddorian died.

'Help, All-Highest, help!' a high Eddorian appealed, finally.

'What is it?' His Ultimate Supremacy, knowing that only utter desperation could be back of such intrusion, accepted the call.

'It is this new Arisian entity . . .'

'It is not an entity, fool, but a fusion,' came curt reprimand. 'We decided that point long ago.'

'An entity, I say!' In his urgency the operator committed the unpardonable by omitting the titles of address. 'No possible fusion can attain such perfection of timing, of synchronization. Our best fusions have attempted to match it, and have failed. Its screens are impenetrable. Its thrusts cannot be blocked. My message is this: solve for us, and quickly, the problem of this entity. If you do not or cannot do so, we perish all of us, even to you of the Innermost Circle.'

'Think you so?' The thought was a sneer. 'If your fusions cannot match those of the Arisians you should die, and the loss will be small.'

The fifth screen went down. Eddore lay bare to the Arisian mind. There were inner defenses, of course, but Kit knew every one; their strengths and their weaknesses. He had long since spread in Mentor's mind an exact and completely detailed chart: they had long since drawn up a completely detailed plan of campaign. Nevertheless, Kit could not keep from advising Mentor:

'Pick off any who may try to get away. Start on Area B and work up. Be sure, though, to lay off of Area K or you'll get your beard singed off.'

'The plan is being followed, youth,' Mentor assured him. 'Children, you have done very well indeed. Rest now, and recuperate your powers against that which is yet to come.'

'QX. Unlace yourselves, kids. Loosen up. Relax. I'll break out a few beakers of fayalin, and all of us – you especially, Con – had better stoke up with candy bars.'

'*Eat!* Why, I *couldn't*...' but at her brother's insistence she took an experimental bite. 'But say, I *am* hungry, at that!'

'Of course you are. You've been putting out a lot of stuff, and there's more and worse coming. Now rest, all of you.'

They rested. Somewhat to their surprise, they could rest; even Constance. But the respite was short. Area K, the head-quarters and the citadel of His Ultimate Supremacy and the Innermost Circle of the Boskonian Empire, contained all that remained of Eddorian life.

But this, Kit knew, was the crux. This was what had stopped the Arisians cold; had held them off for all these millions upon millions of years. Everything up to now the Arisians could have done themselves; but even the totalized and integrated mind of Arisia would hit Area K and bounce.

To handle Area K two things were necessary: the Unit and the utterly inconceivable massed might of the Lensmen.

Knowing better even than Mentor what the situation was, Kit felt again a twinge of panic, but managed to throw it off.

'No tight linkage yet, kids,' Kit the Organizer went smoothly to work. 'Individual effort – a flash of fusion, perhaps, now and then, if any of us call for it, but no Unit until I give the word. Then give it everything you've got. Cam, analyze that screen and set us up a pattern for it – you'll find it'll take some doing. See whether it's absolutely homogeneous – hunt for weak spots, if any. Con, narrow down to the sharpest needle you can possibly make and start pecking. Not too hard – don't tire yourself – just to get acquainted with the texture of the thing and keep them awake. Kay, take over our guard so Eukonidor can join the other Arisians. Kat, come along with me – you'll have to help with the Arisians until I call you into the Unit.

'You Arisians, except Mentor, blanket this dome. Thinner than that – solider, harder . . . there. A trifle off-balance yet – give me just a little more, here on this side. QX – hold it right there! SQUEEZE! Kat, watch 'em. Hold them right there and in balance until you're sure the Eddorians aren't going to be able to put any bulges up through the blanket.

'Now, Mentor, you and the Lensmen. Tell them to give us, for the next five seconds, absolutely everything they can deliver. When they're at absolute peak, hit us with the whole charge. Dead center. Don't pull your punch. We'll be ready.

'Con, get ready to stick the needle right there – they'll think it's just another peck, I hope – and slug as you never slugged before. Kay, get ready to drop that screen and stiffen the needle – when that beam hits us it'll be NO pat on the back. The rest of us will brace you both and keep the shock from killing us all. Here it comes . . . make Unit! . . . GO!'

The Unit struck. Its needle of pure force drove against the Eddorians' supposedly absolutely impenetrable shield. The Unit's thrust was, of itself, like nothing ever before known. The Lensmen's pile-driver blow – the integrated sum total of the top effort of every Lensman of the entire Galactic Patrol – was of itself irresistible. Something had to give way.

For an instant it seemed as though nothing were happening or ever would happen. Strong young arms laced the straining Five into a group as motionless and as sculpturesque as statuary, while between their bodies and around them there came into being a gigantic Lens: a Lens whose splendor filled the entire room with radiance.

Under that awful concentration of force something *had* to give way. The Unit held. The Arisians held. The Lensmen held. The needle, superlatively braced, neither bent nor broke. Therefore the Eddorians' screen was punctured; and in the instant of its puncturing it disappeared as does a bubble when it breaks.

There was no mopping up to do. Such was the torrent of force cascading into the stronghold that within a micro-second after its shield went down all life within it was snuffed out.

The Boskonian War was over.

29
The Power of Love

'Did you kids come through QX?' The frightful combat over, the dreadful tension a thing of the past, Kit's first thought was for his sisters.

They were unharmed. None of the Five had suffered anything except mental exhaustion. Recuperation was rapid.

'Better we hunt that tube up and get dad out of it, don't you think?' Kit suggested.

'Have you got a story arranged that will hold water?' Camilla asked.

'Everything except for a few minor details, which we can put in later.'

Smoothly the four girls linked their minds with their brother's; effortlessly the Unit's thought surveyed all nearby space. No hyperspatial tube, nor any trace of one, was there. Tuned to Kinnison's pattern, the Unit then scanned not only normal space and the then present time, but also millions upon millions of other spaces and past and future times; all without finding the Grey Lensman.

Again and again the Unit reached out, farther and farther; out to the extreme limit of even its extraordinary range. Every space and every time was empty. The Children of the Lens broke their linkage and stared at each other, aghast.

They knew starkly what it must mean, but that conclusion was unthinkable. Kinnison – their dad – the hub of the universe – the unshakable, immutable Rock of Civilization – he *couldn't* be dead. They simply could not accept the logical explanation as the true one.

And while they pondered, shaken, a call from their Red Lensman mother came in.

'You are together? Good! I've been *so* worried about Kim going into that trap. I've been trying to get in touch with him, but I can't reach him. You children, with your greater power...'

She broke off as the dread import of the Five's surface thoughts became clear to her. At first she, too, was shaken, but she rallied magnificently.

'Nonsense!' she snapped; not in denial of an unwelcome fact, but in sure knowledge that the supposition was not and could not be a fact. 'Kimball Kinnison is *alive*. He's lost, I know – I last heard from him just before he went into that tube – but he did *not* die! If he had, I would most certainly have felt it. So don't be idiots, children, please. Think – *really* think! I'm going to do something – somehow – but what? Mentor? I've never called him and I'm terribly afraid he might not do anything. I could go there and make him do something, but that would take so long – what shall I do? What *can* I do?'

'Mentor, by all means,' Kit decided. 'He'll do something – he'll *have* to. However, there's no need of you going to Arisia in person.' Now that the Eddorians had ceased to exist, intergalactic space presented no barrier to Arisian thought, but Kit did not go into that. 'Link your mind with ours.' She did so.

'Mentor of Arisia!' the clear-cut thought flashed out. 'Kimball Kinnison of Klovia is not present in this, his normal space and time; nor in any other continuum we can reach. We need help.'

'Ah; 'tis Lensman Clarrissa and the Five.' Imperturbably, Mentor's mind joined theirs on the instant. 'I have given the matter no attention, nor have I scanned my visualization of the Cosmic All. It may therefore be that Kimball Kinnison has passed on from his plane of exist...'

'He has NOT! It is stark idiocy even to consider such a possibility!' the Red Lensman interrupted violently, so violently that her thought had the impact of a physical blow. Mentor and the Five alike could see her eyes flash and sparkle; could hear her voice crackle as she spoke aloud, the better to drive home her passionate conviction. 'Kim is ALIVE! I told the children so and now I tell you so. No matter where or when he might be, in whatever possible extra-dimensional nook or cranny of the entire macro-cosmic universe or in any possible period of time between plus and minus eternity, he *couldn't* die – he could not *possibly* die – without my knowing it. So find him, please – *please* find him, Mentor – or, if you can't or won't, just give me the littlest, *tiniest* hint as to how to go about it and I'll find him myself!'

The Five were appalled. Especially Kit, who knew, as the others did not, just how much afraid of Mentor his mother had always been. To direct such thoughts to any Arisian was unthinkable; but Mentor's only reaction was one of pleased interest.

'There is much of truth, daughter, in your thought,' he replied, slowly. 'Human love, in its highest manifestation, can be a mighty, a really tremendous thing. The force, the power, the capability of such a love as yours is a sector of the truth which has not been fully examined. Allow me, please, a moment in which to consider the various aspects of this matter.'

It took more than a moment. It took more than the twenty-nine seconds which the Arisian had needed to solve an earlier and supposedly similar Kinnison problem. In fact, a full half hour elapsed before Mentor resumed communication; and then he did so, not to the group as a whole, but only to the Five; using an ultra-frequency to which the Red Lensman's mind could not be attuned.

'I have not been able to reach him. Since you could not do so I knew that the problem would not be simple, but I have found that it is difficult indeed. As I have intimated previously, my visualization is not entirely clear upon any matter touching the Eddorians directly, since their minds were of great power. On the other hand, their visualizations of us were probably even more hazy. Therefore none of our analyses of each other were or could be much better than approximations.

'It is certain, however, that you were correct in assuming that it was the Ploorans who set up the hyperspatial tube as a trap for your father. The fact that the lower and middle operating echelons of Boskonia could not kill him established in the Ploorans' minds the necessity of taking him alive. That fact gave us no concern, for you, Kathryn, were on guard. Moreover, even if she alone should slip, it was manifestly impossible for them to accomplish anything against the combined power of you Five. However, at some undetermined point in time the Eddorians took over, as is shown by the fact that you are all at a loss: it being scarcely necessary to point out to you that the Ploorans could neither transport your father to any location which you could not reach nor pose any problem, including his death, which you could not solve. It is thus certain that it was one or more of the Eddorians who either killed Kinnison or sent him where he was sent. It is also certain that, after the easy fashion in which he escaped from the Ploorans after they had captured him and had him all but in their hands, the Eddorians did not care to have the Ploorans come to grips with Kimball Kinnison; fearing, and rightly, that instead of gaining information, they would lose everything.'

'Did they know I was in that tube?' Kathryn asked. 'Did they deduce us, or did they think that dad was a superman?'

'That is one of the many points which are obscure. But it made no difference, before or after the event, to them or to us, as you should perceive.'

'Of course. They knew that there was at least one third-level mind at work in the field. They must have deduced that it was Arisian work. Whether it was dad himself or whether it was coming to his aid at need would make no difference. They knew very well that he was the keystone of Civilization, and that to do away with him would be the shrewdest move they could make. Therefore we still do not understand why they didn't kill him outright and be done with it – if they didn't.'

'In exactness, neither do I . . . that point is the least clear of all. Nor is it at all certain that he still lives. It is sheerest folly to assume that the Eddorians either thought or acted illogically, even occasionally. Therefore, if Kinnison is not dead, whatever was done was calculated to be even more final than death itself. This premise, if adopted, forces the conclusion that they considered the possibility of our knowing enough about the next cycle of existence to be able to reach him there.'

Kit frowned. 'You still harp on the possibility of his death. Does not your visualization cover that?'

'Not since the Eddorians took control. I have not consciously emphasized the probability of your father's death; I have merely considered it – in the case of two mutually exclusive events, neither of which can be shown to have happened, both must be studied with care. Assume for the moment that your mother's theory is the truth, that your father is still alive. In that case, what was done and how it was done are eminently clear.'

'Clear? Not to us!' the Five chorused.

'While they did not know at all exactly the power of our minds, they could establish limits beyond which neither they nor we could go. Being mechanically inclined, it is reasonable to assume that they had at their disposal sufficient energy to transport Kinnison to some point well beyond those limits. They would have given control to a director-by-chance, so that his ultimate destination would be unknown and unknowable. He would of course land safely...'

'How? How could they, possibly...?'

'In time that knowledge will be yours. Not now. Whether or not the hypothesis just stated is true, the fact confronting us is that Kimball Kinnison is not now in any region which I am at present able to scan.'

Gloom descended palpably upon the Five.

'I am not saying or implying that the problem is insoluble. Since Eddorian minds were involved, however, you already realize that its solution will require the evaluation of many millions of factors and will consume a not inconsiderable number of your years...'

'You mean lifetimes!' an impetuous young thought broke in. 'Why, long before that...'

'Contain yourself, daughter Constance,' Mentor reproved, gently. 'I realize quite fully all the connotations and implications involved. I was about to say that it may prove desirable to assist your mother in the application of powers which may very well transcend in some respects those of either Arisia or Eddore.' He widened the band of thought to include the Red Lensman and went on as though he were just emerging from contemplation:

'Children, it appears that the solution of this problem by ordinary processes will require more time than can conveniently be spared. Moreover, it affords a priceless and perhaps a unique opportunity of increasing our store of knowledge. Be informed, however, that the probability is great that in this project you, Clarrissa, will lose your life.'

'Better not, mother. When Mentor says anything like that, it means suicide. We don't want to lose you, too,' Kit pleaded, and the four girls added their pleas to his.

Clarrissa knew that suicide was against the Code – but she also knew that, as long as it wasn't quite suicide, Lensmen went in.

'Exactly how great?' she demanded, vibrantly. 'It isn't certain – it *can't* be!'

'No, daughter, it is not certain.'

'QX, then, I'm going in. Nothing can stop me.'

'Very well. Tighten your linkage, Clarrissa, with me. Yours will be the task of sending your thought to your husband, wherever and whenever in total space and in total time he may be. If it can be done, you can do it. You alone of all the entities in existence can do it. I can neither help you nor guide you in your quest; but by virtue of your relationship to him whom we are seeking, your oneness with him, you will require neither help nor guidance. My part will be to follow you and to construct the means of his return; but the real labor is and must be yours alone. Take a moment, therefore, to prepare yourself against the effort, for it will not be small. Gather your resources, daughter; assemble all your forces and your every power.'

They watched Clarrissa, in her distant room, throw herself

prone upon her bed. She closed her eyes, buried her nose in the counterpane, and gripped a side-rail fiercely in each hand.

'Can't we help, too?' The Five implored, as one.

'I do not know.' Mentor's thought was as passionless as the voice of Fate. 'I know of no force at your disposal which can affect in any way that which is to happen. Since I do not know the full measure of your powers, however, it would be well for you to accompany us, keeping yourselves alert to take instant advantage of any opportunity to be of aid. Are you ready, daughter Clarrissa?'

'I am ready,' and the Red Lensman launched her thought.

Clarrissa Kinnison did not know, then or ever; did not have even the faintest inkling of what she did or of how she did it. Nor, tied to her by bonds of heritage, love, and sympathy though they were and of immense powers of mind though they were, did any of the Five succeed, until after centuries had passed, in elucidating the many complex phenomena involved. And Mentor, the ancient Arisian sage, never did understand.

All that any of them knew was that an infinitely loving and intensely suffering woman, stretched rigidly upon a bed, hurled out through space and time a passionately questing thought: a thought behind which she put everything she had.

Clarrissa Kinnison, Red Lensman, had much – and every iota of that impressive sum total ached for, yearned for, and insistently *demanded* her Kim – her one and only Kim. Kim her husband; Kim the father of her children; Kim her lover; Kim her other half; Kim her all in all for so many perfect years.

'Kim! KIM! Wherever you are, Kim, or whenever, listen! Listen and answer! Hear me – you *must* hear me calling – I need you, Kim, from the bottom of my soul … Kim! *My Kim!* KIM!!'

Through countless spaces and through untellable times that poignant thought sped; driven by a woman's fears, a woman's hopes, a woman's all-surpassing love; urged ever onward and ever outward by the irresistible force of a magnificent woman's frankly bared soul.

Outward … farther … farther out … farther …

Clarrissa's body went limp upon her bed. Her heart slowed; her breathing almost stopped. Kit probed quickly, finding that those secret cells into which he had scarcely dared to glance were empty and bare. Even the Red Lensman's tremendous reserves of vital force were exhausted.

'Mother, come back!'

'Come back to us!'

'Please, *please*, mums, come back!'

'Know you, children, your mother so little?'

They knew her. She would not come back alone. Regardless of any danger to herself, regardless of life itself, she would not come back until she had found her Kim.

'But *do* something, Mentor – DO SOMETHING!'

'Do what? Nothing can be done. It was simply a question of which was the greater; the volume of the required hypersphere or her remarkable store of vitality . . .'

'Shut up!' Kit blazed. 'We'll do *something*! Come on, kids, and we'll try . . .'

'The Unit!' Kathryn shrieked. 'Link up, quick! Cam, make mother's pattern – hurry it!! Now, Unit, grab it – make her one of us, a six-ply Unit – *make* her come in, and snap it up! There! Now, Kit, drive us . . . DRIVE US!'

Kit drove. As the surging life-force of the Unit pushed a measure of vitality back into Clarrissa's inert body, she gained a little strength and did not grow weaker. The children, however, did; and Mentor, who had been entirely unmoved by the woman's imminent death, became highly concerned.

'Children, return!' He first ordered, then entreated. 'You are throwing away not only your lives, but also long lifetimes of intensive labor and study!'

They paid no attention. No more than their mother would those children abandon such a mission unaccomplished. Seven Kinnisons would come back or none.

The four-ply Arisian pondered; and brightened. Now that a theretofore impossible linkage had been made, the outlook changed. The odds shifted. The Unit's delicacy of web, its driving force, had not been enough; or rather, it would have taken too long. Adding the Red Lensman's affinity for her husband, however... Yes, definitely, the Unit should now succeed.

It did. Before any of the Five weakened to the danger point the Unit, again five-fold, snapped back. Clarrissa's life-force, which had tried so valiantly to fill all of space and all of time, was flowing back into her. A tight, hard, impossibly writhing and twisting multi-dimensional beam ran, it seemed, to infinity and vanished.

'A right scholarly bit of work, children,' Mentor approved. 'I have arranged the means of his return.'

'Thanks, children. Thanks, Mentor.' Instead of fainting Clarrissa sprang from her bed and stood erect. Flushed and panting, eyes flamingly alight, she was more intensely vital than any of her children had ever seen her. Reaction might – would – come later, but she was now all buoyantly vibrant woman. 'Where will he come into our space, and when?'

'In your room before you. Now.'

Kinnison materialized; and as the Red Lensman and the Grey went hungrily into each other's arms, Mentor and the Five turned their attention toward the future.

'First, the hyperspatial tube which was called the "Hell-Hole in Space",' Kit began. 'We must establish as fact in the minds of all Civilization that the Ploorans were actually at the top of Boskone. The story as we have arranged it is that Ploor was the top, and – which happens to be the truth – that it was destroyed through the efforts of the Second-Stage Lensmen. The "Hell-Hole" is to be explained as being operated by the Plooran "residuum" which every Lensman knows all about and which he will never forget. The problem of dad's whereabouts was different from the previous one in degree only, not in kind. To all except us, there never were any Eddorians. Any objections? Will that version hold?'

The consensus was that the story was sound and tight.

'The time has come, then,' Karen thought, 'to go into the very important matter of our reason for being and our purpose in life. You have intimated repeatedly that you Arisians are resigning your Guardianship of Civilization and that we are to take over; and I have just perceived the terribly shocking fact that you four are now alone, that all the other Arisians have already gone. We're not ready, Mentor; you know we're not – this scares me through and through.'

'You are ready, children, for everything that will have to be done. You have not come to your full maturity and power, of course; that stage will come only with time. It is best for you, however, that we leave you now. Your race is potentially vastly stronger and abler than ours. We reached some time ago the highest point attainable to us: we could no longer adapt ourselves to the ever-increasing complexity of life. You, a young new race amply equipped for any emergency within reckonable time, will be able to do so. In capability and in equipment you begin where we leave off.'

'But we know – you've taught us – scarcely anything!' Constance protested.

'I have taught you exactly enough. That I do not know exactly what changes to anticipate is implicit in the fact that our race is out of date. Further Arisian teaching would tend to set you in the out-dated Arisian mold and thereby defeat our every purpose. As I have informed you repeatedly, we ourselves do not know what extra qualities you possess. Hence I am in no sense competent to instruct you in the natures or in the uses of them. It is certain, however, that you have those extra qualities. It is equally certain that you possess the abilities to develop them to the full. I have set your feet on the sure way to the full development of those abilities.'

'But that will take much time, sir,' Kit thought, 'and if you leave us now we won't have it.'

'You will have time enough and to spare.'

'Oh – then we won't have to do it right away?' Constance broke in. 'Good!'

'We're all glad of that,' Camilla added. 'We're too full of our own lives, too eager for experiences, to enjoy the prospect of living such lives as you Arisians have lived. I am right in assuming, am I not, that our own development will in time force us into the same or a similar existence?'

'Your muddy thinking has again distorted the truth,' Mentor reproved her. 'There will be no force involved. You will gain everything, lose nothing. You have no conception of the depth and breadth of the vistas now just beginning to open to you. Your lives will be immeasurably fuller, higher, greater than any heretofore known to this universe. As your capabilities increase, you will find that you will no longer care for the society of entities less able than your own kind.'

'But I don't *want* to live forever!' Constance wailed.

'More muddy thinking.' Mentor's thought was – for him – somewhat testy. 'Perhaps, in the present instance, barely excusable. You know that you are not immortal. You should know that an infinity of time is necessary for the acquirement of infinite knowledge; and that your span of life will be just as short, in comparison with your capacity to live and to learn, as that of *Homo Sapiens*. When the time comes you will want to – you will need to – change your manner of living.'

'Tell us when?' Kat suggested. 'It would be nice to know, so we could get ready.'

'I could tell you, since in that my visualization is clear, but I will not. Fifty years – a hundred – a thousand – what matters it? Live your lives to the fullest, year by year, developing your every obvious, latent, and nascent capability; calmly assured that long before any need for your services shall arise, you shall have established yourselves upon some planet of your choice and shall be in every respect ready for whatever may come to pass.'

'You are – you must be – right,' Kit conceded. 'In view of what has just happened, however, and the chaotic condition of both galaxies, it seems a poor time to vacate all Guardianship.'

'All inimical activity is now completely disorganized. Kinnison and the Patrol can handle it easily enough. The real conflict is finished. Think nothing of a few years of vacancy. The Lens-makers, as you know, are fully automatic, requiring neither maintenance nor attention; what little time you may wish to devote to the special training of selected Lensmen can be taken at odd moments from your serious work of developing yourselves for Guardianship.'

'We still feel incompetent,' the Five insisted. 'Are you sure that you have given us all the instruction we need?'

'I am sure. I perceive doubt in your minds as to my own competence, based upon the fact that in this supreme emergency my visualization was faulty and my actions almost too late. Observe, however, that my visualization was clear upon every essential factor and that we were not actually too late. The truth is that our timing was precisely right – no lesser stress could possibly have prepared you as you are now prepared.

'I am about to go. The time may come when your descendants will realize, as we did, their inadequacy for continued Guardianship. Their visualizations, as did ours, may become imperfect and incomplete. If so, they will then know that the time will have come for them to develop, from the highest race then existing, new and more competent Guardians. Then they, as my fellows have done and as I am about to do, will of their own accord pass on. But that is for the remote future. As to you children, doubtful now and hesitant as is only natural, you may believe implicitly what I now tell you is the truth, that even though we Arisians are no longer here, all shall be well; with us, with you, and with all Civilization.'

The deeply resonant pseudo-voice ceased; the Kinnisons knew that Mentor, the last of the Arisians, was gone.

Epilogue

To you who have scanned this report, further greetings:

Since I who compiled it am only a youth, a Guardian only by title, and hence unable to visualize even approximately either the time of nor the necessity for the opening of this flask of force, I have no idea as to the bodily shape or the mental attainments of you, the entity to whom it has now been made available.

You already know that Civilization is again threatened seriously. You probably know something of the basic nature of that threat. While studying this tape you have become informed that the situation is sufficiently grave to have made it again necessary to force certain selected minds prematurely into the third level of Lensmanship.

You have already learned that in ancient time Civilization after Civilization fell before it could rise much above the level of barbarism. You know that we and the previous race of Guardians saw to it that this, OUR Civilization, has not yet fallen. Know now that the task of your race, so soon to replace us, will be to see to it that it does not fall.

One of us will become en rapport with you as soon as you have assimilated the facts, the connotations, and the implications of this material. Prepare your mind for contact.

Christopher K. Kinnison

Edward Elmer Smith was born in Wisconsin in 1890. He attended the University of Idaho and graduated with degrees in chemical engineering; he went on to attain a PhD in the same subject, and spent his working life as a food engineer. Smith is best known for the 'Skylark' and 'Lensman' series of novels, which are arguably the earliest examples of what a modern audience would recognise as Space Opera. Early novels in both series were serialised in the dominant pulp magazines of the day: *Argosy*, *Amazing Stories*, *Wonder Stories* and a pre-Campbell *Astounding*, although his most successful works were published under Campbell's editorship. Although he won no major SF awards, Smith was Guest of Honour at the second World Science Fiction Convention in Chicago, in 1940. He died in 1965.

For more information see:
      www.sf-encyclopedia.com/entry/smith_e_e